Ken McCoy was born ... and has lived in Yorkshire all his life. For twenty-five years he ran his own building and civil engineering company. During this time worked as a freelance artist, greeting card designer dinner entertainer. He has appeared on television, as a comedian on the Leeds City Varieties' *Good*

is now Ken's first love – not counting of course erie, to whom he has been married since 1973. children and twelve grandchildren.

Visit Ken McCoy online:
www.kenmccoy.co.uk

By Ken McCoy

Almost a Hero

Ken McCoy

piatkus

PIATKUS

First published in Great Britain in 2014 by Piatkus
Copyright © 2014 by Ken McCoy

A CIP catalogue record for this book
is available from the British Library.

ISBN 978-0-349-40401-1

Typeset in Bembo by M Rules
Printed and bound by CPI Group (UK) Ltd, Croydon, CR0 4YY

Papers used by Piatkus are from well-managed forests
and other responsible sources.

MIX
Paper from
responsible sources
FSC® C104740

Piatkus
An imprint of
Little, Brown Book Group
100 Victoria Embankment
London EC4Y 0DY

An Hachette UK Company
www.hachette.co.uk

www.piatkus.co.uk

To my fabulous grandson, Sean Patrick Griffin.

Chapter 1

**The Crazy Dazy Jazz Club, Denmark Street, London
21 June 1935**
There were over a hundred patrons in the club that Friday
night, including Annie Elliker who was celebrating her
twentieth birthday with her fiancé, Ray Dunford. Annie
would have much preferred to be celebrating it with the
young man playing the clarinet, but he probably didn't
know she existed. Even so she knew she was engaged to
the wrong person; she could not possibly spend the next
fifty years with Ray. What she didn't know was how to get
out of it. Her friend Mabel had told her she was lucky to
have such a man ... but what did Mabel know?

Annie came from an impoverished family – not financially impoverished, just lacking in morality, honesty,
compassion, love, generosity, decency, and all of the qual-
ities necessary for us not to be a burden on society.

They were richer by far than any of the people who
paid them protection money, or bought their contraband
cigarettes and alcohol. They were richer than those who
were addicted to the opiates and cocaine they sold in the
belief that this was a business with a big future that the
police hadn't really got a grip on as yet. They were richer

than the women they pimped to pay for the drugs the Ellikers had got them addicted to in the first place, before they sank into prostitution. The Elliker brothers ran a large gang of thieves, extortionists, money launderers, hitmen and men of extreme violence. There was only one streak of decency attached the family and her name was Annie.

She had endured a loveless upbringing, the youngest of four children, after her mother died while Annie was still an infant. When she asked her father if her mother had loved her, he told her that her mother had been a useless bitch and never to mention her again. So Annie didn't ask him again. Her three brothers were all adults by the time she arrived, and treated her as an irritant rather than a sibling. Since she was one year old she'd been brought up by nannies. She was educated at an all-girls school, so her experience of boys was strictly limited until she started university at eighteen. By this time she was aware of the nefarious activities of her family and relieved not to have been asked to join them in some capacity. Her father thought that giving girls a university education was a waste of time, but in the case of his own daughter, who was more than happy to live in university digs, it got her away from home for three years, which suited him.

This paucity of male company in her life to date was why she'd at first welcomed the attentions of Ray Dunford, who came from a world a million miles away from her father and brothers. Ray had a proper job in the City; he made a lot of money and owned a Jaguar sports car, thus proving that you didn't need to be a crook to be wealthy. He was a decent man, six years older than Annie, and he probably loved her as much as he could love any woman. The trouble was that he was the only boyfriend she had ever known, and she had more than a sneaking suspicion she could do better. She was pretty – the mirror told her that – and she was bright and could be funny given the right company. Sadly, Ray was not the right company. He could provide her with a fine home and fine-looking children no doubt, for he was a handsome man – rugged, some might say – but he was as boring as hell, had cigar breath, and no sense of humour. His only redeeming feature was that he'd introduced Annie to Dixieland jazz – the only true love they shared.

As a last resort she'd been prepared to relinquish her virginity to him, to see if had any talent in that direction. Had he been an exciting lover she might have overlooked his other deficiencies but, in the event, although she was inexperienced in such matters herself, she sincerely hoped that there'd be more exciting lovers for her in the future than Raymond Desmond Dunford. On the one and only occasion she'd shared his bed he climaxed within two minutes, and was snoring two minutes after that, leaving her virgo intacta and wondering what all the fuss was about.

Annie had arrived at a crucial point in her life where *she* was going to dictate its course. Her one and only shot at living wasn't going to be ruined by a bunch of crooks who didn't care a hoot for her, or a man who was incapable of providing the deep love she would never know if she stayed with him.

So she was waiting for the opportune moment to dump him.

The trouble was, unlike her father and brothers, Annie wasn't a cruel person and didn't want to hurt him. Ray wasn't cruel or nasty to her. He was a generous man who treated her with respect and affection ... but she didn't love him. She knew there must be more to love than the feelings she had for Ray. Had he gone with another woman she might have been disappointed but not heart-broken; she might even have been relieved. Ray wasn't capable of breaking her heart.

There was nothing else for it, he had to go, but tonight might not be the ideal time. For her birthday he'd given her a beautiful gold necklace with a diamond solitaire pendant. Annie absolutely loved it and wished he hadn't given her it, she'd only have to give it back. Still, it'd do no harm to wear it until the right moment came along.

The room was smoky, the atmosphere relaxed and the audience in good humour because they all had one thing in common – Dixieland jazz – and outside of New Orleans there was no better place than this to hear it. In fact there were few bands *inside* New Orleans as good as the Tubby Blake Band. As in most Dixieland bands the lead instrument was the trumpet. In this band it was played by Blind Oscar McGee, born and bred in New Orleans and brought over to London by Tubby. But as good as Oscar was, his playing was often outshone by the clarinet of Chas Challinor who, besides Tubby, was the only other native Briton in the band.

The laughter and murmur of conversation fell silent and the audience looked expectantly at the stage as Chas got to his feet ready for his solo. The piano player Duke Wellington played him in.

Chas's solo performance of 'Body and Soul' brought an extra thirty people a night into the Denmark Street club. This added around twenty pounds to the night's takings and an extra two pounds a night to Chas's wage packet, although the other band members didn't know this. Tubby Blake had told them all not to discuss money with each other, and warned Chas, 'You're on the higher rate, son, and I don't want the lower-rate guys making a fuss.'

Musicians are rarely short of self-belief. Every man who played in the band believed himself to be singled out by virtue of his superior talent. In fact, Chas, Blind Oscar, Duke Wellington and banjo player Monty Finniston were the star performers in the eight-piece band, but the ensemble playing of the others ably supported them and helped make them the best jazz band in London.

Annie's eyes stayed glued to Chas throughout every note of his clarinet solo. Ray had sneaked a bunch of flowers to the management, to be handed to her by the band. As Chas finished the number the flowers were produced and given to him to present to her. Apart from being a talented young musician he was also the glamour boy of the band. At five feet seven he wasn't a big man, but what he lacked in stature he made up for in good looks and personality. Ray was beginning to think he'd made a mistake in having the flowers presented by the charismatic clarinet player.

'Ladies and gentlemen,' began Chas, 'tonight is the twentieth birthday of a beautiful young lady in our audience and these flowers are a gift from Ray, her lucky fiancé. So could Annie join me on-stage now while we all sing the birthday song?'

Blushing with embarrassment, she made her way to the stage as the audience sang a raucous 'Happy Birthday To You', accompanied by the band. Chas had seen Annie in the audience many times before and, had she not always been accompanied by her boyfriend, would have tried his luck with her. As she arrived on-stage beside him he presented her with the flowers and said, 'Happy birthday, Annie! These are from Ray, who says to tell you he loves you very much. Is that him over there?'

'Yes, it is.'

She said it without taking her eyes off Chas, who gave Ray a wave and asked him, 'Is it all right if I have a kiss?'

'Er . . . yes.'

'Will you come up here, or do you want me to come down to you?'

The audience laughed, as did Annie. Ray sat looking puzzled, not sure what everyone was laughing about. Chas stepped away from the mic and gave Annie a peck on the cheek, murmuring, 'You should come in some time on your own.'

'Tomorrow?' she said.

Annie broke off her engagement in the taxi on the way home. Ray had wanted to take her to the pictures the next night to see Robert Donat in *The 39 Steps*.

'Don't fancy it,' she said.

'But it's an Alfred Hitchcock film.'

She was suddenly tired of having to make up excuses

instead of telling him the truth. Why should she be afraid of speaking out? So she told him the truth – sort of.

'I don't want to go out tomorrow.'

'Why not?'

'Oh, Ray . . . because I don't.'

'That's no excuse.'

Annie saw a window of opportunity to dump him and jumped in with both feet.

'And that's another thing,' she protested.

'What's another thing?'

'Why do I constantly have to make excuses? You want to go out, I don't. If you want to go to the pictures, go with one of your friends or else go on your own. *I* don't want to go with you.'

In the two years they'd been seeing each other this was their first full-blown confrontation. Up until then Ray had pretty much organised their courtship, which had been okay by Annie. He was older and more experienced. He knew all the good places and he had all the money. She was just a student.

The unexpected disagreement quickly flared up into the full-blown argument that Annie was hoping for. It was Chas's off-the-cuff joke about the kiss that had made her see the gap that yawned between the sort of man she really wanted and the one to whom she was engaged.

Their marriage would have met with the approval of both families. Ray's father would have welcomed a family link with the notorious Ellikers, if only to get them off his back. Over the years he'd paid them thousands just to smooth the passage of his many business deals. With Annie as a member of his family, he hoped they might back off.

7

Having got Ray sufficiently riled she screamed at him: 'You can have your ring back if you think I'm going to do your every bloody bidding! I'm my own woman. You don't tell me what to do!'

Ray yelled with equal vehemence: 'Right. I'll have it back then! And you can give me that necklace as well! What the hell am I doing anyway, marrying into a family of low-life bloody crooks?'

Annie's anger overcame her reluctance to give the necklace back, although she did take care to unhook it properly before throwing it at him. She then yanked off the ring and threw that too, saying to the driver, 'Pull over driver. My friend's getting out!'

'Friend? I'm no friend of yours!'

'Just get out, Ray. It's over between us. We're a mistake. I won't marry you.'

The taxi drove off, leaving a fuming Ray on the pavement and Annie in the back seat breathing out a sigh of relief tinged with worry about how she was going to pay for the taxi. She had three shillings in her purse; if it was more than that she'd simply tell the driver who she was and he'd probably let her off paying. She'd done it before in an emergency, though the Elliker family name wasn't one she was proud of.

If Ray made any attempt to get back with her she'd give him the brush-off, no problem. The hard part was done. No guilt, no sympathy. It was over. Pity about the necklace, though.

That night Annie made two vows. One, she would disown her own family, who were indeed a bunch of heartless low-life crooks. And two, she would ensnare Chas Challinor, who had looked and sounded as if he wouldn't need much ensnaring.

The following morning the housekeeper knocked on Annie's bedroom door and told her that Raymond was on the phone. Her first inclination was to ask the woman to fob him off somehow, but Annie knew things needed finishing properly. Ray probably thought that last night's argument was just a lovers' tiff and was ringing to apologise. Annie must put him straight so that she could get on with the rest of her life and meet Chas in the Crazy Dazy without any guilty feelings. She slipped on her dressing gown and went downstairs to the telephone in the hall, ready to rebuff any pleas for them to get back together.

'Hello, Ray.'

She kept her voice purposely toneless. Mustn't get his hopes up.

'I was a bit out of order last night,' he said awkwardly.

'Ray, we're finished. I don't want us to get back together.'

'No, it's not that. It's ... er ... it's what I said about your family. I shouldn't have said that.'

'My family?'

'Er, yes.'

It appeared that Ray was more terrified of offending her family than heartbroken at losing her. Although she had no right, Annie found this insulting. She glanced around to check that no one was listening. No one was.

'You mean about us being a bunch of low-life crooks?'

'Y-yes.'

'Well, I'm forced to agree with you about that.'

9

'What?'

'You're right. They are a bunch of low-life crooks. I'm not, but they are.'

'Jesus, Annie! Can they hear you?' There was fear in Ray's voice, which only amused Annie.

'Not sure,' she said. 'Hang on, I'll have a look, see who's around.'

She left it a full minute before speaking to him again. 'No, we're okay. No one heard me call my family a bunch of low-life crooks.'

'Good God, Annie! Will you stop it?'

'I'm guessing you don't want me to tell them you think they're a bunch of low-life crooks?'

'No,' moaned Ray. 'Please, Annie, if you don't want us to get back together that's fine, but don't tell them what I said . . . please?'

'Ray, if I told them that you'd be a dead man.'

'I know.'

'Which is why I won't tell them.'

'Thank you, Annie.'

'Goodbye, Ray.'

Chapter 2

The following night the band had finished playing and the club was closing. Chas and Annie were sitting at the bar.

'What? Broken it off? Why?'

'Best thing I've ever done. You made me laugh within ten seconds of talking to me. Ray didn't make me laugh once in two years.'

'Ah. Well, I can't say I'm sorry. His loss is my gain. I don't suppose you're rich, are you?'

'You suppose correctly.'

'Curses! Beautiful but poor. Is Ray rich?'

'Rich enough. He's got a Jaguar and pots of dosh.'

'Please tell me you're not trying to do a straight swap, him for me? I'm a bit lacking in the finances department, and my usual mode of transport is the number twenty-four bus.'

'Swap him for you? You're a bit forward, aren't you? I hardly know you. I'm here because I like jazz and you're a great clarinet player. I also suspect there are plenty of women in your life already.'

'Your suspicions are unfounded, madam. I'm a poor judge of character as far as women are concerned – to the extent that I've never had a girlfriend who's lasted more than a month, and that includes a couple with whom I was madly in love. Mostly they dumped me because I didn't pay them the attention they seemed to require.'

'What? Even the ones you loved madly?'

'They wanted to tie me down. I'm twenty-one. Who wants to be tied down at twenty-one?'

'Not me, but there again I'm only twenty.'

'So, you might dump me when my month is up?'

'I can't see you lasting a month.'

He looked at her. She was blonde, blue-eyed and beautiful. 'What if I fall in love with you?'

For the first time in her life Annie felt unconstrained in conversation. With this young man there was no need to watch what she said in case he took offence. He had a warmth and self-confidence that were infectious.

'Oh, you'll fall in love with me, no question, but all I want is a boyfriend to amuse me for a few weeks until I get over the trauma of my broken engagement.'

'You don't look to be suffering any trauma.'

'He bought me a beautiful necklace for my birthday – gold chain and a fabulous diamond pendant. I gave it back to him, plus the engagement ring.'

'Ah, she was poor but she was honest. Foolish girl. Now I understand your trauma. There's one thing you ought to know.'

'What's that?'

'You should know that we musicians are traditionally poor. The only notes I have in abundance are in my clarinet. Any money I earn, I waste on *la dolce vita*. It's all part of my creative spirit.'

'Perhaps I can be part of your *dolce vita* for a month – or part thereof.'

'Perhaps you can.'

'There is one thing *you* ought to know,' said Annie.

'What's that?'

'My surname.'

'Why would I want to know your surname? I'm sure it's a fine surname, but unless you're related to royalty, surnames tend to be a bit humdrum. You're not Lady Anne Windsor are you ... or maybe Countess Anne Saxe-Coburg and Gotha? That's it! You're a German spy sent here by Adolf Hitler to check on our sinful music.'

'See,' she said, 'you're doing it again, making me laugh.'

'Do you have an embarrassing name? I once went out with a girl called Cecelia Clackerbottom.'

'Can't you be serious for one minute?'

'I'm always serious. Right, you were about to tell me your surname.'

'Okay, my name is Annie Elliker.'

'Ah, I see the problem.'

'You do?'

'You're obviously Barry Elliker's sister, the monster Barry Elliker who gave me nits at school, and you're here to continue his fiendish work. What is it you want with me, woman?'

'What are you talking about?'

'You know very well what I'm talking about. The nit nurse made me have all my hair shaved off, which I thought was a bit much. Your evil brother didn't lose a single strand and *he* was the one going round giving nits to everyone.'

'I'm not Barry Elliker's sister.'

'I've only got your word for that. You have a look of him. Blonde hair, blue eyes with more than a hint of devilment lurking there. Did he give you nits as well?'

'I'm not his sister.'

'You'd have thought boarding schools would be nit-free.'

'Boarding school?' said Annie. 'Why, were you rich?'

'My dad has a few bob. He sent me away to boarding school just after my mum died.'

'My dad sent me to a boarding school when I was seven, and I loved every minute of it,' said Annie. 'The worst parts were the holidays when I had to go home to my awful family. Did you enjoy your school?'

'No, it was about the worst thing he could have done to me. I was eight years old. I learned to hate him as much as I loved my mum.'

Annie wanted to tell him then about her own mother whom she didn't even remember, but didn't want to kill the conversation completely. Chas was someone she'd like to confide in. Maybe some other time.

'So, he's rich and you're poor,' she observed instead.

'That pretty much sums things up. As I said, we never had a great relationship after that. I could have gone to work for him after leaving school, but I chose to be a musician instead. Didn't fancy working for him in his boring business.'

'What sort of business is it?'

Chas frowned as he thought about this. 'To be honest I'm not sure – never actually asked him. He seems to dabble in a bit of everything. Buys and sells – that sort of

14

thing. He's got pots of dosh, but life's too short to waste it on buying and selling stuff. The one good thing about my boarding school was that it had a music department, which is where I learned to play the clarinet. It appeared that I had a bit of a gift for it, which was beautiful.'

'Beautiful?'

'No other word for it. To have a gift for something you enjoy enough to make it your life's work is just plain beautiful. I enjoyed football, cricket and shoplifting, but I was never much good at any of them. I tell a lie. I was quite good at shoplifting, but my gang got caught when I wasn't with them. They were expelled and I gave up my life of crime.'

'That was a good move,' said Annie. 'Did you really have a girlfriend called Cecelia Clackerbottom?'

'No, I made that up. Her name was Audrey.'

'Try and tell me something that's true.'

'Three years ago I left the sixth form and auditioned for Tubby's band. Got the job and got my own flat.'

'And is playing in Tubby's band to be your life's work?'

Chas took a sip of his drink as he pondered his answer. 'You know, this is a good life, but I'll need to move on at some stage.'

'What's your ultimate ambition?' she asked.

'When the time's right I'm going over to the States to play with one of the American big bands. Have you heard of the Dorsey Brothers?'

'I think so, but they're not a jazz band, are they?'

'They have a Dixieland group that plays in the intervals while the main band goes off for a break. I'd play in that for starters.'

'You sound very sure of yourself. What if they won't have you?'

'Last year they came over here and needed some British musicians to play with them – all to do with work permits or some such nonsense. Anyway, Tommy Dorsey had heard of me, would you believe, and he came here to see me. Next thing I knew Tubby brought him over and asked me if I wanted to do a short tour with them. Good man, Tubby, most band leaders would have sent Dorsey packing.

'I did nine venues with them up and down the country, playing with the big band as well as the jazz group. The day I left them Tommy came up to me and said if ever I was in the States looking for work, to go and see him. Tommy and Jimmy weren't getting on and Tommy'd just formed his own band. He's got some great instrumentalists and a couple of singers you might have heard of – Jack Leonard and Frank Sinatra?'

He paused, waiting for her to show a hint of recognition. Annie shook her head. 'I've heard of Bing Crosby and Al Bowlly, but that's about all.'

'You're sure you're not Barry Elliker's sister?'

'Positive.'

'Good job, otherwise I'd have had to examine your barnet for nits before I got to know you better.'

She was laughing again. Then her expression turned serious as she said, 'I am related to some more notorious Ellikers.'

He looked at her for a moment and then his face took on an expression of amazement. He put his hand over his mouth and spoke from behind it.

'Whoah! What? You mean *the* Ellikers . . . the baddies?'

She nodded. Chas raised his eyebrows and let her continue. 'I'm an Elliker,' Annie said, 'but like you and your dad, I don't have anything to do with the family line of business.'

Chas put on an American accent. 'So, yer not packin' heat?'

'Sure am. I got me a Derringer pistol stuck down ma knickers, so don't give me any trouble, mister!'

He held up his hands. 'Well, I sure ain't lookin' fer no trouble, ma'am.'

She giggled. 'I'm actually a student at UCL – that's University College London.'

'I do know what UCL is. What are you studying?'

'History.'

'There's no future in that, young lady.'

'I specialise in History of Art.'

'Are you an artist?'

'Not really. It's just that I like art, and I thought if I was to become a Bachelor of Arts my degree might as well be in art.'

'Your logic is impeccable.'

'It's also an easy course – or maybe I find it easy because I'm really interested in what I'm studying. When I do get a job it'll have to have a strong connection with my degree.'

'You should always like what you do for a job,' said Chas. 'My old man wanted me to go to the LSE. In fact he pulled a few strings to get me a place. That's when I left home to join Tubby's band. Studying economics wasn't for me. I was supposed to get all genned up and join him in

17

his business. So, what does the Elliker mob think about you going to UCL?'

'Not much, but with me being female I was never going to be any use to them – thank God.'

'Wow! Do you still live with them?'

'I stay in uni digs during term time. I suppose I spend maybe three months a year living at home with my dad and my brothers. I hate them all with a passion and they know it but they don't do me any harm.'

'Oh, dear, sounds like a difficult three months. From what I hear there's scarcely a crime they haven't committed.'

'And so far none of them has been caught – not my dad nor any of my brothers at any rate. My elder brother Cedric's some sort of legal genius, plus they've got all sorts of people on their payroll – coppers, judges, MPs, you name it.'

'Sounds like Al Capone could have done with Cedric to advise him.'

'He reckons Capone was an idiot to let himself go down on a tax-evasion charge. Capone donated thousands to charity but very little to the taxman apparently. Whereas the Ellikers are meticulous tax-payers.'

'Should you be telling me this?'

'I'm not telling you anything that's not common knowledge. It's not so easy to prove as to talk about. I had a lecture from my dad on my eighteenth birthday to tell me I would never be part of the family business and should always keep my nose out of things that don't concern me. I told the old crook then I never wanted to be part of his business nor would I ever want a share in the proceeds.

Which was a bit drastic, with me having no money. Anyway, he's funding me through university, after which I'm on my own – and I can't wait.'

Chas scarcely took his eyes off Annie as she talked. A thought suddenly struck him. It was something he wanted to share with her because she was the kind of person a man could share his thoughts with.

'All this personal stuff we've been banging on about . . . I've never discussed these things with any woman before. Why have I discussed them with you?'

'You're probably falling in love with me.'

'Am I? I must put a stop to that. Love is for old men of twenty-five and over. I'm too young to be snapped up.'

'I'm told it's unstoppable. It's called love at first sight, only you don't realise what it is at first.'

Annie couldn't believe she had the cheek to say all this to such an attractive and charming young man, and she had more to tell him too.

'How would you know that?' said Chas.

'Because it's happening to me and I can feel you responding. Can't you feel it?'

'I don't know. Maybe if we kissed or something? See if there are any sparks.'

'I think that's worth a try,' she said.

Events overtook Annie to such an extent that she never finished her degree. Their wedding was precipitated by her pregnancy and was attended by the Tubby Blake Band and Annie's friend Mabel. Chas's dad didn't come because he didn't approve of the Ellikers; in fact, he threatened to cut Chas out of his will if he married Annie. Chas was never one to respond to threats.

The Ellikers didn't come to the wedding because Annie didn't tell them she was getting married. She told them later when they wondered why she'd stopped living there during the holidays. Her happy news was met with grunts of disinterest. None of them thought to ask who the lucky man was, so she chose not to mention her other happy news.

Chas and Annie enjoyed four and a half years of wedded bliss before Adolf Hitler's bombers came to town.

Chapter 3

Leeds
1938

Larry Morris attacked his wife in a fit of drunken rage. He felt emasculated, what with Liz being the breadwinner and him being bone idle. He had no job other than thieving, mainly from her; sometimes from the till of the café she owned and sometimes from her purse. He had now further demonstrated his ineptitude by taking to burglary and getting caught on the premises by the householder, who was wielding a gun he'd brought home from the Great War. Larry was currently out on bail pending his trial and had spent the lunchtime in a pub telling his tale of woe to a partially deaf old man who listened patiently for as long as Larry bought him drinks. Larry Morris was a man with few friends and when he ran out of money the old man lost interest in the drivel he was spouting, so Larry went off to his wife's café to replenish his funds.

Liz caught him in the act and slammed the till shut before he could get his hands in it.

'Go home, Larry, you're drunk!'

He hit her full in the face and knocked her on to a nearby table, scattering meals and crockery. Then he opened the till and took out all its contents. As Liz lay unconscious one of her two assistants rang the police, knowing that Liz herself would be reluctant to do so when she came round.

The police station was less than a hundred yards away and by the time Liz was coming round a sergeant and a constable were standing over her and the story was being related by staff and customers alike.

'We've already picked him up,' said the sergeant. 'Staggering down the road. He's in custody, but we need you to make a statement.'

Liz gave this just a moment's thought. A moment that encompassed a brief but awful marriage that was heading for the divorce courts, as well as the miscarriage that had persuaded her to marry him in the first place. Theirs wasn't a marriage built on love. True, Larry was a handsome man who had a certain 'way' with him – one that vanished with drink.

'I'll make a statement if it keeps the thieving bugger away from me,' Liz declared.

The customers gave a shout of approval, as did her staff.

'His bail will be rescinded, that's for sure,' said the sergeant.

Larry's assault on his wife added a year to his eventual sentence. He was in prison when war broke out, and still there when Liz was granted a divorce on the grounds of his cruelty.

Chapter 4

Muswell Hill, London
2 September 1939
Cedric, Edgar and Albert Elliker entered their father's house via a little-used, woodland footpath that passed a gate in the back garden. It was secure, opened only by the key which Cedric had been given as a boy. It was a route they had all taken back then – a short cut on their way home from school.

But that was several years ago and now their father scarcely remembered the gate existed. The grounds were tended by a gardener and rarely used by Montague Elliker, who was currently alone in the house working in his study. Montague spent most of his time there, planning his nefarious business enterprises. He was very much a loner, rarely trusting outsiders. He placed limited trust in Rodney, his manservant, and even less in the cleaner who came in three times a week. In fact, he had limited trust in two of his three sons whose entry into this world he'd brought about with the reluctant assistance of their mother – she had been no more to him than a convenient means of conveying his offspring into this world. Montague's plan all along was to enlist the help of his sons in running the criminal empire he was building.

He'd disposed of the mother once she'd brought a late entry into the world – a girl at that. He'd kept the child, thinking he might find a use for her at some time, but that time had never come and she'd eventually left of her own accord, which suited him. Getting rid of unwanted people was always a messy and sometimes a risky business.

Cedric unlocked the back door. All three brothers entered the house. Cedric led the way into the hall, calling out cheerfully, 'It's me, Dad.'

His father put down his pen and called back, 'I'm in the study.'

Of his three sons Montague had the most time for Cedric, who had turned out brighter than the other two put together. He'd won a scholarship to Oxford and earned a first in law. The other two had struggled to get their School Certificates. Montague was planning on gradually handing over his business to Cedric and going into retirement before the police caught up with him. He was sixty-seven years old, and in his line of work age makes a man careless. He didn't want to spend a single minute of his old age in prison; better to let the sharp mind of his eldest son take over. Besides there was a war brewing and he had plans to move to Ireland, which was unlikely to become involved in a British war.

Cedric entered the room on his own. His father sat back in his chair, lit a cigar and studied his son, who had an educated manner and bearing that Montague liked.

'Just passing,' said Cedric. 'Thought I'd call in and see how you are.'

'I'm getting old, boy. That's how I am.'

'We're all getting old, Dad. Did you get a witness for the will, by the way? Sorry I couldn't do it, but with me being family it's not allowed.'

'No, I understand. I got Rodney to witness it.'

'Rodney? Where is he?'

'It's his afternoon off.'

Cedric knew that.

'I . . . er . . . I'm assuming Annie isn't mentioned in the will.'

'Don't be ridiculous! Of course she isn't. That girl is no part of this family and you should know that.'

'I just wondered.'

'You're wondering if I'm getting old and past it!'

'Not at all.'

'And you're wondering if you get the lion's share.'

'Well, I'm the one who'll be running things, let's face it.'

'If you must know, I'm splitting it forty, thirty, thirty. You get forty per cent, the other two get thirty each. But that's still many years away still. I plan on living at least another twenty.'

'I hope you do, Dad. I won't be able to run things as well as you.'

'Then I hope you learn quickly, boy, because you'll be running the whole show before I get to seventy. Look, there's something I want you to see.'

Cedric stepped around the side of the desk as his father turned over the pages of a thick ledger in front of him.

'This is our family Bible, boy. This is a record of all my business dealings. I've got six of these going back thirty years. The others are in the safe. They contain names, dates, amounts, and records of all the jobs I've been involved in. These books could hang me, boy. These books could hang the lot of us.'

'Why don't I know about these?' asked Cedric, put out by the surprise his father had just sprung on him.

'Because the contents of these books are a burden, boy, and there was never any need for you to know about them until now. The more people know about your business, the less secure it is.'

'Why do you keep them?'

'Because you must always keep things in writing. Many men in our business are afraid of the written word and such fear leads to mistakes. People and places and things forgotten. In these books I store incriminating information about police, judges, members of parliament, and many other people who will go out of their way to make sure none of us is ever arrested, for fear of what we might reveal.'

'I was aware of your hold over your associates, Dad, but not that you had everything recorded in such detail.'

'You're the only one who knows, and I'd like you to keep it that way.'

Cedric nodded without saying a word. As Montague sat studying the ledger, Cedric slid his hand into his pocket and took out a Colt .38. He put the gun to the side of his father's head and pulled the trigger, stepping back in distaste as Montague's brains sprayed out across the far side of the desk. At the shot Edgar and Albert came into the room and stood looking down at their dead father.

'So long, Pop,' said Albert.

'Messy,' observed Edgar.

'Just don't make any prints in the blood,' warned Cedric. He was already wiping his own prints off the gun using a handkerchief. His father's hands rested limply on the desk. Cedric lifted the left hand and wrapped it around the pistol's grip.

'Okay, the old man was left-handed so the gun was in this hand.'

He slid a pen inside the barrel, lifted the pistol out of his father's hand and placed it on the desk.

'He'll have dropped it when he fired, about ... there, would you think?'

Nods from his brothers. Cedric stood back beside them and surveyed the scene. 'Anybody see anything out of place?'

'Is the gun traceable?' asked Albert.

'Not to any of us. The police will assume it's one of Dad's illegal weapons. He's got a Browning in the safe. We obviously know nothing about any weapons found in this house.'

'What about a note?' said Edgar.

'I decided against leaving one,' said Cedric. 'The less information the police have to be suspicious about the better. We just tell them Dad's been feeling depressed lately. No idea why. That's the beauty of depression ... no one knows what causes it or what it may lead to.'

'He looks a bit down in the mouth now,' said Albert, glancing at his father.

'And look what he's gone and done,' said Edgar.

'Oh, yes, we need to get into his safe,' remembered Cedric. 'He's got books in there with records of all his dealings over the past thirty years.'

'Have you got the combination?' Edgar asked.

'I do. Dad thought one of us needed to have it in case of emergency,' said Cedric. 'Such as this.'

'He didn't trust us with anything,' muttered Albert.

'His will's in the safe, and before you ask he left forty per cent to me and the rest split between you two. Any objections?'

Neither of his brothers raised any. They reckoned the old man was worth at least a million, and thirty per cent of that was plenty. Plus his businesses should be bringing in another three hundred grand a year.

'Okay, we just take the ledgers from his safe and check it for anything else incriminating. There'll be money in the safe but we don't take a penny. This wasn't a robbery. Then we give the whole house the once over for the same reason, and we're out of here the same way we came in – off to meet our alibis. With him being who he is the cops will be all over this house like a rash, looking for something to fit us up with. They'll find our fingerprints all over the place, which should be no surprise with us spending so much time here.

'No one must see us leave. Rodney should be back around six to discover his body. He'll most likely ring me first. I'll be home by that time and I'll deal with the police.'

'Sweet,' said Edgar.

Chapter 5

Bermondsey, East London
4 September 1939

Britain had been at war for just over a day. Chas stood at the window looking up at the sky. 'No sign of the Germans yet.'

'No, but there're clear signs of chickenpox,' said Annie, examining Billie's back. 'Have you had it?'

'No idea. I never had a mum around to tell me if I've had it or not.'

'Nor me. We must hope we've both had it.'

'Why's that?'

'Adults get it a lot worse than children ... leads to complications.'

Chas continued looking out of the window. His mind was a million miles away from thoughts of chickenpox, or even the war.

'Have you ... er ... have you seen the paper?' he asked his wife.

'Yes, I've seen it.'

There'd been a piece in the *Evening Standard* about Montague Elliker, who had died of a gunshot wound to the head. The police were saying it was suicide.

'And?'

'And I'm glad he's dead,' said Annie. 'If not for him my mother would still be alive today.'

'Oh, why's that?'

'I don't know. It's just a feeling I've always had. I remember nothing about her. He and my brothers hated her, so she can't have been all that bad.'

'You never talk about any of them. Do you want to talk about your family now?'

'No.' Annie continued without a trace of hesitation, 'They're no part of my life any more. That only began properly four years ago when I met you. I never want to discuss my father or brothers with anyone – and I don't want you to either.'

'Point taken.'

Chas shook his head as he looked at this beautiful young woman who had been treated so abominably by her father and brothers. How could anyone behave so cruelly to a girl like Annie?

'It's a wonder you bother with men at all, the way they treated you in your childhood.'

'It's why I ended up with Ray – any man at all was an improvement on the ones in my family.' She smiled and added dreamily, 'There was one other man, though.'

'Oh?'

'Oh, yes. His name was Charlie, just like you.'

'I've never been a Charlie. So who was he?'

She detected a hint of jealousy in her husband and milked it for all she was worth. 'Oh, he was tall and strong and very handsome, and he really looked after me – made me feel safe.'

'This was before Ray, I take it?'

'Yes, my first Charlie was before Ray, but he was married so I had no chance. I often think about him – wonder if he's still married.'

'Playing fast and loose with a married man, eh?'

'Oh, Chas, he was a lovely man. I'd run away from home, you see, and he found me wandering the streets in tears. He took me by the hand, telling me he'd look after me.'

'I bet he did. And did he look after you?'

'Oh, yes. He took me all the way home and let me wear his tin helmet. You see, he was on his way back to war but he still took the time to see me safely home.'

'Back to war? Just how old were you when you were canoodling with this war hero?'

'We weren't exactly canoodling – I didn't know how to canoodle when I was three.'

'Three! You had me going there, you flipping madam!'

'You were jealous, Chas Chandler.'

'No, I was not . . . well, maybe just a bit.'

Chas turned around and joined her in examining their three-year-old daughter's back, which was showing the raised red bumps of chickenpox.

'How're you feeling, Billie?'

'I feel okay, Daddy.'

'You're going to be a bit spotty for a few days.'

'Why?'

'Because you're a kid. All kids have to get spotty now and again. It's a rule.'

'Oh.'

Chapter 6

Bermondsey, East London
16 September 1940

'Ah, well, Annie. I suppose it had to come sooner or later. I was hoping they'd overlooked me.'

Chas was examining in detail the letter he'd received earlier that day from the War Office. It was addressed to Charles Herbert Challinor. For an inspired second he'd thought of sending it back, saying there was no one of that name here – he'd been known as Chas for as long as he could remember. He'd had the letter now for some ten hours and had come to accept his fate with equanimity, although he'd been secretly hoping that such a summons would never come.

'I'd have preferred later – much later,' said Annie, who was seven months pregnant and currently getting four-year-old Billie ready for bed.

Their daughter had been named after Billie Holiday, an American blues singer who was a great favourite of Chas's. He preferred her to Anne Shelton who was on the wireless right now belting out 'Imagination'. Glenn Miller was due on soon. His was the spot Chas had been waiting for. 'In The Mood', which was charting at number one, was the best swing tune of all time, in Chas's opinion.

He was due to report to Blenheim Barracks for basic training on Monday 29 September. Chas loathed and detested this war, which was damaging his career as a musician, affecting his happy marriage, and was about to make the rest of his life quite a lot worse. They wanted him to go and fight Hitler. The only fight he'd in his life to date was at school against snotty Albert Rowlands, who was a year younger and wore glasses with a corrective lens. Chas had lost that one and vowed to give up the fight game and concentrate on music instead.

'Well, let's hope we can sleep in our own beds tonight. All this bombing's getting to be a bit much. They can't keep this up for long, love, surely.'

'I've no idea,' said Annie, nodding in approval at their daughter who had successfully fastened the buttons on her pyjama jacket. The Luftwaffe had been bombing London day and night for over a week. It seemed they had redirected their aircraft from fighting Spitfires and Hurricanes over the Channel and had picked a softer target ... England's capital city.

'I think we're lucky to still have a roof over our heads,' Annie said. 'The sooner our evacuation's organised the better. What do you say to North Yorkshire? I hear there's some nice countryside up there. Do you know anything about Yorkshire people?'

'Well, they say you can always tell a Yorkshireman, but you can't tell him much.'

'They can't be any worse than my family.'

'I thought that subject was taboo.'

33

She mimed zipping her mouth and said, 'It is.'

'It's maybe as well you're pregnant,' Chas said. 'You can go up north with Billie. I'd hate to leave you here on your own. Then after this war's over you can go back to university and finish your degree.'

'I'd like that, Chas. Not sure if I'd get back in so easily, though.'

'Rubbish. They'll snap you up, bright girl like you.' Chas returned his attention to his letter. 'You should be just about okay for money. Your digs'll be paid for and I'll have most of my wages sent direct to you.'

'I don't want you leaving yourself short. Will you enquire about joining an army band?'

'First words out of my mouth, darling. They'll soon spot I'm not built for fighting.'

'I don't know why they need soldiers. This war's all coming down from the sky. How's it all going to end, Chas? I never thought the Germans'd do this to us. What sort of people are they? We haven't done anything to them.'

'Well, the boys in blue beat the hell out of the Luftwaffe last month. Who's to say they can't do so again?'

'Do you think you'll have to do any actual fighting?'

He shook his head. 'No idea. I personally think this conscription's no more than a precaution.' He didn't believe this for one minute. He was saying it to ease his wife's mind. 'We'll most likely march up and down a barracks square for a few weeks until the RAF have destroyed the Luftwaffe. After that the Jerries'll never dare invade us. Our boys'll sink all their boats in the Channel. Word is that the Yanks'll come over to help if we're struggling. The

34

good thing is that all of us will be out of central London, away from the bombs. Oh, damn!'

The distant wail of the air-raid siren had gradually built up from a frail hum to an ear-piercing whine that would be heard for miles around. Billie was already putting her coat on over her pyjamas without being asked. Her parents got dressed in outdoor clothing and Chas grabbed the air-raid bag, which was always packed in case of emergency. It contained blankets, food, water, a torch and a first-aid kit. They were out of the house within a minute of the siren starting up. Billie galloped on in front. Chas called out to her.

'Straight to the shelter, Billie! We'll catch you up.'

Billie flew through the sandbagged entrance to the shelter and down the steps, where she sat on the end of a long wooden bench already occupied by an elderly couple from the same street as the Challinors.

'Hello Billie.'

'Hello, Mrs Batley. My mum and dad are on their way. Mum's a bit slow because of the baby.'

'Yes, they do slow you down,' agreed Mrs Batley.

Other people were filing down the steps and looking around for places to sit. Many had brought cushions, which they threw on to the floor, using the wall behind as a back rest. Billie's eyes were fixed on the steps.

'Mum and Dad will be here any minute.'

'They need to hurry up,' said Mr Batley as the sound of bombs falling some distance away found its way inside the shelter.

'Are they all right, Mr Batley?' asked Billie, worried now.

The old man said nothing. His wife reassured her. 'I'm sure they'll be here any second, love.'

'I hope so, Mrs Batley.'

More time went by with no sign of Chas and Annie. Billie ran back up the steps to where an ARP warden was standing. The noise of falling bombs was louder than she had ever heard it.

'Can you see my mum and dad?' she asked. 'They were just behind me and now I don't know where they are.'

The warden stepped outside to look up the street.

Annie had stopped walking. She was cradling her stomach. 'Hold on a minute, Chas. I can't go very fast.' Her face creased into a painful grimace. 'Whoa! This is getting nasty. I need to sit down.'

'Sit on this step and catch your breath. No rush, they won't be here just yet.'

She sank down on a doorstep and closed her eyes, breathing heavily. Chas sat beside her and put one arm around her. Distant flashes were lighting the sky but not the blacked-out street they were in. A slim wafer of moon was just enough to illuminate their daughter who was disappearing around the corner, no more than fifty yards from the shelter. A thought struck him.

'The baby's not coming, is it?'

Annie was breathing in short, sharp bursts. 'Chas. I'm not sure what's happening!'

There was the thunder of aircraft in the distance. Approaching bombers. He stroked her hair and said, 'I'll carry you.'

'Chas, you can't carry me. I weigh more than you

do.'

He nodded his acceptance of her reasoning, wishing for the thousandth time that he was a bigger, stronger man and not ten stone two wet through.

'I'll go and get help then.'

'Please don't leave me! I'll be okay in a minute.'

The aircraft sound grew louder.

'Heinkels,' he murmured. Being a musician he had a keen ear for any kind of sound.

Annie sat with her eyes squeezed tight shut, trying to cope with the pain. Chas kept his arm protectively around her. It was all he could do to help. Eventually she opened her eyes as the aircraft noise grew too loud to ignore.

'They'll be here any time. I'd better give it a try, Chas.'

'Good girl. I'll have you in the shelter in two minutes.'

He stood in front of her, placed his hands beneath her armpits and brought her to her feet. She moaned in pain. There were distant explosions. The Heinkels had started unloading their bombs. More explosions followed, getting nearer. He pulled on her arm to hurry her along but Annie's feet began to drag and she screamed in pain. He tried to lift her. Even with the adrenalin pumping through him, he could scarcely get her off the ground. He called for help but the street was deserted. The aircraft were thundering almost directly overhead. Anti-aircraft guns were blazing away from a nearby battery. Their exploding shells were lighting up the sky but having no obvious effect on the bombers, which droned on relentlessly, discharging death and destruction on the helpless innocents below.

Bombs were dropping in nearby streets, causing mind-numbing explosions and throwing up clouds of rubble and sheets of flame a hundred feet high. Chas part-carried, part-dragged his wife to the street corner where they'd last seen Billie. The horrendous noise of the bombs all around was drowning out her screams of agony. They turned the corner and, by the light of the bomb flashes, he saw an ARP man at the entrance to the shelter, the one sent by Billie to look out for them. Chas shouted to him for help. As the ARP man set off towards them a five-hundred-kilogram bomb landed nearby.

The force of the blast hit the sandbags at the shelter entrance, knocking some of them down on top of Billie. The people in the shelter, not knowing what had happened, stayed put, hoping for the best, which was all you could do in an air raid. Meanwhile four-year-old Billie was struggling out from under the bags of sand. She was partially stunned, with sand in her hair, in her eyes and on her clothes. It took her a couple of minutes to collect her thoughts, and when she did she got to her feet and ran out of the shelter shouting at the top of her voice. The wave of bombers had moved on over central London. All Billie could see were destroyed buildings, fire and smoke. No people. No sign of her mum or her dad as she picked her way through the rubble, unaware that she was passing the scattered body parts of the ARP man.

When she got to the corner of the street she could just make out two dark shapes lying in the road, illuminated by the blazing buildings. Her heart was pounding as she ran towards them and made out her mum and dad, lying side by side. The bomb had picked them both up and sent them fifty feet through the air. Chas still had his arms locked around his wife. Billie could scarcely breathe as she approached them. She kneeled down beside them and touched her mum's blackened face.

'Mum, are you alive?'

Annie made no movement. Billie could hardly see through her tears. 'Daddy, are you alive? Please don't be dead.'

Chas's face was scorched and blackened. Had it not been for the duffel coat he was wearing she wouldn't have known it was him. She thought she heard him moan and placed an ear to his mouth, screaming at him: 'Dad . . . Daddy!'

She knew if her dad was alive then her mum must be as well. One would never leave the other. She knew that much about them.

'Daddy, you're not talking to me.'

Billie grabbed his coat and tried to shake some life into him. He reacted by spitting something out of his mouth as he tried to catch his breath. He couldn't hear Billie. The sound of the nearby explosion had deafened him. He could not see anything either. He couldn't see anything and he couldn't feel anything and he couldn't remember anything. What the hell had happened to him? Where was he? *Who* was he?

'Daddy, shall I go and get someone?'

'Billie?'

The shout came from Mr Batley, who had been sent by his wife to find the child. The All Clear hadn't gone and there was still bombing in the distance but there was no sign of any further aircraft approaching the area. Billie looked up and gave him a weak wave. Her face was chalk white and her eyes brimming with tears as she told him,

'It's my mum and dad, Mr Batley. They've been hurt by the bombs. Do you think they're all right?'

Mr Batley looked down at the pitiful sight of the hopeful child kneeling by the broken bodies of her parents and burst into tears at the thought that anyone could be so evil as to do such a thing. He'd fought at the Somme in the last war but he didn't know how to cope with this.

Chas had been drifting in and out of consciousness for twenty-four hours, only he wasn't really aware of when he was awake and when he wasn't. He was lying in hospital along with over forty others who'd been hurt in the same raid. They were among the lucky ones; over a hundred more had been killed in London that night. The attention he was receiving was the best they could manage, which was minimal. He was off the danger list but needed a lot of repair work, especially to his face which was swathed in bandages, leaving just enough of a gap for him to see and talk through. All he could make out was a light, a ceiling and passing shadows.

He'd now been conscious for half an hour and knew just enough to ask where he was and who he was. He tried to speak but his voice wasn't working yet. He didn't know if it ever had worked but instinct told him that it should. He managed a low moan, enough to attract the attention of a nearby nurse.

'Ah, Mr Challinor,' she said. 'You're in Lambeth Hospital. Can you hear me?'

Chas managed a nod.

'You were injured by a bomb but you're going to be okay.'

Another nod. He knew he had questions to ask but he didn't know what they were nor did he yet have any voice with which to ask them.

'You've been in here twenty-four hours. Your daughter's being looked after by your neighbours.'

Daughter? So he had a daughter? All he could do was lie there and listen and nod occasionally. What did she say his name was? He'd forgotten. Would she tell him again? Come on, whoever you are, tell me who I am again. It's only fair. Hospital . . . bomb . . . daughter . . . what was all this about?

He was being drip-fed through a tube. His face was a mass of burns, his left leg shattered. He had three broken ribs, a broken collarbone and two broken bones in his right arm. Chad knew none of this because he'd been given morphine. All he knew was what he could see, plus the limited information that had been given to him. Then he remembered Annie and he remembered her being with him when . . . when what? He now remembered the air raid and everything up to a second before the bomb exploded. So, a bomb had put him in here. Hardly surprising. He remembered his daughter. They said she was being looked after by neighbours but they hadn't mentioned Annie who had been with him. Why hadn't they mentioned Annie? Had they not mentioned Annie because Annie was no more?

Please, no. He wanted to scream but the sound wouldn't come.

Chapter 7

'Mrs Morris?'

'Yes.'

'I saw your card in the post-office window, advertising room and board in your delightful residence.'

Mrs Morris hesitated. Her house was all right, but no one had ever described it as a delightful residence. It was in a cobbled street in a working-class area of Leeds; an end-of-terrace with a small garden, overlooking the cemetery.

'Is it still vacant?'

She looked her caller up and down. He was a youngish man, carrying a suitcase in his right hand and supporting his left leg with a crutch. He was smiling from beneath a mop of the wildest hair she'd ever seen on a man. But it was his face that forced her to take a sharp intake of breath. He had obviously suffered severe burns at some time recently; burns that hadn't healed yet, burns that might never heal.

She gathered her thoughts. Whoever was to rent her

spare room would need to be able to pay, and pay on time, otherwise there'd be no point in her going to the trouble of letting it. A male tenant wouldn't have been her first choice either, but he seemed pleasant enough and he wasn't a big man. The last time she'd let it her lodgers had been forced upon her by a man from some government department, who'd pressed her into taking in two women who were working at a Leeds munitions factory. Their rent was paid regularly but their behaviour left much to be desired. Eventually, after they woke up half the street one night with their drunken shouting, she turfed them out the next morning with all their belongings. They were so hungover they had no fight left in them. This was almost a month ago, since when she'd heard nothing about being allocated further lodgers. She much preferred to choose her own.

She scanned the man's damaged face, trying to detect any trace of guile in his eyes. Detecting guile in people's eyes was something she felt she had a talent for. He sensed her giving him the once-over and offered, 'Don't let the face worry you. I'm told I'll be getting my film-star good looks back before much longer. I'm as harmless as I look, if that's any help.'

'That's just as well, because I'm not. Are you in employment?'

'Will be soon. The rent won't be a problem.'

She detected no dishonesty in the reply.

'It'll be thirty shillings a week, which includes breakfast and evening meal.'

'I assume that's just for one of me.'

'I assume there *is* only one of you.'

43

'One and a bit, actually.'

He held out his left arm and beckoned to someone beyond her line of vision. A small girl appeared beside him. She was an appealing child, maybe five years old, with hair the same colour and in the same wild state as his.

'This is my daughter Billie. We come as a job lot. She could share my room, and if there's only one bed I'm prepared to fork out for another out of my own pocket.'

The girl had the same beguiling smile as her father.

'Hello,' said Billie.

The man gave a wave in the general direction of his face. 'War wound. Not quite fully repaired yet.'

His accent wasn't local. He came from down south, possibly even London.

'So, were you one of our heroic soldiers?'

'Almost. Jerry dropped a bomb on me the very day I got my call-up papers.' The smile disappeared from his face. 'Annie and me were on our way to the shelter. Billie was galloping along in front as usual. I was lagging behind, helping her mum along. My wife was seven months pregnant and ...'

His scarred face crumpled into a frown that told her the full story was too painful to relate. She read what she could into it.

'So are there just the two of you now?'

The frown disappeared. 'That's right, just me and Billie. It all happened six months ago. One minute Billie had a beautiful mum, next minute she just had me – or what was left of me. She was evacuated up here out of the way of the Luftwaffe while her old man was put back together.

I picked her up this morning. Billie wasn't really happy with the people they put her with – good enough types, but it's not the same as living with your own. Mind you, my face takes some getting used to, I suppose. Today's the first time she's seen it since that night.'

'This isn't Daddy's proper face,' explained the child. 'His proper face is much nicer.'

'So,' said Chas, 'here we are, looking for lodgings until we find somewhere a bit more permanent. She's happier now she's with her old dad.'

'Look, you'd better come in and take a look round. If it's the two of you it'll be an extra ten bob a week. I do have an attic we can make into a bedroom for Billie.'

'That's sounds fine,' said Chas.

'You'll want to see the room.'

'I already know we'll like it. The lady at the post office gave you a glowing report, didn't she, Billie?'

They chatted as they went up the stairs. 'She said you were very good at cookin' an' stuff,' called out the little girl, who was bringing up the rear.

'Her mum was a great cook but the people she was sent to weren't, apparently.'

Billie pulled a face to illustrate what she'd had to put up with. 'They kept givin' me pom an' sago.'

This forced a smile from Mrs Morris who was quite taken with this odd-looking pair. They arrived on the landing. She turned, waiting for Billie to catch up. 'The only spuds you'll get from me are the ones I have to peel myself, and as for sago, I expect you used to call it frogspawn.'

Billie nodded.

'So did I,' said Mrs Morris. 'You'll get no frogspawn in this house. I've got a café as a well, so I know a bit about cooking.'

'Must keep yourself busy then,' said Chas.

'Well, I've got a couple of women who help run the café for me. We only open at lunchtimes to feed the workers in a few local factories and engineering works. We get there at half-ten to get the food on, and it's a madhouse between half-eleven and half-two. I shut up shop at around quarter-past three when we've got all the pots done and the place tidied up.'

'Sounds a tidy business.'

'It is. Anyway, this is your room.'

It was quite spacious and had its own adjacent toilet and washbasin on the landing, which had been achieved by knocking through a wall into what had been a box room. Her father, a jobbing builder, had done the work for her just after her now ex-husband got locked up for housebreaking, Mrs Morris explained.

'I had it done especially for taking in a lodger. I think there's nothing worse than not having your own facilities. A lot of the houses round here still use the lavatory in the yard. I have my own facility connecting to my room so there won't be any problems in that direction. There's a bath in the scullery as and when required. Obviously that has to be pre-arranged as it's covered with a wooden lid when it's not in use.'

'Inside lav of our own, that's brilliant,' said Chas. 'We'll take it. What do you think, Billie?'

She dived on to one of the two single beds and claimed it as hers. The room had a large mahogany wardrobe that was more than big enough to take the clothes of the average man and his daughter, plus a dressing table, a large chest of drawers, two chairs, a small table and a three-bar electric fire.

'There are two extra plugs if you have a wireless or anything else you need to plug in,' Mrs Morris told Chas. 'You'll find an electric meter out on the landing which takes everything up to a shilling, and you have my word that the meter is set fairly and I don't make any money out of it. You only pay what it costs me.'

'I think the room is excellent, Mrs Morris. I suppose you need to know who I am.'

'Yes, I need your name for the rent book.'

'My name is Charles Herbert Challinor. My friends call me Chas. If you need to know anything further about me I suggest you read this.' He took a folded sheet of newspaper from his coat pocket and handed it to her. She unfolded what turned out to be page three of the *Evening Standard* dated six months earlier. It carried a family photograph of Chas plus his wife and daughter above an article with the heading:

Tragedy Hits Jazz Musician Chas Challinor.

The journalist reported how he had lost his pregnant wife and been badly injured himself by a German bomb. At the time of the bombing Chas had been playing with the Tubby Blake Band, whose name was vaguely familiar to Mrs Morris. She looked at her new lodger.

'Are you famous or something?'

He smiled. 'Not really. I carry this to prove I am who I say I am. A respectable citizen and not some fly-by-night.'

'So jazz musicians are all respectable, are they?'

'Every last one of us. Do not believe the rumours. I have our identity cards and ration books as well.'

He handed them to her. She stuck the newspaper under her arm, examined them and nodded, as if to say that all seemed to be in order. Then she looked up at Chas again.

'So, what do you play?'

'Mainly clarinet, for whoever wants to hire me.'

'Well, I don't suppose having a wonky leg'll stop you playing.'

'No, but being in constant pain isn't helping. I used to earn a good living from blowing the old liquorice stick.'

She now felt guilty for underestimating how much he must still be suffering. His smile was disarming despite the face surrounding it being scarred and disfigured.

'Is the pain easing at all?' she asked.

'Gradually – the physical pain anyway. Losing my wife and unborn baby's a bit hard to bear at times – most of the time, actually.'

Wordlessly she gave him back the ration books and cards then took another glance at the newspaper article. Chas Challinor had been a good-looking man back then – something else he'd lost.

'Is that still your job then – being a musician?'

'It's something I hope to get back to. In the meantime I've got a job going round Leeds schools teaching clarinet and sax.'

'Will you be wanting to practise here?'

'Not if it bothers you.'

'Well, I'll have to see if it bothers me or not. I'm not averse to a bit of classical music. I passed my grade four at the piano but gave it up when my dad had to sell it to pay the rent. Not too sure about this jazz stuff that you play.'

'I trained as a classical musician, Mrs Morris, so I can give you a bit of Beethoven and Mozart from time to time.'

'Like I said, I'll see if it bothers me. I'll get you a rent book and I'll need two weeks in advance – that's four pounds, please.'

He took out his wallet. 'I insist on giving you eight pounds in advance as proof of good faith. If it's okay by you I'll have the rest of my stuff sent up from London.' He handed her the money. 'I think we're all going to get along fine, Mrs Morris, absolutely fine.'

She left father and daughter to it and went back downstairs, not entirely sure if she'd done the right thing. They had things in common, it was true. He'd lost his wife to a bomb; she'd lost her wastrel of a husband to the law, who didn't like the way he made his money. Chas was no longer handsome and … she looked in the hall mirror at the face that used to turn men's heads. Thirty-one years old and she looked forty. The nine years she'd spent married to that pig Larry Morris had put twice that on her. She'd come through them only to find her home country at war with Germany, and it was a war they weren't having much success with to date. The Germans had even managed to drop a few bombs on Leeds.

When she had the chance she'd change her name back to Liz O'Neill and make more time to recover some of her lost beauty. She'd read in *Woman's Own* how to revitalise her skin using special exercises and nourishing cream. Then she thought of Chas and realised it would take more than skin cream and exercises to help him recover *his* looks. Liz scowled at her own reflection and told herself: Stop feeling so sorry for yourself! Compared to that poor man upstairs you're a lucky lady.

Chapter 8

June 1941

Chas looked up at the place of work he'd never seen before; it was in fact one of several places of work he'd never seen before but would have to accustom himself to if this job were to last. He was now a peripatetic music teacher and would move from school to school instructing the pupils studying clarinet and saxophone. Monday was to be his Roundhay Girls' High School day.

He had a problem He hadn't mentioned his disability to his employers, Leeds Education Department. He'd got the job courtesy of his reputation as a musician. Billie was at a school within five minutes' walk of their new home, Roundhay High School a fifteen-minute tram ride away, so that all worked well for Chas. But he had another problem too: he'd never done any formal teaching before. The doctors said he was six months away from walking without a crutch, although the prognosis was for a complete recovery within eighteen months. In the meantime he needed to support himself and his daughter the best way he could. Since his days as a star performer in a jazz band seemed to be behind him, this teaching job was his best shot at earning a living.

For most of his life Chas had been a happy-go-lucky person and on the outside not much had changed, except that deep down he had an unquenchable hatred for the Germans, matched only by his deep love for his daughter and a bottomless emptiness within at the loss of his beloved Annie.

But as he walked towards the school building the person filling Chas's thoughts was his dad, whose health was apparently failing. Chas had just received a letter from one of his dad's employees who'd been acting as a go-between. Chas was wondering why he should care. His dad had disowned him when he married a woman from the Elliker family. He hadn't even gone to Annie's funeral, saying he couldn't stand to mix with the despicable Ellikers. Nor had he bothered to visit Chas, his only child, in hospital, such was his anger with his son for disobeying instructions and marrying into a disreputable family. In any case Chas hadn't been told his dad had a terminal illness, only that he was just in poor health. It could be that the old man would live for years yet.

The conundrum was: should he visit his father? He hadn't seen him since he'd taken Billie there as a toddler. Back then his father had been barely civil to him and hadn't shown a hint of grandfatherly affection for Billie. If he didn't, it would make Chas just as bad as the old man, but would he be betraying Annie if he made things up with his dad behind her back? Then he told himself not to be so stupid. There was no question of betraying Annie. She was dead. So why did he feel guilty at the thought of doing something so momentous without her being involved? And why was he quite certain that he'd never marry again? Chas smiled to himself at this thought. Who'd even want a washed-up clarinet player who looked as if he'd been ducking for apples in a chip pan?

He was still smiling to himself as he entered the building and asked for directions to the headmistress's office. The girl he asked recoiled from his face and he wondered, not for the first time, if his disfigurement might affect his proposed teaching career.

'It's that door there, sir.'

He smiled at the girl. It was a smile that made up in some part for the cosmetic deficiencies surrounding it. The bomb hadn't damaged his teeth.

'Thank you, young lady.'

The headmistress glanced up at him from her desk as he knocked and entered in response to her call. She didn't recoil from his burned face, simply studied it.

'I assume that was the work of the damned Luftwaffe, was it?'

'It was. You don't seem surprised.'

'When you applied we checked up on you. We knew about your poor wife and that you'd been injured. I find it most commendable you didn't seek to elicit sympathy by mentioning it in your application.'

'That might well have backfired on me. I imagine you want an able-bodied person to do the work – which I am, I hasten to add. Well, apart from a bit of a limp, which will go in its own good time.'

'I'm pleased to hear that. Am I to understand you've never taught before?'

'No, but I was taught music for eight years by excellent teachers and well remember my lessons. To teach music you need to know music. You need to have both a feel for it and a talent for it.'

The headmistress got to her feet decisively. 'I suspect we're lucky to have you, Mr Challinor, or do I call you Chas?'

'I much prefer Chas. I assume I call you Mrs Eames?'

'You do. My first name is Agnes, which means the girls call me Aggie ... but never to my face.'

'My mother was called Agnes so I always feel a certain affection for the name.'

'The virgin martyr.'

'That's what my mother told me. At the time I had no idea what she was talking about. Still don't, to be honest.'

The headmistress raised her eyebrows in disbelief. 'I'll escort you to our music room. You have eighteen pupils but only twelve woodwind instruments. Five clarinets, five saxophones, one oboe and one bassoon. Some of the girls are lucky enough to have parents who'll buy them an instrument of their choice so hopefully it should all work out fine. You've brought with you an air of celebrity, which is why there are six girls present today who have never studied music before. I'll leave it to you to decide which ones they are.'

'I think that'll take me about five minutes. Do you play anything yourself?'

'Why do you ask?'

'I don't know. Just the way you talk about the instruments. You speak with affection of them, and making music is an affectionate business.'

'Is it? Yes, I can bang out a tune on the piano, but only for my own pleasure. I can't sight read or anything.'

'Well today's lesson will be all about reading,' said Chas. 'No one will blow a single note until they know exactly which note they're blowing. That's how I learned and that's how I'll teach. No one learns to read music unless they have a love for the subject. I suspect next week we'll be back down to twelve or maybe thirteen. I can teach the oboe and bassoon up to a certain level, but my principal two instruments are the clarinet and saxophone.'

'We know this and it's satisfactory. If you'd like to follow me?'

The music room was on the ground floor, which suited Chas, who didn't fancy carting his game leg up and down stairs. As Mrs Eames opened the door the sound of girl-ish chattering dwindled to an expectant silence. Chas followed the headmistress in, as nonchalantly as he could, smiling at the group of girls whose ages ranged from four-teen to eighteen.

'Morning, ladies,' he said, before Mrs Eames could speak. 'My name's Chas Challinor. You get to call me by my first name simply because I'm a musician, which also means I don't get lumbered with a nickname. My face is the work of the Luftwaffe and I'm told it's getting better. I play mainly the clarinet but I'm also fairly good on the saxophone. Who among you can play either of those instruments?'

'Is it true that you played with the Dorsey Brothers' band?' asked one girl. About seventeen, a bit spotty but otherwise very pretty.

'Yeah, I played with them for a while when they came over to England back in 1934. What instrument do you play?'

'I, er, I don't play anything yet.'

'No problem. Anyone else play the clarinet or sax?'

A small girl put up her hand. Maybe fourteen, mousy and nervous. Chas smiled at her and said, 'I'm guessing clarinet.'

Nod.

'What level are you on?'

'Level five.'

'Tell me what you can play without reading the music.'

She shrugged, then said, '"Chaconne".'

The girl's eyes strayed to a clarinet case on a nearby table. Chas followed her gaze, walked over to the case and took out the instrument.

'This yours?'

Nod.

He removed the mouthpiece and replaced it with one from his pocket. Then he played Bach's 'Chaconne' for the thousandth time in his life. It was a good piece for practising scales. He played it like the girls had never heard it before.

'Is that what it sounds like?' he enquired of the mousy girl.

'Not when I play it,' she admitted.

The other girls laughed as did Mrs Eames. 'Well, I'm not as good as I used to be before this,' said Chas, jabbing a thumb in the direction of his face. 'But I'm getting my feel for it back.'

One of the older girls called out, 'Can you play "Body and Soul"?'

'I think you know I can. Are you asking me if I will?'

'Yes, please.'

Chas put the instrument back to his lips but was

56

stopped in his tracks by the older girl. 'Can you play it on your own clarinet, please?'

He put the mousy girl's clarinet down, looked at his audience and told them, 'This may not sound quite like it does on the record.'

'We know that.'

He took out his own clarinet and began to play the tune that had been made famous by Ruth Etting in 1930. The girls began to sway in time to it; the older girl, who had asked him to play, began to sing the melody. Chas went up beside her and encouraged her to sing louder; some other girls began to sing harmony. Mrs Eames opened the piano lid and joined in. They'd rehearsed this, they'd set him up, and it pleased Chas no end.

Everyone in the room knew the tune by heart because they'd all listened to the record in anticipation of his coming to the school. The door to the room opened and two passing teachers stood there in open-mouthed amazement. Pupils from a nearby classroom came to see what was happening. They crowded the doorway, forcing the two watching teachers into the room. The music was coming to an end. Chas told his lead singer to go again from the top, and so they all did. They sang and played for six whole minutes, by which time the corridor outside the music room was blocked.

Chas eventually brought the performance to an end to a great round of applause from the girls, from Mrs Eames, and from the dozens of spectators. He in turn clapped his fellow musicians.

'Well, girls,' said the headmistress, 'what do we think? Shall we give this music man the job?'

Chapter 9

Liz was waiting for him when he got back, the same way as a wife might be waiting for her husband to come home after the first day at his new job. This made Chas feel slightly uncomfortable, wondering what Annie would have made of it.

'How did it go?' asked Liz.

'It went well, I think.'

'Any child prodigies?'

'One girl tried to jazz up "God Save The King" on her clarinet.'

'Did any of them know who you are?'

'Actually, yes. The school had one of Tubby's records, with me in the photo on the cover doing a clarinet solo. So they all know I looked like Clark Gable before my boat race got burned.'

'Boat race?'

Chas grinned. 'I'm going to have to teach you primitive Northerners how to speak proper. Boat race is Cockney rhyming slang for face.'

'Oh, right. So, it's not a problem, then?'

'What's not a problem?'

'The boat race.'

'Ah, did I say it might be?'

'Well, I reckon it must have crossed your mind.'

'Woman's intuition, eh? Yes, I did have some reserva-
tions and the obstacle was surmounted, but I've got to
surmount it again tomorrow at another school, and the
same thing every day all week.'

'Sounds like you've got your work cut out.'

'It does, doesn't it?'

'Just tell them you can't judge a book by its cover.'

'Excellent idea. I've got an old Bible with a real tatty
cover. I'll take that to show them.'

'I reckon comparing yourself to the Bible might be
going over the top a bit.'

'Just a bit, maybe. No, I think it's going to be okay. No
doubt they'll all have their nicknames for me, but I'm stuck
with that. I've still got Billie and I've got my life, which is
more than my Annie ended up with.'

Liz felt like putting her arms around him then and hugging him, but she didn't. He was still in love with Annie
and no woman on earth can compete with a ghost.

'I saw Billie playing out in the street. How did she get
on at school?' asked Chas.

'Same as you by the sound of it. When you've got
charm and personality you don't need anything else, and
that kid's got personality plus. Annie would be proud of
you both.'

'I like to think so. I'm thinking of taking Billie to the
first house at the Odeon tonight to see *Pinocchio*. Would
you like to join us?'

Liz almost said, *If you don't think Annie would mind*, but

59

she bit her tongue and said instead, 'Yes, I think I'd like that.'

She thought she might be the only one who could see beyond Chas's ruined boat race to the man beneath the scars. A man she'd fallen in love with. A man who lived in the same house, and who was taking her to the pictures that evening.

Liz stopped to look in the mirror as she followed him into the living room. Did she still look forty-two? Maybe not. Maybe she was beginning to look a bit nearer her actual age – nearer *his* age.

A hour later, as they left for the cinema, across the street at number twenty-six Edna Grimshaw's blackout curtains twitched. Her husband was just coming in from work.

'Looks like Scarface's gorriz feet under Liz's table,' she observed as the trio made their way down the street outside, looking for all the world like a happy little family.

'Yer a rough-tongued woman,' grunted her husband. 'What's fer tea?'

'Owt yer can catch.'

'Yer mean I've been workin' since six o'clock this mornin' and yer've made me no tea?'

'T'fish shop's open.'

'Aye, an' so is your gob. I bet she treats him a damn' sight better than you treat me.'

'Well, he's a lot better-lookin' than you.'

Edna laughed at her own cruel joke as her husband put his coat back on.

'Aw, that's it, yer useless cow!' he said. 'I'm not waitin'

for me call up. I'm signing on for t'army tomorrow.' He went back out of the door before Edna could ask him where he was going. The army was many things, including a refuge for husbands trapped in bad marriages, and there were quite a few wives who didn't see a downside to their husbands being called up.

Larry Morris was currently too old for conscription and there weren't too many decent jobs about for men just out of the slammer. He'd been out a week and had made two decisions. One was to get in touch with his old criminal contacts, and the other was to give his ex-wife a visit to see if he could rekindle the old flame. Liz owned her own house, having been left it by her late father, who had died while Larry was still inside. She also had the café and that made a nice few bob. A woman with her own house and business was worth going back to. A man needed an income and a fixed abode.

There was no light leaking through the curtains when he got to her house. He knocked a couple of times and was about to walk away when Edna called out to him from across the street.

'She's gone out with her lodger.'

Larry walked across. 'Lodger?'

'Yeah. A feller – he's a bit crippled and bashed about. He's got a young girl. They've been gone about an hour.'

'Where've they gone?'

'No idea. I don't s'pose they'll be too late out. Not with 'em takin' t'girl. She's only about five.'

'Has Liz still got the café?'

'She has, yeah. Between that an' takin' in lodgers, she must make a few quid.'

'I imagine she does. A girl, eh? She allus wanted a girl. Mebbe if she'd had one we'd still be together.'

'How come yer never had kiddies?'

'We did, actually. She had a little girl. Died inside her just before she were born.'

'Oh, heck! Liz never mentioned.'

'No, she never spoke about it to anyone, not even me. Ter tell the truth, I weren't all that bothered. Never wanted kids around.' Larry looked at his watch. 'Gone about an hour, yer say?'

'I did. Yer can come in an' wait, if yer like?'

'Well, I don't mind if I do. A cuppa tea'd go down nicely too.'

'I'll put t'kettle on.'

Edna knew about him going to jail, but in her eyes that only added to Larry's glamour. Better him than a useless husband who worked sixty hours a week in a slaughter house for two bob an hour.

'Is yer husband not at home?' Larry asked, as he sipped his tea.

'He's been home an' gone out. Pub most likely.'

'Oh, it's like that, is it?'

'Aye. Useless flamin' lump.'

'Does he still work down at t'abattoir?'

'He does. Slave labour down there. Trouble is, he's good fer nowt else. He's thinkin' of joining up. As if they'd have him!'

'I don't think they're too fussy who they take, Edna. This lodger Liz's . . . got. Is that all he is – a lodger?'

62

A mischievous glint lit Edna's eyes. 'Well, she were linkin' arms with him as they walked down t'street just now, so I'll leave it up ter you ter figure that one out.'

'Big feller, is he?'

'Oh, no ... nowhere near as big as you. The only thing scary about him's his face what's all burned ... ugh!'

'Soldier, was he?'

'No, he's a London lad. Hitler dropped a bomb on him. He's gorra bad limp on him and wouldn't be much competition fer you, I wouldn't have thought.'

'Competition? What makes yer think I'm in the running?'

'What makes yer come back here if not ter gerroff with Liz again?'

He scratched his ear. 'Well, I thought I might give it a try. Yer never know. I've got one or two things lined up that might make her look at me more favourably.'

'I've heard the crime rate's gone up since t'war started,' commented Edna, tactlessly.

'It's due ter go up a bit more if I've got owt ter do with it! There's people makin' millions out of this war and I don't see what's wrong with me making a few quid.'

'Ee, I wish my husband were a bit more like you. He'll be in that pub right now and I won't see hide nor hair of him 'til closin' time.'

Larry studied her face, wondering if she was making a play for him, and wondering if he'd take her up on it if she was. Edna was passable-looking in a bad light, and it'd been a long time.

'What?' she said.

'Nowt.'

'Were yer thinkin' yer've gone without fer a long time?'

He nodded. 'Something like that.'

'Well, we could soon remedy that. If it's what yer want, we could nip upstairs for a bit. I've gone without meself for quite a while, if it comes ter that.'

An hour and a half later they were back downstairs, drinking tea and smoking, when Edna got to her feet and went to the window. She eased the blackout curtain to one side and reported, 'They're back.'

'Right.' Larry stood up and stubbed out his cigarette in an ashtray.

'So, what yer gonna do?' she asked.

'I think I'm gonna join yer husband for a pint or two while I make up me mind about the best way ter go on.'

Edna tapped her nose. 'Fools rush in and all that.'

'I may be many things, Edna, but I'm no fool. I need ter box clever here, and I always think clearer with a pint or two inside me.'

The very thought of any man thinking clearer with a pint or two inside him amused Edna but she kept it to herself.

Liz was down in the cellar doing some washing and Chas was in the back room playing his clarinet. He was using a mute that cut the sound by half, so all Liz could hear was pleasant background music. Billie was fast asleep, dreaming of *Pinocchio*, now her favourite picture of all time. Chas was playing 'Take the "A" Train', the signature tune of the Duke Ellington Orchestra, not written in particular for the clarinet, but the way Chas played any tune was a clarinet tune. It was quarter-past ten when Larry knocked on the door. He'd meant it to be a polite knock but the six pints he had inside him affected his judgement.

Chas heard it and came out of the back room with his clarinet in his hand as Liz emerged from the cellar.

'Could be someone complaining about me playing at this time of night,' he ventured.

'You weren't that loud,' she said, going to the door. Chas stood just behind her so that he could see who it was, and apologise if necessary.

'Hello, Liz. Long time no see.'

She looked down from the entry steps at her ex-husband, an expression of distaste on her face.

'Not long enough, Larry. Why are you here?'

He gave an exaggerated shrug. 'I was just in the area. Thought you might invite me in, for old times' sake. We had some good times, me and you.'

'No, we didn't.'

Larry blinked and scowled at her. This wasn't going quite the way he'd planned. It had all seemed very easy while he was back in the pub. He looked beyond her at Chas.

'Jesus! What the hell's that?'

'Go away, Larry,' said Liz.

'No, what is he? Has he forced his way in here? Is he giving you trouble . . . because if he is, I'll show him what real trouble is.'

'No, he's not giving me tr—'

Larry had pushed his way past her into the room. His fists were clenched and he meant harm to Chas, who was now holding his clarinet like a club. He'd guessed who this man was.

'Just stay back! All I am is her lodger.'

Liz made a grab for Larry. He turned and punched her full in the face. She went down, unconscious. Chas swung his clarinet at Larry's head, delivering what would have been a hefty blow from a more substantial weapon, but it only served to further enrage Larry, who threw punches that had Chas retreating across the room towards the open cellar door. A heavy blow to the side of his head sent him reeling to the floor. Larry kneeled astride him and was punching him about the head when Billie flew at him from behind, screaming and trying to push him off her father. Larry made to get to his feet and was caught off balance when Billie pushed him again. It was only a very slight push but it was enough to send the drunken man falling backwards through the open doorway and down the stone cellar steps.

Billie stood there, shocked. Not knowing what to do. Both her dad and Liz were unconscious and the horrible man might come up out of the cellar for her at any moment. Chas began to stir. Billie took his arm in both her hands and pulled him upright. He rubbed his head and gathered his thoughts, looking round.

'Where is he?' he asked eventually.

'That horrid man? He fell down the cellar steps.' Then she added, with a trace of guilt in her voice, 'He was hurting you so I pushed him.'

'Did you? Good for you, Billie. You saved your old man's skin. Is he still down there?'

'I expect so.'

Chas got to his feet, shut the cellar door and turned the key. He winked at her. 'I think we'll let the coppers deal with him.'

Then he kneeled down beside Liz, who was also coming round. Chas and Billie helped her to a chair.

'We've locked the nasty man in the cellar,' said Billie. 'He was hurting Daddy, so I pushed him down the steps.'

'Saved my skin,' said Chas.

The three of them listened for any sounds coming from the cellar. All was quiet. Both Liz and Chas had the same alarming thought.

'Billie, I think you should go back to bed,' said Chas. 'You've had enough excitement for one evening. School in the morning.'

'Okay, Daddy,' she said, reluctantly. 'Will you be all right to go to work?'

Chad didn't look all right. His already scarred face hadn't been improved by the battering it'd just taken.

'I'll stick some bandages on and tell them it's part of my treatment.'

'But that's a fib, Daddy.'

'I know, but it's a good fib.'

'I didn't know there were any good fibs.'

'You're not allowed to use good fibs until you're grown up,' said Chas.

'I bet that's one of your good fibs,' said Billie.

Chas gave her a hug and a kiss, as did Liz, and they both watched her go up to bed knowing it was their job to protect her from the man in the cellar, no matter what state he was in.

Liz looked at Chas and said, 'We could just call the police.'

'I know. But Billie pushed him down the steps – the *stone* steps.'

'And he'll have landed on the stone floor,' said Liz, quietly.

Chas went to the cellar door and turned the key, half

expecting the madman to come charging through. All was quiet. He opened the door and looked into the darkness. The steps went straight down in front of him but he couldn't see the bottom. He flicked on the light switch and gasped. Liz was behind him.

'What is it?'

'He's still down there.'

'Is he ?'

'I don't know. I'll check him out.'

Hanging in a tool rack on the wall beside the door was a hammer. Chas picked it up just in case Larry was feigning unconsciousness. He descended the steps tentatively with Liz a step behind. Larry was lying with his head at an angle that told Chas all he needed to know. The man had a broken neck. He put his ear close to Larry's mouth and detected no trace of breath.

'I think he's gone, Liz.'

'Oh, God! Can you check his pulse?'

Chas lifted Larry's hand and placed two fingers on the place he thought the pulse usually was. He shook his head. 'I'm not sure if I'm doing it right.'

She knelt down at the other side and took Larry's other wrist. Chas remained motionless as he waited for her verdict. 'He's dead, Chas.'

They both sat back on their haunches with Larry between them, looking at each other. 'Do we ring the police?' said Liz.

'Well, that'd be the right thing to do, but—'

'What else can we do?'

'Should we tell them what happened, that Billie pushed him down the steps?' Chas asked.

'She did it to save you. I could vouch for that. I could tell them I saw it happen.'

'Or I could say he just tripped and fell.'

'That'd do it.'

Chas nodded. 'But Billie knows she pushed him, which means we'll have to tell her to lie, and supposing she caves in and tells the truth?'

'That'd make things much worse for her,' agreed Liz.

'If she tells the truth it'll end up in court and Billie would have to be formally cleared of any guilt.'

'Which is what would happen,' Liz assured him.

'We hope,' said Chas.

'Bloody hell! She's not much more than a baby.'

'I don't want my daughter to have to go to court. I don't want her to know she killed a man. Thing like that could scar her for life.'

Liz shuddered with delayed shock and nodded her head. 'No, we can't let her know what she's done. There must be some way to avoid it.'

'I could tell them he attacked me,' said Chas. 'He tripped and fell down the steps. That Billie had nothing to do with it. I could keep her right out of it.'

'You could, but the court wouldn't accept that as easily as they would Billie telling them she did it. You might end up in prison.'

'Trouble is, whatever we tell the police,' said Chas, 'Billie's going to *know* it was she who killed him. She's not stupid. How will she live with that?'

'I don't know.'

'It's a real mess, Liz.'

'I know, and it's a mess that *he* caused.'

Chas thought for a moment. 'Who else but us knows he's here?'

'Edna maybe.'

'Yeah, she doesn't miss much.'

Chas went back upstairs and opened the front door, standing there for several minutes, during which time Edna's curtains remained drawn and no one else was visible in the street. In other words, their visitor might well have left right then with no one any the wiser, including nosy Edna. Liz was standing beside him.

'If anyone saw him come they can't say for sure he didn't leave around now,' said Chas, looking at his watch. Ten thirty-three.

'We can't keep him here – unless we bury him in the cellar.'

'It's an idea,' said Chas.

They went back inside and both looked at the dead body and then at the concrete floor of the cellar. Chas shook his head.

'This concrete's probably six inches thick at least. I'd need a compressor and jack-hammer to break through it, and it'd make a hell of a noise; complaints from neighbours most probably. I could try to break through with an ordinary hammer and chisel but there'd be hours of banging and clattering.'

'I don't want him kept in this house,' decided Liz, staring down at Larry.

Chas looked at her as his mind ticked over. In the corner of the cellar there was a shovel and a pickaxe.

'There's a cemetery next door,' he said.

'What? Chas, we can't just bury a body in a public cemetery.'

'Why not? That's what cemeteries are for.'

'If the police found out we'd get done for murder.'

'Not if we buried him properly. And even if the police did find him, why would they think we killed him?'

'Because I'm his ex-wife and I live practically next-door to his grave!'

'If we take everything off him that identifies him, they won't know who he is.'

'Can't they identify him from his fingerprints? They'll have a record, with him having been in jail.'

'Dunno,' said Chas. 'Surely they'd have to suspect who he was to make the match. It's not as though they can press a button and say "These are Larry Morris's prints". Anyway, they'd have to suspect something to dig him up in the first place. What would there be to suspect?'

'Nothing, I don't suppose.'

'And by the time he is dug up, in the natural way of things there won't be too much left of him, much less his fingerprints.'

'I suppose not,' Liz conceded.

'Who's going to miss him anyway?'

'His probation officer?'

'Liz, he's a convicted criminal. There's nothing odd about a criminal disappearing. It's what they do.'

She thought about this and nodded. The suggestion seemed drastic but it would be a tidy solution to a potentially messy problem. 'As it happens there was a burial today just over the wall,' she said. 'In a very quiet corner of the cemetery.'

71

'Freshly dug earth,' said Chas. 'The ground'll still be soft.'

'It will, yes.'

'I could easily dig a trench, say, four feet deep.'

'I suppose you could.'

'Lay him to rest and fill it in again – proper burial. Bit of company for the man underneath him.'

'I think it was a woman.'

Without another word, Chas picked up the pick and shovel and carried them up the steps. Liz followed him, determined that he wasn't going to do this on his own.

An hour and a half later, at just turned midnight, Chas had dug a trench in the recent grave, six feet long, two feet wide and four feet deep. The eerie scene was lit by a three-quarter moon. Liz had kept watch although she knew the cemetery caretaker didn't emerge from his lodge after six o'clock in the evening, except in emergencies. Between them they hauled Larry's body up the cellar steps and out of the back door of the house. They heaved him over the cemetery wall, dragged him twenty yards to the trench and rolled him into it. It was an arduous and macabre job that left Liz feeling nauseous.

'Okay?' Chas asked her.

'Not really. Just let's get him buried.'

Chas spent another half hour filling the trench again. The mound was slightly higher than it had been before but it was hardly noticeable.

'How's it looking?' he said, satisfied with his handi-work.

'Like a freshly filled grave,' said Liz, whose nausea had disappeared as Larry's body disappeared beneath the earth.

'All this will settle over the next few weeks, then they'll put a headstone on.'

'I'll have another look in the morning,' said Chas. 'If it needs any finishing touches I can nip over and sort it out while no one's about.'

'There's never anyone about before about ten o'clock,' said Liz. 'Grave-visiting isn't an early-morning thing.'

'Should we feel guilty?' he asked.

'The man was dead,' said Liz. 'All we did was bury him in a cemetery without troubling with the formalities.'

'Do you want to say a prayer or anything?'

Liz closed her eyes and clasped her hands. 'Dear Lord, please slam the Pearly Gates in his face and send him to rot in hell where he belongs.'

'Amen,' said Chas.

Back in the house Liz made them cups of tea while Chas went up to check on Billie, who was sleeping peacefully. He looked down at his innocent child and knew they'd done the right thing. In the morning he'd tell her the nasty man had gone and wouldn't be coming back and that it would be best if they didn't talk about him ever again. Not to anyone. That way they'd forget that this had ever happened. Bad things were always best forgotten in Chas's experience.

He went back downstairs and was drinking his tea when he said, 'Do you know the worst thing about all this?'

'Well, none of it was good.'

'I broke my clarinet.'

'Oh.'

'Oh? What do you mean, oh? It was a Buffet Crampon – the Rolls-Royce of clarinets. Now I'll have to make do with my old one.'

He was holding it up to his eye and, looking down the length of it, he observed, 'It's crooked.'

Liz nodded and said, 'So was Larry.'

Chas put it to his mouth and blew. A squeaky sound came out. 'Sounds like a goose farting.'

There was no humour in his voice and she knew he was trying to take his mind off what had happened. She had no such distraction available. A sudden wave of fear swept over her.

'Chas.'

'What?'

'I need a hug.'

He put the instrument down and went over to her. She stood up and allowed him to take her in his arms. She closed her eyes and wept against his shoulder. He patted her back.

'It's all right. The man's buried. It's all over.'

'Is it all over, Chas? I'm scared.'

He said nothing for a while, he just held her and thought about what they'd done. 'Look,' he said at length. 'I can't guarantee that there won't be police banging on our door tomorrow morning, but if I were a bookie I'd give odds of ten million to one against it. No one knows what happened but us, he won't be missed and there's nothing suspicious about the grave. I'll give it another check in the morning to see if there's anything amiss.'

'I know you're right but it was such an awful thing. I'll never get it out of my mind.'

'Yes, you will. You'll have lots of much better things to think about. In fact we'll make a pact here and now, never to talk about it again and never to think about it ever again. It's done, finished.'

She lifted her head from his shoulder and looked at him. 'What are you thinking about right now, Chas?'

'Oh, the usual.'

'What's that?'

'Annie.'

His hold on her relaxed as he said the name and Liz knew that if an awful incident such as this couldn't bring them together, nothing would. He would never be hers.

Chapter 10

May 1942

'What?' asked Chas.

Liz had been looking at him intently. Billie was in bed and the two of them had been playing dominoes. Liz had just beaten him for the third time.

'Gladys Florence Dickinson's got her headstone at last,' she said. 'Born 1862, died 1941.'

'Who's Gladys Florence Dickinson?'

'She's the one lying under Larry. The day after we buried him it occurred to me that there might be a Mr Dickinson waiting to be planted on top of his wife.'

'Bloody hell!'

'You never thought of that?'

'Well, no, I didn't '

'Don't worry. I called in at the cemetery office and checked in the register. She was a spinster – they have that information in case there's someone else lined up for a double grave. Gladys Florence Dickinson was single, as is her plot.'

'Why didn't you mention it?'

'Because straight afterwards we made a pact never to

76

talk about it again. And I thought I was just being silly, worrying about such a thing.'

'No, you were quite right. Had there been a Mr Dickinson waiting to join her we'd have had to dig Larry up.' Chas shuddered at the prospect.

'Anyway, yesterday was just a year after she was buried. Some relative obviously decided it was time to mark the grave. The stone's very nice. Black marble with gold lettering.' She looked straight at Chas then. 'Do you ever think about what happened that night?'

'Less and less,' said Chas. 'Anyway, now Miss Dickinson's got her headstone I think we can draw a line under that particular episode in our lives.'

'Yes, and I don't suppose there'll be much of Larry left to identify,' said Liz. After saying it she shuddered and added, 'Did that sound callous?'

'Not really. There wouldn't have been too much of me left by now if Billie hadn't come to my rescue that night.'

Liz began putting the dominoes back in the box. 'By the way, your boat race is looking much better nowadays.'

Chas instinctively ran his fingers over his scars.

'You think so?'

'I know so. In the time you've been here it's healed enormously.'

'Hmm. I suppose I was luckier than the lads in McIndoe's Army.'

'McIndoe's Army? What's that?'

'They call themselves the Guinea Pig Club. Blokes who got it a lot worse than me. There's a plastic surgeon called Archibald McIndoe who's a genius at rebuilding hands and faces. He works at a hospital in East Grinstead. I was taken there so he could have a look at me, to see if I needed his help, and he said nature would heal my scars a lot better than he could.'

'It looks as if he was right.'

Chas stared into the fire and remembered what he'd seen in McIndoe's clinic. 'Some of the lads'd had most of their faces burned off and McIndoe still managed to rebuild them. But he knew their physical recovery was nothing compared to the challenges they'd face in the outside world, so he arranged for them to go to all sorts of events such as film premieres and theatrical first nights, dressed in their uniforms or street clothes instead of hospital gowns, and walk around as if they looked like Clark Gable. Eventually other people stopped staring at them.'

'Did you go on any of these outings?'

'Well, I was only there for a few days but I did get to see the premiere of *Sea Wolf*. I was actually introduced to Edward G. Robinson — well, me and about twenty other blokes.' Chas frowned at the memory of the men who'd become his friends during his brief stay.

'He's still doing it. Great man, McIndoe. They call him "The Maestro". I knew I wouldn't need him as soon as I got there. Compared to some of the other blokes I probably did look like Clark Gable. Brave lads, every one of them. It put my little scratches into perspective.'

He looked at Liz then and noticed the tears filming her eyes. 'You okay?'

She nudged away the tears with the crook of a finger. 'Yeah, I'm fine.'

'You're not fine, you're crying. It's me who should be —

crying after the drubbing you've just given me! What's the matter?'

She looked down. 'Nothing.'

'Is there anything I can do?'

She sighed. 'Unfortunately not.' She smiled at him and added, 'You still love Annie, don't you?'

He hesitated then said, 'Yes ... I do. I'll always love Annie.'

Liz shook her head and got to her feet. 'I'll make us a cup of tea.'

He stood up and grabbed her hand. 'Won't you tell me what your problem is?'

'No, because it's not fair on you ... or Billie. If I told you it'd just ruin things between us all.'

Chas's curiosity was aroused. 'Is it something you've done in the past? Liz, do you have a skeleton in your cupboard?'

She laughed and stood facing him. 'You know, Chas, if there was another woman in this room – any woman – you wouldn't need to ask me what the problem was, you could just ask her.'

'Oh, so I can't see the problem because I'm a man, is that it?'

'Correct.'

Chas sat down again, without taking his eyes off her. 'This has something to do with me, hasn't it?'

She held up her hands in despair and confessed, 'Oh my God! Chas, my problem is that I'm ruddy well in love with you, and I know you don't love me.'

He sat back in his chair, completely non-plussed, then said, 'Well, I'm very fond of you, Liz.'

'Chas, I know you are, and I'm very happy that you're fond of me. I couldn't stand it if you weren't fond of me. Unfortunately, for me it goes a bit deeper than that. You see, I've never been in love with a man before and I've fallen for one who's ... er ... unavailable.'

'I don't know what to say, Liz. I find you a very attract-ive woman and I know any man would be lucky to have you as his wife.'

'You find me attractive?'

'Of course I do. Good Lord, Liz! There are mirrors in this house. You don't need me to tell you that. But as for me, I don't know if I'll ever look upon another woman the way I looked upon Annie. I certainly can't see myself getting married again, and it's nothing to do with my face.'

Liz went over to the window and drew back the cur-tain a few inches to see who it was she could hear walking up the street – Edna Grimshaw. She wondered how her neighbour was managing without a husband in her life. Judging from the frequent male visitors to her house it seemed she wasn't missing Mr Grimshaw much, though strangely she'd once asked Liz if Larry would be moving back any time soon. Liz had brusquely assured her he cer-tainly would not – without, of course, any indication of why she was so sure.

A carnal thought occurred to Liz then that she'd already dismissed from her mind several times since her lodger first arrived. She sat down again, looked into his eyes and said, 'Chas, do you miss the, erm, physical side of marriage?'

'What?'

Liz said nothing by way of further explanation. She just shrugged and raised her eyebrows, awaiting an answer.

Chas coloured slightly and said, 'Well, I'm a normal bloke and I'd be a liar if I said no.'

'So do I.'

Liz's reply came straight back at him. Her eyes held his. The message in them was unmistakable. He smiled, shook his head and lowered his eyes. She smiled too and dropped the subject, for the moment at least.

Chas was lying in bed, pondering what Liz had been saying to him and wishing he'd taken her up on her implied offer. He heard a quiet knock on the door. Billie had bad dreams from time to time and always brought her troubles down to him.

'Come in, Billie.'

The door opened revealing a silhouette in the doorway, backlit by the landing light. It wasn't the silhouette of a little girl, but of a naked woman.

'I'll only come in if you want me to,' Liz whispered.

As his eyes grew used to the dim light Chas could see more of her and he didn't want to turn her away.

'Come in, Liz.'

She moved to the side of his bed. She'd let her hair down and it tumbled around her shoulders. Her breasts were full and firm and her figure looked beautiful in the half-light from the landing.

'You look lovely,' he said.

'Thank you. Mind if I join you?'

'Not at all, although I think I should shut the door.'

He got out of the bed as she got in.

'You'd better lock it too,' she said. 'We don't want any small intruders with what I've got in mind.'

81

Chas shut the door, turned the key and made his way back to the bed in the dark, pausing only to slip off his pyjamas. Her open arms welcomed him as he got in beside her and pulled the covers over them both. They kissed, tentatively at first, and then their nakedness kindled desire.

An hour later Chas looked up at the ceiling, beyond which was Billie's attic bedroom, and asked, 'Did we make much noise?'

'Not enough to wake her up. She's a good sleeper is your Billie.'

'True, and that might come in handy in the future.'

'I don't think I should move into your bed permanently, Chas. Billie would never understand that.'

'I didn't mean that. I just meant—'

Liz stopped him with a kiss, then said, 'I know what you meant, and I'm happy to have as much of you as you can spare, just so long as I'm not sharing you with anyone.'

'Sharing? There's hardly enough of me to go round.'

It was crossing Liz's mind then that, given time, she might be able to make herself an indispensable part of Chas's life – too indispensable for him ever to let her go.

Chapter 11

16 September 1943

Chas was beginning to feel guilty as he walked past recruiting posters, especially the one showing Winston Churchill pointing accusingly at him and saying, 'Deserve Victory'.

At first it hadn't bothered him much, what with having had to sacrifice his wife and his good looks, but today it did – the third anniversary of Annie's death. A soldier wearing sergeant's stripes was standing at the door to the recruiting office on Briggate. He watched Chas approach and was about to ask him if he was home on leave when he spotted the fearfully scarred face and thought better of it. Chas glanced back at him and said, 'I suppose you're wondering if I'm in the services.'

'Well, son, it looks to me as if yer've been in the wars right enough.'

'Me? No. I've never served a day in uniform. A bomb did this to me three years ago today. The day I got my call-up papers, as it happens. I spent the next six months in hospital.'

'I'm sorry ter hear that.'

'Who are you recruiting? I assume conscription took care of most of it.'

'Women mainly, and men with special trades who haven't been called up for some reason.'

'Would that include musicians?'

'Well, the army needs good bandsmen.'

'Do you think I'd pass the medical?' Chas asked, suddenly. 'I'm a musician.'

'If yer otherwise fit, I don't see why not. There's a big push coming up and the upper age limit for volunteers is now fifty-one.'

'Well, I'm only twenty-nine.' Chas mentioned that because his scars made it hard for others to tell, 'but I've been declared medically unfit for active service.'

'And *are* you medically unfit?'

'I hope not. My leg was badly damaged at the time but it seems okay now.' He thought of Annie for the millionth time and added, 'I wouldn't mind having a go against that bastard Hitler before it's over.'

There was enough venom in his last sentence for the sergeant to ask, 'Am I right in thinking you lost someone dear to you when the bomb dropped?'

'You are,' said Chas.

'There's a medic in here right now, if you want to step inside and take the King's shilling.'

Chas smiled. 'They still give you that, do they?'

'Not really. It's just an old saying that I use.'

'Meaning once I sign up, there's no way I can change my mind?'

'No way at all. Do you have any dependants?'

'I have an eight-year-old daughter.'

It didn't occur to Chas to mention Liz, who was his lover, his landlady and his friend, but definitely not his dependant. Though she might have given him an argument there.

'Then you have a big decision to make and I'll expect you back tomorrow if you do decide to join us.'

Chas was totally preoccupied with his forthcoming decision as he boarded the tram back to Liz's house; the house he'd thought of as his and Billie's home for the last three years. Liz's friendship and support had made life bearable for him, albeit still tinged with constant bitterness against the Germans for killing his beloved Annie. Of all the vile crimes that were being committed in this war that, in Chas's mind, was the worst.

He sat next to an elderly man who was probably wondering why such a young chap wasn't wearing uniform. Was Chas home on leave or was he a conchie or was he unfit for active service? Usually one look at his face would put paid to any such curiosity. But people sitting next to you on trams tend not to look at your face.

'Home on leave, are you?' asked the man, without looking up from his newspaper.

'No,' said Chas, not wanting to explain himself for the hundredth time.

The man turned to look at him, about to say something, but thought better of it.

'Satisfied?' said Chas.

'I meant no offence, son.'

'None taken,' said Chas. He sometimes wondered the same himself when he saw men of call-up age in the streets. At the four schools where he taught music he was the only man under forty-one except for an emaciated maths teacher and a Latin teacher with a glass eye and a club foot. A lot of the forty-ones to fifty-ones were now being called up.

Chas had joined a local jazz band to supplement his income. The other musicians, trombone, trumpet, sax, banjo and piano, had all come from different bands which had been decimated by conscription. When Chas joined them he brought the average age down to fifty-five.

He was saddened that he couldn't make it down to London today to visit Annie's grave. He'd made the trip on the last two anniversaries of her death but this year he couldn't really afford to go, as it'd cost him the fare plus the lost day's pay. Instead he'd been into St Anne's Cathedral, said a prayer and lit a candle for her. He wasn't a Catholic but he assumed that God couldn't afford to have favourites in this wicked world.

As he walked into the house Liz and Billie got up to greet him, studying his face for signs of grief. They both knew what day it was. Chas gave Billie a big hug. She was now eight, very pretty, very bright, and very understanding.

'How are you, Daddy?'

'I'm not good, Billie. They're calling up men of fifty nowadays to go and fight the men who killed your mum, while I stay here playing my clarinet. God knows what she'd think of me.'

'She'd want you here to look after Billie,' said Liz. 'You've suffered enough in this war.'

'But I haven't *done* anything, Liz. They killed my wife and I haven't fought back.'

'Do you honestly think you'd make a difference?'

Chas shook his head. 'What if every man in the British

army thought like that? To be honest, I'm struggling to live with myself.'

Billie squeezed him tightly. 'Are you going off to war, Daddy?'

'Only if I knew you'd be okay, darling.'

Liz lit a cigarette and exhaled loudly and irritably. 'Of course she'd be okay. I'd look after her like she was my own, which is exactly how I see her anyway. She'd be just like all the other kids in the street whose dads are away at war.'

'That's right,' said Chas, kneeling down in front of his daughter. 'So, in future, when the other kids start making fun because you're the only one whose dad's not away fighting Hitler, you can tell them that he is.'

'I'm not bothered what they say, Daddy.'

'I know, darling, and if you say so I'll stay at home.'

'That's not fair on the girl,' protested Liz. 'It should be your decision, not hers.'

Chas sighed. She had him there. 'Okay then, my decision is to stay with my daughter.'

Billie let go of him and went upstairs to her room. Chas sat down and lit a cigarette of his own. He and Liz sat in unbroken silence, each with things on their mind. Liz had given up all hope of Chas ever truly loving her, but it didn't stop her loving him. They'd slept together many times and had intimate conversations, but the love wasn't mutual. He was a good man who would never sleep with another woman while they were involved, something for which she would in fact have forgiven him if only he'd loved her. Still, it was as much of a relief to Liz as it was to Billie that he'd decided to stay at home.

'You know, I can't play like I used to,' Chas said

suddenly. 'I can't think of any good reason why. I'm technically as good as I was but I'm nothing special. I've lost whatever edge I had.'

'You always sound okay to me.'

Chas got to his feet and walked over to the gramophone, a present from him to the house. He selected a Tubby Blake 78 and placed it on the turntable. Before switching it on he turned to Liz.

'This is "Mood Indigo" and I do a one-minute solo in the middle. I vowed I wouldn't play this again until I'd got my old edge back. I'm guessing you've never heard it before.'

'Not if you've never played it. I only listen to the records you put on.'

They both listened in silence as the band gave way to Chas's clarinet solo and the honeyed notes from his Buffet Crampon floated through the speakers and filled the whole house. After a minute the band came back in and Chas looked at Liz.

'Have you ever heard me play like that?'

Her eyes were moist. 'It's fabulous, Chas,' she said quietly.

'Yeah, I was pretty good. At first I thought the problem was with the clarinet not being fixed properly, but I took it to Kitchen's in town and tried it against an identical one of theirs and mine's still the better of the two.'

'So what do you think it is?'

'I think when I lost Annie, I lost my edge. To play like that you've got to almost forget you've got a musical instrument in your hand and just allow your soul to play the notes for you.'

'And now?'

'And now it's as though there's something inside me holding me back, not allowing my emotions through, and I don't know how to shake it off. I play okay, but I seem to play by numbers.' He tapped his chest at heart-level. 'There's nothing coming from here. If Tubby reforms the band after the war he won't have me back. In fact, I would refuse to go back. I'd only be an embarrassment to him.'

As Chas sat down Liz got up and switched on the Bush radio, another present he'd bought for the house. A burst of laughter came though the speaker, causing Chas to look up. He smiled when he realised the cause of the laughter was Tommy Handley in his new show *ITMA (It's That Man Again)*. Liz sensed the laughter didn't match his mood, and asked, 'Do you want me to turn it off?'

'No, no, leave it on. I'm just being grumpy and unreasonable, that's all.'

'I don't think you're being unreasonable, Daddy.'

'They both turned to see Billie standing in the doorway. She came into the room and stood in front of Chas, looking at him eye to eye. 'At school today Mrs Beecham said everyone had to do their bit in the war and I don't think it's fair of me to stop you doing yours.'

'Don't you, darling?'

Liz opened her mouth to interrupt but thought better of it as Billie continued speaking.

'I've never heard you play like that. Is it because you've some stuff you need to get out of your system?

Not for the first time Chas smiled at her perspicacity, which went way beyond her years. 'I'm not sure but I think it might be, darling.'

Billie looked down at the floor as if she were in deep thought. The two adults waited without interrupting her. The girl looked up again with sufficient resolve on her face to hold back the tears that weren't far away.

'Daddy, you should go to war if you think it's the right thing to do. I think Mum would be proud of you if you did. I know I will.'

Chas took her in his arms. 'Do you remember Mum, darling?'

'A bit,' said Billie. 'I remember hearing that bomb go off and some stuff before then. She used to read me bed-time stories. She was very pretty, wasn't she?'

There were photos in her room to verify that, but Chas assured her that her mum was the prettiest woman in the world. Liz was now wishing she'd put a bit of make-up on. Chas had often passed compliments on her appearance, but never with the same look in his eyes as when he talked about his Annie. He was a good man who would never knowingly hurt her, but he often did.

Chapter 12

December 1943

As Chas stared out of the window of the train his eyes were focused a thousand miles beyond the passing Yorkshire countryside. He'd completed his basic training at Beckett's Park Barracks in Leeds and he'd done all the marching, rifle drill and assault courses. He'd had his interviews and inoculations and had just had two weeks' home leave before joining the Herts and Essex Yeomanry at Slingsby in East Yorkshire. What the Herts and Essex Yeomanry were doing in Yorkshire was beyond him, but the army had their own ways and a lot of them didn't make sense.

After his initial interview in the recruiting office he'd assumed he'd be sent off to be a bandsman, perhaps in the Royal Marines. But the colour sergeant had different ideas.

'So you're a musician?'

'I am, yes.'

'Have you ever been on the wireless?'

'A few times, yes.'

'Excellent. I'm putting you down for the Herts and Essex Yeomanry, they're short of wireless operators. After your basic training you'll be given a rail warrant to take you to the barracks in Slingsby and I expect you'll do your wireless training in Scarborough.'

With that he disappeared, giving a dumbstruck Chas no time to argue. Not that arguing would have done any good. Wireless operator? Sounded interesting.

He was missing his daughter and wondering at the wisdom of joining up when all he had to do was sit out the war safe in civvie street. Was he being fair on Billie, leaving her behind? The truth was though that he was now feeling better about himself than he had done in over three years. A man who's suffered a heavy loss needs to take every opportunity for revenge that comes his way. He knew he hadn't joined up to fight for king and country. He was out for vengeance.

He thought about Liz and, not for the first time, wondered about asking her to marry him. He'd never find another Annie, but there again, he'd struggle to find another Liz.

Marrying her would make her more of a mother to Billie, but was this a proper reason to take a wife? Was it fair on Liz? She'd never be another Annie, he knew that. Maybe after this war was over he'd give it more thought.

Chapter 13

Just as the colour sergeant had predicted, Chas was sent from Slingsby to Scarborough to do a wireless signalling course that was due to last two months. It suited him insofar as uniforms weren't insisted upon. He took full advantage of the wear-what-you-like regime as he knew it wouldn't last any longer than his training period at Scarborough.

The instructors were good and kept them at it, and Chas very soon became proficient at Morse and semaphore; skills he didn't see lasting into civilian life, but skills nonetheless.

Where his colleagues were missing their wives and girlfriends, and in some cases their mothers, Chas missed Billie, but he also found himself missing Liz, not just Liz the lover but Liz the friend. Once again he wondered about proposing to her and once again Annie's memory gave him an argument.

After their week's training, the barracks routine was that on Saturday mornings they had to clean up their rooms and wash the floor next to where they slept. After this they were free until the following Monday morning, provided they didn't leave the Scarborough area.

It seemed an unnecessary restriction to Chas who would don his uniform and board a train to Leeds without wasting his short supply of money on a ticket. On the return journey, when the ticket inspection was a bit more rigorous, he would jump off as the train was slowing down between Seamer and Scarborough, and leave the track by climbing over a fence on to the road into town.

He completed his course by March and was sent back to Slingsby for weapons training: Bren and Sten guns, grenades, bayonet practice and the Lee Enfield rifle. He surprised himself with his proficiency at all this. It was early May before he got his next home leave – a full week. He wasn't told as much, but the general feeling was that this was embarkation leave, prior to active service.

Chapter 14

In 1895, two Frenchmen, Pierre le Rouzic Grene and Philipus Fforde, established a Methodist temperance house in Harehills, Leeds. In 1944 the Fforde Grene was owned by the Melbourne brewery. It was the biggest pub in Leeds and regularly held jazz nights on a Thursday.

On Thursday 4 May Chas was home on leave and had called in the Fforde Grene to see a couple of friends who played in the band. Through force of habit he'd taken his mouthpiece with him and within half an hour of walking through the door he'd become part of the band, playing a clarinet belonging to the saxophone player – and playing it better than it had ever been played before.

Ten o'clock came, closing time. Chas had mentioned that this leave would be the last for a while as he expected to be going overseas any time soon. That was as much as he knew. He'd learned there'd been a big build-up of Allied troops on the south coast and that they weren't there on holiday. What he didn't know was when and exactly where he'd be going.

The drummer suggested a lock-in for a game of poker. Ernest, the pub landlord, took little persuading and, as soon as the pub emptied, he locked the doors and prepared a large round table at which he set five chairs. He took their orders for after-hours drinks and they settled down to what they hoped would be an enjoyable couple of hours' gambling.

Chas liked a game of cards. It was around eleven-thirty when he picked up four queens. By this time he was also certain that Ernest was cheating and in league with the drummer who had suggested the lock-in. When Chas was a boy his father hadn't taught him much, but he'd taught him to play poker, along with all the odds, the tells, the tricks and the cheats to watch out for

Chas had a good idea how it was being done, but to make an outright accusation would cast a cloud over what had been up to now an enjoyable evening. Because of this he had decided to make an excuse and leave, but now he had a rare hand indeed and had picked it up straight from the dealer without changing any cards, thereby giving no clues as to what he held in his hand. Based on what he suspected, he'd obviously been dealt this hand by mistake. It was an occupational hazard when people used this method of cheating, his dad had taught him that.

This wasn't a hand that merited a minimum bet, but Chas didn't have enough money on him to take it far. He also knew that the landlord would have been given a good hand by the dealer, Maurice. Chas didn't know how good, but cheats rarely give themselves major hands ... just enough to win nine times out of ten. Maybe a flush or a full house. Maurice must have stacked the deck wrongly and given Chas four queens instead of three. His other card was a ten and he was pretty sure that one of his queens should have been another ten, and a full house, had the deck been properly rigged.

Chas raised the bet to five shillings; two players threw in and three remained. After another round it was just Chas and Ernest, who raised to a pound. Chas looked at him, as if studying him for a tell.

'You're bluffing,' he said.

The landlord grinned. 'Could be. It'll cost you a quid to find out.'

Chas put in a pound. Ernest raised it to five.

'Aw, c'mon, fellers,' said Wilf, the saxophone player. 'This is supposed to be a friendly game.'

Chas held up both hands. 'I've got thirty bob in my pocket and fifty quid in my bank account. So,' he looked at the landlord, 'the question is, will you take an IOU?'

'I hardly know you,' said Ernest.

'We do,' said two of the band.

'I'll stand surety,' said Wilf.

'No need for that,' said Chas, looking at Ernest. 'I'm either out or I'm going to call your bluff big time. But if I lose I can't pay until tomorrow. What's it to be?'

'Okay, I'll trust you for it,' said Ernest. 'What's your bet?'

Chas grinned triumphantly. He took his bank book out of his pocket and pushed it across the table. 'Fifty quid. Everything in there.'

The landlord looked down at the bankbook and then at Chas. 'Your hand's that good, is it?'

'I don't need a good hand to beat what you've got, and you know it. You tried to force me out with a fiver. I'm definitely forcing you out with fifty quid. Unless you want to cover it.'

'I haven't got fifty quid,' said Ernest.

'Then it's my kitty.'

'I've got a car worth at least seventy.'

'What sort of car?'

'Austin 10 1934, good runner.'

'Do you have the logbook and the keys?'

'I do.'

'I'll value it at fifty.'

Ernest drummed his fingers on the table, then said, 'Okay, what the hell? I'm hardly going to lose it.'

'Can you put them in the kitty?' asked Chas.

'Why should I? You can't put your fifty quid in the kitty.'

That's because I don't have my fifty right now but you've agreed that my credit's good.'

'Okay. I'll get the logbook and keys.'

Ernest put his hand face down on the table and said to the drummer, 'Keep an eye on those, Maurice.'

Two minutes later he was back. He had in his hands a key ring with two keys, along with a logbook. 'It's in the top car park,' he said. 'The tax has run out but it's got half a tank of petrol.'

The atmosphere was now tense. Fifty pounds was over four months' army pay for Chas. The landlord grinned. 'You think I've been bluffing, do you?'

Chas grinned and said, 'I know you're bluffing. No way will you throw your car into this kitty.'

'That's what you think, is it?' Ernest made a show of dropping his keys and logbook on to the table and said, 'There you go, I'll see your pair.' He looked at Chas, expecting a worried expression in return.

'Are you sure?' Chas said.

'Never been surer, lad.'

Chas turned over three of his queens. Ernest's grin broadened at first, then froze in horror as Chas turned over another one.

'Four ladies. Can you beat that?'

The landlord threw his cards away and made to retrieve his keys from the kitty, but Chas's hand was there before his.

'Mine, I believe.'

'He's right,' said Wilf, who'd turned over the landlord's hand. 'He's got a full house, kings over eights.' Ernest got to his feet, glared at Maurice, and walked out of the bar.

'We'll just push the door shut, will we?' called out Wilf.

Chas swept up the coins with a cupped hand and picked up his bank book, the keys and the logbook, then he looked at Maurice and asked, 'How many decks are you carrying?'

'What?'

'You're a card mechanic. You've got a few stacked decks about you. Trouble is, you stacked one of them to give me four queens instead of a queens over tens full house. What happened?'

Maurice said nothing. Wilf said, 'He used to do a magic act with cards.'

'I'm amazed you haven't been caught out before,' said Chas. 'Switching decks is the oldest trick in the book and you aren't all that good at it, which is how I ended up with this car. Thanks very much, by the way.'

Maurice still had nothing to say. He dismantled his drum kit in sullen silence.

'No one likes a cheat,' said Chas. 'Did the landlord think I was made of money?'

'He knew you were a well-known jazz musician,' said Wilf. 'Maybe he thought you had a few quid to lose.'

As Maurice packed his drums into their boxes Wilf went with Chas to the car park. The Austin was the only vehicle there apart from Maurice's van. It was a solid-looking square box on wheels, a design that had gone out of fashion before the war, but it had a ten-horsepower engine that could propel the car at over fifty miles an hour given a following wind. Under the gas lights it looked to be painted maroon and black with little rust evident; the running boards seemed to be in good condition and it had a wind-out windscreen to allow in a breeze on warm days. Chas gave a nod of approval. 'It'll do,' he said, 'seeing as it cost me nothing. Did you know he cheated?'

'We had our suspicions but we never said anything. This is a pretty good gig and he never cheats us, only newcomers.'

'Such as me.'

'We honestly didn't think he'd try it on with you.'

'What would you have done if he'd beaten me?'

'We'd have split on him.'

'What, and lost your good gig?'

'Doubt it. But he'd have lost the tenancy if we told the brewery what he'd been up to. No, we wouldn't have let you be cheated out of fifty, mate. Not by anybody.'

'That was never going to happen,' said Chas. 'If he'd looked in my bankbook, as I invited him to, he'd have seen I've only got ten bob in there.'

'What? You cheated the cheater?'

'I actually won the game fair and square – apart from exaggerating how much I had in the bank. I just double bluffed him into believing I thought he was bluffing. He'll have thought I had a good hand, but not as good as his. No way did he know Maurice had made a mess of stacking the deck and given me four ladies. You'd be as well not mentioning any of this to Ernest, by the way.'

'If he lets us keep the gig, I'll keep my mouth shut.'

Liz was still up and waiting for Chas when he got back. She heard the car pull up outside and went to the door as he was getting out. He walked around the car, proprietorially, examining his very first vehicle.

'Who's is that?' Liz asked.

'Mine. Won it in a card game. What d'you think? It's ten years old but it'll get us from A to B.'

'I didn't know you could drive.'

'They let me drive stuff in the army.'

'Do you have a driver's licence?'

'Not as such.'

'You're supposed to be insured against accidents and stuff.'

'I know that.'

'Is it taxed?'

'Tax? Erm, I believe that's run out.'

'You're supposed to have insurance before you can tax it. And you can't drive round without one of those disc thingies in the front window.'

'God grief, Liz! Can you hear yourself? You're a real nit-picker, you know that, don't you?'

'I don't want you getting into trouble, that's all.'

'Oh, heaven forbid that I should get arrested and locked up. Wouldn't be able to go off and fight for king and country then, would I?'

Liz didn't know why she was being so negative. It wasn't like her at all. She was acting just like a nagging wife – only without the security of a ring on her finger.

'Sorry. Yes, it looks a good car. Well done.'

'Look, with Billie being on half-term holiday, why don't we all go for a drive in the country tomorrow? It's her birthday on Sunday and I won't be here then. Let's have a good day out – just the three of us.'

Chapter 15

Liz leaned forward to examine the window. She turned to Chas. 'Hmm, funny sort of tax disc.'

'It's just to stop the coppers nosing round before I get it properly taxed.'

'It's a Guinness label.'

'I know. Looks just like a tax disc, from a distance.'

She thought about mentioning insurance and a driver's licence again but decided against it. Billie was already in the front passenger seat, all excited about the day ahead.

'Where are we going, Dad?' she called out.

'Anywhere you want.'

'I'd like to go to Scotland.'

'That's a bit too far.'

'You said anywhere I want.'

'All right, anywhere you want in Yorkshire. It's the biggest county in England according to the natives. They've got fields and trees and rivers and hills and lots of sea.'

Billie narrowed her eyes. 'I want to go to the seaside. Is Filey in Yorkshire?'

'It most certainly is.'

'Hilda McGilly's been to Filey. She says it's smashing.'

'Filey it is then.'

'Do you know the way?' Liz asked, still looking at the bogus tax disc.

'More or less. Filey's on the east coast. All I have to do is keep the sun on my right-hand side and head east till our hats float.'

'I hope you're not in charge of navigation when you lot invade France, you'll most likely end up invading Norway.'

'It's very pleasant in Norway, so I hear,' said Chas. He got out the starting handle and cranked the engine into life. Liz got in the back. Chas slid into the driver's seat and took off down the street. He knew exactly how to get to Filey, having studied maps of Yorkshire as part of his course in Scarborough. No fun in telling Liz that though. As far as she was concerned he'd be navigating by the sun.

The spring weather was fine and sunny that day. Liz had packed a picnic in a hamper that had been handed down through her family for several generations but never used by her since she was a child. Chas had found that amusing too.

'I never knew a picnic hamper could become a family heirloom. My old man has a painting of some fisherwomen done by a world-famous artist I've never heard of. You get a picnic hamper.'

'What was his name?'

'I called him Dad.'

'No, the artist.'

'Can't remember. Funny sort of a name.'

'What? Like Picasso?'

'Could be Picasso, yeah.'

'You're joking!'

'Could be. I told the old man it was worthless, so he stuck it in the attic.'

'Is it worthless?'

'Probably. Someone gave it to him in part-payment of a debt. The old man knows nothing about art ... or music for that matter. With me being a musician, he assumed I knew all about art as well.'

'Why did you tell him it was worthless?'

'Because he was a bully.'

'Oh, dear,' sighed Liz, knowing only too well how stubborn Chas was once he'd made his mind up. It was a pity he couldn't be reconciled to his father, though, for Billie's sake if no one else's. The poor child didn't seem to have a relative in the world apart from her father.

He drove for an hour along the A64, which took him through the ancient city of York and the market town of Malton. They passed a sign saying Picnic Area along with an arrow pointing along a narrow track. Chas brought the car to a stop.

'Shall we have our picnic over there?'

'Oh, yes,' cried Billie. 'I've never been to a proper picnic area.'

'Neither have I, come to think of it,' said Chas. 'We must investigate.'

The track led to a field that served as a car park. It was deserted. Nearby was a farm house and as soon as they'd parked an elderly woman appeared and pointed to a discreet sign saying *Car Parking 2/6d*.

'Bit steep that, isn't it?' said Liz. 'Half a crown to park a car. I'm not surprised we're the only ones here.'

'That's because we've only just started doing it. This field used to be our garden. It includes lavatory facilities and spring water, plus the prettiest stretch of river in Yorkshire. And the girl can have a ride on a donkey if she dun't mind riding bareback.'

They looked around and the woman was quite right about its being a pretty stretch of river. The grass ran almost to the water's edge and was kept short by two munching donkeys. It was edged by a variety of mature trees: oak, ash, horse chestnut, and copper beech. There were azalea shrubs in full flower, pink, purple, orange, yellow and white and best of all, in Billie's eyes, a host of shimmering bluebells growing in the shade of the trees. She said she'd never been anywhere quite so beautiful. Chas gave the woman half a crown and asked where the spring was.

'Over there.'

She pointed to a stone wall. Inset was a stone carving of a peeing boy. Billie ran over to it and laughed with delight.

'Daddy, look! There's water coming out of his willy!'

'Hmm, I'm not sure she should know about such things,' he murmured to Liz.

'She goes to school. She'll know about willies.'

'Not *all* about them, I hope.'

'Not yet. She'll find out all about them in good time. There'll be no need for you to have that talk you've been dreading. I never had one, and I knew all I needed to know by the time I was fifteen.'

'Fifteen? So she has another seven years of innocence.'

'Make the most of them. It's after that you need to start worrying.'

106

'I've worried about Billie since the day she was born.'

Liz laid out a checked tablecloth on the grass and provided lettuce and tomato sandwiches, biscuits and scones. Then she surprised them with a birthday cake complete with eight candles.

'But it's not my birthday till Sunday,' said Billie.

'No, but it's your party today,' Liz told her, rather than point out that Chas wouldn't be with them then.

The weather was warm and sunny. They all sat on the riverbank with their bare feet dangling in the water while they ate their picnic lunch, then queued up to take a drink from the peeing boy. Chas got his clarinet from the car and played 'Happy Birthday To You' with Liz singing along as Billie blew out her candles. Then, with her father holding on to her, she spent ten minutes riding the donkeys – five minutes on each animal because she said it wasn't fair to have a favourite. They spent a magical two hours in the picnic area before moving on to the coast.

Chapter 16

The small fishing town of Filey is half a mile south of a promontory of land that juts out into the North Sea, tapering off into a line of rocks known as Filey Brigg, a paradise for kids who like fishing or just playing in rock pools.

Chas parked the car in a field at the top of the steep cliffs overlooking the Brigg. He'd been there before during his time at Scarborough, just nine miles to the north.

'We can park up here and walk down the cliff path then out on to the Brigg,' he said.

Liz and Billie got out and looked down towards the sea. Clouds were moving in and a cool wind was blowing.

'It's not as warm as it was at the picnic place,' Billie commented.

Liz shivered. 'I don't fancy the climb back up if the weather turns nasty.'

Chas was forced to agree. He glanced back the way they'd come in towards a Thrift Store that seemed to sell most things. 'Tell you what, I'll go to the shop and get us some goodies – sweets and stuff. How about that?'

'I'd better come with you,' said Liz. 'We've nothing in for tea tonight.'

'Do you mind if I stay in the car?' asked Billie. 'I'm cold.'

'Okay,' said Chas. 'We'll go to the shop. If the weather's looking bad we can either drive up to Scarborough and go in the amusements, or we can go straight home. Billie makes the choice.'

Billie nodded, excited now by the prospect of visiting the amusements in Scarborough. Because that's where they'd be going, no matter what the weather. She got back in the car as Chas and Liz headed for the shop.

Ten minutes later the shopkeeper was bagging up their purchases in a carrier when he glanced over their shoulders and exclaimed, 'Aw, no, not again!'

Chas and Liz turned around and looked in the same direction. Both of them gasped with horror.

Two youths were pushing his car towards the edge of the cliff. Chas ran out of the shop and shouted at them: 'Stop that! There's a child in the car!'

The youths either couldn't hear him or weren't interested. The car gathered speed as they both put their shoulders to it. Chas set off running with Liz in pursuit. The shopkeeper was phoning the police. Ten yards from the edge the youths figured the car would make its own way over the cliff so they ran off in the opposite direction. Chas was within fifty yards when the Austin disappeared from view. He screamed in horror and fear for his daughter, then went to the cliff edge to see the car on the rocks, sixty feet below, now burning. There was an explosion as the petrol tank went up.

Chas stood there screaming at the top of his voice. Nothing intelligible, just venting his every emotion at seeing his daughter killed before his eyes. Liz arrived behind him. She was screaming as well. Chas began to clamber down the cliff face, calling out Billie's name and weeping. It was steep but there were pathways and handholds. He was part running, part stumbling, part falling down. When he got to the bottom the blazing car was just thirty yards to his left. He ran towards it and was immediately forced back by the flames. He was still yelling his daughter's name and trying to see beyond the flames and dense black smoke. He knew she must be in there and he knew she must be dead. He sank to his knees, heaving out great sobs of despair. His whole world was inside that blazing car. His darling daughter, and he'd let her down. Why had he let her stay in the car on her own?

The heat from the blaze was singeing his hair. As far as he was concerned his life had ended at that moment. Nothing left for him now. Might as well go and throw himself on the fire. It crossed his mind, but such intense heat is impossible to run into without being forced back. He struggled to his feet and moved back a couple of paces, eyes fixed on the centre of the inferno where Billie was. He felt it was his duty as her dad to watch over her until the bitter end; until the flames had died down and she was nothing but ashes. He'd been charged with the safekeeping of two wonderful people and they'd both died in his care. What use was he in this world anymore? Had he really thought he'd make a soldier? He would have laughed if he hadn't been on the verge of tears.

He remembered pacing up and down outside the delivery room and hearing Billie's first cries. The nurse coming to the door and telling him he had a daughter

110

and she was perfect. He remembered shivering with wonder when his baby was taken from Annie's arms and handed to him. This beautiful tiny person who was look-ing up at him and loving him despite not having a clue who he was.

'Hello, I'm your daddy. Welcome to the world.'

And he had suddenly realised the enormous responsi-bility he had taken on. This beautiful child's future was entirely in their hands – his and Annie's. This child was entirely dependent on them.

He had been there when Billie took her first steps, from him to Annie. Three whole steps without toppling over. They had clapped their encouragement and Billie had smiled, knowing she'd done well. Then Annie had turned her round and she'd taken four steps back to Chas. More clapping. Billie had brought them great joy, and he'd let her die an horrific death. Billie and Annie both.

He'd taught her to ride a two-wheeler bike only a few months ago. She'd mentioned that she was too old for her tricycle, so for Christmas Chas had bought her a small two-wheeler from the cycle shop on Harehills Lane. It had a basket at the front and he'd taken her into the park to learn to ride on the tarmac paths there; much safer than the bumpy cobbled streets. She'd fallen off once and grazed her knee. She'd cried but the tears vanished as soon as she saw the size of the plaster she'd been rewarded with – a giant affair that had covered her whole knee like a badge of honour. She'd worn it to school long after her graze had healed.

Happy memories mingled with Chas's abject misery. Other people began to arrive. First some small boys who had been fishing in the rock pools, then some adults, probably the boys' parents. Faces appeared along the cliff top, looking down on the sad scene below. Chas found himself surrounded by a semi-circle of kids and adults.

Liz was up there as well, shouting down at him. Two voices now, both of which he recognised. He squinted upwards through tear-sodden eyes, wanting to believe what he saw, but scarcely able to. Just one of them shouting now.

'Daddy, I'm all right!'

He shuddered with shock, not quite knowing how to handle this amazing turn of events – from deep despair to great joy in the space of seconds. He turned and looked at the group gathered around him. 'Your daughter's okay,' said a man. 'She's up there, look.'

They all followed the direction of his pointing finger. A couple of them waved back at Billie. The kindly man stepped forward and put his arm around Chas's shoulders.

'Did you think she was in the car, mate?'

'I did, yes. I don't know how she—'

Chas shook his head, lost for words.

'She's okay, mate. She's up there, waving at you.'

'She . . . she is, isn't she?'

A woman called out then, 'Jim, bring him up the cliff path. He's not fit to go up on his own.'

'Aye, I'll do that. Come on, pal. I'll see you up to the top.'

'Thanks,' said Chas to his new-found friend. His eyes were still fixed on Billie, to make sure she wasn't a mirage, and then at the blazing car that was no longer turning her to ashes. He waved at her and she waved back. Both of them were in tears, as was Liz and some of the watchers who had been caught up in the emotion of the incident.

'Yer car's a write-off,' said Jim, climbing the path behind Chas. 'Still, Third Party Fire and Theft should cover it, eh?'

'Yes,' said Chas, who wasn't insured and didn't give a damn.

The three of them were sitting in the back room of the Thrift Store drinking tea made by the shopkeeper, who had been haranguing the two uniformed constables sent to investigate the crime.

'It's the third time in the last twelve months them buggers have pushed a car off the cliff! I can tell you who they are, y'know.'

'I think we know who they are,' said one of the constables. 'Trouble is, when it comes up in court the witnesses don't turn up. They've been scared off.'

'We won't be,' vowed Chas. 'That was one of the worst moments of my life.'

'I'll be able to recognise them,' said Billie. 'They opened the car door and said I'd got two seconds to get out or I'd go over the cliff with the car. I got out quick!'

'Thank God,' said Chas. 'Listen, do you want us to come with you to arrest them?' he asked. 'It might help me to overcome my shock if I could see them both arrested.'

'And I'd be able to identify them,' put in Billie.

The constables looked at each other and shrugged. *Why not?*

'I want to come as well,' said Liz. 'I want to see them buggers brought to book.'

*

113

The two suspects lived on a caravan site a little further up the coast. The constables seemed reluctant to go in there without reinforcements. They stopped off at a police box and called the incident in, asking for help. The constable who'd made the call came back to the car and said to his colleague, 'There'll be another car here in five minutes.'

'Good There could be any number of them hanging around them caravans.'

'They're over there,' said Billie from the back seat. Four pairs of eyes followed her pointing finger. Two youths, both aged around seventeen, were sitting on a nearby stone wall, talking to a couple of girls of similar age. None of them had spotted the police car.

'That's definitely them, is it?' said Chas.

'Definitely.'

'Right,' said the driver to his colleague. 'We need to be a bit canny here. As soon as we get out of this car they'll take off. I'll drive straight up to them, you have your door already open so you can be out the second I stop. I'll be straight after you.'

'So will I!' said Chas.

'We'd like you to stay out of this, sir.'

'Okay, I'll stay out of it,' said Chas. Both Liz and Billie knew he was lying.

The four youngsters turned in surprise as soon as the car drew up next to them. The youths set off running. Both constables were out of the car in a second, Chas in half a second. He collared one of the youths instantly. The boy snarled and swore at him. Chas head-butted him viciously, fired up by his recent anguish. The youth sank to the ground with blood pouring from his nose. The second youth had been caught by the two constables. The girls were by now nowhere to be seen. Billie looked from one youth to the other.

'That's them,' she confirmed. 'They're the ones who did it.'

'Did what?' said the youth who wasn't injured.

'I was there as well,' said Chas. 'I saw you both.'

'You can't have. You were miles away.'

Chas laughed. 'Gotcha!'

'You bloody idiot!' cursed the injured boy.

'We're arresting you for vehicle theft, arson, threatening behaviour, causing damage to property ...'

'What about assault?' said Chas, pointing to the injured youth. 'This one attacked me with his nose. If I hadn't ducked my head I'd have been severely injured.'

'And assault with intent to cause grievous bodily harm,' added the constable. 'You are not obliged to say anything unless you wish to do so, but whatever you do say will be taken down in writing and may be given in evidence.'

'I should write down that bit about him saying I was miles away,' said Chas.

'I've duly noted that, sir.'

'And don't think you can scare us off,' said Billie to the youths.

'We'll see about that.'

Chas leaned right into the face of the boy who had replied and hissed, 'You really don't know who you're up against here, do you?'

The scarring on his face and the chill in his voice wiped the sneer off both boys' faces. The support car arrived and the two boys were handcuffed and taken away. One of the original officers turned to Chas.

'You scared the living daylights out of them.'

'It's the face,' he said. 'It has its uses.' Then, by way of further explanation, added, 'Bomb, four years ago. It killed Billie's mother.'

'What you did to that lad was assault, but we both know he deserved it so we're putting his injury down to self-defence by you.'

'He put something into my system that I needed to get out,' said Chas. 'For a few minutes that seemed like a lifetime I thought my beautiful daughter had burned to death in that car.'

'And have you got it out of your system now?'

'No, I don't think I'll ever be able to get that out of my system.'

'They'll both do serious time for this.'

'That'll help.'

'Dad, tomorrow, before you go back to camp, can we go to the pictures?' Billie piped up then.

Chas looked down in amazement at Billie. Their car had just gone over a cliff – and she was talking about going to the pictures.

'*Meet Me in St Louis*'s on at the Odeon. It's got Judy Garland in it. You like her, don't you? Do you like her, Auntie Liz?'

'You and your dad are best going on your own this time. I think I need a quiet day to get over all this,' said Liz, who for once meant what she said and was not just tactfully leaving them alone together.

'Okay,' said Chas. 'We'll go to the matinee and have a

wander round town to see if we get you a birthday present.'

'We'll need you down at the station now,' said one of the constables, 'to give your statements.'

'And we'll need to get back to Leeds without a car,' said Chas. 'I don't suppose you have any rail warrants floating around at your place, have you?'

'I'm sure we can fix you up with free travel, under the circumstances. Oh, and we'll need your written authority to pay the recovery costs out of the scrap value of the car. We'll send you a receipt for your insurers. It's the way we did it for the other two cars those jokers pushed off the cliff. It'll help if you send the logbook through to us.'

'I'll do that.'

'And sorry about your car, sir – bad luck, that.'

'Far outweighed by the good luck I ended up with.'

'I should say so, sir.'

It was then that Chas realised what else he'd lost that day – his precious clarinet had been in the car. Then he looked down at Billie and saw the whole thing in its proper perspective.

And he smiled.

Chapter 17

They left the cinema at four fifteen and headed for Kirkgate Market where the prices suited Chas's limited funds.

'Okay, what would you like?' he asked.

They were standing by a toy stall. Billie's eyes lit up as she pointed to a model car that was an exact replica of the one that had gone over the cliff.

'What? Won't it bring back bad memories?'

'It wasn't the car's fault and it'll remind me of the best picnic I ever had; the best birthday party I ever had; that lovely picnic place with the beautiful flowers and the trees and eating our sandwiches with our feet in the river and the donkeys and my birthday cake and you playing "Happy Birthday" on your clarinet and Auntie Liz singing along.'

This all came out in one impressive, breathless burst.

'Wow!' said Chas.

'Whenever I look at that car I'll think of our picnic.'

'Just the good stuff, eh?'

'It's not wrong just to remember the good stuff, is it, Dad?'

Chas squeezed his eyes shut as the horror of the previous

day came back to him. Was there ever a kid with a more beautiful mind?

'Dad?'

'No, it's not wrong, Billie. In fact, it's a one-way ticket to a happy life.'

On their way back to the tram they walked along Harewood Street and looked in Barker's toy shop window. There was a delightful doll on display. Billie pressed her nose against the glass and told her dad that this was the most beautiful doll in the whole world, and Chas sighed as he looked at the price: £19 17s 6d. He guessed that the doll had been put in the window more for show than for sale. After paying seven and threepence for the toy car he had twelve shillings in his pocket, which was a lot more than he normally had. Billie's board and lodging were now being paid for by the army, but his army pay of seven and six a day didn't leave him with much for luxuries, such as the most beautiful doll in the world.

'When I come home on leave again I'll get you that doll, Billie,' he promised rashly.

'Honest, Daddy?'

'Honest.'

It was a promise Chas knew he had to keep. That evening, before his tearful farewells to Billie and Liz, he'd emptied his kitbag of all his civvies, knowing he could exist until his next leave without any civilian clothes. At seven p.m. he caught the tram into town in plenty of time to catch the eight fifteen train to Malton. Leeds City centre was dark and empty, as he knew it would be. Not a light on anywhere due to the blackout regulations. Very few coppers about and the only civilians were the men heading for the pubs. There was one pub on Harewood Street, the Market Hotel, also known as the Madhouse. That night it was closed due to recent trouble.

Chas walked quietly along the street. He knew what he had to do and intended doing it with the minimum of fuss. In his kitbag he had a lump hammer. As he approached Barker's he glanced all around to ensure he wasn't being watched then took out the hammer and swung it at the glass with as much force as he could muster. The glass cracked but didn't break. He glanced up and down the street again to see if anyone had been alerted by the loud bang – apparently not. He swung the hammer again, and this time the window shattered and collapsed, noisily, half into the shop and half into the street. Within seconds the doll was in Chas's kitbag and he was marching away at the double. He turned left up Sidney Street, across Vicar Lane, up the County Arcade and into Briggate, well away from the scene of the crime. His heart was thumping when he passed a beat copper.

'Going back or coming home?' asked the copper.

'Going back to see my dear old sergeant.'

'Invasion soon, eh?'

'If I answered that I'd have to shoot you, and I haven't got me gun.'

The policeman laughed and wished the criminal well.

Chapter 18

As the train approached Malton Chas felt in his pocket for his rail warrant and cursed under his breath when he remembered it was on the dressing table back in Leeds. If he couldn't produce a ticket he'd have to pay the full fare plus a fine, which he could ill afford. Nothing else for it but to jump off before it came to a halt as he'd done many times before on the Leeds to Scarborough route. In Scarborough the railway line had been easy to negotiate. Not so in Malton where a large policeman was on the lookout for fare dodgers. He collared Chas and marched him into the station-master's office.

'Caught this one jumping off before the train stopped. I'm guessing he hasn't got a ticket.'

'I left my rail warrant behind in Leeds,' explained Chas.

'No warrant, no ticket. That makes you a fare dodger,' said the station master.

Chas was worried in case this ended up with the copper searching his kitbag. He was busy dreaming up a good reason to have the stolen doll in there when he decided to change tack and go on the offensive.

'This uniform makes me a soldier who'll soon be off to

France to fight the Germans. You know I'm entitled to a rail warrant.'

'You're also supposed have it with you whenever you travel, otherwise you pay the full fare in cash plus a fine.'

'Okay, I'll pay. How much do you want to take off me?'

Chas stuck his hand in his pocket and put a ten-shilling note and some coins on the desk. 'Ten and sevenpence ha'penny. That's all I've got. Do you want it all or are you going to leave me my bus fare to Slingsby Camp?'

The policeman and the station master exchanged help-less glances. His uniform gave Chas the moral high ground. The station master sighed and pushed the money back to him.

'All right, I'll let it go this time, but think on, we've all got a job to do. That uniform doesn't make you a law unto yourself.'

'Indeed it doesn't. You're a good man, sir.'

Chas touched his beret by way of salute, thanked them both for their understanding, and marched away carrying the kitbag containing the world's most beautiful doll. His mind was haunted by thoughts of how it might all have gone badly wrong for him. Still, he was a soldier now, a professional risk-taker, and any risk that'd put a big smile on Billie's face was a risk worth taking.

Chapter 19

'Auntie Liz, do you think Daddy might come home today?'

Billie was staring out of the window at the rain bouncing off the stone cobbles in the street. Liz was busy arranging washing on a wooden clothes horse in front of the fire.

'Doubt it, love. He's back at Slingsby now. I think they're a bit stricter there. He wasn't supposed to come home from Scarborough, you know.'

'Wasn't he? How did he manage it, then?'

'Because he's your daddy, that's how.'

This was explanation enough for Billie.

'Do you think his face will get really better? I think it's healed a lot since we came here.'

'I agree,' said Liz.

'Daddy used to be very handsome, didn't he?'

'Like a Hollywood film star.'

This made Billie smile with pride. 'I love him, you know.'

'I think I know that, Billie. He certainly loves you.'

'Do you love him, Auntie Liz?'

'I like him very much.'

'That's the same as loving him. When we were in town last Saturday we saw a beautiful dolly in the toy-shop window. Daddy said he'd get me it.'

This kindled a recent memory in Liz's mind. She'd read in the *Yorkshire Evening Post* about a smash and grab raid at a toy shop in town where the only thing taken was a very expensive doll from the window. Surely Chas wouldn't ? Jesus! She wouldn't put it past him, having promised Billie. He'd be off to war soon. Men going off to war like their last flings and tend to throw caution to the winds. She decided not to mention this to Billie, who wouldn't have read about it. The only reading she did was the *Dandy*, the *Beano* and *The Wind in the Willows*. The dreary daily news in the local paper wouldn't interest her.

'Really? How much was it, did you notice?'

'Nearly twenty pounds.'

Liz's heart sank. The same price that was given in the paper. There weren't too many toy shops in town, maybe a couple that she knew of, and what were the odds against both of them having an expensive doll in the window?

'I don't think Daddy can afford that. Maybe he was just saying it to cheer me up,' Billie continued.

'Have you ever known your daddy not to keep a promise?'

Billie didn't have to think about this one. 'No, never.'

An hour later a GPO van pulled up outside. A delivery man got out and knocked on Liz's door. As soon as she opened it Liz knew what was in the large parcel he was holding. A sticker on it read *HANDLE WITH CARE*.

'Parcel for Miss Billie Challinor.'

Billie appeared beside Liz. 'That's me.'

The postman smiled and handed it to her before returning to his van and driving off. Liz watched him disappear, hoping he didn't have a clue what was in the parcel. Get a grip, Liz! How could he know? She went inside where Billie was tearing off the wrapper. Inside this this was a cardboard box stuffed with straw. Billie looked up at Liz.

'What do you think it is?'

'I think it's something very fragile.'

Billie plucked at the straw and revealed the face of the most beautiful doll Liz had seen in her life. Billie screamed with delight. 'This is it! He's bought me it!'

'Careful,' said Liz. 'You don't want to break it.'

'Okay.'

Very carefully Billie removed all the straw that was packed around the doll inside the box and took it out. It was a porcelain doll, two feet tall, modelled to resemble a beautiful young woman, not a child. She had a perfect face with shining blue eyes that looked real, and golden hair that also looked and felt real because it was. She had it tied back with a multi-coloured silk scarf and was dressed in a blue silk dress that stopped at the knee, revealing fabulous legs ending in gold, high-heeled shoes. This was a miniature woman of immense beauty. A woman-doll a man might secretly fantasise over, a doll whose beauty many women might aspire to, a doll that every girl in the world would adore ... and Billie was no exception. She looked up at Liz with tears of joy in her eyes.

'He kept his promise, Auntie Liz.'

'He did indeed. Now I want you to make me a promise.'

'What sort of promise?'

'I want you to keep that doll in your room and not show it to anyone.'

'What? Why?'

'Because it's the sort of doll that will make every girl in the world jealous. No friend of yours will have a doll like that or can ever hope to have one. The last thing you want is to have jealous friends.'

Billie was already planning on showing it off to Peggy Gill, next door but one.

'I bet Daddy would let me show it to my friends.'

'In that case you can write to him and ask him.'

Liz was already planning on writing a letter of her own; a letter that wouldn't make easy reading for Chas.

'Promise me, Billie. This is very important. I'm sure your daddy will agree with me. If he doesn't then you can show it to your friends, but until such time as we hear from him I don't want you to show it to anyone. In fact, it might be as well if you don't even talk about it, because they'll only think you're showing off.

Billie grimaced and said, 'I promise.'

'Good, now why don't we give her a name?'

'It'll have to be a beautiful name.'

'Why not give the name of a flower, such as Rose?'

'My favourite flowers are bluebells. Like the bluebells at the picnic place.'

'Well, she's wearing a blue dress and bell means beautiful.'

'Does it, honest?'

'It does if you stick an e on the end.'

'In that case I'll call her Bluebelle with an e.'

Billie picked up the doll and hugged it to her, then kissed her on the end of her nose. 'Hello, Bluebelle,' she said. 'I'll find you a special place in my room where we can talk.'

Chapter 20

5 June 1944

Chas was thinking about the doll a month later when he boarded a 10,000-ton cargo ship called the *Princess Portia* in East Ham Docks. It wasn't much of a ship but it didn't need to be to get them out of the Thames estuary, south into the Channel and over to France.

They'd been moved two hundred miles south from Slingsby into a compound near the docks where they'd been kept sealed off from the outside world for two weeks. The highlight of their stay was being issued with two hundred francs in French coinage which gave them a clue as to where they were headed. The invasion was obviously imminent but no one talked about it because no one really knew anything about the plan.

It was seven in the evening of 5 June when they were marched from the compound to the docks where they boarded the unimpressive-looking ship that went off in a convoy and sailed all night, with Chas trying to snatch some sleep up on deck. The following morning, just before dawn, they were standing to off the French coast between two British battleships that were firing broadsides to shore. Around them were hundreds of other vessels ranging from 10,000-ton tramps to cruisers, destroyers, corvettes, and tiny assault craft.

The RAF was supplying a constant covering patrol but the Germans were returning fire from just beyond the beach. Operation Neptune, the landing phase of Operation Overlord, had begun. They were standing off the Normandy beaches two hundred and fifty miles south-west of Calais where Hitler had amassed his army, thinking they were going to land there. By using double agents feeding the Germans false information about the invasion, MI5 had successfully carried out the biggest hoax in history. Even as 150,000 Allies were landing on the five Normandy beaches selected for the invasion force, the double agents were telling the Germans that this was just a diversionary tactic to get their armies away from Calais . . . and the Germans were still believing it.

Chas knew nothing of this. All he knew was that he was in an assault party and he'd never assaulted anyone in his life – well, apart from the youth in Filey. The weather was overcast and rainy, and visibility poor, which helped the invaders, although Chas would have preferred a nice sunny day for his first visit to France.

It was four in the afternoon when they went over the side. One of the skills they hadn't been taught was how to climb down the nets into the landing craft. Chas had to be helped by a US sailor otherwise he'd have dropped between the two vessels and probably drowned under all the kit he was carrying. He thanked his American saviour and found time to shudder with apprehension of what awaited them on shore. There was sporadic shelling and machine-gun fire coming their way and above all this was

129

the thunderous booming of the battleship's guns firing broadsides to shore, along with the guns of every other vessel. On any other occasion this would have seemed like the most magnificent firework display Chas had ever seen, but the noise brought back a memory of the bomb that had killed his wife and he froze for a while, closing his eyes and breathing deeply to take control of himself. In his mind he spoke to Annie.

'This is for you, Annie. Maybe I'll be seeing you soon, eh? God, I hope so. Billie'll be okay with Liz.'

The landing craft stopped fifty yards from the beach. The door dropped open and became a ramp for the disembarking troops who waded ashore, through chest-high waves, at the mercy of incoming fire, with weapons and equipment held aloft lest it became damaged by saltwater. Nothing for it but to wade as fast as they could. Most made it unscathed; some didn't. Their reception was nowhere near as fierce as the Yanks were getting on Omaha Beach over to the west, but it was bad enough for these young men who had never experienced live fire.

Chas was wading behind a pal of his, Wilkie, a Scot, who took a bullet and went down under the waves. Chas lunged forward, grabbed him by the scruff of the neck and pulled his head clear.

'Wilkie, where are you hit?'

'Shoulder.' He inclined his head to the left. 'Left shoulder ... Jeez, I'm strugglin', man.'

'Can you walk?'

'Aye, I can do that, only just but –'

Chas moved to Wilkie's right and took the Scotsman's arm around his shoulders. A bullet ripped through Chas's tunic but there was no cover for him here; all he could do was carry on and hope for the best. He got Wilkie ashore and was met by a corporal medic who laid the wounded man on the sand and ordered Chas to move up the beach and dig himself in.

In quick time Chas dug a slit trench and memory returned to him of the last trench he'd dug – Larry Morris's final resting place. Chas lay down in his trench, hoping it wouldn't be *his* last resting place. After a while sleep overtook him and he was awakened by a sergeant bawling at him.

'Wakey, wakey, Gunner! We've got a bleedin' war to fight. Would you care to join us?'

'Sarge.'

It was now dark. They formed a column two abreast and set off marching through the night. Chas was now glad of the odd hours of sleep he'd had since leaving England. One of the men was talking about them getting their own back on William the bleedin' Conquerer, which amused some of them. A few German planes flew over and dropped bombs, but none dropped anywhere near their column. They marched for three hours, by which time Chas was exhausted and his legs rubbed sore by the harsh material of his wet uniform trousers. It was one o'clock in the morning when they reached their position. He dropped into a hedge bottom and slept until it was light.

The sergeant major was bawling out an order to dig themselves in, set up Bren guns and wait for Jerry to arrive. It was around noon when Chas heard the most welcome order any soldier could receive.

'Come and get your mail!'

It had travelled with them from England. Chas had just one letter, from Billie. She wrote to him twice a week.

Dear Daddy,

As usual I hope you are safe and well. I have some bad news for you. I disobeyed Auntie Liz and took Bluebelle to show Geraldine. Her daddy is a policeman and he asked me where I got the dolly from and I didn't see any harm in telling him you bought it for me and the very next day a man from the toyshop came round with Geraldine's daddy and asked to take a look at Bluebelle. Then they took her away because they said she had been stolen. I said she could not have been stolen because you bought her for me so when you come home you must tell them this and then I can get Bluebelle back. Auntie Liz was very upset.

Lots of love and kisses,
Your loving daughter,
Billie xxxxx

Chas would have much preferred another bomb to drop on him than to have received this letter. He couldn't think of anything worse. How the hell could he get out of this? Billie would have told the police about their trip to town on the day the doll was stolen and how they'd seen it in the window and that her daddy had promised to get it for her. They'd have put two and two together and made four.

He was known to have gone back to camp that evening, and it would easily be presumed that he'd made a detour via the shop on his way to the station. When he got back he'd be charged with the crime, which was bad enough, but nowhere near as bad as Billie finding out that her daddy was a thief who had stolen her cherished doll.

This was by far the greatest burden Chas was carrying when they took up position in Herouvillette to the north of Caen, their main target. Chas's job would be to work from an observation post from where he could get clear sight of the enemy target and direct the gunfire using his radio transmitter. It was a job that wouldn't start for another day. Some US 6th Airborne troops were already there. One of them came over to talk to Chas.

'You know your officer's an asshole, bringing you guys here in broad daylight?'

Chas didn't have a high opinion of the major himself but took this as an insult to his regiment and walked away. The American called after him.

'Hey, buddy. I didn't mean nothin' by it. I was tryin' to help, is all.'

'Help how?' asked Chas.

The American pointed to a nearby hill. 'Jerry's got a mortar battery up there. As soon as it gets dark he'll just plaster this area. You guys won't stand a chance.'

Chas squinted at the hill but saw nothing.

'It's up there, soldier. Take my word for it.'

'Thanks,' said Chas, who didn't quite know how to use this information. He'd never spoken to Major Bowyer. Do no harm to pass the info up the chain of command, though. He went to Sergeant Dodsworth.

'Sarge, one of the American Airborne blokes reckons Jerry's got a mortar battery on that hill and as soon as it gets dark they'll open up on us.'

'Does he now?'

'Yeah. Do no harm to mention it to the major.'

'No harm at all, gunner. You've given me the info, I must pass it on.'

Darkness fell with no sign of them moving position. They'd got themselves a comfortable billet in a farm building that had been knocked about by the war but which still had a roof and most of its stone walls. Chas wasn't thinking about the mortar battery; he was kicking himself for being so stupid as to give such a present to Billie. Giving her that thing was like giving her one of the crown jewels to play with. Not that she didn't deserve the crown jewels but he'd set her up to be noticed. It was all his fault and she thought it was hers. Hell! Now he was a smash-and-grab thief who'd end up in court when he got back to Blighty; might even get a dishonourable discharge from the army when they found out. He wouldn't want that. In the time he'd been in the army he'd developed a loyalty to his regiment, as did the most reluctant of conscripts, and Chas had been a volunteer.

Would he be locked up for this? He didn't know enough about the law to say one way or the other. Nor was he all that worried about being locked up. He'd been through a lot worse and survived. What he couldn't handle was losing the respect of his daughter.

The light went out of the gloomy sky at around ten o'clock. The German mortar batteries opened up and one landed right outside the window where Chas was sitting.

Fortunately there was no glass in it but the force of the explosion blew him clear across room where he lay shocked and winded on the floor. More bombs were dropping all around as the Germans sought to get their range. Men were now taking cover under anything they could. Chas was crawling under a substantial-looking table when a mortar shell came straight through the roof into an adjoining room and exploded with an ear-shattering boom. Smoke filled the room where he and ten others were taking cover. He could hear one of the men in the next room crying for his mum and recognised the voice as that of young Eric Payne who'd had his twenty-first birthday the previous day. His final cry turned into a choked-off gurgle and Chas knew the lad had died. There was a stunned silence then Sergeant Dodsworth's voice came booming out.

'Set up two Brens and take them bastards out! Robertson, follow Gunner Challinor. He knows where they are.'

Chas and another gunner grabbed their Brens and ran into a room where they'd have sight of the mortar battery. Chas pointed out its position. There were two glassless windows in a wall that faced the right way. Chas pushed a chest of drawers up to one window, set up his Bren on its bipod and trained it on where he thought the mortar battery to be. Robertson did the same with a table set under the other window. Jerry was out of sight, taking cover just over the crest of the hill. Their guns were being directed by a spotter. The actual position of the mortar battery soon became apparent as a flash lit up the hilltop about three hundred yards away, and a few seconds later a mortar landed just beyond the wall that was giving them cover. Chas managed to duck in time but Harry Robert-son took the blast full in the face.

Chas emptied a thirty-round magazine at the mortar position but the tracers showed that every round was going straight over Jerry's unseen head. He clipped another round into the curved magazine. The sergeant was kneeling behind him. A medic was declaring Harry Robertson dead.

'How're we doing, Sarge?' asked Chas.

'Not good. Four dead, half a dozen wounded. We've lost our cook, our QM and young Payne.'

'Why did we stay here, Sarge?'

'Stupidity, son. Sheer bone-headed stupidity.'

Chas fired another burst at the flash from the mortars, then braced himself for it to land. An explosion at the back of the building told him they'd received another direct hit.

'We're sitting ducks here, Sarge.'

But the sergeant had gone to see what further damage had just been done and also to find out if Major Bowyer had any bright ideas for them. Chas peered through the darkness at Harry Robertson, who was lying on his back. His face was no longer there. Chas found a cloth to cover him with. Harry had a weapons pouch slung around his shoulders in which, Chas knew, would be at least three grenades. He himself carried only two in his tunic pock-ets. He opened Harry's pouch and found five grenades inside. The room lit up from the flash of another mortar heading their way. He lay flat on the floor as a bomb came through the roof and exploded in a passageway, showering him with dust and rubble. Screams of pain were coming from all around. Sergeant Dodsworth was bellowing orders but Chas could hear nothing from their officer. Maybe he was dead. That wouldn't have bothered Chas. The major wasn't much of a leader.

He shook his head at the hopelessness of their situation. Someone had to do something otherwise they'd all be wiped out without ever fighting back, and fighting back was what Chas was here for. He slung Harry's weapons pouch over his shoulder and added his own two grenades. For a second he wondered if he should take the Bren but thought it might hinder his progress up the hill.

Chas tilted his steel helmet forward and ran out of the door. He knew the Jerry battery wouldn't see him from where they were but their spotter might so he kept low, trying to work out the observation post from where their spotter might work. To his right, high above him, were several large rocks about two hundred yards away. He thought back to his training which had covered all this. Yes, if he'd been wanting an OP he'd have run a wire to there. Another flash from the mortars. He waited for the shell to land, which it did, just behind the farmhouse, doing further damage and probably injury or worse to his friends. He left it a few seconds then set off running towards the rocks at full pelt, knowing the spotter would now be on the radio back to the battery to tell them where the last shell had landed. He got to within fifty yards of the rocks and flung himself flat on the ground. He took out two grenades and watched the rocks for a sign of movement. The spotter should be back at work now. If the spotter could see the farmhouse, Chas should be able to see the spotter. Which he did. Just a dark, moving shape between two of the rocks.

Chas didn't excel at many sports but at cricket he was a very fast, if inaccurate, bowler. However, his main talent lay in throwing the cricket ball at which he was very accurate and the only boy in the school who had ever thrown it over a hundred yards. The spotter was well within his range.

He pulled out the pin and hurled the grenade in an overarm action. It exploded just beyond his target. Chas immediately sent another on its way, using the first as a range-finder. This one did the trick. Chas ran forward to check and stared down at the first man he'd ever killed. He felt no guilt whatsoever. He could only think of Annie. This dead man belonged to the army that had murdered his Annie, and there were more he needed to kill. Men who were trying to kill him and his friends. He swung over to his left and headed for the battery that would now be working blind and wondering what had happened to their man.

In the farmhouse, Sergeant Dodsworth was peering over to where he'd seen the grenade explosions. It solved the mystery of where Gunner Challinor had gone. He also noticed that Harry Robertson's weapons pouch was missing. He looked up at the hill with a proud glint in his eye, growling, 'Go on, my son.'

Another flash sent a mortar shell hurtling down on the farmhouse. It went through the roof and exploded inside. More of his friends dead or wounded. Chas was now picturing Annie down there, an innocent victim of German murderers. He was around sixty yards from the battery. A machine gun opened up from above, raking the hillside. Chas tried to bury himself in the ground as a bullet ricocheted off his helmet. He was hoping his comrades would work out where he was and wouldn't return fire. Maybe he should have told someone where he was headed.

Back down at the farm a gunner was taking aim with Chas's abandoned Bren. He felt the sergeant's hand on his shoulder. 'Don't shoot, son. We have a man out there.'

The enemy machine gun stopped firing. Chas took out all five of Harry's grenades and laid them in a line in front of him. He knew this must be done quickly and accurately. The first two he'd thrown had given him a good idea of the range. He hurled one high in the air so it would arrive from above with no warning. As far as he knew it exploded right on target. The screams of pain from up there told him he was right. He sent three more in the same direction. Boom, boom, boom. All on target. He thought he heard cheers from the farmhouse. He saved the last one as a just-in-case weapon and headed up the hill. There was another burst of machine-gun fire that took him down.

In the farmhouse the sergeant cursed loudly and screamed at the gunner, 'Take out that bloody machine gun!'

The gunner had already fixed his target and sent thirty rounds straight at the machine-gun flash. It flashed no more. The sergeant set off up the hill at the double with a medic hard on his heels. Some of the surviving men followed.

When Sergeant Dodsworth got to Chas he was still conscious but had taken several rounds right across his stomach and was leaking a lot of blood. The sergeant bent down beside him.

'That was well done, Gunner. Bloody well done.'

'Did I get them all, Sarge?'

Chas was in deep shock that was anaesthetising the pain. He felt as though he'd been punched in the stomach. There was a shout from above where other soldiers had arrived at the German battery, indicating that the enemy posed no further risk.

'You got them, son.'

The pain was kicking in and Chas looked down at the damage 'Have I had it, Sarge?'

The sergeant said nothing. A medic was peeling back Chas's battledress which was sodden with blood. The look on his face told the sergeant that Chas had no chance.

'We'll do what we can, son.'

'Thanks. It hurts quite a lot.'

'I'll give him some morphine,' said the medic, taking out a syringe.

'Sarge,' said Chas. 'There's a letter in my top pocket I'd like you to read.'

'No problem, son.'

The sergeant took Billie's letter from Chas's pocket and read it by the light of a torch as the medic injected morphine into the dying man's arm.

'What's this about, son?'

'It's about a doll that I stole from a shop to give to my daughter. I broke the window and stole it. It looks like I'm in trouble with . . . er . . . with the police.'

'That's nothing son, not to what the thieves and vagabonds in this mob get up to.'

Chas's voice was now breaking up as his strength left him. 'I wonder . . . if you could somehow square . . . square things with my daughter . . . when you get back home.'

'When I get back there I'll tell your daughter she's got a very brave man for a father. The best of the best is what you are, son. I'll make her proud of you.'

Chas managed a bleak smile. 'Hey, Sarge . . . When I see Annie . . . I'll get my . . . my edge back.'

Dodsworth was still wondering if he should ask Chas what he was talking about when he died. The sergeant frowned away a tear and looked up at the men around him. There was no sign of the major.

'Anyone know where Major bleedin' Bowyer is?'

'Wounded, Sarge. In his arm.'

'Badly?'

'I don't think so, Sarge.'

'Pity. This man's bravery saved many lives tonight. I want to put him up for a VC. Anyone got a problem with that?'

There were murmurs of approval all round. The sergeant only hoped his recommendation was taken up. It was no less than Gunner Challinor had deserved.

Chapter 21

'We're here to speak to Miss Billie Challinor.'

Liz was standing at the door looking from one man to the other. One was in the uniform of an army officer, the other wore a civilian suit and trilby, which he had removed when she came to the door. It was he who spoke.

'Billie? Well, she's at school. What's it about?'

Even as she asked the question she was beginning to suspect the answer. 'It's to do with her dad, isn't it?'

The men introduced themselves. One was from the War Office and the other was a captain in the Herts and Essex Yeomanry.

'I'm sorry. We didn't know her age. Our records aren't quite as up-to-date as they should be. How old is Miss Challinor?'

'She's eight.'

'Might I ask who you are? Are you a relative?'

'No, just the person nominated to look after her while her dad's away. The appropriate authorities have been informed of this, so everything's above board.'

'I'm sure it is. And your name?'

'Elizabeth Morris. I think you'd better come inside,' she said, 'and if it's bad news I think you'd best tell me first.'

The two men came into her front room and stood there until she invited them to sit down. Both of them looked very solemn. Liz's heart sank. It could only be one of two things.

'Is he dead or just missing in action?'

The two men glanced at each other then the army man said, 'I'm sorry to inform you that Charles Challinor was killed in action.'

Liz fought to hold back the tears and lost the battle. She leaned forward with her elbows on her knees and head in her hands. The two man waited with the patience and understanding of those who'd seen all this before. She lifted her head, wiped her eyes on her pinafore and asked, 'Do you want me to tell Billie?'

'We'd like you to be present when we tell her ... is it *Mrs* Morris?'

She hesitated before saying it was.

'She's in school and won't be back until a quarter past four.'

The army man looked at his watch. It was just after midday. 'I think we'd better bring her out of school.'

'Okay, I'll go. It'll be dinnertime, so I won't be bringing her out of her classroom.'

'We should all go,' said the man in the suit. 'Maybe the head teacher will give us use of his office while we tell Billie what's happened, then we can bring her back in our car.'

'It's a her,' said Liz. 'Her name's Mrs Leeney, she's the headmistress.'

Chapter 22

Billie looked up at the four adults who were standing in a solemn semi-circle around her.

'Is this about my dolly?' she asked. 'Because if it is I don't want her back if she's been stolen only I can tell you now that my daddy didn't steal it because he always told me that honesty is the best policy . . . '

'It's not about the dolly, love,' said Liz. Her eyes were streaming with tears, as were Mrs Leeney's who'd already been told the bad news.

The man in the suit leaned down so that his head was level with Billie's. 'We've come to tell you about your daddy who was involved in a battle in France. He was very, very brave. In fact, he's been recommended for a very important bravery medal.'

'You mean my dad's a hero?'

'Well, we don't know what he'll get yet, but for what he did he deserves a Victoria Cross. He saved the lives of many men.

'The trouble is, Billie,' the man went on, 'in saving all those other men's lives your daddy was shot, and I'm really sorry to tell you that he didn't survive.'

Billie stared at him for a very long moment. The office

was completely silent, except for the noise of children playing outside.

'What do you mean?' she asked, innocently.

Liz leaned down and hugged her. 'Your daddy died, Billie,' she said.

The child froze in her arms as realisation began to sink in, but somehow it still didn't make sense to her. Stuff didn't kill her dad. If a bomb couldn't kill him nothing could. He'd told her that.

'So, when will he be coming home?'

'He won't be coming home, darling. He's to be buried in France with military honours.'

'You mean I won't see my daddy again . . . ever?'

No one could summon up the self-control to answer this without blubbing, so no one did. Billie's face was ghostly white and she was shivering with shock. Liz held her in her arms and stroked her hair. Mrs Leeney left the room, she wasn't needed there. She went to the staff common room to break the news to the others. It reduced most of them to tears, although Billie wasn't the only one to have been orphaned by this war. She was just such a popular kid.

Billie was taken home by car and sat quietly all afternoon while Liz watched over her, not really knowing what to do or what to expect. She herself was grieving for this lovely man but Billie's grief took precedence over hers. Evening came and Liz switched on the wireless to break the gloom. A new show called *Much Binding in the Marsh* was getting people laughing. It seemed so wrong, people laughing when her dad was dead. She went over to the wireless and pushed it off the sideboard on to the floor where it lay with the laughter and wisecracks still coming from it. She stamped on it to make the laughter stop. Liz, who had been watching this, came over and picked it up.

'I'll shut the buggers up,' she said, and threw the wireless with some force down the same cellar steps that had ended Larry Morris's life. It did the trick. They then clung to each other, having vented their rage on the now silent Bakelite box.

'Your dad bought us that,' Liz said eventually.

'That doesn't make it right for them to laugh on a day like today.'

Liz understood her logic and said, 'I'll get us another . . . when we're ready.'

'I'm not sure I'll ever be ready, Auntie Liz.'

It was a week before Billie went back to school and almost two months before Sergeant Dodsworth arrived at their door.

Chapter 23

He was in uniform, had one arm in a sling and was carrying a large parcel under his other arm. Billie answered the door. It was late August and during the school holidays.

'Am I right in thinking you're Miss Billie Challinor?' the big man asked.

'Yes,' she said.

Liz came to stand behind her.

'My name is Dodsworth. I'm a friend of your father.'

'My daddy's dead.'

I know, miss. I was, er, I was with him when he passed away.'

'You'd better come inside,' said Liz.

'Thank you.'

Dodsworth removed his beret and stuck it under his epaulette as he followed them into the house.

'Can I make you a cup of tea, Sergeant?' asked Billie, having counted his stripes.

'That would be most welcome. The last cup I had was in Nottingham station. It was like drinking dishwater.'

Billie smiled and asked, 'Have you been wounded, Sergeant?'

'Look, you can call me Jim if you like. In fact, I'd prefer it.'

'OK, Jim,' said Liz. 'So, have you been wounded?'

'Er, yes, bit of shrapnel. Which is why I'm here not over there, although I'll be going back in a few weeks for the final push, hopefully.'

Billie went into the scullery to put the kettle on the gas ring. She was back out within seconds, not wanting to miss anything.

'Have you come to tell us about Daddy?'

'Erm, yes. An officer was going to come but I volunteered as I knew Gunner Challinor personally.'

'And you were there when the Germans shot him,' added Billie.

'I was, yes. He acted on his own initiative to destroy a German mortar battery that was raining shells down on us. Had it not been for your father I wouldn't be here today, nor would many of our men.'

'He's supposed to be getting a medal for it,' said Liz. 'But we haven't heard anything yet.'

'No, well, that's one of the reasons I'm here. Gunner Challinor is to be awarded the Military Medal for his bravery in action.'

'Is that as good as a Victoria Cross?' asked Billie.

'Not quite,' said Dodsworth. 'The recommendation was for a VC as I've never seen bravery like that before, but there was a bit of a complication so it was downgraded to an MM, which is still a very high decoration.'

'What was the complication?' asked Liz.

Dodsworth looked embarrassed. 'Well, before he died, Challinor asked me to read a letter he'd got from Billie about a doll that had been stolen. The police think he might have had something to do with it.'

'Well, we don't think that, do we, Auntie Liz?' Billie broke in.

'No,' said Dodsworth, 'and even if he had it shouldn't be a good enough reason not to award him the VC after what he did. But someone sitting behind a desk somewhere in London must have seen a police report and altered his award from VC to MM. Either that or a certain useless officer in command of our unit might have had something to do with it.'

'A VC would have made Daddy a real hero, wouldn't it?' said Billie.

'He *was* a real hero, young lady.'

'Not according to those people who took his VC away. *Almost* a hero, but not a real one.'

'No, no, no, you must never think like that. Out there in Belgium right now there are over thirty men who know they owe their lives to your daddy. I'll never forget what he did, nor will they.'

'Thank you,' said Billie.

'Oh, and this morning I checked with the shop owners about the stolen doll. I told them all about Gunner Challinor and how he'd been accused of stealing it, so the owner of the shop, Mr Cecil Barker, has written a letter for me to give to you, along with this present.'

He handed Billie the parcel and a white envelope, inside which was a letter which Billie read first.

Dear Miss Challinor,

We at Barker's are proud to associate ourselves with a soldier as brave as your late father. His action saved the lives of many other brave men, but none so brave as he. I know his passing must be a great loss to you but you must always remember him with enormous pride. As a small token of our appreciation we'd like you to accept the gift the sergeant is bringing to you.

Yours sincerely,

C. G. Barker

Billie opened the parcel and squealed with a delight that Liz hadn't seen in her since Chas died. 'It's my dolly! It's Bluebelle! I knew my daddy would get her back to me.'

'Well, it's your daddy's doing all right.' Dodsworth grinned. 'He saved me and my men and now he's saved Bluebelle.'

Liz gave him a hug. 'Thank you for this, Sergeant. It's made a difference.'

Chapter 24

4 September 1944

It was over a week before Billie asked the question that had been worrying her. She was just about to leave for the first day of the new school term and had presented herself to Liz for inspection as she often had with her dad, whose inspections often ended with them both in fits of laughter after Chas had found a potato in her ear. Billie could never figure out how he did it.

Sleight of hand was not Liz's forte so she resorted to examining Billie's hair for insects in the manner of a monkey. Daft humour played a big part in their relationship, as it had with Chas. Liz pretended to throw something on the floor and stamped on it.

'Large earwig.'

'Oh, Auntie Liz, that was Harold, my pet earwig.'

'Well, Harold's now at peace in earwig heaven.'

But Billie didn't laugh. She had a question to ask. 'Auntie Liz, do *you* think Daddy stole Bluebelle for me?'

'I never had your daddy down for a thief, Billie.'

'No, but he was going off to war, not knowing if he'd be back, and he'd promised me a dolly he couldn't afford to buy.'

'Would you forgive him if he had stolen it?'

'Of course I would.'

'In that case, I think he probably did steal it for you . . . and good luck to him for doing it. I think Mr Barker thought the same thing as well.'

'What about the sergeant?'

'Him too, love. But neither of them thought your dad did too much wrong. He took a very big risk just to put a smile on your face.'

The following Friday another visitor came to the door.

Chapter 25

8 September 1944

The man came in a taxi, not a common sight in Gascoigne Street. A few curtains twitched, including those of Edna Grimshaw. Someone got out of the taxi and knocked on Liz's door. He doffed his trilby when Liz answered it. He was tall, middle-aged, and wore a dark Crombie overcoat.

'Mrs Morris?'

'Yes.'

'My name's Cedric Elliker. I believe my niece lives here.'

He had a southern accent, not unlike Chas's but not quite as friendly, although he was obviously doing his best to be charming.

'Your niece? You mean Billie?'

'Yes. I'm one of her late mother's brothers.'

'Oh, I didn't know she had any relatives. Billie's never mentioned you.'

He was carrying a briefcase in his right hand which he patted with his left. 'I appreciate your caution, Mrs Morris, and in anticipation of there being any problem I've brought my credentials along. Identity card, passport, and photographs of me and Billie's mother taken when

Billie was very small. I also have a photograph of me, Billie and my sister Anne, which I'll be pleased to let you have.'

'Oh, right, you'd better come in.'

'Thank you.'

He entered the house and stood there politely, awaiting Liz's permission to sit down.

'Oh, sit down, please. You say you're Billie's uncle?'

'I am. She's my late sister's girl. I've only just found out that Chas was killed in France. I've come to offer my condolences and to offer any help I can.'

'Where have you come from?'

'London. I have a practice there.'

'Practice? Are you a doctor or something?'

'Heavens, no. I'm a solicitor. I don't think the sick would benefit from my healing hands.' Cedric smiled at his own joke and Liz smiled too, out of politeness.

'How did you find out about Chas?' she asked.

'Well, there was a newspaper article about the band he was in and it was mentioned there that he died in heroic circumstances.'

'He did, yes.'

'Might I ask if he received any recognition of this bravery?'

'He got the Military Medal.' Liz looked at the clock. It was showing three-forty-eight.

'Billie'll be home from school in half an hour. Would you like a cup of tea?'

'I'd love one, thanks.'

Billie arrived home full of bounce. The thought of her daddy taking such a big risk just to put a smile on her face had given her a great memory she'd always cherish. On top of which the shop he'd stolen it from didn't mind at all and had given Bluebelle back to her, and on top of all *that* she could now show the doll off to whoever she wanted, although taking her to school was strictly banned.

'She's a very precious toy, darling,' Liz had told her. 'And she needs to be kept safe whenever she's not with you.'

Billie had agreed with this and only allowed her very best friends to have an audience with the magnificent Bluebelle. Her uncle got to his feet when she came through the door. Billie gave him a polite smile as Liz introduced them.

'This is your Uncle Cedric, he's from London.'

'I come from London,' said Billie, 'so did Mummy and Daddy.'

'I know,' said Cedric. 'I'm your mother's brother.'

Billie's eyes widened incredulously. 'I didn't know I had any uncles.'

'Well, you've got three. I have two brothers.'

'He has a photo of you with him and your mummy,' said Liz. 'It was taken when you were just a toddler.'

Cedric got his photos out and handed them to Billie who examined them eagerly. She looked from the photo to Cedric and back to ascertain that it was indeed him in the picture. 'It is, it's you!' she exclaimed.

Cedric smiled. 'Of course it's me.'

'Why didn't anyone tell me about you?' Billie asked.

Liz looked at him. She'd been asking herself the same question. The smile went from Cedric's face.

'Well, I didn't know you hadn't been told about me, but I think the reason might be that grown-ups sometimes aren't very sensible. Your father's father didn't approve of my sister.'

'My mummy was lovely,' said Billie stoutly.

'I know she was. It wasn't so much your mummy as our whole family. There'd been some silly disagreement between your grandfather and my father that got out of all proportion.'

Liz knew about Chas being disinherited by his father because he'd married Annie, so Cedric's story had the ring of truth.

'Yes, grown-ups can be silly,' Billie agreed. 'Do I have a big family in London?'

'Well, my parents are both dead, my father died just before the war, but my two brothers both have children. I haven't, I'm afraid. Just me and your aunt Lavinia.'

'Aunt Lavinia? Wow! I didn't know I had an Aunt Lavinia. Is she nice?'

'Well, I think so. She bosses me about a bit but maybe I need bossing about. She'd love to meet you.'

'You mean I could go to London to see her? I've never been back to London since the horrible bomb dropped. Do they still drop bombs?'

'Not bombs, we get doodlebugs nowadays.'

'Doodlebugs? I've heard of doodlebugs,' said Billie. 'What are they?'

'It's what we call the German V1 rockets,' said Cedric. 'They send them all the way from Germany and fill them with just enough fuel to come down on London. They make this horrible whining noise, and if that noise stops overhead it means it's run out of fuel and you know you're for it. Most of them are shot down by our fighters.'

'Isn't Auntie Lavinia scared of them?'

'Oh, no ... I work in London but we actually live about ten miles from where they're dropping so we're safe enough – and it won't be long before the war's over, hopefully. Our boys have already booted the Nazis out of France.'

'I wish it had never started,' said Billie, 'then I'd still have my mummy and daddy.' She looked up at Cedric and asked, innocently, 'Did you fight in the war, Uncle Cedric?'

He looked uncomfortable. 'I ... erm ... I was called up, but at my age and with my feet it turned out that I was much more useful being in the Home Guard.'

'You scarcely look old enough for the Home Guard,' commented Liz, a shade tartly.

'I'm forty-five,' said Cedric. 'Annie was a lot younger than me.'

Billie turned to Liz. 'Auntie Liz, when can I go and see Aunt Lavinia?'

Billie didn't notice the expression of anxiety that flashed across Liz's face, but Cedric did. He raised his eyebrows as he looked at her. 'Billie,' he said, 'your Auntie Liz and I have something we need to discuss in private, like us adults do sometimes.'

The concerned expression returned to Liz's face. 'Why don't you go out and play, love? See if Jean's playing out.'

Billie shrugged, said, 'Okay,' and went out of the door.

'Great kid,' said Cedric.

'Yes, she is. I love her as if she were my own.'

'I can see that, and on behalf of my sister and brother-in-law I thank you for what you've done for her, but she's really my responsibility now with me being the eldest of her three uncles.'

'You mean, you want to take her from me?'

'Well, I wouldn't put it like that but I suspect she might have a better life with us. I have a large house and, with no disrespect, can afford to give her a fine education which will ensure she makes the most of her talents.'

'What she has around here is a lot of love and friendship. Don't you think that taking her away from everyone she knows will be a bit too much for her, so soon after losing her father?'

'It could be that a complete change of lifestyle might be just what she needs. While she's here there'll be people and places that remind her of her father.'

'What wrong with that?'

'What's wrong with it is that she might be in mourning for years, constantly reminded of her dad.'

'I'm sorry but I don't agree.'

'Look, the last thing I want to do is argue with you but I suggest that Billie comes back with me now. Give it a couple of months then you can come down to see her. If she wants to come back with you then I won't stand in her way. You have my word on that.'

'Oh, I don't know . . . '

'Mrs Morris, I could simply exercise my rights and take her. You have no legal right to be her guardian, whereas I do. I can assure you that I'm acting purely in Billie's interests. She'll have an excellent chance to make the most of her life if she comes to live with us. It's what my sister would have wanted.'

Liz was struggling to hold back her tears. Billie was the

daughter she'd always wanted. She'd replaced the child who had died inside Liz, and now this child too was about to be taken away from her.

'You can't do this to me.'

'To you? I'm sorry but this isn't about you. This is about my dead sister's girl having the life she deserves.'

'I can give her the life she deserves,' Liz protested.

'Really? And what sort of life's that? I'm a wealthy man, Mrs Morris, and you're a woman on her own who's obviously struggling to make ends meet. When Billie comes to live with us she'll want for nothing and she'll have a mother figure *and* a father figure to look after her. We'll love her like our own.'

Liz looked up at him with misting eyes. 'Will you?' she said. 'Will you really love her? How do you know?'

'Because she reminds me of my sister when she was a girl – and I loved my sister dearly.'

So there it was, Liz was defeated. When Chas died she'd lost a man who had never been hers but had still left a big hole in her heart. Now she was about to lose the small person she thought had replaced Chas in her affections. Not so.

She could fight Cedric for custody of Billie but he was a rich London lawyer and she was a woman struggling to make ends meet and who had no legal right to the child. What chance did she have? And maybe she had no right to stand in the way of Billie's chance of leading the good life. The kid's life hadn't been a bed of roses up to now.

'You can come down to visit her just as often as you like,' he said. 'We've got plenty of room to put you up for a few nights.'

159

'It's all happening a bit too quickly,' Liz said. 'One minute I've got a little girl whose been daughter to me for the past three years and the next minute she's being taken from me.'

'In my experience the quicker things are done, the quicker you get over the shock. Just remember, you can see Billie whenever you like and I'll make sure she always calls you Auntie Liz, because that's how we'll always refer to you.'

Liz went to the window and saw the taxi still waiting outside. 'Must you take her right now?' she said. 'Supposing she doesn't want to go with you. I mean, she doesn't even know you.'

'And that's where I'll need you on my side, Mrs Morris.'

'I'm not on your side.'

'Okay, then we'll both need to be on Billie's side. All I want is to do my duty by her. It's my job as her uncle – I'm also her godfather, by the way.'

'What religion?'

'C of E. We're not particularly religious, it was Annie who wanted her christened. The fact is that I have every right to take my niece away and you've no right to keep her here. We don't want Billie caught in a tug-of-war which can only have one outcome, so be on my side, for her sake. Tell her it's better for her to come with me, and if she doesn't like it there, she can always come back to live with you. Tell her this and let her come with me, with a smile on her face.'

Liz's was streaming with tears.

'You know I'm right,' he said persuasively.

'I know no such thing, except that if I fight you I can't win.' Liz wiped away her tears with her pinafore and got to her feet. 'I'll go and fetch her. You can do all the talking and persuading. I don't want her thinking I had any ruddy part in this!'

Billie wasn't too unhappy at being recalled to the house. Her hitherto unknown Uncle Cedric was a subject of great interest to her and she didn't want to miss anything. He and Auntie Liz were both standing there looking serious. It seemed as though her auntie had been crying, which wiped the expectant smile from Billie's face.

'What's up, Auntie Liz?'

'Your uncle had better explain this to you. It's out of my hands ... apparently.' Liz didn't even try to hide the bitterness she felt.

'What does that mean?'

'Look, I've got a headache coming on,' said Liz. In truth she felt more tears about to fall. 'I'll just go upstairs for a lie down.'

Without another word she left the room and made her way upstairs. Billie heard her burst into tears before she reached the landing. Something bad had obviously happened and Uncle Cedric had brought the news.

'What's happened, Uncle Cedric?' Billie asked him.

'Nothing's happened. It's just that your Auntie Liz is very sad that you're coming to live with us.'

'Live with you? Why must I live with you?'

'Well, because it's the law, young lady. I'm your mother's brother and you're my responsibility. I'm sorry to have to take you away but you can come back to visit and your aunt can come to see you at our house. We have a beautiful home near London and you'll be going to a lovely school where you'll make many new friends. It'll be a great adventure.'

He thought that Billie might be the type of girl to be persuaded by the chance of an adventure and he wasn't wrong.

'Does Auntie Liz want me to go with you?'

'No, she doesn't, and having met you I can understand that. I can see so much of your mother in you. What I can't get through to Auntie Liz is that she isn't losing you. She'll always be your Auntie Liz and she can visit whenever she likes.'

'I think I'd better go and see her.'

Liz was staring out of the window when Billie tapped on her door.

'Come in, love.'

Billie went in and stood behind her. 'I'll stay with you if that's what you want, Auntie Liz.'

Liz smiled and shook her head, still looking through the window. 'It's not up to me, love.'

'Okay, I want to stay here whether you like it or not.'

Liz turned and put her arms around Billie. 'It's not up to you either. Your uncle's a lawyer. He knows his rights and responsibilities, and apparently he has a right to be your guardian.'

'But he doesn't know me.'

'He's met you, Billie. That's all he needs to know about you. There are some people you can weigh up in a couple of minutes, and you're one of them.'

'So I have to go with him, whether I like it or not?'

'It seems so. Look, I imagine you'll love it where you're going. Nice house, nice clothes, great school, holidays abroad I shouldn't wonder, when the war's over. He just wants to make it up for you losing your mum and dad. He's your godfather, did you know that?'

'My godfather? Wow! I wonder why my dad didn't mention any of this to me.'

'Because your dad was a typical man. Men have different priorities from women. Look, I'll keep in touch as much as I can. I'll write to you and come to visit as often as I can get down there.'

'When am I going?'

'My guess is right now. I think he came here to take you back with him today.'

'But I need time to say goodbye to my friends at school.'

'Billie, it's Friday. You won't see them until Monday. I doubt your uncle will wait that long.'

Chapter 26

Only Billie and Cedric were in the first-class compartment to London but, despite its comparative comfort, the girl felt uncomfortable. Cedric was deeply engrossed in the six newspapers he'd bought in Leeds City Station and had paid her little attention since stepping into the taxi that had brought them here. It was dark outside with nothing to see so Billie passed the time by calling out the stations.

'Doncaster, Uncle Cedric.'

He glanced through the window at the passing station sign.

'So it is.'

Half an hour later she called out, 'Newark.'

Just a grunt this time.

She was asleep when they pulled into King's Cross Station four and a half hours after leaving Leeds.

'Wake up, Billie, we're here.'

With her trailing in his wake, Cedric carried her suitcase out of the station and past the taxi rank to a large black car parked on Euston Road. He gave a brief wave to the driver, opened a back door and waited for Billie to arrive, out of breath. He indicated that she should get in the back seat, took her suitcase from her and threw it into the boot. Then he got into the front passenger seat and the car drove off without anything else being said. Billie wasn't particularly bothered about not being introduced to the driver, but it was bad manners and she didn't like bad manners.

The two men talked of things Billie knew nothing about, nor was she interested. The only thing she knew was that manners would have to improve if she were to stay here.

After twenty minutes' driving through a heavily built-up area the buildings seemed to thin out, giving way to trees and general greenery and fine-looking houses.

'Is this where you live, Uncle Cedric?'

It was as if he'd only half heard her question and was more interested in talking to the driver so it went un-answered. She didn't repeat it.

They eventually turned up a street of very grand houses and pulled into the driveway of one of the smaller ones, although it would dwarf Auntie Liz's house in Leeds. The driver got out and opened the boot, took Billie's case out and carried it to the front door. She and Cedric followed him. The door was opening as they got to it. A woman was standing there.

She was tall, about the same age as Cedric, and had bright red lipstick on her thin-lipped mouth. Her dark hair was swept up from her face into a roll on the top of her head, very much like a picture of Veronica Lake that Billie had seen on the cover of one of Liz's magazines. Only this woman was no Veronica Lake. She attempted a smile, but it didn't come naturally to her.

'You must be Billie.'

'Yes.'

'I'm Aunt Lavinia, welcome to your new home.'

'I'm very pleased to meet you, Aunt Lavinia, and thank you for letting me come and live with you.'

It was a line she'd been given by Liz but Billie struggled to make herself sound sincere.

'You can leave your case in the hall. I'll show you your room later.'

'Thank you.'

Billie followed them into a large, extravagantly furnished room. It was bountifully carpeted from wall to wall, the curtains were silk and the wallpaper sumptuous. A fire was burning in a huge marble fireplace in front of which were two leather settees facing each other over a low, marble-topped table. There were books on the table with glossy covers but they didn't look to have been read much. Other comfortable-looking chairs were scattered around the room, enough to seat another half a dozen people. On one wall an antique longcase clock inlaid with walnut marquetry chimed out the hour. Antique vases, silver, porcelain and china ornaments were on display in a mahogany cabinet; lavishly framed oil paintings and photographs hung on the walls, all illuminated by a sparkling crystal chandelier. Billie had never been in such a room. It was a place that had probably never known a muddy boot, much less a boisterous child. Above the fireplace was a large oil painting of a severe-looking man. Cedric saw her looking at it.

'That's your grandfather, Montague Elliker.'

'Wow!' said Billie, impressed. 'Didn't even know about him. Does he live here with you?'

'No, he's dead.'

'Oh, heck,' she said, disappointed at the loss of her newfound granddad.

On another wall was a family photograph portraying a stern-looking group, including her grandfather and one smiling girl. Billie pointed at her.

'Who's that?'

Cedric followed her pointing finger. 'That's my sister Annie.'

'You mean my mum?'

'How many sisters would I have who are called Annie?'

Cedric was trying to be funny and failing. Billie didn't like jokes about her dead mother and her uncle shouldn't be joking about his own sister either. She kept her eyes on the photograph and pointed at a scowling young man. 'Blimey! He looks miserable. Who's that?'

'That would be me,' said Cedric.

'Oh, sorry. I didn't realise it was you. I didn't mean to be rude.'

Lavinia tried a joke. 'That's him when he's in a good mood.'

It fell on stony ground. Billie pointed to another photograph, a larger copy of the family photograph he'd shown her in Leeds with both him, Annie and an infant Billie. 'Isn't that the same one you showed me?'

'It is. Taken on your christening day. Your mother brought you to see us quite a lot in those days. His quick glance at Lavinia told her to back him up on this lie. Annie and Billie had been to visit just once and there had been no christening.

'And you're my godfather?'

'I am.'

'Do I have a godmother?'

'She's standing right behind you.'

Billie turned and looked up at Lavinia. 'You're my god-mother?'

'I am,' lied Lavinia. 'Come on, I'll show you to your room. I'm sure it's way past your bed time.'

It was gone eleven but Billie couldn't sleep. She got out of bed and opened the curtains so that she could see the sky. It was a cool, clear, early-September night. There was a radiator under the window and she warmed her hands on it, revelling in its luxury. The only radiators she knew were the ones at school. Her aunt and uncle must be very rich to own a house with four bedrooms and central heating. She looked up at the stars and wondered if they were the same stars that she could see from her bedroom window in Leeds. She scanned the skies for the Plough and issued a squeak of delight when she found it. She knew that the two end stars pointed to the North Star. Her daddy had taught her that. He'd told her how the black slaves in America didn't call it the Plough, they called it the Drinking Gourd, and when they escaped their evil mas-ters they followed the Drinking Gourd because freedom was in the north. He'd even sung her a song called 'Follow The Drinking Gourd' which the slaves used to sing as they marched to freedom. Her daddy knew a lot of songs, with him being a musician. This one had been taught to him by a black friend of his who was very funny and played the piano. His name was Duke Wellington but he wasn't really a duke. She sang the song to herself as she looked up at the night sky and felt a sense of comfort from knowing her daddy would be listening somewhere, Mummy as well probably. It was good that they were together again. She wondered if they approved of her coming to live with Uncle Cedric.

Or would she end up following the Drinking Gourd herself? Follow it north to where her own freedom might lie. She hoped not. She hoped her aunt and uncle might one day come to love her like Auntie Liz did.

Chapter 27

St Ethelburga's Preparatory School for Young Ladies was a different world from Gipton School on Harehills Road in Leeds. It was a private day school. Cedric could easily have afforded to send her to a top boarding school but he wanted Billie near to him where he could keep an eye on her. Given the choice he'd have kept her off school altogether until his business was concluded, but he needed to prove to the authorities that he was a suitable guardian.

Lavinia took her to get kitted out for a school uniform consisting of a dark green and purple striped blazer, dark green beret for the winter and straw boater for the summer, three pleated grey skirts, three white shirts, two green pinafore dresses, a green and purple striped tie, and two pairs of sensible black shoes. As she stood in front of the mirror in the school outfitter's Billie thought she'd never looked as smart.

'Would the young lady like to look at the school sportswear?' enquired the assistant.

'What sort of sportswear?' asked Lavinia.

'Well, it's the hockey season now so . . .'

'I've never played hockey,' said Billie.

'You soon will be,' said Lavinia. 'We'd better have a pair

of hockey boots, shin pads, socks and couple of shirts – one white, one in school colours.'

'Won't I need a stick as well?' asked Billie, who was becoming interested in this idea.

'You will indeed,' said the assistant, 'and a pair of young lady's shorts no higher than four inches above the knee.'

'We'd better have a couple of pairs two inches above the knee,' said Lavinia. 'They grow so quickly at this age.'

'How old is your daughter, madam?'

'She's eight.'

Billie looked up at her aunt, wondering why she hadn't corrected the man. Lavinia didn't meet her gaze. It seemed to Billie that she'd acquired a new mother and she wasn't too sure about this. Her aunt said and did all the right things but she lacked the obvious affection that Billie felt radiating from Liz, who wasn't even her proper aunt.

There were fourteen girls in Billie's class. She'd been in a class of forty-four in her last school. Most of her classmates had been at the school for three years. They knew each other well and they all came from a higher echelon of society than Billie was used to. From day one she was a fish out of water. The three years she'd lived in Leeds had given her original London accent a distinctive Yorkshire twang, which was a source of great amusement to the other girls.

Most of the girls were okay but there was a clique of four who set themselves apart from the rest. These girls were four of the brightest scholars and the best at games. They had a leader called Delma Beddington-Croft, who had been picked to play for the school junior hockey team despite being only eight years old. She was a tall girl and destined to be quite beautiful. She was also a bully.

The lessons were probably a year ahead of what Billie had been doing in Leeds, where she'd been consistently top of the class. At the end of day one she was asked by her class teacher, Miss Molloy, if she'd been following the lessons all right. Billie saw no advantage in lying.

'No, miss. We didn't do fractions and long division or nouns and verbs and things, but I am good at reading so I might be able to catch up.'

'Your aunt has asked for extra tuition if required to bring you up to the other girls' standard. You must ask me if you think you need it. In the meantime I'm going to loan you three books that should help you. One on arithmetic, one on English Grammar and a General Studies book. There's also hockey practice after school on Wednesday. You might want to join in. I understand you haven't played the game before.'

'No, miss.'

'You might also wish to polish away your Northern accent. The girls can be cruel without knowing it.'

'Yes, miss.'

Delma and her four cronies were waiting for Billie later at the school gates. One of them called out to her, 'Hey, you, Northern oik! What are you doing in our class?'

Billie walked over to them.

'I beg your pardon,' she said, politely.

'You heard,' said Delma.

'I heard you ask what I was doing in your class and it seemed such a silly question that I thought I might have misheard.'

172

'Are you calling me silly?' snarled Delma.

'Well, if you don't know what I'm doing in your class it means you are a bit silly.'

Delma clenched her fists and advanced on Billie. She was probably three inches taller and ten pounds heavier. What she lacked was the hard life Billie had known thus far. A life that had left her totally unafraid of the Delma Beddington-Crofts of this world. Billie clenched her own fists and stood her ground.

'Thump her, Delma!' shouted one of the other girls. 'Thump the oik!'

Billie went over to the girl who had shouted and asked her, 'Why don't *you* thump me?'

The girl went quiet and looked at the ground. Billie went over to face Delma. 'Are you the class bully, then? The girl who likes to pick on the small kids. I might be smaller than you, but I bet I can beat you in a fight.'

She struck a boxing stance that her dad had taught her. Sideways on to Delma. Left fist ready to jab, right fist protecting the chin, looking ready to fight. *You stand like that, Billie, and look fierce, they'll probably back off without aiming a blow. It got me out of a lot of trouble when I was a kid.*

As it happened Billie didn't know much more than the correct stance but it had scared off one or two bullies in Leeds so she figured it might also work on Delma. And it would do no harm to throw a lie into the mix.

'My dad taught me how to box. I'm pretty good, as you're gonna find out.'

She was sincerely hoping none of them would call her bluff. Delma stepped away, muttering something about not wanting to dirty her hands on the Northern oik. Billie was tempted to call her a coward but she decided not to push her luck. Hopefully they might leave her alone from now on.

It didn't actually help Billie that the confrontation had been witnessed by other girls who soon spread the word that the bullies had met their match in the new girl from Yorkshire. It gave her a reputation that would allay further physical assaults by bullies, but clever bullies have clever ways of hurting people.

That evening, after tea, Billie took her three books up to her room and by nine that night she had taught herself the basics of fractions, long division and multiplication, surprising herself with how easy she was finding it. Then, using a torch under the bedclothes, she taught herself the definitions of grammatical terms: a noun is a person, place or thing – a woman, a shop, a car; a verb is a *doing* word; run, jump, sing. An adjective describes a noun: a nice woman, a cuddly toy, a fast car; an adverb describes a verb; run quickly, walk slowly, sing softly. Before sleep overtook her she'd read about pronouns and learned how to conjugate the verb 'to be'.

In one evening of intense study she taught herself enough to be able to hold her hand in the air a couple of times to answer the questions Miss Molloy threw at the class the next day. Her teacher didn't praise her any more then she'd praise any girl who had answered a question to which she was expected to know the answer, but when the bell went, she asked Billie to stay behind for a few minutes.

'Challinor, would you have been able to answer those questions yesterday?'

'No, miss.'

'I'm impressed with you, Challinor.'

'Yes, miss.'

'Just one thing.'

'Yes, miss?'

'Stay out of trouble. You seem to have speedily acquired a reputation as a girl to be reckoned with.'

'I haven't done anything, miss.'

'Nor will you, Challinor, if you have any sense.'

'Yes, miss.'

Billie went away wondering if this meant her teacher had found out about her confrontation with Delma. If so, what had she heard? And what did she mean – a girl to be reckoned with? Just what did that signify? If Liz were around Billie would ask her, but no way was she going to ask Aunt Lavinia or Uncle Cedric. She didn't feel comfortable around them. She couldn't put her finger on why and told herself it was perhaps because she was eight and you're not expected to know such stuff when you're eight.

The following day Delma and her cronies confined their bullying to sniggers and remarks made at Billie's expense, but they were frustrated by the fact that every one of the girls in the class knew that Billie had faced down all four of them. Also by the fact that Billie totally ignored them. Her dad had taught her that. If you want to get the better of some people, the best thing to say to them is nothing.

This all added fuel to the fire of hatred burning inside Delma Beddington-Croft. It was a fire that could only be quenched by a suitable revenge on this upstart northerner. She and her three cronies put their heads together.

Chapter 28

St Ethelburga's had extensive playing fields which included three full-size hockey pitches. It was on one of these that Billie found herself being introduced to the game. She also found her very first friend at the school, Margaret Ashmore, or Mags as she was more popularly known. Mags was a shy girl who had been Billie's predecessor as the target of Delma's bullying and she was secretly relieved to have some of the pressure taken off her.

'She can be really horrid,' Mags told Billie. 'I hate this school because of her but I can't leave because my parents won't hear of it.'

'Have you told them about Delma?' Billie asked.

'I have, and my dad says I have to learn to deal with it myself.'

'He's probably right.'

'Delma's dad is my dad's boss,' said Mags. 'He's a really rich man and I don't think my dad wants to get on the wrong side of him.'

'Yeah, and I bet Delma's a real daddy's girl.' Billie thought about what she'd just said and added, 'Mind you, so was I when my daddy was alive.'

'Your dad's dead?'

'Yeah, so's my mum. Both killed in the war.'

'Oh, Billie, I'm so sorry. Who do you live with?'

'My aunt and uncle.'

'Are they nice?'

Billie had to think about this. 'They're okay, I suppose.'

They were to have a practice game against a fourth-year team. Delma put Billie in goal, the least enjoyable position in the game. She gave her instructions.

'Your job is to stop the ball going in the net.'

'Thank you,' said Billie. 'I'd never have known.'

Delma glared at her. 'You can use your stick or any other part of your body. The rest of us can only use our sticks.'

'Right.'

Billie had let a goal in within two minutes. Their opponents were a year older and fully expected to win by a good margin, but this didn't stop Delma screaming at Billie.

'Are you blind, you oik? My grandmother could have stopped that.'

Delma was a forward, as were two of her cronies. Within five minutes she'd levelled the scores with a shot from the twenty-five-yard line. The other team came back at them. Billie went to the edge of the shooting circle to meet the onslaught. An opposing forward picked up a pass and was turning to shoot when Billie charged her down. The whistle went for a penalty.

Delma was screaming at her again.

'Don't you know the rules, you oik?'

Billie retorted, 'No, I don't know the rules. I've only been playing ten minutes.'

The ball was placed on the penalty spot. The referee, who was a games teacher, told Billie to stand with both feet on the line and not to move until the ball was played.

The attacker walked up to the ball smiling to herself, confident of an easy goal against this girl who hadn't played before. Billie sensed her confidence and called out to her.

'Hey! Better not miss against me. I'm useless. They'll all laugh at you if you don't score.'

With her confidence wounded the girl scowled and took the shot, which hurtled straight at Billie. She stopped it easily, to the delight of most of her team. All except Delma and two others.

For the rest of the game Billie acquitted herself with increasing skill. They lost the match 10–3 but it had increased Billie's popularity somewhat. She thought she might learn to enjoy this game, provided they let her play in the outfield and not in goal.

Ten minutes after the game finished Miss Wilde, who had been refereeing the game, came into the girls' changing room. She called for quiet and looked quite stern.

'A gold watch has gone missing from the staff changing room. Does anyone in here know anything about it?'

The girls looked at each other then back at Miss Wilde, all shaking their heads.

'No, miss.'

'I left it in my property box along with all my things and now it's missing. I can only assume it has been stolen.'

'It wasn't any of us, miss,' called out one of the girls. 'We all came straight in here.'

'Yes, but you had to pass the staff changing room to reach here.'

Another teacher, Miss Ramsden, arrived and stood beside Miss Wilde. She called out, 'Girls, we need to eliminate all of you from suspicion so I want you to come forward, one by one, and allow me to search you. You will then wait outside until we have searched this room. The watch is very valuable and we would much rather not involve the police.'

Delma stepped forward immediately and allowed herself to be searched, as did her three cronies. Then, one by the one, the other girls submitted to this before going to wait outside. Billie was sixth in line and somehow felt very uncomfortable about this. Mags was in front of her.

'Mags, does this happen a lot?' she hissed.

'No, it's never happened before.'

Billie was searched and nothing was found. She waited outside as instructed and her eyes were drawn to Delma and her friends who were standing by the groundsman's hut, grinning.

'I wonder what they're smiling at,' Billie said to her new friend.

'Dunno, but I don't trust Delma.'

'No, nor me.'

Miss Ramsden came out and stood with her hands behind her back, awaiting her colleague. Ruth, one of Delma's cronies, the one who hadn't been playing, walked over to Miss Ramsden and spoke to her quietly. Miss Ramsden nodded briefly and dismissed the girl who went back to stand with Delma. Billie noticed all this. Miss Wilde came out holding the watch by its gold bracelet.

Miss Ramsden spoke to her. Miss Wilde's eyes fixed on Billie.

'Challinor, come here.'

Billie's heart sank. She could hear Delma laughing out loud, along with shocked gasps from her other school friends.

Miss Wilde turned on her heel and walked back inside. Billie followed her into the changing room. The teacher turned to confront her. 'Challinor, I found this in your satchel. What do you have to say for yourself?'

Billie was shocked. 'I . . . I didn't take it, miss.'

'Then why was it in your possession?'

'I don't know, miss.'

'You were seen going into the staff changing room.'

'No, I never went into the staff changing room, miss. I've never been here before.'

'Then perhaps you went in by mistake and thought you'd pick up a souvenir while you were about it.'

'I didn't, miss. I didn't go in there.'

'Then how did this watch come to be in your satchel?'

Billie was in tears now. 'I don't know, miss. Honest, it wasn't me.'

'Tomorrow morning, Challinor, I want you to be in Mrs Leverton's office at nine o'clock sharp. Do you understand?'

'Yes, miss,' said Billie miserably.

Mags was waiting outside for her.

'What happened?'

'They found the watch in my satchel. I didn't steal it but whoever did put there.'

'Ruth Allison took it,' said Mags quietly.

'What?'

'When Miss Wilde took you inside, Delma and that lot were laughing like mad. They were all leaning against the groundsman's hut. I went inside from round the back so I could listen to them talking about it. I think it was Delma's idea. Ruth took it while we were playing and stuck it in your satchel.'

Billie shook her head then looked at Mags. 'Why don't you come back with me and tell Miss Wilde that?'

Mags blanched at the prospect. 'If it gets Delma into trouble it might get my dad into trouble with his boss.'

'Mags, I've got to see Mrs Leverton in the morning. She'll expel me for sure and I've only been here three flippin' days.'

'Oh, no!' said Mags. 'Tell you what. I can speak to my dad and see what he says. Trouble is, they'd expel Delma and the others if the truth came out. I don't think his boss'd be so pleased if that happened.'

'It'd be Delma's fault, not ours.'

'I know but . . . '

'Okay, see what your dad says. With any luck my Uncle Cedric'll boot me back to Leeds, which'll suit me down to the ground.'

'What? You prefer living in Leeds to living here?'

'I prefer living with my Aunt Liz to living here.'

'Isn't it all flat caps and mill chimneys?'

Billie burst out laughing. 'Plenty of flat caps, but not many chimneys that I know of. No snobs either.'

Billie didn't mention her plight to Uncle Cedric or Aunt Lavinia. She knew they'd find out about it at some time

181

but it would be better if Mags was able to help her out with the true story. One thing she did miss were the Leeds neighbours and their children. No one here seemed to have any. The next-door neighbours were both elderly, presumably with grown-up children, and Billie had seen a girl of around fourteen riding around on her bike and a paperboy much the same age, but no kids of eight or so. She'd been hoping that some of the girls at school lived nearby, but the way things were going she herself wouldn't be at there much longer. She gazed out of her bedroom window wondering what tomorrow might bring.

Billie's hopes were dashed by the look on Mags's face when they met outside the school gates.

'Sorry, Billie. Dad says it's nothing to do with me.'

Billie shrugged and headed for the headmistress's office without Mags's testimony to help her. Delma and her cronies were standing near Mrs Leverton's door.

'I don't know why you've bothered turning up,' sneered Delma. 'You're going to get expelled anyway, you thieving Yorkshire oik.'

Billie saw an opportunity to hit back. 'Someone was in the groundsman's hut and heard you lot talking. They told Mrs Leverton it was Ruth who took the watch and stuck it in my satchel. It's you lot who're gonna get expelled.'

The shocked expressions on their faces brought a smile to Billie's. 'You can always go in and tell her the truth,' she said. 'Say it was just a silly prank and that you're sorry.'

For a moment she thought they were going to do it. The four of them were looking at each other as if pondering the suggestion. Then Delma turned to Billie and snarled, 'You're a liar!'

'But you know I'm telling the truth. If I'm lying, how would I know what happened?'

Delma hustled the other three away without looking back. Billie called after them, 'If you walk off now you'll all be expelled for sure.'

Ruth stopped and was about to turn round when Delma grabbed her and virtually dragged her away down the corridor. Billie sighed and thought, *Nearly*.

Mrs Leverton was sitting behind her desk. She was a large, strict-looking woman. Miss Wilde was already there, sitting in a chair. Billie knocked and was told to enter. She stood in front of the headmistress with her hands clasped together. The woman glared at her.

'You are a thief, Challinor.'

'No, I'm not, Mrs Leverton. Another girl took the watch and put it in my satchel to get me into trouble.'

'What other girl?'

'Ruth Allison.'

'Do I just have your word for this, or do you have some sort of proof?'

'It's what happened, Mrs Leverton. Another girl heard them talking but she can't say anything because her dad says she mustn't.'

'She heard who talking?'

'Ruth and Delma and two other girls. I don't know their names but they're always with Delma, who's a bully.'

'Really?' said Mrs Leverton. 'I'd like to know who the girl is who heard them talking.'

183

'I don't think I can tell you that, Mrs Leverton, because I don't want to get her into trouble with her dad.'

The headmistress looked at Miss Wilde. 'Do you believe any of this?'

'I do not. I know this girl was seen to go into the staff changing room.'

Billie remembered Ruth talking to Miss Ramsden. 'I bet it was Ruth Allison who told Miss Ramsden that.'

'How would you know?' asked Miss Wilde.

'Because I saw her talking to Miss Ramsden. None of the other girls will have seen me go into the staff changing room, because I didn't.'

The headmistress took off her glasses and rubbed her eyes. She didn't know this girl, other than from the good report she'd had from Miss Molloy about her. She also knew that Delma Beddington-Croft was a bully. The trouble was that her father was a valued patron and governor of the school.

'Wait outside, Challinor. I wish to have a word with Miss Wilde privately.'

'Yes, Mrs Leverton.'

After Billie left the headmistress looked at Miss Wilde and sighed. 'You know, I'm inclined to believe this girl.'

'Yes, so am I.'

'The trouble is, what to do? If we bring in the girls involved and they admit what they've done I will have no option other than to expel them all. Expelling Beddington-Croft will prove difficult, considering who her father is. If he withdraws his financial backing the school might well go under.'

'It seems wrong to risk the future of the school just to

save a pupil who's only been with us few days,' said Wilde.

'You think we should sacrifice Challinor for the greater good?'

'Mrs Leverton, I love my job. If the school goes under, so do we, and all the other staff. Can we not just give the Challinor girl a ticking off and leave it at that?'

Mrs Leverton considered this and shook her head. 'The problem is that the whole school knows what's happened. We have a valued reputation for setting an example. We stand no nonsense of any kind and turn out well-behaved and disciplined young ladies of the highest quality.'

'I'm afraid Beddington-Croft doesn't come into that category, Mrs Leverton.'

'No, she doesn't, and her father is aware of it, but we can but try with the girl, for his sake. If word gets back to the other parents that we've taken no action in this matter our reputation will be severely damaged. There's also the fact that Challinor is the niece of Cedric Elliker and in his care, and I'm not too happy about the school being associated with him. Next thing we know is we'll have half of London's underworld sending their kids here.'

'That does add weight to the theory that the girl is a thief,' said Miss Wilde. 'Dishonesty running in the family and all that.'

'Trouble is we don't believe that for a minute, do we?' said Mrs Leverton.

'No.'

'Oh, bloody hell! Best get this over and done with. Bring Challinor back in.'

Billie came back expecting the worst and she wasn't

disappointed. Mrs Leverton's gaze was directed downwards as she pronounced her verdict.

'We've considered the matter, Challinor, and you leave me no alternative other than to expel you from this school.'

Billie waited until Mrs Leverton looked up before saying defiantly, 'I didn't do it. It was Ruth Allison and Delma Beddington-Croft.'

'Please leave the school, Challinor.'

Chapter 29

Without saying a word Billie turned round and walked out of Mrs Leverton's office in tears. It wasn't until she was outside the school gates that she realised she'd have to walk the two miles or so to her home and she wasn't entirely sure of the way. She normally went home by school bus and had no idea which other bus to catch. In any case the injustice of the situation left her feeling aggrieved to the extent that all she wanted to do was leave this horrible place and go back to her Auntie Liz in Leeds. But Leeds was hundreds of miles away and she only had . . . Billie felt in her pocket to see what money she had. Her uncle had given her two shillings pocket money of which she had a shilling left. Better go back to Uncle Cedric's and run back to Leeds another day. Maybe tomorrow. She could nick some money off them, enough to get her back to Leeds, but right now she had a more immediate problem. She didn't know her own address!

Uncle Cedric's house had been of so little interest to her that she hadn't even bothered to ask. When she got on the school bus it had been right outside the front door. Blimey, Billie, you don't know where you live! Should she go back to the school and ask Mrs Leverton? No. The woman would only tell her how stupid she was as well as being a thief. She tried to remember the direction the school bus had taken, but it was complicated. She thought it turned left just after setting off and then it turned right ... or did it? She'd been taking little notice. She'd only travelled home on it three times. Each time she'd got off opposite St Paul's Church, along with some other girls. She knew her way back from there.

Last night the bus had been half empty, just taking the hockey players home, and she'd sat on her own downstairs, away from the rest of them who all thought she was a thief. Mags lived near the school and walked home. Last night Billie had taken no further notice of anything at all.

A bus appeared in the distance. Billie ran to a stop and stuck out her arm. Its destination board said City, which was good enough for her.

She boarded and went upstairs. In Leeds she'd always travelled upstairs on the tram or bus when she could. Lots to see from an upstairs window. Maybe she'd recognise something. A conductor followed her up, calling out, 'Fares, please.'

She held out her shilling and asked, 'Do you go past St Paul's Church?'

'Don't know the churches,' he said, 'we go to the City, like it says on the front of the bus.'

'Oh, half fare to the City then, please.'

'To the terminus?'

'Er, yes.'

'That'll be sixpence.'

As he clicked a ticket out of his machine a thought occurred to Billie. 'Do you go anywhere near the station?'

'You mean King's Cross?'

The name rang a bell with her. It was definitely the station where they'd got off the train. So there should be a train there that would take her back to Leeds.

'Er, yes,' she said, then added, to allay any suspicion, 'I'm meeting my daddy there.'

'Yes, we go right by King's Cross. If you'd told me before it'd have saved you tuppence.'

'Could you let me know when we get there, please?'

'Of course. I always call out the King's Cross stop.'

Billie had been staring at a station notice board giving train times for five minutes before she realised she was looking at the Arrivals Board. She moved to the Departures Board and looked up at the station clock. It was ten past ten and there was a train leaving platform two at ten forty-five for various destinations culminating in Leeds. All she had to do was get on it.

She remembered Roy Morley from her Leeds school had once boasted that he'd bought a platform ticket for a penny at Leeds City Station and got on a train that took him to Wakefield where he'd got off and taken another train back to Leeds, all for a penny ticket. Billie saw no reason why this wouldn't work just as well going all the way to Leeds. Once she was there she'd tell them she'd lost her platform ticket. What would they do to an eight-year-old girl who'd lost her platform ticket? Not much. She still had sixpence for her tram fare to Auntie Liz's house; in fact that was only tuppence so she could buy herself a cup of tea and a bun on the train. Roy Morley said they sold all sorts of food on a train. All of a sudden her future looked a lot brighter.

She was still wearing her posh school uniform and had her satchel slung over her shoulder so no one would mistake her for an urchin who was going to cause trouble. There was an office with several windows above displaying the word *Tickets*. She went over and asked if she could buy a platform ticket.

'You get them from the machine, miss,' said the man inside, pointing to a platform ticket machine not far away. 'You'll need a penny.'

'I've only got a sixpence.'

'Here, I'll change it for you.'

'Thank you.'

It seemed that everyone was being very helpful. Billie went to the machine and put in a penny. Out came her ticket to Leeds. She located platform two then found a wooden seat to sit on while she waited. After a while an echoing announcement came over the loudspeakers.

'The train now standing on platform two is the ten forty-five to Peterborough, Grantham, Newark, Doncaster and Leeds.'

With her ticket clasped in her hand Billie strolled over to the platform gate and gave the ticket to a man who clipped it and waved this respectable schoolgirl through. No way would he have done that for any of the local young ruffians who couldn't be trusted not to board a train and go joyriding.

As she passed the locomotive it let out a noisy burst of steam that made Billie jump. A nearby man and woman smiled and asked if she was all right.

'Yes, thank you,' she said politely and followed them up the platform as though she belonged to them, catching them up as they boarded a first-class carriage. Once inside

Billie turned the other way and headed down a corridor to find an empty compartment. Roy Morley had said that first class was best because there were always loads of empty compartments. This proved to be the case.

She settled in her seat and waited for the train to move. Once it was she'd feel safe in the knowledge that she was leaving London and all its miseries, not the least of which was that a London bomb had killed her mum and badly injured her dad. After a while there was a whistle, a slamming of doors, a loud hiss of steam and the train moved off, clanking gently over the rails. *Clankety clank . . .clankety clank . . . clankey clank*, faster and faster as it built up speed.

Billie unhooked the leather strap that let down the window and stuck her head out to see the station marshalling yards receding behind them. A railway worker looked up from his work on a line and waved to her. She waved back and thought how friendly people were. How easy it would be to get back to Leeds with all these people on her side.

The lines gradually reduced to the one they were travelling on and its incoming partner and they entered a dirty urban landscape of high stone walls littered with graffiti which Billie didn't understand. Then came a tunnel, which had her pulling the window back up. Beyond the tunnel were more dirty walls which became industrial buildings, smoky chimneys and factories and now rows of houses. She smiled broadly and in her mind she spoke to her daddy.

Hope you're not too cross, Daddy. I didn't like it in London.

She knew he wouldn't be. She bet he'd have done the

same when he was eight if he'd had the chance. Her brave daddy, who would have won the Victoria Cross if he hadn't nicked a beautiful doll for her. Bluebelle was still in Leeds and Billie was glad she'd left her there. Somehow it hadn't seemed right taking her to live with Uncle Cedric. Had things turned out okay she'd have asked Auntie Liz to send her on, but things hadn't turned out that way at all. *Clankey clank . . . clankety clank.* Her eyes were still glued to the passing landscape when she heard a voice behind her.

'Tickets, please.'

She turned round to face a ticket inspector who had slid open the door to her compartment.

Are you with someone, miss?'

'Er, yes.'

It was a lie but it was all she could think of. What would he say if she told him she was on her own? She added to her lie.

'My parents have gone to get something to eat.'

'They'll be lucky. The restaurant's car's not open yet.'

'Oh,' said Billie. 'They didn't know that.'

'I'll pop back.'

He slid the door closed as she contemplated her next move. Then she remembered something else Roy Morley had mentioned.

'If yer see a ticket inspector all yer 'ave ter do is hide in t'lavvy. There's loads o' lavvies on trains. If it says "vacant" on t'door it means no one's using it and you can go in. Yer slide t'lock back an' that makes it say "engaged" outside, which means someone's in. Then yer can stay in as long as yer want.'

Billie slid open the door and looked to her left where the inspector had gone. She went to the right and moved through two compartments until she came to third class, which was much more crowded. The toilets both declared themselves to be vacant so Billie went inside one of them, locked the door and settled herself down on the seat. After a while she became bored so she opened her satchel and took out her General Studies book which she found interesting. She soon became engrossed and took little notice of the door being occasionally rattled by people who obviously hadn't read the engaged sign. Time went by, a lot of time, she wasn't sure how much, but the train had already stopped once and she was becoming hungry. The door rattled again. A voice said, 'Whoever's in there's been in a long time. I hope they're all right.'

Another voice suggested mentioning it to an inspector. Billie became frightened, not knowing what to do for the best. Maybe it would be a good idea to swap toilets. Just walk down the train and find another one. Maybe go to the restaurant car to get something to eat. She had fivepence. Tuppence for the fare from the station and threepence to spend on a cup of tea and a sandwich. Roy Morley had said you could get a cup of tea and a sandwich for threepence. She put the book back in her satchel, opened the door and looked up into the face of the ticket inspector she'd met earlier. He shook his head in disappointment.

'I was hoping it wouldn't be you who'd locked herself in there but I was wrong, wasn't I?'

Billie said nothing. She'd been caught and that was that. At least she'd been caught for doing something she'd actually done, which made a change.

'You got on in London, didn't you, young lady?'

Billie said nothing because sometimes nothing is the best thing to say.

'You're not with your parents, are you?'

Same answer.

'Well, I'm afraid I'm going to put you off the train at Grantham and give you to the Transport Police to deal with.'

This broke her silence. Sometimes saying nothing is just not possible 'Police? I haven't committed a crime or anything.'

'I'm afraid you have.'

'What?'

'I'll let the police explain that to you.'

Billie was worried to the point of tears. 'Are they going to lock me up?'

'I imagine they'll take you back to where you belong.'

'I belong in Leeds.'

'Then that's where they'll take you.'

'My name's Arthur and I gather you're Billie.'

'I am, yes.'

'What's Billie short for?'

She'd been asked this before, many times. 'It isn't short for anything. It's my name.'

'I thought it might be short for Wilhelmina or something.'

Arthur wore the same uniform as an ordinary policeman except that his helmet bore the insignia *British Transport Police*. He took it off and sat down opposite Billie, who was now in an office in Grantham Station.

'Where do you live, Billie?'

'Number twenty-seven Gascoigne Street, Leeds.'

'Why were you on a train coming from London and what's the school uniform you're wearing?'

'I don't live in London, I was only there to visit my uncle.'

'And your uncle sent you back to Leeds without buying you a ticket, is that it?'

No answer.

'Pass me your schoolbag, Billie.'

She dutifully handed it over. He took out several books which still belonged to the school – something Mrs Leverton had overlooked when she'd expelled her. The name of the school was stamped inside the covers.

'St Ethelburga's in Chigwell,' read Arthur. 'That's in London, not Leeds. And your name's Billie Challinor. Where do you really live, Billie?'

'My mum and daddy are both dead from the war. I'm s'pposed to live with my Auntie Liz in Leeds but I was sent to London to live with Uncle Cedric and I don't like living there. Everyone's horrible to me.'

'Can I have your uncle's address in London?'

'I don't know what it is.'

It was the truth but Arthur didn't believe her. He sighed. She was a bright, personable child despite her stubbornness. 'All right, have it your way. You stay here, I need to make some phone calls. Do you need to go to the toilet because I'm locking you in, or is that a daft question considering you've been sitting in one for the last two hours?'

'I'm okay, thank you. Please don't send me back to London. I want to go back to Auntie Liz.'

195

'I'll do what I have to do, Billie.'

This told her she was definitely going back to London, which depressed her. She'd been so near to getting back to Leeds. If only she'd swapped toilets a few times no one would have been suspicious. Still, there'd be a next time. If at first you don't succeed, try, try again. She'd learned that at school. A Scottish king used to say it all the time to a spider.

Arthur came back half an hour later and sat down. 'I've been speaking to Mrs Leverton at your school. Your Aunt Lavinia is very worried about you.'

'I don't think she is,' Billie said. 'And Mrs Leverton expelled me for pinching a watch when it was Ruth Allison who did it. I never touched her rotten watch.'

'Your aunt was so worried she rang the police.'

'She doesn't love me like my Auntie Liz loves me.'

'Billie, I've got good reason to believe that Chigwell is the place you're supposed to be living and that's where you're going as soon as I can arrange transport.'

'What sort of transport?'

'You'll be going back on the next London-bound train and I'll be going with you. Your Aunt Lavinia will be in King's Cross Station to pick you up.' He looked at her tearful face and felt sorry for her. 'Billie, do your Uncle Cedric and Aunt Lavinia hurt you in any way?'

'You mean, do they hit me?'

Billie thought about this for a few seconds. If she lied and accused them of hitting her then she might not have to go back to them. But it was too big a lie for her to tell. They might not love her, but they weren't cruel to her.

'No,' she said. 'They don't hit me.'

'And I understand they live in a very nice house.'

'So does Auntie Liz.'

It wasn't what Lavinia had told Arthur, but he let it go. He looked at his watch. It was almost half past one. 'The London train's due in about fifteen minutes. I'm having to work overtime today because of you, young lady. I won't be back until after seven tonight and I've been on duty since six this morning.'

'Sorry.'

Chapter 30

Lavinia had taken the call from Mrs Leverton.

'Expelled? Why has she been expelled?'

'I'm afraid she was caught stealing a valuable gold watch from one of our teachers.'

'Caught? Who caught her?'

'The watch was found in Billie's satchel.'

'And has she admitted taking it?'

'No, she compounded her offence by blaming it on one of the other girls.'

'How long ago did this happen?'

'At nine this morning. The theft was carried out at games practice yesterday evening.'

'It's half past twelve. Where is she now?'

'On her way home, I imagine.'

'That's what you imagine, is it? Did she leave the school at nine?'

'Yes. Well, possibly quarter past.'

'That's three and a quarter hours ago and she's not home yet!'

'I tried to ring you earlier but the line was engaged.'

'Mrs Leverton, Billie's home is two miles from the school, she's eight years old and she doesn't know the area.

Did you take that into consideration when you were expelling her?'

'I'm sure she'll be all right.'

'I'm ringing the police. If anything has happened to the girl I will hold you personally responsible.'

Chapter 31

By the time Cedric arrived home from work Billie was back. She'd already explained to Lavinia why she'd run away.

'I hate that rotten school. They say you've done stuff you haven't and there's bullies there.'

'Why did you run away to Leeds instead of coming back here?'

'I didn't know the way so I got on a bus and it took me to the train station, so I thought I might as well go back to Leeds, 'cos you'd be cross about me being expelled.'

'If what you say is true I'm cross with the school, not with you.'

'It *is* true.'

When Billie repeated the story to Cedric his brow furrowed as she spoke and he shook his head in anger.

'This Beddington-Croft girl, do you know if her father's an investment banker?'

'I dunno what one of them is. I think he's very rich 'cos Mags's dad works for him.'

'Mags ... who's Mags?'

'Mags Ashmore.'

'Ashmore, yes, Beddington has an assistant called Ashmore. Got to be the same man. How many Beddington-bloody-Crofts can there be?'

'I dunno.'

'No matter, I'll deal with it.'

Billie didn't know what he meant by *dealing with it* but she didn't query it. She didn't understand her uncle at all, nor her aunt. She had a sudden urge to write to her Auntie Liz.

'Is it okay if I write to Auntie Liz to tell her how I'm going on?'

'Of course you must,' said Lavinia. She got to her feet. 'I'll get you some writing paper and an envelope.'

'When you've written it, give to me. I'll stick it in the post at work,' said Cedric. 'Save a half-mile walk to the letter box.'

'And the cost of a stamp,' added Lavinia.

Cedric smiled. 'I'm sure my firm can afford a tuppenny stamp.'

'Look,' said Lavinia, 'I wouldn't mention what happened today. No point worrying Auntie Liz unduly. As far as the school's concerned, it may be that your uncle can clear that little matter up without you having to leave.'

'Okay,' said Billie.

Dear Auntie Liz,
I am writing to tell you that I am doing all right with Uncle Cedric and Aunt Lavinnia so you have not to worry. I started school this week and the girls are nice but the lessons are quite hard but I think I will soon catch up. The uniform is very posh.

We live in a very big house with lovely furniture
but I still prefer living with you because I don't
think my Uncle Cedric and Aunt Lavinnia love
me as much as you do. I hope they will get to love
me one day.
Your sincerely,
Your loving niece,
Billie

'Aunt Lavinia, what's our address?' she called.

'What? Have you written the letter without putting the
address at the top?'

'Yes, I forgot. I put the date on, though.'

'Then I don't think it'll matter. Your Auntie Liz knows
our address. Have you sealed it properly?'

'Yes.'

'Good, give it to your Uncle Cedric. It'll be posted
tomorrow.'

'Thank you.'

Billie was asleep in bed when Lavinia steamed open the
envelope and read the letter. She took it over to Cedric for
his opinion. He read it and shrugged.

'She says she's doing all right with us – all right's good
enough for me. The important thing is that she didn't put
our address on it.'

'Nor the name of her school,' said Lavinia.

'No mention of us living in Chigwell either.'

'She's eight years old. You don't bother with details like
that when you're eight.'

'Okay,' he said, 'I'll send it off to Auntie Liz. She'll send a reply to the Hackney address I gave her, and when Billie doesn't receive it she'll wonder why and maybe write again, with the same result. Eventually she'll get fed up and forget her Auntie Liz.'

'We hope,' said Lavinia. 'What about school? Will she be allowed back?'

'Not a problem. I've made a few calls and sorted out Beddington-bloody-Croft, but it may be that we'll end up having to take her out of school and get a home tutor until this thing's settled. We nearly lost her today. We can't afford to take that risk again.'

'Agreed.'

The following morning as Billie arrived at the school gates Delma and her cronies were waiting for her. Billie tensed, ready for a confrontation. Her uncle had told her to go straight to Mrs Leverton's office and that everything would sort itself out. Billie had no idea how this was supposed to happen. But Delma was trying to smile at her.

'I'm really sorry about yesterday,' she said.

'Yeah, so was I.'

'I didn't know you were an Elliker.'

'I'm not an Elliker, I'm a Challinor.'

'No, but your uncle's an Elliker and you live with him.'

'That's right.'

'So, are we okay?'

'I don't know what you're talking about.'

'Well, we're all going to see Mrs Leverton to tell her what we did and we're hoping she won't expel us.'

'We're going to tell her it was just a silly prank,' added Ruth.

'Okay,' said Billie. 'I'm going there as well.'

She let them walk on in front. Mags had just arrived and ran to catch up.

'Billie, I thought you'd been expelled!'

'So did I, but Delma and the others are going to tell Mrs Leverton the truth.'

'Wow! Why are they doing that?'

'Dunno. I think my Uncle Cedric had something to do with it.'

'Is that what Delma was talking to you about?'

'She was going on about not knowing I was an Elliker, which I'm not.'

'So why did she say it?'

'Well, I suppose it's because my Uncle Cedric's called Cedric Ellliker.'

'What? Is he a real Elliker?'

'What's a real Elliker?'

'Everybody knows the Ellikers.'

'I only know two. Well, three, if you include my mum who used to be one. What's so special about Ellikers?'

'I don't really know but I've heard my dad talk about them as though they're gangsters or something and everyone's frightened of them. Hey, if your uncle's a real Elliker and he's spoken to Delma's dad about her getting you into trouble, they'll be scared stiff.'

'What? Frightened of Uncle Cedric and Aunt Lavinia. Don't make me laugh. Uncle Cedric's a lawyer not a gangster.'

A man was in Mrs Leverton's office when Billie arrived, as were Delma, Ruth and the other two girls. The man was small and corpulent and looked as if he might be rich. He turned to look at Billie and gave her an apologetic smile.

'This is Mr Beddington-Croft,' said Mrs Leverton. 'He confirms your version of yesterday's events which leads me to apologise for misjudging you.'

'Does this mean I'm not expelled, Mrs Leverton?'

'Yes, it does. Take a seat, Challinor. I want you to witness justice being done.'

She turned her attention to Mr Beddington-Croft. 'As you know I expelled Challinor yesterday for the offence that your daughter and these other girls committed. Only their offence was graver insofar as they did it to get Challinor into trouble.'

'Yes, I understand that.'

'So, Mr Beddington-Croft, I'm honour-bound to expel your daughter and her three friends.'

'Of course you are. Unless I can plead mitigating circumstances.'

Mrs Leverton looked at him sternly. 'What circumstances are these?'

'Well, Delma has been an innocent victim of certain domestic problems my wife and I have been having. Problems which I explained to you earlier. She's a troubled child and being expelled from here will only add to her problems.'

Billie focused her attention on this troubled child and struggled to feel sorry for her. Delma was a bully, plain and simple. Billie didn't believe this man. Mrs Leverton looked at Delma, then back at her father who added, 'I'm willing to make reparation to the young lady by paying her school fees for this year.'

Billie had no idea about school fees so this didn't impress her. Delma and her cronies should be expelled.

'So, you suggest we keep your daughter and expel the other three girls?'

'I understand this theft was committed by only one of them,' said Beddington-Croft. 'I suggest you expel her. My daughter and the other two girls were foolish and misguided but they're not thieves. *Such a solution would keep me happy with your school.*'

He emphasised the last sentence with his eyes fixed on Mrs Leverton. She lowered hers, having received his message.

'It was Delma's idea!' blurted out Ruth.

'No, it was not,' said Delma.

The other two girls, seeing a way out here, decided to take her side.

'Delma's right,' said one.

'We knew nothing about it,' said the other.

Mrs Leverton had been given a way out that would apply some sort of justice to the situation, keep Mr Beddington-Croft happy and the school's finances intact. She sat back in her chair, nodding to herself. Billie could see who was going and who wasn't.

'Thank you, Mr Beddington-Croft,' said the headmistress. 'I imagine Mr Elliker will be happy to accept your generous offer. Your daughter and the two girls who were party to the theft but didn't actually take the watch will be given one hour's detention every night for two weeks.'

'That should teach them a lesson,' said Delma's father.

Mrs Leverton glared at Ruth. 'Allison, you are expelled forthwith!'

Ruth burst into tears. 'It's not fair. Delma told me to do it. It's all her fault!'

Everyone in the office knew she was speaking the truth and Billie learned then how grown-ups often bend the truth to suit themselves. As she got to her feet to follow Delma's father and the three fortunate girls out of the office a fact occurred to her that seemed to have had a strong bearing on the whole incident. She glanced at Mrs Leverton and said innocently, 'I s'ppose you all know that my uncle is Cedric Elliker.'

Beddington-Croft stopped momentarily, as if waiting to hear an answer from the headmistress, but none came so all five of them filed out of the office, leaving the head-mistress alone with the weeping girl.

Chapter 32

Liz received three letters of significance within the space of three days. The first was from Billie who *seemed* to be doing okay, although the term 'damned with faint praise' wasn't far from Liz's thoughts. The second letter was from Fallon & Fallon, solicitors in Leeds, asking her to call into their office as soon as possible on a matter relating to the estate of the late Charles Herbert Challinor, MM. Although she was aware that Chas was unlikely to have left anything of any significance she went down there the following day purely for Billie's benefit. It did, however, intrigue her that the letter was addressed to her and not to his daughter. She was taken to the office of a Mr Fallon, who shook her hand, asked her to sit down and opened a slim file.

'We're retained to act on behalf of the War Office in certain legal matters and it transpires that Mr Challinor left a will that hasn't been dealt with. It's an unforgivable oversight considering he died in action most heroically, but it may well be that it was overlooked because there was little of any value in his estate apart from some musical instruments. Or it may have been overlooked because no relatives came forward to enquire. I would add that this is an oversight of the War Office, not ours.'

'I think I already have some of his instruments in my house,' Liz told him 'He lost his clarinet in a car fire just before he went away.'

'I imagine that was a blow to him,' said Fallon.

'He didn't mourn it, considering what he thought he'd lost.'

'I have his dog tags, medal ribbons, a campaign medal and various other things – some letters, a cigarette lighter, a watch, penknife, that sort of thing. There is some money due to his daughter Billie, but I'm not sure how much as yet. The War Office have sent a cheque on account for one hundred pounds, which is in our client account at the moment.'

'A hundred quid!' said Liz.

'Three months' wages for most men,' said Fallon.

'Six months for most women,' said Liz, thinking of her own employees. 'I've got Chas's Military Medal, although it belongs to Billie, of course.'

'Ah, yes, Billie. She's the main reason I've asked you here. Mr Challinor attached a codicil to his will which I'll read out to you, if I may.' Mr Fallon took out a pair of reading glasses, put them on and scanned the writing until he came to the relevant part,

... with regard to my beloved daughter Billie. In the event of my death it is my wish that she be placed in the care of Mrs Elizabeth Morris, 27 Gascoigne Street, Leeds 8, and all monies due to me to be administered by Elizabeth Morris on my daughter's behalf.

The solicitor looked up at Liz. 'He made you her legal guardian. Was this something he agreed with you before he left?'

'Erm, actually, no.'

'In that case this depends on whether or not you agree to be her guardian.'

'Well, yes, of course I do.'

'Is Billie currently living with you?'

'Er, no. She was taken away quite recently by her late mother's brother, who told me he's her legal guardian, with him being the elder of her three uncles.'

'And normally he'd be quite correct but her father's will supersedes any claims of bloodline. How recently was this?'

'About two weeks ago.'

'Then he probably hasn't had time to be appointed by a court. We can block this by notifying him of the request in Mr Challinor's will.'

'Okay.'

'I have two copies of this will. Do you wish me to retain one for safekeeping?'

'Yes, please.'

'Whereabouts is Billie living?'

'In London. Her uncle's a solicitor.'

'Well, hopefully you can sort this matter out with him. If you have any problems, please don't hesitate to call me.'

'Thank you.'

'Before you go, as her legal guardian, I need you sign a receipt for the effects I'm handing over to you. Would you like me to send the money on to you?'

'Er, no. Keep it until we know where Billie will be living.'

Liz left the office feeling light-headed. She'd be going down to London to find out how Billie was really doing, and if she wanted to come back and live in Leeds. If so Liz would remove her from Cedric's care with as much speed and compassion as he'd showed her.

The next day she received a letter from PC Arthur Harris of the British Transport Police in Grantham. Arthur had felt guilty about sending Billie back to London and had memorised the address in Leeds she'd given him.

Dear Liz,

I only know you as Auntie Liz so you must excuse the familiarity. I came across your niece, Billie Challinor, on Thursday 14 September of this year. She had got on a train at King's Cross in London bound for Leeds, using only a platform ticket. Needless to say she was caught by a ticket inspector and put off at Grantham from where I returned her to London. She was met at King's Cross Station by her aunt Lavinia. I assume her aunt and uncle in London have already informed you of this incident but just to make sure I thought I should write this letter. Billie seemed to favour living in Leeds with you to living in London, which is why she was heading back to you.

Yours sincerely,

PC Arthur Harris

British Railway Police

Liz was packing her bag within minutes of reading the letter. She left a note in the café leaving Connie in charge for a few days until she got back. Connie was middle-aged and trustworthy, unlike young Alice who was hard-working but with a tendency to help herself to tea, butter and sugar. Liz had threatened to sack her if she didn't pack it in but the girl was pretty much the bread-winner at home so Liz's threats were as empty as Alice's purse.

Chapter 33

It was now over four years since the Blitz had done serious damage to the centre of London. The only damage caused recently was by the V1 rockets. The streets had long since been cleared of the vast acres of rubble, and rebuilding had begun. Liz looked out of the taxi window and was shocked at the number of cleared areas that had once been houses, shops, churches, cinemas and the like, most still awaiting reconstruction, maybe as something completely different from before. Some were already rebuilt, some still under construction. In one place a block of flats was being built. It looked to be at least eight storeys high, the highest building she'd ever seen. She'd witnessed bomb damage in Leeds but nothing on this scale and she marvelled at the resilience of the Londoners who had withstood nightly assaults on their city for years. The taxi driver looked at her reflection in his mirror.

'First time you seen this lot, madam?'

'What makes you think that?'

'I can tell by your accent that you're not from London, and I just wondered . . .'

'I'm from Yorkshire and, yes, it's the first time I've seen this lot.'

'It's nuffink to what it was. Time was when the whole of central London was like one big smokin' demolition site. Me 'ouse went in nineteen forty. Me an' the missis was in a shelter, thank gawd. We went ter live wiv me sister, then *she* got bleedin' bombed! I saw enough meself in the first lot. I had me mates dyin' all around me. Young men dyin' fightin' old men's wars, that's what that was all about. Young men dyin' fightin' old men's bleedin' wars. Hitler done this to us, just like Kaiser bleedin' Bill did in the first lot.'

'He's destroyed millions of decent lives,' said Liz, thinking about Chas once again, 'and for what?'

'You might well ask, madam. Anyway, here we are, Tunstall Road. What number we looking for?'

'Sixty-three.'

There were gaps between the houses that obviously hadn't been created by any builder. It struck Liz then that this wasn't the sort of street she'd expect a wealthy solicitor to be living in. It had a mixture of semi-detached and terraced houses and wasn't much more salubrious than her own neighbourhood in Leeds.

'Here we are, sixty-three. That'll be three and sixpence, madam.'

She gave the driver four shillings including a tip. He gave her a card with the phone number of his office if she needed a cab again. She could even ask if he was free. His name was Sid.

'I wonder if you could just wait here a minute?'

'No problem.'

She stood in front of number sixty-three and was somewhat perturbed that it looked unoccupied. Not just

214

unoccupied but not lived in. All the curtains were drawn despite its still being mid-afternoon on a sunny day. It was a terraced house with a small, unkempt garden and a front door that needed more than a lick of paint. She knocked and listened for signs of life. Nothing. She knocked again, louder this time. Loud enough for the next-door neighbour to pop her head out to see what the noise was about.

'There's nobody in,' she said.

'You mean, they've gone out?'

'Never been anybody livin' there since I moved here three years ago.'

Liz tried the door. It was locked as expected.

'Do you know who owns it?'

'No idea, love. We sometimes see someone call in for a few minutes and I know the postman delivers letters there. Maybe they come to pick up the mail.'

'This person who calls in, is it a man of about forty-five?'

'Could be. I don't take too much notice. Not a nosy person me. Not like some round here I could mention. I know he drives a big posh car. Humber it is – Humber Super Snipe, accordin' ter my boy who knows his cars. It's a sin and a shame to leave a house empty like this. There's a shortage of good houses round here.'

Liz stood there, not knowing what to do. She went back to Sid's cab and sat in the back, deep in thought. What on earth had happened? Had Billie been abducted by this man who claimed to be her uncle? Why would anyone do that? He'd showed her a photo of himself and Billie's mum. That had been genuine enough, and she'd seen his identification – Cedric Elliker. She knew Annie's maiden name was Elliker. So why had he given her a false address?

'Problem?' said Sid.

'Yes. I came to see a girl I'd been looking after up in Leeds until she was taken away by her uncle. This is the address he gave me, but the place has been empty for at least three years.'

'Close to the girl, were you?'

'Very. Her father died in the war and he wanted me to be her guardian – something I wasn't told about until yesterday.'

'Sounds to me like you need to tell the police. Would you like me to take you there?'

'Erm, yes. Yes, I think I should go to the police.'

'If you need any ferrying about you only have to ring our number and ask for me. I'll just charge you for the journeys, not for waiting time or anything else.' Sid started the cab. 'I'll take you to Highbury Vale nick. That's the nearest to here. When you get inside, say you need to speak to an inspector on a very important matter. Don't be fobbed off by no sergeants or constables. Ask for a senior man.'

Liz still wasn't sure what she was going to say as she stood at the bottom of the steps that led up to the narrow door of Highbury Vale police station. Above her to her right was an iron post with a blue lamp on top. It was there to give her confidence in the knowledge that she'd come to the right place. She didn't feel very confident.

She pushed open the door and walked towards a desk at which a uniformed sergeant was writing in a ledger. She stood in front of him, politely waiting until he finished. He couldn't fail to be aware of her presence but he didn't look up. After two minutes she began to feel annoyed at such rudeness – annoyed enough to add some steel to her voice.

'I wish to see an inspector.'

He froze for a second then looked up, slowly.

'Why's that, madam?'

'I want to speak to someone who can deal with a most urgent matter and you don't appear to be that person.'

He put his pen down. 'What matter would that be, madam?'

'The abduction of a child. I insist on seeing an inspector.'

'The inspector's busy, madam.'

'Well, I'll have to wait until he's less busy. We must hope this doesn't affect the safety of the child.'

'If you'd like to give me some details, madam.'

'No, I would not like to give you any details. I wish to speak to a senior officer, not someone who believes that scribbling in his book is more important than dealing with a member of the public who has come in here for help.'

He stared at her, at a loss for what to say, then turned and went through a door behind him. A few minutes later he reappeared and lifted a flap in his desk.

'If you'd like to come through, madam. Detective Inspector Anderson will see you.'

'Thank you.'

Anderson was a middle-aged man with a bushy moustache and a bald head. The sergeant had forewarned him of Liz's belligerent attitude.

'What is it you wish to see me about? Something far too important for my sergeant to deal with, I assume.'

He hadn't invited her to sit down so Liz didn't, simply put her bag down on the chair and remained standing.

'My very presence at his desk seemed too much for him to handle with any measure of alacrity, Inspector.' She spoke in an articulate Northern accent and she wasn't going to be as easy to handle as he'd thought.

'This is about a missing child?'

'I believe she has been abducted.'

He opened a notebook and said, 'You'd better start from the beginning. First your name and address.'

Liz gave him her and Billie's details; how the child had ended up living with Liz and how her Uncle Cedric had come to take her away. Then she showed him the will that gave her the right to be Billie's guardian.

'Why didn't you tell the uncle about this?'

'I didn't know about it until first thing this morning. I came straight down to London to check on Billie. Had she been happy I'd have allowed her to stay, but in the event I found I'd been given a false address. The house was deserted and had been for at least three years. You can imagine my concern.'

'I can indeed. The problem is that when Mr Elliker took the child neither of you knew that he wasn't her rightful guardian. So he hasn't committed any crime in that respect. In fact, in law the girl hasn't been abducted.'

'That may be true, but in law it's my right to become her guardian which I can't do because Mr Elliker, for reasons I know nothing about, has taken her beyond my reach. Plus he's a solicitor, so it may be he somehow knew about her father's will.'

'Unlikely.'

'I need your help to track him down,' Liz persisted stubbornly.

'Well, if he's a solicitor with a practice in London we should be able to trace him easily enough.' The inspector got to his feet. 'If you'll excuse me for a few minutes I'll check through our records. Cedric Elliker, did you say?'

'Yes. I don't know what his practice is called.'

'Well, if he's a partner, his name should be in there somewhere.'

'Thank you.'

She picked up her bag and sat down, confident that her search was over almost before it had begun. The inspector was gone a full fifteen minutes and came back shaking his head.

'Drawn a blank, I'm afraid. There are only two Ellikers practising in the London area, one's an Edward Elliker who's in his sixties and the other's called Vera Elliker. You say he has a practice in Central London?'

'That's what he told me. I also saw his identity card and his passport – Cedric Elliker.'

'Hmm, but do you know for sure he's a solicitor with a practice in London?'

'That's what he told me.'

'He lied about where he lived. For all we know he might have taken the girl up to Scotland or over to Ireland or even overseas. Travel to the United States is easier now for a man with money, and wherever he is he might well be using a false identity.'

'But why would he take Billie?'

'Who knows why anyone takes a child? But it happens all the time.'

'And he was in a photo with her mother.'

'There's a mystery attached to this and no mistake, Mrs Morris. But it may well be that when we find her we'll also find he hasn't committed a crime, other than giving you a false address which, in itself, isn't illegal. The problem we have is that we're undermanned with so many of our people engaged in the war. All I can do is put her on our Missing Persons List along with the name of Cedric Elliker.'

'But she's an eight-year-old girl who might be in danger!'

'It seems she's with her uncle, Mrs Morris. I doubt she's in any danger.'

Liz stared at him and shook her head in disgust. 'Is this because I gave your sergeant a piece of my mind?'

'No, it's because to search for a missing child takes up enormous resources and manpower. Unless we're certain the child's life is in danger we can't afford to deploy such resources.'

Liz got to her feet. 'Okay, I get the picture. I'll find Billie myself without your help. And when I do I'll tell the newspapers I had no assistance from you.' She thought about what she'd said and added, 'In fact, I think I'll go to the papers now. See if they can help.'

'That might scare him deeper into hiding,' warned Anderson.

'You're a very negative man, Inspector.'

But Liz thought he could be right. She left without

saying goodbye. A minute later Anderson picked up the phone and dialled a familiar number.

'Put me through to Cedric Elliker, please.'

Liz got back into Sid's cab with a heavy heart as the real-isation that she might never see Billie again sank in. Another idea struck her.

'Sid, do you know anything about London jazz bands?'

'Not a lot, no. Why, do you like jazz?'

'Kind of – Billie's dad was a musician in a London jazz band. I'm wondering if I could track them down. Then some of the band members might be able to help.'

'How could they do that?'

'I don't know until I ask them, but right now I've got nothing else to go on. The police won't help, and for all I know Billie's so-called uncle might have taken her off toTimbuktu. Do you know anyone who might know about jazz bands?'

Sid smiled as he drove. 'I know a whole street full of people – Denmark Street, better known as Tin Pan Alley.'

'I thought that was in New York.'

'This is the British version.'

'Okay, let's go there.'

Denmark Street was narrow and barely a hundred yards long. It was populated by shops selling all kinds of musi-cal instruments and sheet music, a school of music, two music clubs, a recording studio, a rehearsal room and a café. As Sid dropped her off Liz said, 'I'll need somewhere to stay the night. Can you recommend anywhere?'

'There's a B&B just around the corner. A lot of musi-cians use it, so it can't be all that expensive.'

'Sounds just the place. Thanks, Sid.'

Liz walked up and down the street, passing shops selling pianos, guitars, saxophones, and the one she was looking for – clarinets. In the window she saw a Buffet Crampon very much like the one Chas had lost in the fire. It had a price tag of £195 – the cost of a small car.

She went inside. An elderly man stood behind the counter. Very few young men were to be found working in shops. Very few young men were to be found working anywhere. Britain was now a strange world of women, old men and children.

'How can I help you, madam?'

'I'm ... erm ... I'm not looking to buy I'm looking for information about the Tubby Blake Band.'

'Ah, no longer in existence, I'm afraid. Tubby went to war along with half his band.'

'What about the other half?'

'Well, a few of them formed another band who play in the Crazy Dazy over there.' He pointed to a sign of that name across the street.

'Will they be there right now?'

'Possibly. They like to rehearse on an afternoon.'

'Thank you.'

She turned to go and had a last thought. 'Did you know of a clarinet player called Chas Challinor?'

The man's face broke into a broad smile. 'Know of him? I knew him very well. I sold him the Buffet Crampon you can hear on all Tubby's records. He struck a hard bargain did Chas but I didn't mind dropping the price, not for a player like him.' The smile faded.

'You do know he passed away, don't you?' he said.

'I do, yes.'

'Were you close?'

'Yes.'

'I'm sorry. He was a very popular young man.'

'Yes, he was. Could you tell me the name of the new band?'

'Of course. It's the Duke Wellington Jazz Band.'

'Duke Wellington? Bit of a corny name for a jazz band.'

'I believe it's his real name. Black American, you see. They like to give themselves fancy titles. Wonderful musicians though.'

'What does he play?'

'Piano, and he plays it very well. Do you have Chas's Buffet?'

'No, it was destroyed in a fire before he died.'

'Ah, great pity. It was a rare model.'

'Chas valued it highly.'

She could have added, *But it counted for nothing against the life of Billie, who could have been killed that day.* Chas hadn't shown the slightest hint of distress at its loss, only relief and joy at his daughter being brought back to him. He'd had his priorities right.

Chapter 34

It was late afternoon but Liz could hear music coming from the Crazy Dazy. She opened the door and stepped into a passage. The floor was covered in well-worn linoleum and the walls were wood-panelled and hung with dozens of posters advertising events long gone by. The Tubby Blake Band featured on many of them. She studied a few to see if she might see the name Chas Challinor. Perhaps he'd played here, but there was no evidence of it.

At the end of the passage was a sort of foyer with an unattended counter, behind which were more posters, some advertising the Duke Wellington Band. Not too much trouble had been taken to smarten up the place, which probably hadn't had a face-lift since the turn of the century. It had a lived-in look that probably suited jazz fans.

Liz noticed Duke Wellington was due to play tomorrow night and she wondered if he might be one of the musicians currently practising behind the double doors in front of her. She pushed them open and entered a large, brown-painted room with a few tables and chairs, a bar, plenty of space for standing, and a low stage. The floor was once again lino-covered and the ceiling stained brown from fifty years of nicotine fumes. There were a couple of worn leather Chesterfields up against one wall but the other chairs were all of plain wood as were the tables. Nothing too breakable in here. The smoky air in the evening would be circulated by a large wooden fan suspended from the ceiling, currently turning very slowly.

On the stage a group of men holding musical instruments were gathered around a piano, discussing something and laughing out loud. The piano player, a large black man, began to play a jazz tune Liz recognised but couldn't name. The others joined in.

What started out as a cacophony merged into pleasing but raucous harmony, if jazz can ever be called harmonious. Liz sat down at one of the tables to listen. No one took any notice of her. No one objected to her being there either. For all they knew she might have as much right to be there as they had. When they'd finished playing she walked over to the stage and asked, 'Is one of you gentlemen Duke Wellington?'

The piano player answered her question with one of his own. 'How come you don't know that already?'

'Because I hear he's a brilliant piano player and that didn't sound too great to me.'

The band howled with laughter. 'We was just practisin',' said Duke. 'It ain't s'posed to sound great when you're practisin'. Who told you I was brilliant?'

'Chas Challinor.'

There was a silence that she took to be out of respect for his name.

'Chas is dead,' said Duke.

'I know that.'

'You knew him?'

'I did.'

'You're from up north. Chas and his daughter moved there after the bomb dropped on him, right?'

'Correct. I was his landlady and his friend, and now I'm trying to find his daughter Billie who was taken from me by a man who says he's her uncle.'

It was a simple sentence but it contained enough information to have them mulling it over for a while.

'I was a good friend of Chas's,' said Duke finally.

She stared at him, remembering that Chas had told her many stories about the band and its black piano player.

'I know, but I'm guessing you're not really a duke?'

'Part of me's a duke. My full name is Marmaduke Wellington Junior. We're jazz musicians, which means we're not who we say we are, exceptin' me of course.'

'My jazz name's Blind Oscar but I got eyes like an eagle,' said the trumpet player.

'Ozzie, you talkin' to your own reflection in my trombone. The lady's over here.'

More laughter from these musicians who didn't take much too seriously. Liz could see how Chas would have felt at home among them.

'Perhaps you and I should retire to the bar to discuss your problem,' suggested Duke.

Liz looked around. 'The bar doesn't look open to me.'

'No, but it'll be open to me in a minute. Carry on, gentlemen, I have business with the lovely lady.'

The band struck up with a tune Liz might have recognised as 'Piña Colada' had she known anything about jazz, but to her it sounded like a man playing one tune on his

226

trombone and everyone else playing something else more suited to their own instrument. But somehow it all sounded okay and it did remind her of Chas. Duke went behind the bar and threw a light switch which operated several bulbs.

'What's your pleasure, lady?'

'I'll just have an orange juice if you have one.'

'Juice of the orange fruit coming up, lady.'

'My name's Liz, and did you get that off Chas?'

'Get what off Chas?'

'Juice of the orange fruit. He used to say that.'

'No, if anything Chas would have got it from me, and I got it from my old grandma in Jamaica where they grew in her yard.'

Liz smiled. She already liked this man who had known Chas and had the feeling that she'd like everyone who had known him.

'Did you see him after the bomb?' she asked.

Duke poured her an orange juice and himself a large whisky. 'Yep, we all saw Chas, but we didn't see too much of him with his face being all bandaged up. We went to visit him reg'lar. The next thing we knew he had up and left town and no one knew for where, except word was that his girl had been evacuated north an' maybe Chas had gone to join her. Next thing we hear is that he's been killed in France. Died a hero so I read in the paper.'

'He did. He was recommended for a VC but it was downgraded to an MM due to a misdemeanour that had been reported to the police.'

Duke laughed out loud. 'Well, that sounds like our

227

Chas! He was a great man for the misdemeanours. Never knew a man get up to so many pranks as Chas Challinor!'

'I think he might have calmed down by the time he got to me. Losing your wife and your face does that to you.'

Duke's smile vanished. 'Hey, lady, I didn't mean no offence to Chas. You say he lost his face? I never saw him without his bandages on.'

'Well, let's say he lost his good looks. Not that I ever saw them, but I've seen photos of him before he was injured.'

'Goddamn! He certainly was one good-lookin' dude. He used to draw in the gals like flies to a jam pot, even gals who weren't interested in the way he played. Not that we minded. Losin' his wife knocked the hell out of him. He sure did love that little lady.'

'Yeah, I know,' said Liz. She then asked, 'How come you're not in the army?'

'Because I was in the Royal Marines. Signed on back in nineteen forty-one. Marine Wellington, M.' He saluted smartly. 'Invalided out in 'forty-two with a leg missin'. Blown up by a torpedo. I was one of the lucky ones.'

'I didn't notice you limping.'

'Blown off below the knee, so I've got two working kneecaps, which make walkin' a mite easier. It don't stop me playin' the piano. Could Chas still play when he came to you?'

'Oh, yes, he could play but he thought he'd lost something. I think he called it his edge. He told me that Tubby wouldn't have him back. In fact, Chas said he wouldn't go back because he'd only be an embarrassment to Tubby.'

She saw Duke's eyes misting over. He was shaking his head. 'Man, if that ain't the saddest thing. Y'know, Chas without his edge'd beat the hell out of most players who only *think* they got the edge. Tubby would've had him back, no danger. I sure would've had him back.'

Liz felt her own eyes filling up then. She pushed her glass of orange juice back over the bar to him. 'I think I'll swap that for a whisky.'

He poured her a glass and leaned against the bar, looking at her. Duke was a good-looking man, she had to admit, probably around Chas's age. She noticed his hands, which were beautifully manicured. The nicest hands she'd ever seen on a man.

'So, why d'you wanna see me?' he asked.

'Well, it's not so much you in particular . . . just someone who knew Chas and maybe his wife's family.'

Duke's eyes hardened at this. 'You mean the Ellikers?'

'That's right.'

'Do you mind if I ask why you wanna know about the Ellikers?'

'Well, Chas's daughter Billie lived with me after he died, then a couple of weeks ago an uncle appeared out of the blue and took her away, saying he was her rightful guardian. I believed I had no legal rights over her, and he was a lawyer so I had to let her go. No sooner had she gone than I found out that Chas wanted me to be her guardian so I came down here to see how she was going on . . . and found the home address her uncle gave me is just an empty house. No sign of Billie or her uncle and aunt.'

Duke swished his whisky around in the glass, then

229

drank it in one go. Liz continued: 'I also know she tried to run away and get back to Leeds, but the police caught her and took her back to Cedric.'

'Cedric Elliker,' said Duke thoughtfully.

'Yes, have you met him?'

'No, I ain't never had that displeasure, but I heard Chas speak of him. Not in very glowin' terms, I might add. He sure as hell wouldn't like his Billie livin' with no Cedric Elliker.'

'Why ever not? He is her uncle.'

'Because the Ellikers have a reputation in this city of bein' big-time bad people. Criminals and fraudsters, thieves, blackmailers, and goddamned murderers.'

'So, why aren't they locked up?'

'Mainly because of Cedric. He's a top-notch genius lawyer who'd have got Crippen off scot-free. Plus they got judges an' police in their pockets. No one in London dares go up against 'em.'

'I wonder why Chas never warned me about them.'

'He never did speak about them much. Him and Annie had a pact not to speak about them at all, so if you never knew about them he most probably wouldn't have mentioned them out of respect for his Annie.'

'It would have helped if I'd been forewarned. When Cedric came to my house to take Billie away I thought it was strictly legitimate. No way would he have got his filthy hands on her otherwise.'

'Yeah, well, maybe if Chas had been able to see into the future he might have told you about them.'

'True, he wasn't to know,' conceded Liz. 'I went to the police today and spoke to an inspector. He told me there was no solicitor of the name of Cedric Elliker practising in London.'

'Could be he's in Elliker's pay,' said Duke. 'Old man Challinor hated the Ellikers, who had done him great harm at some time or other. Didn't stop the old man gettin' back on his feet but he never did forgive that family. Chas marrying an Elliker woman was like bein' stabbed in the back by his own flesh an' blood to old Challinor.'

'So, Chas's wife Annie, what was she like?'

'Aw, lady. Her an' her goddamned family was chalk an' cheese. She weren't nuthin' like them. She was sweet an' kind and she hated her own folks just as much as old man Challinor did, only he couldn't accept her, no way. He sure was a stubborn old guy.'

'Is he still alive?'

'No, he ain't. He died a few weeks ago. Rich as Croesus and with no one to leave his fortune to.'

Liz stared at him. Silence hung between them for a while, then she said quietly, 'No one?'

Duke returned her gaze. 'Goddamnit, lady! I know what you're thinkin'.'

'I'm thinking the obvious. Chas was a good man, his father must have known that. Do we know for certain that he cut Chas out of his will?'

'Chas was pretty certain he would do. In any case, he'd told the old man he could stick his money where the sun don't shine. Chas Challinor was his own man.'

'Yes, he was, but he left a daughter who was the old man's only grandchild. Did you ever know a granddad who held a grudge against his own granddaughter?'

'Nope, can't say I ever heard of such a person.'

'Did the old man ever meet Billie?'

'Yes, I believe he did. Chas felt duty bound to take the girl to see his old man. Just once, as far as I recall.'

'Really? Billy never mentioned it.'

'Well, I would imagine she was too young to remember. Chas only took her once because the visit didn't go down too well. Once would be enough for Billie to charm the old man's socks off,' said Liz.

'I sure can't wait to meet this little lady.'

Liz smiled. 'She'll have you eating out of her hand. I don't suppose you know where Cedric lives, do you?'

Duke poured himself another whisky and offered the bottle to Liz. She put her hand over her glass, which she'd scarcely touched.

'No,' he said, 'the domicile of Cedric was always a mystery to Chas. Could be the house ain't even in his name so there ain't no record of him livin' nowhere. And there's maybe no record of his legal practice anywhere in London. Chas figured he ran his legal business under another name. Why, what are you thinkin'?'

'I'm thinking of going to his house and bringing Billie back with me. I have a legal document that gives me that right and I know she wants to return to Leeds.'

'I don't think no legal document is gonna be enough to persuade Cedric. I hear he's one deadly dude. Seems to me that young Billy is a property worth many millions and Cedric is her guardian. He ain't goin' to let her go to some lady who just knocks on his door, even if you can find that door.'

'Many millions?' said Liz.

'Yep. I do believe the war was good to old man Challinor. He had factories that manufacture all sorts of machinery and he had many lucrative gover'ment contracts.'

'Well, that doesn't sound right to me. His son getting killed in the same war that made him a fortune. Mr Challinor doesn't seem much better than the Ellikers to me.'

'Except he made his money legal and maybe had a conscience that led him to leave his fortune to his granddaughter, who never did him no harm.'

'Well, we don't know that for certain, but it would explain why Cedric Elliker wants Billie in his care.'

'Maybe he's already got his hands on the money,' said Duke. 'All he needs is to be given power of attorney and he can do what he likes with it.'

'Power of attorney?'

'Yes. I studied law for a whole year at one time. Didn't pass no exam due to my lifestyle, which weren't conducive to study, so I was obliged to give up.'

'Chas's solicitor doubts if Cedric's been able to obtain legal guardianship as yet,' said Liz. 'He's only had Billie for two weeks.'

'Then I doubt if he's got power of attorney yet. I think the first thing you need to do is to take a look at the old man's will,' said Duke.

'No, first I need to take a look at Billie to see if she's okay.'

The band played away on the stage, unaware of the drama that was playing out at the bar. Duke glanced across at them, then back at Liz.

'Look, Liz. All I know best is how to play piano. I ain't no Dick Barton Special Agent, nor is any of the band, but for Chas's sake I'll give you whatever help I can.' He thought for a while and added, 'If I was to give you any advice right now it'd be not to say anythin' to the Ellikers about Billie maybe inheritin' old man Challinor's fortune or about you bein' her official guardian. All you is to them at the moment is a harmless pain-in-the-ass. Better make sure it stays that way.'

Liz remembered arranging to telephone the Leeds solicitor and give him Cedric's address, but events had overtaken her fortunately. Cedric was still in the dark about Chas's will and that's how it should remain until she got Billie away from him. But for now she had another priority.

'You know, I've had a full day today. Right now I think I need to find myself somewhere to stay.'

Duke shrugged. 'I reckon you can stay right here. There's a spare room on the top floor for overnighters.'

'Will that be okay with the owner?'

'Well, me and the bank are the owners, and it's certainly okay with me.'

'Your club, really? Am I allowed to use your telephone? I'll pay for the room and all my calls.'

'No payment required. Feel free to use whatever you like. Anything you need, you only have to ask.'

'What I need is someone who knows where Cedric Elliker lives.'

'Then what would you do?'

'Tell the police and insist that Billie be handed over to me.'

'Somehow I don't think it'd be that simple. I think you might have to beat him at his own game.'

'You mean snatch her?'

'It's not the term I would use, but it'll do.'

A sudden idea hit Liz. She picked up the phone and dialled the operator. 'Hello, I wonder if it's possible to put me through to Grantham Railway Station in Lincolnshire?'

A minute later she heard, 'Hello, Grantham Station. How can I help you?'

'I wonder if I could speak to PC Harris of the British Transport Police. Is he on duty right now?'

'One moment please ... Putting you through.'

'Hello, this is PC Harris, who am I speaking to?'

'Liz Morris from Leeds. You wrote to me about Billie.'

'Ah, Auntie Liz. You come well recommended by your niece.'

'Actually she's not my niece, just the daughter of a friend. She lived with me after my friend died.'

'And now she lives with Uncle Cedric and Aunt Lavinia who don't love her like you love her.'

Oh, dear. She told you that, did she?'

'Yes, she did.'

'Look, I'm in London. The address her uncle gave me was wrong but I'm on his trail.. Trouble is, I think they're trying to make it difficult for me to talk to Billie. Did she tell you what her London address was?'

'She said she didn't know. I wasn't sure I believed her. I just took her to King's Cross and handed her over to her aunt, who'd already contacted the police in London.'

'So they should know Billie's home address?'

'Possibly. When I rang London Transport Police in King's Cross they already knew she was missing. Standard procedure for a missing person, especially a child – alert all train stations. I assume they rang the aunt when Billie was returned to London.'

'So, if no one else, King's Cross police should have her aunt and uncle's phone number?'

'I assume so.'

'Thank you, PC Harris.'

Liz put the phone down and looked at Duke. 'The police at King's Cross will have Cedric's phone number. They should be able to track his address from that.'

Duke looked at her. 'Didn't the police at Highbury Vale give you the run around? If Cedric knows the coppers at King's Cross have his phone number I'm guessing he already took measures to protect his privacy.'

'What? Surely he hasn't got that much clout?'

'From what I hear he's a man who knows exactly how to cover his back. Look, leave it 'til tomorrow. I'll come over to King's Cross with you and see what can be done then.'

'Thanks, Duke,' said Liz, stifling a yawn. 'Look, if you meant what you said about that spare room ...'

'I'll take you up now,' he offered. 'Then it's back to band practice for me, I'm afraid. We open tomorrow.'

Chapter 35

Liz's room had two decent-sized beds and was next door to a bathroom which Duke said she could consider her own as he had a separate toilet and washing facilities.

The following morning she was up and about at eight o'clock. She went downstairs and found the kitchen, which was poorly stocked with food. It had a pantry at the top of the cellar steps which would have kept supplies reasonably cool had there been much there. She found four eggs, some thick-sliced bacon on a plate, a loaf, half a pint of milk, a jar of coffee, half a packet of tea and a box of cwornflakes. She decided on the cornflakes as the safest option.

By half-eight there was still no sign of Duke so Liz went outside to take a look at London. She walked to the end of the street affectionately known as Tin Pan Alley, into Charing Cross Road, and marvelled at the stoicism of the Londoners who seemed to be going about their business as if the devastation still being wreaked upon them by the German rockets was merely an inconvenience. Pure chance had so far spared this particular area from the new rockets but there was plenty of bomb damage visible, most of it dating back to the early part of the war and cleared in readiness for rebuilding when the men came back. Traffic was at its rush-hour heaviest: cars, buses, horse-drawn vehicles, many bicycles, two policemen on huge horses, and a bin wagon with two boys standing on the rear platform, hitching an illegal ride. Then she looked up into the sky at the barrage balloons, tethered there like air-borne whales, and knew the war wasn't over yet. Not the war against Germany or her personal war against the Ellikers; both were battles which had yet to be won. She turned and walked back to the club hoping that Duke might be up. She smiled. Musicians, it seemed, kept different hours from normal human beings.

Duke had risen early for him. He was in the kitchen studying the contents of the pantry when Liz got back.

'Want some bacon and eggs?' he said.

'You've barely got enough for yourself. You need to go shopping.'

'Never was much good at shopping. There's a café down the street does a good breakfast. Care to join me?'

'Yes, thanks. I've had some of your cornflakes, but I'm still peckish.'

The enquiry office at King's Cross Station directed them to Camden where the Transport Police were based. They'd gone there in Sid's taxi. He was waiting for them outside the station.

'We need to go to Camden police station,' Liz told him.

'That's five minutes from here.'

'Could you drop us off and wait for us again?'

'No problem,' said Sid, who seemed almost as keen to find Billie as Liz was.

When they entered the police station Liz had a feeling of déjà vu. A sergeant was standing behind the desk poring over a ledger. She got the distinct impression that he'd been studying the ledger for just two seconds, since he'd heard the door begin to open. Maybe that was part of his training – always look as if you've something more important to do than attend to casual enquiries. There was a brass bell on the desk just a foot away from the policeman. She and Duke had been standing there for ten seconds when Liz smacked her palm down on it. The policeman looked up, very slowly.

'Yes, madam?' he said, sourly.

'I need information about a missing child. Her father was killed in the war and he requested that I be her guardian, only she's been taken aware by a man purporting to be her uncle having left me a false address.'

Liz placed a copy of Chas's will on his desk and pointed to the relevant clause. The sergeant scratched his chin as he took in what she'd told him so far, then he read the document, then he looked up at her, then at Duke.

'Are you together?' he asked.

'Yes. This is Mr Wellington,' said Liz. 'He was a friend of the girl's father. Mr Wellington was injured in the war.'

'Was he now?'

'Yes, part of his leg was blown off.'

The sergeant leaned over the desk to get a clearer view of Duke's leg which seemed intact. Duke bent down and gave his left calf a hollow tap. 'Part me, part mahogany,' he said, politely. 'The missing girl's dad was a hero – got the MM.'

'The girl's name is Billie,' said Liz, 'as you can see from

her dad's will. She ran away from her so-called uncle and tried to get back to me in Leeds.'

'Leeds?'

'Yes. Only she was caught by the police in Grantham, returned to London and handed over to the Transport Police at King's Cross Station. I understand they're based here.'

'They are indeed.'

'So ... could I speak to one of them?'

He stayed pondering her request for a full five seconds, drumming his fingers on the ledger before saying, 'I'll see if there's anyone in their office.'

'Thank you.'

As he disappeared through a door Duke murmured, 'It might be better if you were real polite. Upsetting these guys is gonna get you nowhere fast.'

'I'm just hoping Cedric hasn't beaten us to it,' Liz said. 'He'll know the Transport Police will have his phone number, and if he doesn't want to be found ... well, he might try and use his influence on them.'

'I understand he's a big man for the bribe,' said Duke.

'Do you think I should tell the police why we think he's taken Billie?'

'We don't know for sure ourselves that she's due for an inheritance. Maybe you should just use Chas's will as your, er, credential. You're trying to carry out her dead father's wishes and Cedric Elliker is obstructing you.'

'The sergeant never asked me for the so-called uncle's name,' said Liz.

'I know,' said Duke, 'and that's a worry.'

'You think he knows it already?'

'Maybe. Let's see.'

The sergeant returned with a uniformed constable in his wake. 'This is PC Hetherington,' he said. 'He can deal with your enquiry.'

'Hello. My name's Liz Morris. I assume the sergeant's told you why I'm here.'

'Briefly. You'd better come through.'

Liz and Duke followed him to a door leading on to a short corridor where they went through another door with *British Transport Police* written on it. It was a large room with three desks, a stack of filing cabinets, a typewriter and telephone. The walls were decorated with photographs of men in uniform, mainly police uniform but some from the services. PC Hetherington looked to be of the right age for call-up. Liz assumed the police force was a reserved occupation

Hetherington invited them to sit down in two of the many chairs available. 'We have the place to ourselves today, my two colleagues are out on duty.' He opened a large notebook. 'So, if I might take some details.'

Liz told the story once again and showed him Chas's will, but omitted to tell him Cedric's name, purposely this time.

He got to his feet and went to the filing cabinets. 'Do you know the date this happened?'

'Yes, it was September the fourteenth.' Liz took the letter from PC Harris out of her bag and handed it to him. He studied it for a few seconds then gave it back to her and took out a thick file which he placed it on his desk.

'This is our missing persons file. Whoever dealt with the matter should have entered it in here.' He turned to what Liz assumed was the relevant page and shook his head. 'Hmm, I'm guessing it was a problem that was solved almost before it became a problem.'

'Billie was missing for about three hours before she was handed to PC Harris.'

'Well, that explains it,' said Hetherington, sitting back in his chair. 'We don't record anyone as missing after just three hours, unless there's been an obvious abduction. I suspect one of my colleagues will have dealt with it as a matter of course without writing it down in here – problem arose, problem solved. No need for any record-keeping.'

'But one of your people must have rung Billie's aunt to tell her she'd been found and to come to King's Cross station to collect her. If you've got the phone number presumably you can trace the aunt's address.'

'I'm sorry but there's no phone number recorded in this book, nor any mention of the incident. All I can do is to ask my colleagues if they recall the girl and her aunt, and if they made a note of any phone number.'

'If? Surely there shouldn't be any *if* about it,' said Liz.

'I thought you guys were s'posed to keep a record of everything,' added Duke.

'Everything important,' replied Hetherington.

'So, a missing child isn't classed as important?' said Liz.

'She wasn't exactly missing though, was she?'

'Yes, she was, and she's still missing now.'

'Okay, I'll report her as missing. I have all the details, we'll set the wheels in motion.'

'Oh, you have all the details, have you? But you still haven't asked me one all-important question,' said Liz, whose hackles were rising

'What question's that?'

'You haven't asked me the name of the uncle who took her. Why haven't you asked me that?'

Hetherington shifted in his chair, uncomfortably. Liz continued: 'You haven't asked me because you already know the answer, don't you? You already know it was Cedric Elliker, a man you daren't go up against.'

Hetherington tried to maintain his composure. Her verbal assault had unnerved him, she could see it in his face.

'Madam, I . . . I don't know what you're talking about.'

Liz got to her feet, as did Duke. 'Yes, you bloody well do,' she said, coldly. 'You're the second copper who's fobbed me off. When I get to the bottom of all this you'll have some explaining to do!'

Hetherington's face went white as they stormed out of his office. Liz stopped in front of the desk sergeant and hissed, 'If you're in this with him, you're for the bloody chop as well!'

In the taxi she was still fuming. 'Damned coppers. Are they all bent in London?'

'Don't think so,' said Duke as Sid drove them back to the club.

'The one in Grantham was all right,' said Liz. 'Trouble is, he didn't know anything.'

They drove for a while, all deep in thought. Sid broke the silence. 'Did you say Billie ran away straight from school that day they took her off the train?'

'I believe so, yes.'

'And would that be a private school?'

'I believe it would be, yes.'

'So she'll have been wearing a school uniform . . .'

'Sid, you're a genius!' said Liz.

'I'm glad you've rung,' said PC Harris. 'This school thing occurred to me as soon as I put the phone down.'

'So, was Billie wearing a uniform?'

'She was.'

'If you could describe it we should be able to identify her school.'

'I can do better than that. She was wearing the uniform of St Ethelburga's Girls' School. I've got the phone number and the name of headmistress – Mrs Leverton. I should have told you that when you last rang.'

'That's okay. I'm just hoping Billie's uncle hasn't taken her out of school.'

'St Ethelburga's will have her home address.'

'You would think so. He's doing his best to make sure I can't track Billie down.'

'Have you reported this to the police down there?'

'I have . . . and I get the impression that they're in his pocket.'

'That's a very serious allegation.'

'I know.'

'Who is this man?'

'His name is Cedric Elliker. If you check with the London police you'll see what I'm up against.'

'Cedric Elliker,' wrote down PC Harris, unsure how to react to such an accusation. 'I'd, er, I'd be obliged if you could keep me informed of progress.'

'I'll do that, PC Harris, and thank you again.'

Chapter 36

That same evening Billie was in her bedroom reading her schoolbooks when she heard men's voices coming from below. Her room was directly above Cedric's office.

She put her ear to the floor in the hope that she might hear what they were saying. Not that she was interested, but being able to listen to private conversations is always exciting to a child. The sound was muffled so she pulled up the carpet square and tried again, with her head against the floorboards. This wasn't much better but she did notice one of the floorboards seemed to be loose so she wedged her narrow fingers in at one end and pulled it clear of the joists. It was about six foot long and four inches wide and below it was a space about eight inches deep before she could see the wooden lathes supporting the plaster ceiling of Cedric's office. The voices were much clearer clear now, almost as though they were speaking in her room.

Billie recognised the voices as those of Cedric's two brothers who had arrived at the house earlier in the evening. They were talking about cigarettes and whisky, and something called cocaine, and about people buying and selling stuff for large amounts of money. She was becoming quite bored when someone mentioned Cedric's book.

'Just how safe is that book you keep, Ced?'

Billie was wondering what the man meant, then she realised that Ced was short for Cedric. This amused her. Would she ever dare call him that herself? Uncle Ced? Probably not.

'It's safer with me than with any of you lot,' Cedric replied smartly. 'I need to keep it up-to-date constantly. It never leaves this office. Either I'm working on it or it's in the desk drawer.'

'And you always keep that drawer locked if you're not in the room?'

Billie heard a rattle of keys 'With this key that never leaves this key ring that never leaves my pocket.'

Billie knew this was not true. She'd often seen her uncle's bunch of keys on the hall table. She replaced the floorboard and the carpet, happy in the knowledge that she knew something Uncle Cedric didn't. She knew how to listen to his private conversations, which would probably be all about gangsters and robbers and stuff next time. Not about boring cigarettes.

She went back downstairs, ostensibly to make herself a cup of cocoa but in reality to see the gangsters once again. They came out of Cedric's office into the hall where Billie was standing drinking her cocoa. She smiled politely but her smile wasn't returned. One of them turned to Cedric.

'What's the story with this kid? You some sort of do-gooder or somethin'?'

'She's Annie's daughter. We're her uncles. We Ellikers are a family, or hadn't you noticed?'

One of the others laughed. 'Not like any family I've ever known.'

This set them all laughing as they trooped out of the door. Cedric followed them to their cars, spoke to them for a while, then came back into the house, locked the door and threw the keys down on the hall table, as was his habit.

Chapter 37

Ten minutes later Cedric was concentrating on his ledger when Billie walked past the half-open door of his study. She peered inside at her uncle, who was writing busily in a thick black ledger. Billie assumed this was the book they'd been talking about earlier in evening; the book that was always kept under lock and key. A book that was of great interest to her.

She didn't knock because to knock meant she'd be refused entry. When in doubt do it and *then* ask permission. Her dad had taught her that, but not when it applied to him. She must always ask his permission first, which she did in silent supplication.

Shall I go in, Daddy?

Of course you must, my darling girl.

She went in quietly, so quietly that she'd been standing at the other side of Cedric's desk for a full minute before he became aware of her presence. He looked up, slammed the book shut with great force and screamed at her.

'OUT!'

'Uncle Cedric, I only came to ask you something.'

It was a lie but it was an easy one to justify. All she

needed was a question, any question. A question about her homework perhaps.

'I said, get out! You bloody stupid girl!'

Billie stood her ground. She'd never been sworn at by an adult. A few of the kids at her Leeds school had mouths on them but she could give as good as she got with that lot.

Cedric got to his feet, rounded the desk and grabbed her by the scruff of the neck with one hand. She screamed in protest as he dragged her out into the hall, opened the understairs cupboard with his free hand, threw her in and locked the door. Billie was more astounded than shocked. What on earth was all that about?

She shouted in protest for a while but her protests were nothing compared to the volume of abuse coming from Cedric, to the extent that she thought she might be safer where she was. He was shouting at Aunt Lavinia now and she was shouting back, trying to tell him not to make a fuss over nothing. The girl meant no harm; you shouldn't have left your office door open if you didn't want her to come in; she's an eight year old – what harm can she do to you?

And so it went on. Lavinia wasn't defending Billie, she was simply angry at Cedric for losing his self-control. After a while Billie closed her ears to it all. She hadn't done any harm. She'd watched him writing in his stupid book but she couldn't see what he was writing because it was all upside down to her, and in any case she wasn't interested. She'd gone in there because she was curious about this mysterious book but once she saw it her curiosity had melted away. It was just a boring old ledger with boring old writing in it. Lists of stuff. Who was interested in lists? She wasn't. Lists were boring.

It was dark in the cupboard. Billie banged her head against something metallic and cried out. She rubbed her head then felt around and realised she'd probably bumped against a gas meter like they had at the top of the cellar steps in Leeds. A floorboard beneath her wobbled. Purely because she had nothing else to do she scrabbled around and found she could lift it up, just like the one in her bedroom. It was something to do in this darkness; only a thin shaft of light filtered through under the bottom of the door, nothing more. The loose board was two feet long. It had been cut away by a plumber who had needed to gain access under the floorboards. Billie stuck her hand through the four-inch wide gap and reached her arm down as far as she could. She could just touch her fingers on something hard – concrete as it happened, but all she knew was that it was another floor underneath the one on which she was already sitting. To an adult this discovery would have been singularly uninteresting; to a kid it seemed a great place to hide stuff.

It was over an hour before Lavinia opened the cupboard door and sent Billie off to bed. Lavinia had won the battle of words. Cedric had already stormed off to his bed, his anger fuelled by an irrational sense of self-disgust that he had allowed himself to be witnessed making an entry in the incriminating ledger. The girl after all had no idea of the information it contained.

Billie lay sleepless in her bed for a long time. She seemed to have lived a life overflowing with injustice. A bomb had killed her mum; the Germans had killed her dad; Cedric had taken her away from the only person she loved and trusted; Delma had tried to get her expelled as a thief. But she'd got her own back on Delma and she'd felt good about it, so maybe she should get her own back on Cedric.

Chapter 38

Billie awoke in the early hours from a dream in which she was still locked under the stairs. As she lay there, a plan evolved in her brain. A great and simple plan. Simple plans are always the best, her daddy had told her that. It some-times amazed Billie how much stuff her daddy had taught her in their hundreds of conversations. How she wished he was here now to give her his opinion.

In the sort of silence that could only be achieved by a lightweight child she crept downstairs. The house was dark; she daren't switch on any lights, but she had the torch she used for reading in bed. She'd brought it with her from Leeds, one of her most valued possessions. The battery was running low but it had enough power to show her the way to Cedric's study. The keys were still on the hall table and it was just a process of elimination to find the ones that fitted the office door and the desk, which had only one drawer that locked. Inside it was the book.

The ledger was big and heavy, too heavy for her to lift with one hand so she had to switch off her torch, stick it in her pyjama pocket, heave the book out with two hands and place it on the desk while she locked the drawer again.

All this she did by the dim light seeping through the curtains, her young eyes accustomed to the dark by now. Once outside the office she placed the book on the floor so that she could lock the door to the study and put the keys back on the hall table, then she picked up the book again. She wasn't going to take it far, just to the cupboard in which she'd been imprisoned earlier – the cupboard with the cunning hiding place. The key was always kept in the cupboard lock. She opened it and, in less than a minute, the Elliker family Bible was hidden under the floorboards.

Billie had just reached the top of the stairs when she heard a bedroom door open. She darted forward into the bathroom directly in front of her, turned on the light and closed the door behind her. Within seconds the handle turned.

'I'm in here,' she called out.

Cedric made a grunting sound and trudged off to the downstairs toilet. Billie breathed a sigh of relief, left it a couple of minutes then pulled the chain and came out. Cedric was doing the same downstairs. By the time he arrived on the landing Billie was in bed. Justice had been served.

What do you think, Dad?

I think you did well, Billie.

Chapter 39

The noise Cedric was making woke Billie up. He was banging and shouting and slamming doors, and she knew it was only a matter of time before he came to question her. When her bedroom door burst open, she pretended the noise had just woken her up. Cedric was standing over her bed.

'Where is it?' he screamed.

Billie rubbed her eyes and sat up. Lavinia was standing in the doorway. Cedric screamed at her again.

'Where's the ledger? I know you took it!'

'What?' said Billie.

Cedric yanked her out of bed. 'Tell me what you've done with it!'

'Done with what?'

'You know what!'

'I don't know.'

His rage had Billie crying in fear. She was already thinking that taking his book hadn't been such a good idea, but she couldn't admit to it now. Judging by the look on his face he'd probably kill her. Aunt Lavinia was looking concerned for her welfare.

'Auntie, he's scaring me! I don't know what he's talking about.' Billie's genuine tears added credibility to her lie.

'Leave her, Cedric. She doesn't know where it is.'

'She was out of bed last night.'

'I had to go to the lavvie,' protested Billie.

'And now I come to think of it, your bedroom light wasn't switched on. Why would you leave your light switched off unless you were up to no good?'

'The switch is by the door. I used my torch.'

'Torch, what torch?'

Billie produced the torch that she kept on her bedside table. Cedric took it and switched it on. It gave a dim light.

'It needs a new battery,' said Billie. 'Do you think I could have a new battery, Uncle Cedric?'

He wasn't satisfied with her explanation. 'I'll search this house high and low, and if I find that book I'll know it was you who took it, girl!'

Billie said nothing because it was the best thing to say.

'Well, it's a big book so it shouldn't be hard to find,' commented Lavinia. 'That's if it's still in this house.'

'How do you mean, if it's still in this house?' howled Cedric. 'She hasn't taken it out of the house, the doors are locked.'

'I'm not talking about her, I'm talking about your damned brothers! I don't think they're very happy that you've got that book. They both know how to pick locks and close doors behind them.' She stared at him, accusingly, as she remembered something. 'In fact they wouldn't have to pick too many locks, with you always leaving your keys on the hall table. It wouldn't surprise me if one of them's got a copy of our front-door key.'

Cedric looked suitably guilty.

'I'll help you search the house,' said Lavinia, 'but don't be surprised if we don't find it. Billie, get dressed and go downstairs for your breakfast.'

'Yes, Aunt Lavinia.'

Chapter 40

Billie spent the whole of that day worrying about Cedric finding the book. It even crossed her mind to put it back, but she could think of no way of doing this without getting caught. She paid little attention to her lessons and was reprimanded several times by Miss Molloy, who told her to stay back after the afternoon bell.

'Is anything wrong, Challinor?'

The teacher knew all about Billie's difficulty with Delma, and she also knew the fearsome reputation of the uncle with whom the child was now living.

'No, I'm okay, miss.'

'You would tell me if anything was wrong?'

'Yes, miss.'

Billie left to go home and Miss Molloy stopped by Mrs Leverton's office. 'I'm worried about Billie Challinor. I hate to think of an innocent child living among those damned gangsters. Mr Beddington-Croft was obviously terrified of them, what chance does a small girl have?'

'I don't know,' said the headmistress. 'She tried to run back to Leeds. Maybe it's a pity she didn't succeed.'

'There's no "maybe" about it.'

*

Uncle Cedric's car wasn't in the drive when Billie got back, which meant he was still at work. If Aunt Lavinia told her he'd found the book Billie would immediately run out of the house and make another attempt at getting to Leeds.

She opened the front door tentatively and went inside. The wireless was on in the living room, so she headed there. She'd left the front door open and taken out the key, which she stuck in her pocket. Should the need arise she'd run out of the front door and lock it behind her before making her getaway. This was a plan she'd formulated on the bus home. She was a fast runner and felt that with a bit of a lead she could lose her aunt. Lavinia was sitting in a chair, reading a newspaper. Billie called out to her from the hall.

'I'm home, Aunt Lavinia.'

'Oh, hello, Billie. Good day at school?'

So far, so good. No annoyance in her aunt's voice.

'Yes, thanks. Is Uncle Cedric okay?'

'Cedric? Oh, God, no. Still like a bear with a sore head.'

'He scared me this morning.'

'Yes, I know he did. He scared me.'

'Did he find his book?'

'He didn't, no, which didn't surprise me.'

Billie stuck the front door key back in the keyhole. No need to do a bunk yet. There was still time to plan that properly.

'I hope he's not still angry when he gets home.'

'Me too, Billie.'

*

Cedric came in at six-thirty and sat down for his dinner. Billie had already eaten. She'd previously explained to her aunt that in Leeds people sat down to tea at five o'clock and then maybe had a bit of supper before bedtime. Leeds people had their dinner at dinnertime, which was what Londoners called lunchtime. Lavinia went along with this because she had decided it was better to befriend the girl rather than make an enemy of her. Billie hovered out of sight but near enough to the dining-room door to listen to the adults' conversation.

'So,' said Lavinia. 'Did you find out who took it?'

'No,' grunted Cedric.

'But you asked, surely.'

'Lavinia, for me to ask was for me to admit that I'd lost it. I'm pretty sure one of them took it, but I'm not sure who.'

'And you think whoever took it is keeping it to himself and not telling the other?'

'That's exactly what I think and that's why I haven't mentioned it to them. One knows I've lost it, the other doesn't. No idea which one but he'll make himself known at some stage, otherwise there's not much point in him having it.'

'He might use it to do a deal with the police if things get too hot. Sell you out in exchange for his own freedom.'

'That thought had crossed my mind, but whoever did that wouldn't survive long and he'd know it.'

'This is very dangerous ground, Cedric.'

He nodded. 'The quicker we sort out this other business, the quicker we can get away from both of them. I'll leave them each a note telling them the ledger's gone and one of them has it. It's their problem after that.'

'What about the girl?'

'I don't know. We might have to take her with us.'

'I can think of a more permanent solution,' said Lavinia.

'So can I, but not while that busybody aunt of hers is nosing around.'

'What do you mean, nosing around?'

'I mean I heard from the police that she's trying to locate us.'

'So she's in London?'

Cedric nodded. 'She was over at Highbury Vale police station yesterday and Camden today.'

'Why Camden?'

'That's where the King's Cross transport coppers are based. There's a limit to how many bent coppers there are in this town. The Highbury Vale man's been in my pocket on and off for five years. The Camden coppers I managed to anticipate, knowing you'd given them our phone number. I had to put two of them on wages.'

'Ah – I had to give them the number to get the girl back here.'

Cedric grunted. 'So far it's costing me a lot of money to keep that damned woman off our backs – too much money. It might well be her who needs the permanent solution.'

Billie wasn't entirely sure what her uncle meant by 'permanent solution' but it didn't sound good, so she knew she had to run away again. Maybe not tonight because she needed to get some money. Steal some from Aunt Lavinia's purse perhaps. Do no harm to wait for an opportune moment.

Chapter 41

Liz spent that same day working out her strategy along with Duke. She favoured the direct approach.

'Why can't I just go to the school and bring her out? I've got Chas's will giving me the authority to be her guardian.'

'Liz,' said Duke, 'I've been talking to some people who know a lot more about the Ellikers that I do and they are very dangerous people.'

'All the more reason Billie shouldn't be in their care. Surely not all the police in London are in Cedric's pocket?'

'True, but so far our record is two out of two who are. We don't want to make it three out of three.'

'Couldn't we go to Scotland Yard or somewhere and ask to speak to a very senior officer?'

'I'm told Cedric has some of them in his pocket too. Are we willing to take that chance?'

'That's got to be one chance in a hundred, surely.'

'I don't know, Liz. The Ellikers are scary people.'

'What about Billie's school? Do you think they might have influence there?'

'I don't know. All I do know is that we need to be real

sneaky about this. First, you need to ascertain that she's still at the school.'

'And how do I do that?'

Duke suddenly held up a finger to indicate the arrival of an idea. 'Well, I do believe our banjo player married briefly into money and their son's daughter might well go to that very school if I'm not mistaken. He'll be in for rehearsal late this afternoon.'

Monty Finniston, the banjo player, wasn't absolutely certain which school his granddaughter went to, other than it was a private school and that his ex-wife's family thought themselves to be a cut above Uncle Monty, the lowly musician.

He was originally from Mississippi and had been brought over to England by Tubby Blake, who had been playing over there and needed a good banjo player. Monty was in his sixties, had a mop of white hair, three gold teeth, and was as tall as Duke but nowhere near as broad. He still hadn't lost his Deep Southern accent.

'My grandson Elmo is away fightin' in France right now. I've always got on with his wife Maisie, who's a lady of substance and not unappreciative of my personal charms.'

'I don't suppose she's on the telephone?' asked Liz.

'Like I said, she's a lady of substance. She most certainly is on the telephone. Do you wish me to get hold of her?'

'Yes . . . but just hang on,' said Liz. 'I need you to word this correctly. I don't want anyone, no matter how innocent they are, to get wind of what I'm about.'

'Just ring her and ask her to ask her daughter if there's

a girl called Billie Challinor at school,' said Duke. 'Tell her you think it might be Chas's daughter. She'll know who Chas is.'

'Okey-dokey, I got the lady's details in my numbers book.' He picked up the receiver and dialled.

'Hello, is that Maisie? . . . Thought so . . . Your good ole father-in-law Monty here . . . Oh, so-so . . . I'm wonderin' how my boy Elmo's doin'? . . . Well, no news is good news in these goddamned times . . . Look, d'you remember a clarinet player called Chas Challinor? Stupid question – everyone knew Chas. You know he bought it in France? . . . Tragedy . . . Look, I hear me a whisper that his daughter Billie is a pupil at St Elthlburga's School. Now ain't that jes' the same school as Belinda goes to?' Monty stuck a thumb up. 'Y' know, I thought it was. Look, could you ask Belinda if she knows Billie? Is she home from school yet? . . . Great, put her on. Tell her it's her crazy old grandpa.

'Hi, Belinda, how're you doin'? . . . Oh, I'm still pluckin' the ole banjo. You must ask your mom to git you a guitar for your birthday and take some lessons . . . Look, what I wanted to ask you was about the daughter of the finest man who ever blowed down a liquorice stick . . . that's a clarinet to you. Her name is Billie Challinor and I believe she goes to your school. Maybe she's about your age . . . What? A year below you? Well, pardon me, miss, for making you younger than you is. She's still at the school, is she?'

Monty held the phone to his ear as Belinda spoke at some length, nodding and shaking his head. He eventually said goodbye and looked at Liz and Duke.

'Billie's a pupil there right enough. Apparently there was some trouble recently when she got herself expelled just after she started, but it was all cleared up. She'd been accused of stealin' a golden watch from a teacher but it turns out she'd been set up by some other girls. Hoity-toity schools, eh? Who'd pay to go to one?'

'So she's still there?'

'Yup, Belinda saw her on the school bus today.'

Liz was struggling to wipe a beaming smile off her face. 'So,' she said, 'I know where she is and I know she wants to come back to me. All I have to do is collect her from school before she gets on the bus.'

'I should come with you,' said Duke. 'I've got a van.'

'No, I'll do the collecting along with Sid. I'll bring her back here.'

Chapter 42

St Ethelburga's was situated about two miles east of Cedric's house, just on the edge of Epping Forest. Sid picked Liz up at two. The plan was to get to the school mid-afternoon and see if she could spot Billie on her afternoon break.

'Fine-looking school,' remarked Sid as he pulled up at the gates. Liz agreed. It was a substantial stone building with extensive grounds and playing fields. It was just the sort of place Liz would have liked Billie to be at, under other circumstances.

The gates were closed and Liz was trying to work out the best plan. Some girls were about but not many and not Billie. Liz had told Sid the full story and he'd suggested she walk in through the gates, have a good look round, grab the girl and bung her in the cab.

'Sounds like a good way to get the police hotfoot after us,' said Liz. 'No, I've got the school's phone number. I'll find a phone box and ring up the headmistress.'

'And tell her what?'

'Who I am and that I'm concerned for Billie's welfare. I'm the one Billie tried to run back to. What harm can the truth do?'

'I don't know.'

'Neither do I, but the truth is all I have.'

'I can't argue with that. We passed a phone box about half a mile back.'

'Mrs Leverton? My name is Liz Morris. I'm ringing to talk about Billie Challinor.'

The headmistress seemed pleased to hear from her.

'Then you know who I am?' said Liz, surprised.

'Yes, I do. I've heard Billie speak of you in glowing terms.'

'Good, that saves a lot of explanations. How does she speak of her uncle and aunt?'

'She doesn't.'

'I've heard disturbing stories about them.'

'Yes, so have I,' said Mrs Leverton.

'I'm relieved to hear you say that.'

'I'm quite curious to know how and why she came to be living with them.'

'She and her father lodged at my house in Leeds,' said Liz. 'When Chas – her father – died, she stayed with me, right up until recently when an uncle turned up out of the blue and more or less laid claim to her. I've since found out that in his will her father said he wanted me to be Billie's guardian. Apparently the War Office messed up and the will was mislaid or something.'

'So, you came down to take her back with you?'

'I came down to see if she was happy living here and if she was I'd have said hello and left her in peace, but the address her uncle gave me was bogus, which wasn't a good sign.'

'Really? I do have her home address if you need it.'

'Thank you, but it appears that the Ellikers are trying to make it difficult for me to talk to Billie. I found out about this school from a policeman who picked her up in Grantham after she tried to get back to me.' Liz paused then said, 'I'm hearing very bad things about the Elliker family, Mrs Leverton.'

The other woman tapped her fingers on her desk, deep in thought. 'I have to admit that I'd prefer this school to have no connection with the Ellikers, but if I were party to you just turning up and taking the girl away I suspect the family would give me a lot of trouble. They seem to have influence everywhere, including this school.'

'Really?'

'Yes, in her first week here some of the girls tried to get Billie expelled for theft. Her uncle found out about it and used his influence on the ringleader's father, who himself is a very influential man. The guilty girls confessed. The ringleader's father, by way of reparation, has paid all Billie's school fees for the year.'

'They're obviously not a family to be crossed.'

'No.'

Liz let a long moment go by then asked, 'Could you manage to have a quiet word with Billie and tell her I'll be at the school gates at home time and would like to see her then?'

Mrs Leverton gave this some thought then said, 'I see no harm in that.'

'Good . . . And Mrs Leverton?'

'Yes.'

'If Billie wants to come back to Leeds with me it's best I take her here and now.'

'Oh, dear, best for you perhaps, but it could get both me and the school into a lot of trouble.'

'I understand, so I imagine it's in your interest that this conversation never happened.'

'You imagine correctly. What exactly is it you want of me?'

'What time's home time?'

'Four o'clock.'

'Okay, at four o'clock Billie goes to the school gates as usual and there I am. Lots of girls will see her getting quite happily into a taxi with me instead of on to the school bus. You know nothing about it. Once I get her back to Leeds I'll ring your local police and let them know what's happened. I assume they'll know all about the Ellikers and they won't think too badly of me for taking her in this fashion. As far as you know she left school at home time and got on the school bus.'

There was a pause as Mrs Leverton thought about the implications of all this. Both she and Miss Molloy were worried about Billie living with the Ellikers, but to get involved in such subterfuge on the girl's behalf . . . was this wise?

'Mrs Morris?'

'Yes.'

'Where are you now?'

'In a phone box not far from your school.'

'Do you by any chance have proof of who you say you are and that you're Billie's rightful guardian? It's not that I don't trust you but—'

'Mrs Leverton, your job is to safeguard Billie's welfare. I'd expect no less. You mean do I have her father's will with me? Yes, I do. I also have my identity card. I brought them as a precaution. Do you want me to bring them to you?'

'I don't know. That might expose our little subterfuge.'

'My cab driver could bring them. I've got to know him well while I've been here, his name's Sid.'

Mrs Leverton was still hesitant.

'Unless you can think of another way?' added Liz. 'I don't mind coming to your office in person then Billie can identify me as her Auntie Liz.'

'I think a visit from Sid will suffice.'

At four o'clock Mrs Leverton was waiting by the school door as the girls tumbled out, pursued by shouts of 'No running!' from a teacher inside. When Billie approached her the headmistress laid a hand on her shoulder and spoke into her ear.

'Challinor, walk straight to the gates, say nothing to anyone. Your Auntie Liz is waiting for you there.'

She was walking away before Billie could react. In the distance she could see the familiar figure of Auntie Liz. Billie ran as fast as she could, flinging herself into Liz's open arms.

'Auntie Liz, can I come home with you? I hate living with Uncle Cedric. He's a bad man. He shouts at me and locks me up in a cupboard. Can I come home, please?'

'Yes, that's why I'm here.'

Mags was watching and listening. Billie spotted her and said, 'This is my Auntie Liz.'

269

'Pleased to meet you. I'm Mags.'

'She's my best friend,' said Billie, then to Mags she said, 'I'm going to Leeds.'

Mags looked at Liz. 'Will she be coming back?'

'Er, no, she won't. Would you do us a favour and tell Mrs Leverton that Billie got into a taxi with her Auntie Liz?'

'See you, Mags.' Billie grinned at her. 'I'll write to you care of the school.'

Liz took her hand and took her to the taxi. Sid asked where to.

'Tin Pan Alley, please.'

Their destination didn't sound very appealing to Billie, but anywhere was good so long as her Auntie Liz was with her.

Chapter 43

Around the time Liz, Billie and Sid set off for Denmark Street the Germans launched a V2 rocket from a site just west of Calais in northern France. The V2 was faster, quieter and far more destructive than its predecessor the V1, or doodlebug as it was more commonly known by the British. The V2 was fired sixty miles up into space where it arced over the English Channel and headed down towards London. The first thing Londoners knew of an approaching V2 was the double sonic bang as it broke the sound barrier. It was due to hit the ground at four times that speed.

On their way back into central London Billie noticed a bus with the words *Finsbury Park* on its destination board.

'My mum's grave's in Finsbury Park Cemetery,' she said.

'That's just down there, next right,' said Sid.

'Would it be okay if I went to see it? I've never seen it. Daddy used to go every year. Maybe we could get some flowers.'

'I don't see why not,' said Liz. It was hardly a request she could refuse.

The V2, at the mercy of the capricious wind, had been

calibrated wrongly. It was meant to land on central London but was overshooting by several miles. Sid stopped his cab by a flower-seller who had set up a stall near the cemetery gates. Liz and Billie got out.

'Mum liked red roses best,' said Billie. 'Daddy told me that.' She looked up at the sky. 'I bet he's giving her a bunch of red roses right now.'

Liz bought a bunch of red roses for two and fourpence. Sid said he'd be waiting for them. Liz waved her thanks and took Billie to a stone lodge just inside the cemetery gates.

'We'll need to see the manager to find out where your mum is buried.'

'Okay.'

The lodge had a window with a sign announcing *Ring bell for attention*. Billie darted forward and rang it. A man in dark uniform appeared at the window. Liz stepped in front of Billie.

'I wonder if you could direct us to the grave of Mrs Anne Challinor.'

The man stepped away from the window, ran his finger down an alphabetically arranged list then referred to a plan of the cemetery.

'E26,' he said. 'First right, second left, third right, and it's the third grave on the right.'

Billie ran the directions through her head. Everything concerning her mother was of the utmost importance to her. First right, second left, third right, third grave on the right. Etched into her memory.

'Will I ever be able to see Daddy's grave?' she asked as they walked along the pathways.

'I imagine so,' said Liz. 'He wasn't posted as missing or anything. I expect Sergeant Dodsworth will know where he is.'

'We should have asked him when he came. He might get killed, then we'll never know.'

'Your dad's regiment will be able to tell us after the war's over.'

'That's good. We go right here, then it's the third grave on the right.'

Annie's gravestone looked quite new compared to the decrepit monuments they'd just passed. It was in white marble with gold, engraved lettering. The inscription was simple:

HERE LIES ANNE MARGARET CHALLINOR
BORN 21ST JUNE 1915
KILLED BY A GERMAN BOMB 16 SEPTEMBER 1940
BELOVED WIFE OF CHARLES
DEVOTED MOTHER OF THEIR WONDERFUL
DAUGHTER BILLIE

Wonderful daughter. Billie hadn't expected to see her name on anything so grand. It gave her a permanent connection to her mum and dad and brought immediate tears. Liz put an arm around her as she fought against her own reaction. There was an earthenware vase on the grave into which Liz placed the roses. She stood back and clasped her hands together, as did Billie.

'What do I say, Auntie Liz?'

'Just talk to her as if she was here.'

Billie stared at the inscription and began to speak.

'Hello, Mum. It's me, Billie. I've grown a lot since you last saw me.' She bit her lip before she went on: 'Daddy was killed by the Germans but I expect you know that. I hope he's with you, and if he is will you tell him I miss him awfully? Uncle Cedric took me to live with him and Aunt Lavinia who I don't think are very nice people, but I expect you know that as well. I should be okay now I'm back with Auntie Liz.'

Liz squeezed her hand reassuringly as Billie continued:

'On your birthday I'm going to come here every year to bring you roses, and when we find where Daddy's buried we'll bring him back here to be with you. He never stopped going on about you. I bet no man ever loved anyone as much as Daddy loved you.'

The V2 had passed its zenith and was now heading for earth at two thousand five hundred miles an hour. It was just ten seconds away from hitting Finsbury Park eight miles below. Liz and Billie heard the double sonic boom and ignored it; the skies of London were not the quietest of places during this war. The V2 carried a warhead containing one tonne of high explosive, enough to destroy a whole street. In the event it was mercifully heading for an area mostly devoid of human life. Plenty of human death, but not much life.

It landed in the back garden of the cemetery manager's lodge, blasted a crater twenty feet deep and disinterred many nearby bodies, some of them over two hundred years old, their coffins having rotted away a century or more ago. Shattered bones and bodies in various stages of putrescence flew a hundred feet into the air and were scattered over the cemetery grounds.

Liz and Billie were standing a hundred yards from the explosion. Both of them were lifted off their feet and catapulted through the air. Liz landed on soft earth; Billie wasn't so lucky. Being lighter, she travelled further than Liz, landed on a stone-flagged path and rolled on to the last resting place of Honoria Constance Quinn who had died in 1825. Earth, bones, rotting flesh, vegetation and gravestones were still raining down on Billie when she rolled to a halt.

Liz pushed up on to her feet and tried to orientate herself. Her mind was numb with shock. Billie . . . where was she? She tried to shout but it came out as a cough. Her throat was clogged up with dirt and dust; the noise of the bomb was still ringing in her ears. Her strength left her and she dropped to the ground again, unconscious.

Two V2 rockets landed at around that time, both dispatched from the same launch site. The other landed on Norwich and did more serious damage. Two fire engines, four ambulances, a van full of ARP volunteers, and three police cars were sent to Finsbury Park Cemetery. Rubble blocked the road, mainly from the lodge which was no longer there; nor were the manager and his wife who had both disappeared along with their home. The boundary wall to the side of the house had been blown down and Sid's taxi, which had been parked at the other side on the road, was upside down, having travelled thirty feet through the air and landed on its roof. Sid was still in the driver's seat, crushed to death. The flower-seller was lying dead under a pile of rubble.

Along with Liz and Billie there had been eight other people visiting graves in the cemetery. Some were killed outright, some survived. Liz was the first one to be found alive. She regained consciousness for the second time just as she was being lifted on to a stretcher. Billie was in her thoughts immediately.

'Billie was with me. Is she okay?'

'Who's Billie?'

'She's my ... er ... my niece. She's eight.'

'And she was with you?'

'Yes ... right ... right beside me. Is she okay?'

'I don't know. We're still looking for survivors.'

The ARP man shouted across to his colleagues, 'There's an eight-year-old girl in here. Has anyone seen her?'

Searchers looked up but didn't react. The man shouted again, louder this time. 'An eight-year-old girl. Has anyone seen her?'

Still no reply. Liz began to shudder with grief. 'Please, you've got to look for her.'

Occasional shouts of 'Over here' meant someone had been found, either alive or dead. But Billie wasn't among them. Liz sat up on her stretcher.

'Let me off, I need to find her.'

She swung her legs around and stepped off. The stretcher bearers were protesting but she brushed them aside. 'Just help me look for her, please.' Liz's voice was parched and weak. 'Her name's Billie. Can you shout it out, please?'

The two men began to shout out Billie's name with Liz standing between them, her arms around their shoulders.

'She can't be too far away. She's a lot smaller than me but I doubt she was blown much further. Oh, please be alive, Billie! It's this way. I was blown this way.'

The three of them stepped over fallen gravestones, bones and loose earth. They came to a path beyond which Liz saw a pile of debris lying across a grave. Some sixth sense told her that Billie was underneath it, but didn't tell her if she was dead or alive. Liz's voice was tentative as she asked, 'Is she over there?'

One of her helpers let go of her and went over to inspect the grave of Honoria Constance Quinn.

Chapter 44

Five o'clock came with no sign of Billie's return. Lavinia rang the school. Mrs Leverton answered.

'Hello, this is Lavinia Elliker. I'm a little concerned that my niece Billie Challinor hasn't returned from school.'

'Oh, I assumed you knew.'

'Knew what?'

'One of the girls saw her getting into a taxi with a woman your niece said was her Auntie Liz.'

'WHAT?

'I assume you know this woman, Mrs Elliker. According to the girl, Billie seemed more than happy to go with her.'

'What? Yes, I do know her. But that woman has no right to collect my niece!'

Mrs Leverton, who had had seen Chas's will, thought differently, but she kept this to herself.

'Have you any idea where she has taken my niece?' demanded Lavinia Elliker.

'The girl who saw them leave came straight to my office and said Billie had told her she wasn't coming back.'

'Not coming back? Not coming back from where?'

'I'm simply repeating what was said, Mrs Elliker. I assume you know where this Auntie Liz lives.'

'My husband will have something to say about this! You have a duty to look after the children who attend your school.'

'I'm sorry. This happened outside the school gates so it was beyond our control. If you feel it's a serious problem then you must report it to the police, especially if you know the woman who took Billie. As I said, she wasn't coerced into going with her aunt or I'd have rung the police myself.'

Mrs Leverton strongly suspected that neither Lavinia nor her husband would want the police involved. The line went dead. Mrs Leverton smiled and put down the receiver with a satisfying clunk.

Chapter 45

One of Liz's helpers was on his knees, scrabbling away at the debris. He stopped and sat back on his haunches.

Liz said, 'What is it?'

The man shook his head and said nothing. He continued with his search, but with less enthusiasm. Liz took a step towards him and almost vomited with anguish. A small hand had been uncovered. The man still supporting her asked her if she was okay. She didn't reply but he let go of her anyway and went to help his colleague. Bit by bit they uncovered the whole of Billie's body. Liz daren't ask the one question that urgently needed answering. One of the men bent right over the child and listened for breathing. He looked up at Liz and said, 'She's alive. We need the ambulance people.'

Liz dropped to her knees beside Billie, wanting to hear what the man had heard: Billie breathing. She was, faintly but regularly. Liz could see little blood, just a graze on her forehead.

'Billie, it's Auntie Liz. Can you hear me?'

She let out a moan which brought a smile to Liz's face.

'Billie, can you open your eyes?'

Billie frowned then opened her eyes a little, enough to see Liz, who asked her, 'Can you talk?'

Billie moaned again.

'Okay,' said Liz. 'Don't try. There was a bomb, but we're both safe. There's an ambulance to take you to hospital. I'll come with you.'

Both Billie and Liz were taken to the ambulance on stretchers. It was a short but horrific journey for a seated Liz, through the shattered cemetery with body parts visible everywhere. Luckily Billie was lying down and could only see the sky above her. As they came through the gate Liz saw Sid's crushed taxi across the road from where she'd last seen it. She called to a nearby policeman.

'That's our taxi. Is the driver okay?'

He shook his head. 'I'm afraid not, madam.'

'Oh, no! It's because of us he's dead. We shouldn't have brought him here.'

'It's because of Hitler he's dead, madam. We can't blame ourselves for any of this.'

Liz was put in the same ambulance as Billie, who was being given an injection of morphine.

'What's wrong with her?' Liz asked the doctor who'd accompanied the ambulance.

'Well, as far as I can see she's got a broken left arm and right leg. Hard to say what else until we get her into X-ray.' He looked speculatively at Liz, who was filthy from head to toe with blood seeping through a deep cut on her scalp.

'What about you?' he asked.

'I think I've hurt my ribs. Can't breathe properly, my head hurts, and I think I've done something to my ankle.'

'Your head needs stitching. I might as well do that now before you lose any more blood.'

'What about Billie? Is she going to be okay?'

'We need to check her for internal injuries before I answer that.'

The doctor put ten stitches in Liz's head wound and left them in the care of the ambulance people since he was needed back in the cemetery. Liz and Billie were rushed to St Bartholomew's Hospital in Smithfield, with bells ringing and lights flashing. For the time being all thoughts and worries about Cedric Elliker were completely forgotten.

Four more survivors of the explosion followed them there, all of them badly injured, one not expected to live. Fortunately Billie's X-rays showed no internal injuries but a double fracture of her right tibia and fibula, fractured radius in her left arm, two cracked ribs, severe bruising and concussion.

Liz had three cracked ribs, a twisted ankle, a cut to the head and severe bruising. Two hours later, suitably swathed in bandages and plaster, they ended up in a two-bed ward side by side. Billie had been allocated a bed in the children's ward but Liz put in a request for them to stay together.

'She's been through a lot recently. I think it might help her if I'm by her side.'

'Hmm, well, we do have a two-bed ward empty at the moment,' said the ward sister, undecided.

'I definitely want to be with Auntie Liz, if possible,' confirmed Billie. Sister asked if there was anyone she needed to contact. Billie said simply, 'No, Auntie Liz is all the relations I have.'

Liz gave the nurse two phone numbers. One was of the café in Leeds, which would be closed now but perhaps Sister could speak to them in the morning? And then there was Duke's number at the club. Could he be asked to call in to see them as soon as possible? There were things Liz needed to know. Or rather there were things she needed Cedric Elliker *not* to know, such as that his niece and her rescuer were both immobile in hospital and therefore extremely vulnerable. She wondered if she could request police protection, but on what grounds? Would her PC pal up in Grantham be able to advise on that matter or should she ask her Leeds solicitor for advice? Tell him about the Ellikers being notorious gangsters. All these thought flashed through Liz's mind while Billie sank into a morphine-induced sleep.

Chapter 46

Liz was discharged two days later. On that same morning Percy Cudlipp, editor of the *Daily Herald*, called Helen Hawkins into his office. She was a nineteen-year-old junior reporter and this was the first time she'd spoken to him one-to-one. Up until then she'd worked on local news in the south-east of London.

He looked up from reading a memo and smiled at her. 'Ah, Helen, I have a job for you which is possibly beyond the scope of what you've been given so far, but you appear to be a young lady of some talent and this war is thinning out our stock of reporters at an alarming rate. As you know, Henry McFadden has just been called up and he's older than me.'

'I believe he enlisted, sir.'

'Yes, he did, and hopefully by the time he finishes his basic training the war will be over.'

McFadden was a distinguished senior reporter whose younger brother had recently been killed in France.

Cudlipp continued: 'We have interesting information from a stringer about the V2 rocket that dropped on Finsbury Park Cemetery. I'm of the opinion that a little research may well unearth a most intriguing story. I'd like you to take it on.'

'Thank you for the opportunity, sir.'

'Please sit down and take notes.'

Helen sat down and took out her shorthand notebook as Cudlipp read from the memo on his desk.

'One of the injured people was an eight-year-old girl called Billie Challinor. Her mother was killed by a bomb in 1940 and is buried in that same cemetery. I assume the girl was visiting the grave.'

The name rang a bell with Helen. 'Challinor? Isn't she the daughter of Chas Challinor the jazz musician?'

Cudlipp smiled. 'She is indeed. Are you a jazz fan?'

'Not really, sir, but I remember that story from my first week here. Her father was badly burned.'

'You have an excellent memory, Helen. And there's another strand to this story with which you'll have to tread most carefully.'

'Would this have anything to do with the Ellikers, sir?'

He raised his eyebrows in admiration. 'My word, you're a well-informed young lady.'

'I remember the dead woman was an Elliker, that's all.'

'Her daughter was recently living with Cedric Elliker. So we have a high-profile solicitor whose family is inextricably linked with major crime; his niece has been injured by a German bomb, and her father was a well-known jazz musician who died a hero's death just after D-Day.'

'Oh, I didn't know he was dead?'

'He was awarded the Military Medal for the action that killed him. In my experience when people and events such as this are linked it often provides a story that is more than the sum of its parts. I'd like you to put this one together. Are you up to it?'

'I believe I am, sir.'

'Excellent. You can travel by taxi and use a photographer as and when you need one.'

'May I make a suggestion, sir?'

'You may.'

'Could I start by running a short item containing everything we know so far, but excluding the Elliker connection, and see what interest it stirs up?'

He gave this some thought and nodded. 'Poke the hornet's nest, eh?'

'I suspect I'll get phone calls filling in gaps I might struggle to work out otherwise.'

'Yes, you will. Just so long as the competition doesn't pick up on it too.'

'The phone calls will be to me not them, sir.'

'And the by-line will be yours, so the Ellikers might not be too pleased with you if the story develops into something involving them.'

'Isn't that all in the job, sir?'

Chapter 47

The two thugs entering the Cosy Café on Ashley Road in Leeds weren't the usual type of customer. Alice Morley indicated that they should wait few minutes until a table became available.

'Busy time right now. There should be space for you in five minutes.'

They were both big men wearing expensive suits and trilby hats; Sunday wear for most men around there. 'We're not here to eat, we're here to talk to Liz Morris,' said one.

'Liz is away at the moment. Can I help?'

Connie and Alice had been forewarned by Liz that someone might come looking for her and Billie.

'No. Where is she?'

The man's manner was belligerent, his accent Southern. Connie heard the exchange and called out from behind the counter.

'London lads, are yer?'

'Where is she?'

'She's minding her own business, love. I'm sorry but if yer don't want to eat yer need ter bugger off. We're too busy ter waste time natterin'.'

Connie's manner was pleasant if firm but it annoyed the

men. The one doing the talking said, angrily, 'No, we haven't got time to waste either.'

'What's that supposed ter mean?' said Alice.

'I mean Liz Morris has abducted a child and we need to find out where she is.'

'Are you the police, then?'

'No, we're private investigators and we want answers.'

'Really?' said Connie. 'If she's abducted a child why aren't the coppers 'ere asking questions?'

'Have yer got any identification?' asked Alice.

The customers were beginning to take an interest in this. Four men from a nearby engineering works were sitting at one table. Two of them got to their feet.

'Yer've been asked ter leave, gents.'

The two thugs looked as though they could handle themselves but, on glancing around, they realised that there were many men in the café who looked ready to give them trouble. They'd got the name of the café from a neighbour of Liz Morris's called Edna Grimshaw, who'd told them she hadn't seen Liz for over a week. Connie walked past them to the door and opened it. The thugs hesitated. Alice looked outside at a black Rover 16 parked by the kerb and asked, 'Is that your car?'

'It is,' said a woman customer sitting by the window. 'I saw 'em gerrout of it.'

Connie stepped out of the door with her order pad and wrote down the car's registration number, then went back inside. 'We get lots o' coppers come in here,' she said. 'I'll give 'em yer car number just in case yer thinkin' of causin' us any bother. They'll have you London lads fettled in no time.'

The thugs looked at each other. These were men used to their threats having the desired effect, but they were in Yorkshire, foreign territory, among people who didn't take kindly to threats. A huge customer got to his feet then. He wore a white overall spattered with what looked like blood. 'D'yer want rid of 'em, Connie?' he asked.

'Aye, yer can tek 'em down ter t'abattoir an' hang 'em from them 'ooks.'

The whole café laughed at such a thought. The two men turned and walked out. Connie followed them to the door and called after them.

'An' yer can think on what I said about yon coppers. They'll have yer car number soon enough. You mark my words!'

The men got into the car and looked at each other, baffled. One said, 'Jesus! What was all that about?'

'No idea.'

'So, what the hell are we supposed to do next?'

'No idea.'

'Well, I think we should get the hell out of this town. It's full of bloody lunatics. We can tell Cedric we've put the squeeze on the locals and she's definitely not here.'

Cedric put the phone down. Lavinia looked at him, expectantly. She'd answered it originally and knew the call was from one of the men who'd been sent up to Leeds to find Liz.

'Well?'

'Well, what?'

'Damn it, Cedric! Are they in Leeds or what?'

'Not as far as I know. Liz Morris has taken the girl and

she's lying low. When we catch them I've a good mind to put them both down. Save a lot of time and trouble in the long run.'

'You do that and you're number one suspect. We've been through this before. What we planned is legal, all signed, witnessed and sealed. They can't touch you for it.'

Cedric grunted.

Chapter 48

The following morning Cedric had just arrived at his office when his receptionist called out to him.

'Mr Elliker, have you read the *Daily Herald* this morning?'

'No, I don't read that socialist claptrap.'

'There's something in it about your niece. She was injured by the V2 that landed on Finsbury Park Cemetery.'

He spun on his heel. 'What?'

The receptionist handed the newspaper to him. 'She's all right, sir. They took her to hospital.'

Cedric snatched it away from her and took it into his office. It was a short article just listing the dead and injured. It included the names Billie Challinor and Elizabeth Morris. The reporter had singled out Billie as being jazz musician Chas Challinor's daughter. It was said she had been visiting the grave of her mother, who had been killed in 1940 by a bomb. It also gave the name of the hospital to which the injured had all been taken – St Bart's in Smithfield.

Cedric banged a clenched fist on his desk and exclaimed, 'Gotcha!'

*

Billie was sitting up reading *Schoolfriend* when Liz and Duke appeared by her bed. Liz was holding a newspaper. Neither she nor Duke was smiling.

'Who's this?' said Billie.

'He's a good friend of mine,' said Liz.

'I got a phone call this morning from our banjo player,' said Duke.

'Banjo player?' said Billie.

'He's got a band,' explained Liz. 'He knew your dad.'

'He told me you were in the paper,' said Duke.

'Who did?'

'My banjo player.'

Liz handed the paper to Billie and pointed at the relevant column. She read it and looked up at him. 'Wow! I've never been in the paper before. You're in it as well, Auntie Liz.'

'I know,' said Liz, still not smiling.

Billie wondered what was wrong, then she realised.

'Oh, heck! What if Uncle Cedric reads it?'

'Oh, heck's right,' said Duke. 'Cedric will most likely know by now. Someone's bound to have told him.'

'Do you know Uncle Cedric?'

'Not personally.'

'I don't like him.'

'Not many people do,' said Duke.

'Were you a friend of my dad's?'

'I was, yes. We played in the same ban—'

The ward sister interrupted them then, sounding annoyed. 'This isn't visiting time,' she said.

'I'm sorry, Sister,' said Liz, 'but we needed to see Billie on an important personal matter.'

'I suppose the people downstairs are here on a personal matter as well.'

'What people?' said Liz.

'Reception's just rung to check that Miss Challinor is on this ward. Apparently her uncle and another man are here on an urgent matter as well.'

'Uncle?' said Liz.

'I haven't got any uncles,' said Billie, who had realised what was happening. 'I've only got Auntie Liz.'

'I bet they're from one of the papers,' said Duke. 'There's something in the *Herald* about her.'

Billie handed the ward sister the newspaper. She read it and spun on her heel, saying, 'Well, we'll soon get rid of them!'

'Do you think she will get rid of them?' asked Billie when Sister had departed.

Duke shook his head. 'My guess is that they're on their way here right now. Cedric's type don't get fobbed off by receptionists. The one downstairs is probably a fiver richer and they're on their way up. They'll know which ward and which bed number.'

'Surely they can't just snatch Billie away from hospital?' said Liz.

'Liz, that man has influence in all sorts of places. It's a risk we shouldn't take.' Duke looked around and saw an empty wheelchair out in the corridor. Within twenty seconds it was by Billie's bed.

'Billie, you need to get in this chair. They could be here any minute.'

Duke helped her into the chair as Liz grabbed her clothes from the bedside cabinet. They rushed her down a corridor to the lifts just as one was arriving. Duke accelerated and pushed Billie around a corner, out of sight, as the lift doors opened. Liz stood there, knowing that if Cedric were in the lift he wouldn't recognise her. He was and he didn't.

He and his companion strode purposefully down the corridor. Liz stuck a raised thumb around the corner, indicating that it was safe for the others to get in the lift. Two minutes later they were on the ground floor heading towards the exit just as Cedric was asking a nurse where the occupant of bed nine was.

'She must have gone to the toilet. A nurse will have taken her.'

A girl in the next bed said, 'Some people came for her. They took her away in a wheelchair.'

'When?'

'Just now. It was a man and a woman. The lady had a bandage on her head. The man was a big black man.'

'Did she know them?' enquired the nurse.

'The lady's the one who came to visit her,' said the girl. 'She was hurt at the same time as Billie. I think she was Billie's aunt. She's a really nice lady.'

Cedric cursed under his breath, 'Liz bloody Morris!'

His companion remarked, 'Could have been the woman outside the lift just now. She had a bandaged head.'

'Hardly unusual in a hospital,' said Cedric, disparagingly. 'And where was the black man and the kid in a wheelchair?' He turned to the girl in the next bed.

'How long since they left?'

'Just now.'

'They had no right taking her away!' snapped the nurse. 'She needs a lot of treatment before she can be discharged.'

But Cedric and his heavy were already running out of the ward.

'I don't like those men,' said the girl in the next bed.

'No,' said the nurse. 'I wasn't too struck on them myself.'

Liz, Billie and Duke were approaching the hospital exit when Duke said, 'He'll probably know by now that Billie's just been taken away. My guess is that he'll have a car waiting outside whereas we need to find a taxi. We can't afford to be hanging around waiting for one. I'd have brought the van but it's got a flat tyre and the spare's a bit dodgy.'

'That way.' Liz pointed to some double doors on their left, above which a sign read *Men's Surgical, Men's Medical, X-ray.*

They went through the doors and hurried past crowded waiting areas. They found a sign directing them to a non-denominational chapel, into which they pushed Billie. There were just three rows of pews inside the dimly lit room. There was an arched, stained-glass window, a small pulpit and half a dozen flickering candles alight in a rack. Liz sat down, gratefully. Duke was positioning Billie's chair when he introduced himself.

'I'm Duke, by the way.'

'Duke Wellington?'

'That's me.'

'Hello, Duke. Liz told me about you but I heard Daddy talk about you as well. You're not really a duke, are you?'

'Nope. I'm Duke as in Marmaduke Arthur Wellington.'

'Marmaduke? I must say that's too fine a name only to use the Duke bit.'

'Why, thank you, young lady.'

Billie looked at the candles, then at Liz. 'Auntie Liz, can I light a candle for Mum and Daddy?'

Liz was looking at the door, hoping that Cedric hadn't followed them, wondering if it was possible to lock it. Billie's question distracted her.

'What? Yes, light two.'

She opened her handbag and her purse. 'Here's a shilling, light one for us as well. We might need a bit of divine intervention.'

Duke smiled as he pushed Billie over towards the candles. 'How're you feelin', Billie, with all your aches and pains?'

'Well, they give me tablets for the pain and I'd only just had some before you came so I should be okay for a bit.'

With Duke's help she lit three candles, after which he stood by respectfully as she said a silent prayer.

'Your daddy was a fine man,' he said, after she'd finished praying. 'And your mom was a fine lady.'

'You knew my mum?'

'Sure did. In fact I knew you as well. First met you when you was a tiny baby.'

'Wow! I never knew that.'

Liz came up beside them. 'Duke, what are we going to do now?'

'Not sure. We haven't had too much time to think this through.'

'We haven't had *any* time to think this through. We

can't just take Billie out of hospital, she needs care and attention for weeks yet.'

'I don't want to stay if Cedric knows I'm here,' said Billie.

'Right now,' said Liz, 'he doesn't know *where* you are.'

'He'll know who took her,' said Duke. 'Other kids in the ward will have seen us. We're a bit conspicuous. Big black guy and a woman with a bandage on her head.'

'The hospital might well report this to the police,' Liz said. 'In fact, with Billie being a child, I think they'll definitely report it to the police.'

'Which means we gotta get out of here without *anyone* seein' us. Never mind Cedric.'

'How do we do that?'

Billie was looking up from one to the other as she followed the conversation.

'We need a vehicle,' said Duke. He looked at Liz. 'Did we just see a sign saying *Ambulance Station* and *Exit*?'

Liz nodded, nervously.

'I'll go and check it out.'

'No,' said Liz. 'How many big black guys do you think there are around here? I'll check it out.'

She unclipped the safety pin holding her bandage in place and began to unwind it. Duke helped her until her wound was revealed. The stitching had been done without her hair having been shaved so the wound was easy to cover.

'There,' she said. 'No big black guy, no woman with a bandaged head. I'll need to keep the walking stick, though.'

There was a door to one side of the chapel. Liz opened it to investigate. Behind it was a small ante-room. On the wall were several clerical-looking robes. She tried on a couple until she got a reasonable fit, and presented herself to Duke and Billie.

'What do think? Do I look like a woman of importance?'

'Yes, you do,' said Duke. 'Not sure what exactly, but you sure look like a person who commands a certain amount of respect.'

'So, I don't look like an ambulance thief?'

Billie was astounded. Duke shook his head. 'You look like a hand-maiden of the Lord.'

'Good,' said Liz. 'Now I must hope that the Lord leads me to an empty ambulance with a key in the ignition.'

'You sure you can drive an ambulance?'

'Duke, I can't drive anything. You're the driver, I assume you can drive it.'

'I can drive it.'

'If I don't come back for you, I suggest you ring the police and tell them our story and how we need to get Billie away from the Ellikers. The police will know of them so some of them at least should be on your side, especially if Billie backs you up. You haven't taken her out of the hospital, you just brought her down to the chapel to pray for her mum and dad, so you haven't done anything wrong.'

Duke grinned. 'No, that starts when we drive away together in an ambulance. We'll take her to the club and make our plans from there.'

*

298

Liz left Billie and Duke sitting side by side, both deep in thought as befitted people inhabiting such a place, only their thoughts weren't spiritual. They were both wondering if Liz could commandeer an ambulance or, if not, what? The 'what' seemed the most likely outcome, and was occupying most of their thoughts until Billie broke the silence.

'If she's caught, will she go to prison?'

'No, no, of course not.'

'Good.'

The silence resumed. Liz walked along the corridor, following the signs for the ambulance station. Right turn down here. Double door in front of her leading outside. It opened up on to a concrete platform beyond which were parked two ambulances. One was backed right up to the platform so that the occupant could be wheeled straight out without having to be carried down any steps. A door to her right was just closing, presumably behind the ambulance driver who had parked there. She took the three steps down from the platform, walked around the side of the vehicle with fingers crossed and looked in the cab. Sigh of brief exultation that ambulance drivers are such a trusting breed. A key was sticking out of the ignition. She opened the door, took out the key and stuck it in her pocket.

Three minutes later she was back in the chapel. 'Okay, we're in business.'

'You got the key?'

She handed it to Duke. He spun the wheelchair around and they headed out of the door.

Liz was suddenly aware that any sighting of them would

make them suspects in the theft of the ambulance, which was surely a much greater crime than keeping an eight-year-old girl out of the hands of the Ellikers.

'Run, Duke. I'll try to keep up.'

Ten minutes later, when the ambulance driver came back through the door to park up his vehicle, it was gone. He stood on the edge of the platform looking down at where it had so recently been, as if it might give him a clue as to where his vehicle had gone. He was now in serious trouble. He'd left an expensive ambulance with its key in the ignition, but everybody did that. It was on hospital grounds. There was a war on. What sort of low-life steals an ambulance?

Meanwhile the people responsible for his problems were parking in a deserted side street near Lincoln's Inn Fields. Duke got out and walked around the back to open the door. 'We can leave the ambulance here and walk it in ten minutes.'

He lifted Billie and her wheelchair out, shut the doors and stuck the key back in the ignition. One minute after he'd parked up the unlikely trio was heading west to Tin Pan Alley. One hour after that a passing vagrant took an interest in the ambulance, hoping it contained the drugs he needed to take away the pain of his existence. The ambulance contained no drugs but it did have a key in the ignition and he knew how to drive. Three hours after that he ran out of petrol in Folkestone and thus started a new episode in his life. A stay by the sea.

Chapter 49

'Fallon and Fallon.'

'Hello, my name's Elizabeth Morris, I'd like to speak to Mr, er ... oh, dear, I don't know which Mr Fallon I want.'

'There is only one nowadays. Mr Fallon Senior died a few years ago.'

'Oh, I didn't know.'

'I'll put you through.'

Liz was ringing from Duke's club where she and Billie had been given a comfortable refuge away from the clutches of Cedric.

'Hello, Mrs Morris, how may I help you?' asked the solicitor.

Liz told him the whole story, including the V2 rocket explosion and how they'd sneaked Billie out of hospital, ending with her asking how much trouble she might be in with the police.

'Hard to say. Possibly none, possibly some. I need you to give me the name of the hospital so I can inform them that you've been in touch and are applying to be the girl's legal guardian ... something you are legally entitled to do. I'm puzzled as to why this Cedric Elliker even wants to be the child's guardian, given the animosity he seems to feel towards her.'

'It was puzzling me too, but an old friend of Chas's thinks it might be something to with her grandfather's will. He died some months ago and although he cut Chas out of his will it doesn't mean to say he'd cut his grand-daughter out.'

'He cut his son out? Any particular reason?'

'Yes. Chas marrying an Elliker. His father disapproved strongly.'

'Ah, the dreaded Ellikers. I must learn more about them. Are there any other possible beneficiaries to this will?'

'I believe Chas was an only child and Billie is Mr Challinor's only grandchild, but who knows what a man puts in his will?'

'Mr Challinor's solicitor will know.'

'How do I find out who Mr Challinor Senior's solicitor is?'

'Do you know his company address?'

'Hang on . . .' There was a pause as Liz took a piece of paper from her pocket. 'It's called H. G. Challinor Limited and the address is forty-three Temple Place, Highgate.'

Fallon wrote these details down. Liz asked him, 'Do you want my address and phone number here?'

'Mrs Morris, as a solicitor I'm an officer of the court. If the police ask me where you are I'll be obliged to tell them . . . that's if I know. So, where are you staying?'

'None of your business.'

'Ring me back tomorrow morning. I'll see what I can turn up.'

*

The following morning Billie's analgesic had worn off and she was in considerable pain. Liz had been sleeping in a camp bed beside her.

'Bad, is it?'

'They gave me injections in the hospital so that it didn't hurt.'

'That was a children's dose of morphine. You can only get that in a hospital, we can't do it here. All we can give you is aspirin. I'm sorry about this but we didn't have much time to think things through.'

'Will the pain go away?'

'Of course it will. I'll see if Duke's got anything. Can you handle it in the meantime?'

'Dunno, but I don't want to go back to Uncle Cedric.'

'That's not going to happen.'

Duke said he might be able to get hold of something stronger than aspirin but: 'I ain't no doctor, Liz. I think it better she handles it without anything too strong until it goes away.'

'I'll give her the aspirin. She's a tough kid.'

'If it gets too bad I know a doctor who'll take a look at her and maybe give her something, but in my opinion the fewer people who know about Billie being here, the better.'

'Who else knows?'

'Just us three. You ringin' that lawyer guy today?'

'I am, yes, but he doesn't even want to know where we are.'

'Sounds like one of the good lawyers. I don't know too many of them.'

*

Liz rang Fallon an hour later. 'Do you have anything for me?'

'I do. Chas's father was called Herbert Gordon Challinor and his solicitors are Blackburn, Fielding in Watling Street in the City. I've taken the liberty of arranging an appointment for you to meet Mr Fielding at ten tomorrow morning. You'll need to take Chas Challinor's will and Billie with you. Can you manage that?'

'I can.'

'You'll be given a copy of Herbert Challinor's will. I've asked for this meeting to remain highly confidential in case Cedric Elliker gets wind of it. Mr Fielding knows of the Elliker family and fully understands the need for caution. He's also informed me that Cedric Elliker has recently been given power of attorney over Billie Challinor's estate. Does she know this?'

'I doubt if Billie even knows she has an estate. Can this power of attorney be rescinded or something?'

'Once you become Billie's legal guardian you can have it transferred to you.'

'How long will that take?'

'We could do the whole thing in a week or so if we start now. Do you wish me to go ahead with it?'

'Yes, please. Will we have to come up to Leeds?'

'No, we have an associate practice which handles our business down there. How is the girl?'

'She's in pain. If it gets too bad we'll call in a doctor to see her.'

'Good.' The lawyer paused then added, 'This is very much off the record but I'm given to understand, from our London associates, that the Ellikers have undue influence in London. They have people in their pockets in many places, including the police and the courts. Even if you get guardianship and power of attorney it might not stop them trying to get their hands on the Challinor fortune.'

'Fortune? Just how much money is involved?'

'This is also very much off the record, but according to our London associates Mr Challinor had extensive business interests so it could amount to well over a million – perhaps several millions. The will hasn't been finalised yet but Blackburn, Fielding are the executors and I'm told it may take several more weeks, if not months, to administer the will properly.'

'Did they say if Billie's in it?'

'If she's to be given a copy, we may assume so.'

'So she could be rich?'

'She could be the beneficiary of something large, something small.'

'Cedric seems to think it's something large. How would he know?'

'I raised this very point with Mr Fielding and it's a matter of concern to him that someone in his firm may have been giving out confidential information.'

'Could this person have already told Elliker that Billie and I are going to see Fielding tomorrow?'

'Mr Fielding assures me that no one else in his firm knows of the meeting. Only him.'

'I hope he's right.'

'Ring me as soon as the meeting is over.'

Chapter 50

Detective Chief Inspector Dundas of the Metropolitan Police tried to conceal his exasperation with Cedric, who was berating him.

'It's a bloody ambulance, for God's sake. A big white van with *Ambulance* written on the side. How the hell can your people not find it?'

Dundas wanted to tell him that looting in London had reached an all-time high and his men were struggling to cope as it was without chasing stolen ambulances, but he didn't want Cedric as an enemy. He had influence much higher up the ranks, possibly as high as Assistant Commissioner. Dundas would love to have something cast-iron on Cedric Elliker; something that wouldn't just go away when it came to the notice of the police hierarchy. Elliker had begun shouting the second Dundas answered the phone and so far the inspector hadn't been able to get a word in.

'We have found it,' he said, when Elliker finally paused to draw breath.

'What?'

'I said, we have found it.'

'Where?'

'In Folkestone.'

'Folkestone? What the hell's it doing there?'

The Folkestone police had found the ambulance with its driver's door swinging open and key in the ignition. Had it not been out of petrol it would have been at the mercy of another thief. It had been easy to trace it back to St Bart's but the thief or thieves had not been found nor were they likely to be. Folkestone had bigger problems to solve apparently, with it being right under the flight path of the V2s.

'And have you found my niece, who was in that ambulance?' Cedric hectored him.

'I'm afraid not.'

'Then I suggest you get your bloody finger out and find her or I'll know the reason why!'

'That's up to the Folkestone police right now, Mr Elliker. They have been notified that your niece might have been in the ambulance.'

'Might? How do you mean, might? Of course she was in the bloody ambulance!'

Dundas knew he was being berated by one of the biggest crooks in London and was powerless to retaliate.

'We have no jurisdiction in Folkestone, Mr Elliker, and we are rather busy ... what with there being a war on.'

'Really? It's not as though you're out there fighting on the frontline, is it? If our boys out there were as useless as you we'd have lost the war years ago.'

Dundas had had enough of this man. 'Until I was invalided out I spent three years fighting in Africa, Mr Elliker. How does that compare with your war record?'

Cedric slammed the phone down. Dundas cursed at the receiver and immediately dialled his superior.

'Sir, I've just had a roasting from Cedric Elliker about us not finding his missing niece. He was most insulting to the police and I'm afraid I lost my temper with him. I only hope this doesn't come back to haunt me.'

'Yes, I've heard about his missing niece from higher up. Been told to make a special effort to find her.'

'It seems to me that Mr Elliker wields undue authority with our superiors, which makes our job much harder.'

'It does indeed.'

There the conversation ended, but Dundas was happy he'd made his point.

Chapter 51

Duke came upstairs to pass on a piece of news to Liz and Billie. His clientele included quite a few jazz enthusiasts from the ranks of the police. There had been a piece in the *Evening Standard* about the stolen ambulance and Duke took the opportunity to bring it up in conversation as he poured one of the coppers a drink.

'I was readin' about an ambulance bein' stolen from a hospital. What the hell is the world comin' to? People stealin' ambulances. Have you guys found it yet?'

'Apparently it turned up in Folkestone.'

'Folkestone, eh?' said Duke, taking the policeman's money. 'Must be a joy rider. Stealin' an ambulance and taking it to the seaside. Some people, eh?'

'Yeah, some people.'

Later Duke knocked politely on Liz's door and entered when she said, 'Come in, Duke.'

He came in and sat on Liz's empty bed. 'Are you two okay in here?'

'So far so good,' said Liz. 'I'll be glad when we can get this thing settled legally. Trouble is the solicitor reckons that me having legal custody of Billie might not stop Elliker trying to get his hands on the Challinor money.'

'I might be rich, Duke,' put in Billie.

'I sure do hope so, honey. How's your aches and pains?'

'Not bad. My leg's beginning to itch now and I can't scratch it.'

Duke laughed. 'Oh, ain't I been there, Billie? Broke my leg once and the itchin' nearly drove me mad until I got me a drumstick to poke down my pot an' give it a good ole scratch.'

'Could you get me a drumstick, Duke?'

'Sure can, honey. In fact, I still got that very same drumstick in my room just in case I ever break my leg again. I'll bring it to you right this very minute. Oh, before I do, I need to tell you the ambulance has been found.' He paused for a while before adding, with a broad grin, 'In Folkestone. Some chancer must have jumped in and taken it for a drive to the seaside.'

'Where's Folkestone?' asked Billie.

'Many miles from here.'

'Which is where the police will think we are,' said Liz.

'Oh, good. Can you get me that drumstick, Duke?'

'Sure can, honey.'

Chapter 52

Lavinia entered Cedric's office without knocking. He looked up, ready to slate whoever it was who had walked in without his permission, but held his tongue as his wife sat down in front of him.

'So?' she said.

He threw down his fountain pen on the document in front of him and spilled ink all over it. 'Blast and damn it! I need another copy of this bloody thing now! What the hell do you want?'

'What the hell do I want? I'm in this thing as well, you know. What have you found out from Folkestone?'

'Nothing as yet.'

'Because you've got no one in the Folkestone police in your pocket?'

'What I've got are connections. One connection connects with another and so on until we make the right connection.'

'And?'

'And it's cost me an arm and a leg for a Folkestone detective inspector. I've put him on wages to track the girl down.'

'Anything so far?'

'I only set him on an hour ago. Folkestone's not a big town, they should find her soon.'

'And when they do?'

'When they do my legal people will remind the courts and the police that I'm her legal guardian, and the courts will uphold it.'

'How do you know it'll go in front of the right judge?'

'Trust me, that won't be a problem.'

'What if she tries to run away again?'

'Right now she can't run anywhere without help. All we have to do is make sure she doesn't get any. Hopefully she'll be disabled right up until this will is settled. Which might well turn out to our advantage.'

'If we find the girl.'

'If she's still in Folkestone we'll find her.'

'What if she's not in Folkestone?'

'Lavinia, she's an eight-year-old girl with a broken leg, on the run with a woman who doesn't know her arse from her elbow. How long do you think it'll be before she comes to my attention? I've got two coppers in Leeds on the lookout as well.'

'All this must be costing a fortune.'

'But it's chickenfeed compared to the millions that're waiting there for us to collect once we get Billie back.'

Chapter 53

Duke and Liz lifted Billie and her wheelchair into the back of Duke's van and headed for Watling Street and the appointment with Mr Fielding, Herbert Challinor's solicitor. Billie's pain was becoming manageable and she was feeling quite chirpy; in fact, embarrassingly so.

'How old are you, Duke?' she asked.

'As old as my feet and a bit older than my teeth.'

This amused Billie who decided to memorise it. 'My dad always said he was twenty-one when I asked him, but I know he wasn't. He didn't tell lies but he did like joking. My daddy was twenty-nine when he died. He was born on the seventeenth of July nineteen fourteen and he died on the seventh of June nineteen forty-four. That's not very old for a man, is it?'

'It's very young,' said Duke.

'So, how old are you?'

'I'm thirty-five, young lady.'

'And are you married?

'Nope.'

'Why not?'

'Billie!' scolded Liz.

'I was just asking. He's very handsome and he make us laugh and he plays the piano.'

'That's very kind of you. Maybe if I wait a few years you might marry me.'

'I'd have to be at least twenty. Would you wait that long?'

'For you, I'd wait twice as long.'

'Wow!'

Billie went quiet for a while then said, 'I wouldn't mind if you married Auntie Liz. Then neither of you would have to wait any longer. How old are you, Auntie Liz?'

Neither Liz nor Duke was comfortable with the direction this conversation was taking. 'Billie,' Liz said, 'don't you know it's rude to ask people their ages?'

'Don't see why. People always ask me how old I am. I just tell them I'm eight because it's what I am.'

'I'm guessin' your Auntie Liz is about thirty,' said Duke.

'That's what I thought,' said Billie.

'Okay,' said Liz. 'I'll be thirty if it makes you both happy.'

'We're here,' said Duke.

'Not before time,' said Liz.

Luckily there was a lift to Mr Fielding's third-floor office. Duke travelled up with them and waited outside in a reception area as Liz and Billie were shown into Mr Fielding's office by his secretary.

Fielding got to his feet and came round his desk to greet them. 'I'm sorry if it's been a problem for you to bring Billie here, Mrs Morris, but it is necessary, with her being the major beneficiary.'

'How do you know this is Billie?' asked Liz, curiously.

Fielding smiled. 'Excellent question, and the answer is there was a recent photograph of her in Mr Challinor's effects. His son must have sent it to him some time before he went overseas.'

'I get the impression his father died before Chas?' said Liz.

'Only just. He passed away on the fifth of June.'

'Three days before.'

'A father shouldn't outlive his son,' said Billie.

Fielding and Liz looked at her with some amazement. Billie smiled. 'I heard it on the wireless last week and it made me wonder if my granddad had died after my dad, but he didn't, so that's the proper way, isn't it?'

'Yes, it is the proper way, young lady,' said Fielding. 'Did you ever meet your grandfather?'

'I think so, when I was very young. I don't remember him so I don't know if I liked him or not.'

'I suspect he liked you.' He put on his spectacles and turned his attention to Liz. 'Did you bring Charles Challinor's will?'

Liz got it out of her bag and handed it to him. He scrutinised it and nodded with satisfaction at the part where Chas requested that Liz be Billie's guardian. He then took Herbert Challinor's will out of a drawer and untied the ribbon holding it closed. Liz felt a surge of excitement she hadn't expected. This was the first time she'd been to the reading of a will, much less the will of a millionaire. She looked at Billie, who seemed more interested in a picture of the king on the wall. Fielding cleared his throat to attract her attention.

'Right. This is a fairly complicated document so I won't read it out in detail or we'll be here all day. There were several small bequests made to employees and a couple of charities, but the important bequest is that the deceased left his companies, which are listed, and all of his properties, also listed, and all his investments . . . once again there are details of each one . . . ' He looked up at Billie and Liz as he itemised the extent of the legacy. 'He left all of this to his son, Charles Herbert Challinor, and then in trust to his granddaughter Billie Challinor.'

This didn't register with Billie but Liz was stunned. 'You mean, Billie gets the lot?'

'Yes, that's what it means. I'm afraid I can't give you a final figure or anything because it's still with the accountants, who are negotiating with the Inland Revenue and various other creditors, but I am empowered to give Billie an advance from our client account of one thousand pounds.'

'Wow!' said Billie, who understood that bit.

'I understand you'll be requiring a transfer of power of attorney, Mrs Morris, so first of all you must establish yourself as Billie's legal guardian. After that it's a formality.'

'What about Cedric Elliker?'

'Mr Elliker cannot interfere with the wishes of the girl's late father, nor has he any cause to object to the transfer of power of attorney.'

'I'm told he won't need any cause,' commented Liz.

'His consent or lack of it is immaterial. After the transfer has been made the court will notify him that he no longer has power of attorney.'

'But he can't do anything right now because things haven't been settled?'

'Correct. The wheels of the law turn very slowly.'

'Lucky for Billie they do, otherwise her uncle would have taken everything from her.'

'It would certainly have been possible. Anyway, after you've established power of attorney I'll send the cheque for a thousand direct to you.'

Chapter 54

'Auntie Liz, if I get to the door and back three times can we go out somewhere?'

'In the wheelchair maybe. I'm thinking this Folkestone thing might have put Cedric off our scent.'

Duke had acquired a pair of crutches from an injured soldier customer who had ceremonially thrown them away in his club. Duke had had to do quite a lot of work to adjust them down to Billie's size, but they were serviceable and she was getting quite proficient with them.

'Wow! Do you think he's got spies all over London?'

'Don't know what he's got, Billie. I know a lot of people work for him one way or another.'

'I bet he's got their names in his stupid book.'

Billie was on her second journey from the bed to the door, swinging her injured leg quite expertly. Liz was nodding her head in approval.

'What book's that?' she asked, conversationally.

'Oh, it's something I nicked off Uncle Cedric, to get my own back for him shouting at me.'

'Did he shout at you a lot?'

'Not really. But that one time I walked into his room when he was writing something in his stupid book he went bonkers. He locked me in a cupboard under the stairs.'

'Did he now? I wonder why he went so bonkers?'

'I think it was because of the book. When I nicked it I was really scared. Wished I hadn't actually, 'cos if Uncle Cedric had found out it was me I reckon he might have killed me, he was so mad.'

'Oh, I don't think he'd have killed you, Billie. You're much too precious to him.'

'So's his stupid book. I once heard him talking about it to his brothers. They were arguing about him not keeping it safe or something.'

'How come you could hear all this?'

Billie grinned as she commenced the last leg of her third lap. 'His office was just under my bedroom. I lifted the carpet and found a loose floorboard. When I lifted that up I could hear what they were talking about.'

Liz was by now keenly interested. 'And what were they talking about?'

'Aw, stuff about millions of cigarettes mainly. There were going to get a big truckload of cigarettes from somewhere and sell them to someone. I think smoking's a bad habit. You shouldn't smoke, Auntie Liz. The teacher at my new school says we shouldn't start to smoke when we grow up because it's very bad for us.'

'So, what were they saying about the book?'

'Auntie Liz, I've done it three times, can we go out now?'

'What? Oh, yes, of course we can go out. But first, Billie, I'd like you to tell me as much as you can about this book.'

Billie pulled a face, wishing she'd never mentioned the stupid book if it was going to get in the way of her going out. She sighed and sat down on her bed. 'He called it his leg . . . .led . . . '

'Ledger?' said Liz.

'That's it. His ledger. When I went into his office I stood there for ages without him knowing I was there. I watched him writing stuff in it.'

'What sort of stuff?'

'Dunno, it was upside down from where I was standing, just lists of stuff – writing and numbers and stuff. It must be important because his brothers were worried that he might lose it or something.' She grinned. 'He's lost it now because I nicked it! Serves him right as well.'

'What did you do with it?'

'I hid it in the cupboard he locked me in.'

'So, he might have found it by now?'

'Don't think so. I hid it under the floorboards. It's a massive big book. There must be loads of loose floorboards in that house. Dropping to bits, if you ask me.'

'Well, it's an old house,' said Liz, her brain going into overdrive.

'So, can we go out now?'

'Later. I'm just going to have a word with Duke.'

'Aw, blimey, Auntie Liz. You promised!'

Chapter 55

Four days had gone by with no sign of Billie. Cedric was becoming increasingly worried, not just about his missing niece but also his ledger. The two items were of equal importance so far as his future was concerned. One guaranteed his financial security; the other guaranteed his freedom from prosecution. If either of his brothers had the book they were expert at concealing the fact, more expert than he'd ever given them credit for. He was beginning to fear the worst: that someone from outside the family had taken it. But how? There had never been any sign of a break in. He'd blamed the girl at first, but she couldn't have got it out of the house. It was much too big for her to smuggle out unnoticed, much too big to fit in her school bag, probably too heavy for her to carry any great distance, and it most certainly wasn't in the house. He and Lavinia had almost taken the place to pieces in their search for it. He'd even found a loose floorboard in Billie's bedroom and for a moment he'd had a feeling of triumph, but it was short-lived. The ledger wasn't there.

He was having difficulty concentrating on what was supposed to be his proper job, as a solicitor in a busy central London practice. That day he was at home, pacing across the carpet in the living room and annoying Lavinia with his restlessness.

'For God's sake, Cedric, go to work. Take your mind off things. Like you say, you'll probably get the girl back, and even if you don't it's not the end of the world. You haven't done anything illegal so far as she's concerned.'

'It's the damned ledger as much as anything! I've a good mind to confront my bloody brothers and see what comes of it.'

'That might not be a bad idea.'

'Trouble is, if they both deny knowledge of it, where does it leave me?'

'One of them's got it, Cedric. They're a lot more devious than you give them credit for. Nearly as devious as you.'

This drew a wry smile from her husband. 'Yeah, you're right. How could they not have it? No, I'll just let whoever nicked it stew for a while.'

'Who do you think it is?'

'I think the hot favourite's Edgar.'

'So do I.'

'Might have a quiet word in his ear.'

'Wait a bit. What about the other ledgers?'

'You mean my dad's?'

'Yes. I think you should burn them.'

Cedric paced up and down the room. 'Yes, you're probably right. There's nothing in them I need any more. All the good stuff's in mine.'

'But they're historically incriminating. Records of the things you did for him when he was in charge. No good stuff in them, just stuff that's bad for you.'

'You're right. I'll burn them.'

A van pulled up outside. Lavinia slid aside a net curtain to see who it was. It was a small van with *Chartered Gas Light and Coke Company* written on the side. A uniformed man got out and walked up the drive.

'Gasman,' she said. 'I'll go.'

Cedric continued with his pacing as his wife, out in the hall, unlocked the door to the meter cupboard under the stairs. She came back into the room and shook her head at him. 'For God's sake, go and see Edgar then. This is getting ridiculous!'

'I can't, he's out of town today.'

The gasman gave a shout from the hall to say he'd finished and would show himself out. Lavinia shouted back 'Okay' and picked up the telephone receiver. 'I'm going to ring Edgar's house myself and tell them to get him over here as soon as possible,' she informed Cedric.

Half an hour later the same small van pulled up outside the Crazy Dazy Club on Denmark Street. The uniformed man got out and went inside. Liz was waiting for him. He took Cedric's ledger from his bag, put it on the bar and said, 'Sweet as a nut.'

Liz looked from the ledger to Duke, who was in the gasman's uniform which a theatrical costumier had made for him. The van was Duke's and was a similar basic colour to the company's van. He'd had it lettered with transfers to make it look more or less genuine. Liz wondered what they'd have done without him. He gave her one of his broad smiles. She stood up on tiptoe and kissed him on the lips. Just a peck, but full on his lips.

'My, my,' he said. 'Such a handsome reward for so little work.'

'It went okay, then?'

'Like I said, sweet as a nut. There was a second when I thought she was going to stand over me, but I went right inside the cupboard and she left me to it. The place was just as Billie described. Loose board, and the book right where she said it was. I was in and out in half a minute. The only thing I omitted to do was read the meter.'

Liz laughed and opened the ledger. It had times, names, dates, various notes and amounts of money dating back to 1939. Duke took a look too and flicked through the more recent pages. He glanced up at Liz.

'There was a jewel robbery on Bond Street back in May. There's a note in here naming the very shop, the people the stuff was fenced to, the amounts paid and who was on the job – one Elliker and three others. Jesus, Liz, this book is dynamite! We need to get it to the police straight away.'

She gave the matter some thought. 'I don't want to rush into this. I'm going to speak to Mr Fallon first and see what he says.'

'You're telling me you don't trust the police?'

'Not all of them, Duke. We have to find someone the Ellikers haven't got to first – and that could take a while.'

Chapter 56

The following day Cedric was speaking to Edgar in his office. Lavinia went into the hall to put a pair of wellington boots she wore in the garden away in the understairs cupboard when she noticed something slightly amiss. A floorboard was sticking up slightly, as if it had been taken out and not put back properly. In their search for the ledger she'd checked this cupboard and hadn't noticed any loose floorboard then. Feeling puzzled, she went into the kitchen for a torch and checked more closely. She lifted up the floorboard and shone the torch into the cavity that was revealed. Beneath the wooden floor joists was a ten-inch gap and then rough concrete. Lying on the concrete was a rectangular piece of card, an inch wide and four inches long. She reached down and picked it up, recognising it instantly. The card had the flags of the Allied nations printed on both sides. She closed her eyes as she untangled her racing thoughts then cursed out loud at such stupidity. Seconds later she was bursting through the door of Cedric's office, waving the card in her hand. She put it on the desk in front of him. 'Do you know what this is?'

He looked down at it then at her. 'Yes, it's a bookmark I use in my ledger. Where did you get it?'

She looked closely at her brother-in-law Edgar. 'Has he asked you about the ledger?'

'Yes. I haven't got it.'

'Oh, I *know* you haven't got it.'

'How do you know that?' asked Cedric.

'Because it was hidden under the floorboards in the meter cupboard. That is where I found this bookmark. It must have dropped out of the ledger.'

'*Was* hidden,' said Cedric. 'You mean it's not there now?'

'No, not since that gasman came to read our meter.'

'WHAT?' Cedric sprang to his feet.

'The girl obviously took it from your office and put it there,' said Lavinia, 'which means the gasman's teamed up with her somehow ... only he isn't really a gasman. I imagine that woman who calls herself Auntie Liz is behind it all.'

'And they've got the bloody book!' roared Edgar. 'Jesus, Cedric, you've dropped the lot of us right in it!' He was on his feet by now, his face puce with rage. 'I knew that book wasn't safe with you, you bloody idiot!'

Cedric squared up to him, equally angry that his younger brother should disrespect him like this.

'Don't you call me an idiot! If it weren't for me you'd be doing time in Pentonville right n—'

Lavinia interrupted them both. 'Just calm down. I think I know where they are, and it isn't Folkestone.'

Cedric and Edgar stared at her in amazement. 'How the hell do you know where they are?' asked Cedric.

'Because when the gasman came I thought I'd seen his black face before. At the time I assumed it was because he'd been here to read the meter, but now I remember exactly where I've seen him. He's the nigger who plays the piano in that band Chas used to play in, and now he's got his own club on Denmark Street. It's called the Crazy Dazy. You've been there with me, Cedric.'

'I know the place,' said Edgar. 'Never been in, but I've heard of it.'

'I hate jazz,' Cedric exclaimed. 'Don't remember the feller, but if that's the case we need to get some people down there right now. I want that girl back here with me so we've got some leverage to do business with.' He looked at Edgar. 'Can you arrange that?'

His brother was still angry. 'I think someone'd better arrange it, pretty damn' quick. And it'd better be someone who knows what they're doing.'

'Don't harm the thieving little bitch!' snarled Cedric. Then added, 'Any more than you have to.'

Chapter 57

That same afternoon Liz was in the club preparing for that evening. Duke was busy rehearsing at the piano. She called out to him.

'Do you think we're safe here, Duke?'

'As long as Elliker thinks you're in Folkestone.'

'Have you ever had any Ellikers come in here?'

'Just once to my knowledge – about three months ago. I didn't see them personally. One of my guys mentioned Cedric had been in with his wife. I remember it because I didn't want my place to become a venue for villains.'

'Do you think it's safe for me to do bar work?'

'You wanna work the bar?'

'I need to do something while I'm waiting for the solicitors to sort things out and I daren't take her up to Leeds just yet.'

He stopped playing and gave this some thought. 'Should be okay. Whatcha gonna do about the book?'

'Nothing until I get proper custody of Billie and power of attorney. I've got an appointment in court in a couple of days. It can all be sorted out then. After that I'll notify Cedric that I've got his ledger.'

'I'm not sure that's such a good idea. Why not just hand it over to the police?'

'I'm not sure I trust the police, Duke. It might fall into the wrong hands.'

He resumed playing. Liz walked over and sat down to listen. He turned and smiled at her and she saw something in his smile that she'd never really seen in a man before, certainly not in Larry Morris. In Chas's smile she'd always seen friendship, but this wasn't a friendly smile. This was something else. She saw real affection in Duke's smile . . . and perhaps something more.

Whatever it was it made Liz feel good. She liked being around this man, and Billie was right, he was handsome, no mistake about that. How a handsome man like Duke had remained unmarried for so long suddenly puzzled her.

When he stopped playing Liz asked him, 'Duke, how come you're not married?'

He played a few bars of 'Little Woman Blues' then paused. 'I was married,' he said.

'Oh.'

'My wife died.'

Liz wanted to ask how it had happened but that seemed too intrusive a question somehow. If Duke wanted to tell her he would.

He played a few more bars then added, 'It was most prob'ly my fault she died.' He played some more then stopped again. 'It was back in Jamaica. I ran with a bad crowd. I wasn't so bad myself, but they was bad dudes and they moved among other bad dudes who was inclined to fightin'. One night I was out among my bad dudes, my Valeria was with me, and another crowd arrived who had

329

started a ruckus which ended in people getting stabbed, includin' my beautiful Valeria. She died in my arms. She was twenty-one years old. Never met anyone like her since. My God, she was a beautiful lady. Worst thing she ever did was to take up with a big lug like me.'

He played on with tears rolling down his face.

'I'm terribly sorry, Duke.'

'She was three months pregnant at the time.'

Liz waited until he'd finished playing the song, then asked, 'Did the police find out who did it?'

'Oh, I knew who did it. There was no need to inform the police, who was very open to bribery. We took care of our own problems back then. I took care of that one personally.' His gaze met hers and she knew exactly what it meant.

'I don't blame you,' Liz told him without looking away.

'I needed to do that thing and I did it. Then I came over here. My daddy was an Englishman, did I tell you that?'

'No, you didn't.'

'It's why I can live over here. I'm a bona-fide suntanned Englishman. Meant I had to go an' fight ole Hitler in a British regiment, but that was okay by me.'

Liz stepped up on to the stage and walked over to him. She took his tear-stained face in her hands and said, 'I know you'll never meet another Valeria but this is from me.'

She kissed him on the lips and felt him responding, although his hands still rested on the piano keys. She broke off and said, 'Billie wants to go for a walk, which means me pushing her wheelchair up to Oxford Street. I might need you to help her downstairs.'

Edgar and one of his men had been parked outside the Crazy Dazy for half an hour, waiting for a carload of hired thugs to arrive as back-up. The plan was to break into the club mob-handed, do whatever was necessary to subdue any resistance, and come away with the girl and, if possible, the book.

Edgar's face broke into a broad grin when he saw Duke and Liz helping Billie out of the front door in her wheelchair. He gave the matter a minute's thought as he watched them head off down Denmark Street and turn left at the bottom. He could get the girl without any problem but what about the damn' book? It was probably still in the club. But what if it wasn't? Picking up the girl and then going into the Crazy Dazy for the book would take more time than he wanted to spend in Soho during daylight hours. He wasn't exactly unknown in these parts. He'd handled abductions before and the secret was always in the timing. Scoop up the mark and be away before anyone around could react to what had happened. To hell with it! He'd take the girl and let his useless brother worry about reclaiming the book he'd lost to the kid. He signalled to his accomplice to start the motor.

'Follow them closely and pull up by the kerb just in front. No screeching of brakes, make it look as if you're parking the car.' The driver did as instructed. Edgar got out just as Liz and Billie were passing. He aimed a punch at Liz that knocked her to the ground. Almost in the same movement he lifted Billie from her wheelchair, threw her in the back of the car and jumped in after her. The car sped away down Charing Cross Road, the whole abduction having taken less than half a minute. Liz was sitting on the pavement, dazed. Passers-by ran over to her. The wheelchair lay on its side. Questions were coming at her from all around.

'Are you okay? Do you want us to ring the police? Did anyone get the car number?'

Liz looked down at the wheelchair that had a sticker saying *Property of St Bart's Hospital* on the frame. It was insignificant enough, but not when subject to police scrutiny. Was she ready to tell the whole story to them? Billie had been taken, it seemed the logical thing to do, but something was telling her not to. Not just yet.

'I'm okay,' she said. 'No need to involve the police.'

'Are you sure?'

'Who was in the wheelchair?'

Questions she was struggling to answer. She picked herself up and pushed the wheelchair back to the club as the bemused crowd dispersed.

Liz had been back in the club just half an hour when the phone rang. At this point she wasn't aware that Cedric knew she had the ledger. He'd obviously tracked her to the club somehow. Duke answered the phone.

'Put me on to Liz,' Cedric said, almost pleasantly.

Duke handed her the phone. 'I think it's him.'

'Yes,' said Cedric, overhearing this. 'It's him. I want to know where my niece is. I know you've got her.'

Liz put her hand over the mouthpiece and spoke to Duke. 'He wants to know where Billie is.'

'Tell him you're wondering the same thing yourself.'

Liz did just this and added, 'She was snatched off the street, as you well know, in front of dozens of people. The police have the car number so I should soon get her back.'

'That's if they didn't put a false number plate on the car,' said Cedric. 'I hear that villains do that, you know. Anyway, why should you get her back? I'm her legal guardian.'

'Because her father left instructions in his will that I should be Billie's guardian. His last wishes supersede any claim you might have made on her. The courts already know this. They also know you're just trying to get your slimy hands on her granddad's fortune.'

Cedric wasn't expecting this. His thoughts raced. 'So, you say she was kidnapped or something?'

'You know she was.'

'And you've reported this to the police?'

Liz hesitated then said, 'I had no need to. The, er, people who saw it rang them.'

Cedric spotted her hesitation. 'Have the police interviewed you?'

'Not yet, but they will.'

'Now that's very odd. You've had a child snatched from you in the street and the police haven't interviewed you yet? I'm not sure I believe any of this.'

'There's one thing you'd better believe,' retorted Liz. 'As soon as the police do turn up, I'll tell them where your book is.'

'Ah, my stolen ledger.'

'It's a bit more than that. I've had a good look at it. There's enough in there to have the whole Elliker family swinging from the gallows.'

'If it's so damning, why haven't you given it to the police already?'

'I have my reasons. And we both know how damning it is.'

'The tragedy is, you might never see Billie again if that ledger isn't returned safely.'

'You wouldn't dare harm her!'

'How could I harm her? I don't know where she is. The last I heard of her was when you abducted her from the hospital. In fact, I think it's my duty to report you to the police for doing that.'

'You'll only get your book if I get Billie back. You bring her here right now and I'll give you your rotten book. Billie's no use to you anyway. In two days I'll be her guardian and I'll have power of attorney. Plus, it'll be months before her granddad's will's sorted out. Everyone's rumbled your crooked game, you won't get away with it.'

Cedric was inwardly seething. Liz was right. If the courts had any grounds for suspicion he wouldn't be granted power of attorney, regardless of any claim Liz might make. He gave the matter some thought before he answered. She was also right about the danger to him and his family if the book got into the wrong hands. It had been risky keeping such a record but it had been necessary to maintain a hold over the underworld organisation he controlled. It occurred to Cedric that he might just be able to regain the book *and* keep the girl, but his devious scheme was already being foiled by Duke who was whispering to Liz. She nodded her agreement and waited for Cedric to speak.

'I want you to bring the book t—'

In a fit of anger she stopped him mid-sentence. 'I don't give a damn what you want, you bloody crook! I don't trust you as far as I can throw you. You bring her here personally in one hour from now or that book will be handed in to the police and I'll let *them* get her back for me.' Liz looked at her watch. 'That's ten past five on the dot. I want you and Billie to be coming through the front door of this club at exactly ten past five. There'll be a wheelchair in the entrance. You drive her here on your own, carry her from the car and put her in the wheelchair, then you bring her inside. The book will be on the table in front of you. Meanwhile I will be keeping a shotgun trained on you. Our people will be watching you arrive so don't try coming mob-handed. If you come in with anyone else we'll lock and bolt the doors from inside and ring the police.'

'My, my, you have people,' he said, sarcastically.

'I have *friends* – not a word I expect you to be familiar with. You come through the door on your own, except for Billie. You pick up your book and leave without her. Any funny business and I will shoot you.'

'How do I know I can trust you?'

'You don't. You just have my word, which is worth a lot more than yours. Ten past five, on the dot.'

Liz put down the phone and asked Duke, 'Is this going to work?'

'I think you're holdin' all the aces, honey. Billie ain't worth nuthin' to him no more. The book is vital to him. His whole life depends on it.'

'So, you think he'll turn up?'

'Oh, yes. I think he'll be hoping he can trust you.'

'Do you actually have a shotgun?'

'I do.'

'You're really sticking your neck out for me, Duke. I appreciate that.'

'Maybe I think you're worth it.'

Under less trying circumstances Liz might have pressed him to explain himself but Billie was foremost in her thoughts so she didn't. Perhaps when this was over . . .

At ten past five Liz was standing behind the bar, apparently on her own, when she heard the outer door to the club open and Billie talking to someone. Her heart quickened. Duke had been watching the street from an upstairs window and had seen Cedric pull up and carry the child inside. He was now behind a door at the back of the bar, talking through it to her.

'He's come on his own.'

Liz picked up the shotgun that had been resting on the bar. She'd had a few rudimentary instructions on how to hold it and where to point it, but nothing more. She aimed it at the opening door and was delighted to see Billie coming through it, pushed by Cedric. She lowered the barrel slightly and before Cedric could speak she rapped out an order.

'Shove Billie to one side!'

Liz indicated which side with the barrel of the gun. Cedric did as she asked and gave the wheelchair a shove that had it rolling ten feet away from him. His eyes were now fixed on the ledger that lay on a table before him.

'If this is a trick,' he warned, 'I'll come after you, be sure of that.'

Hatred of him welled up inside Liz then. She aimed the gun just to the left of him and pulled one of the two triggers. The recoil sent her staggering backwards and the deafening noise reverberated off the brick walls of the club. Cedric howled in pain as a few of the pellets ripped his sleeve and hit his left arm. He threw his right hand into the air in terror that she would fire the other barrel. Duke shot through the door just as Liz was regaining her composure.

'What the hell . . . ?'

'He threatened me,' she explained, meanwhile aiming the barrel at Cedric's face. 'If he threatens me again I'll blow his bloody head off!'

'You shouldn't threaten my auntie,' said Billie, now wheeling herself over to Liz.

Cedric's face was white, his whole body shaking. Blood was dripping down his sleeve on to his hand. 'All right, all right, just don't point that bloody thing at me!'

'Take your book and go, before I lose patience with you completely.' Liz walked around the bar, still aiming the gun at his head, and advanced on him until she was almost at the table where his book lay. Cedric took a couple of tentative steps forward and picked it up with his good hand.

'I assume it's all here.'

'Every vile page of it. We want you out of our lives for good, don't we, Billie?'

'Yes,' said the girl. Then added, mischievously, 'Why don't you shoot him properly, Auntie Liz?'

With beads of sweat glistening on his face, Cedric tucked the book under his right armpit and backed out of the door without saying another word. Liz moved out from behind the table and followed him until he'd gone through the street door, which she slammed and locked behind him. Duke went upstairs to ensure he'd driven away. When he came back down Billie and Liz were hugging each other. Liz was apologising profusely for allowing the girl to be taken.

'I heard Uncle Cedric talking to Auntie Lavinia,' Billie told her. 'He said something about once they got the book back, you had nothing on him so he could come and get you.'

Liz smiled at Duke, who was grinning broadly.

'What are you both grinning at?' asked Billie.

'I've got a copy of Cedric's book,' said Liz.

'But there's thousands of pages of stuff. Millions of words. I didn't see you copying anything.'

'Three hundred and twenty pages, actually,' said Liz. 'We had them all photographed by a pal of Duke's who's a photographer.'

'Have you got them back from the chemist yet?'

Liz and Duke laughed at this engaging child. 'Not yet, the man's developing them himself, but the book's all been photographed. It took him hours but we'll have clear photographs of every single page, just as Cedric wrote them.'

'Will it get him into trouble?'

'Yes, it will,' said Liz. 'Quite a lot of trouble.'

'I'm glad. He's horrible. So are my other uncles. I don't like any of them. I bet my mum didn't like them either.'

'She didn't,' said Duke, ruffling her hair. 'Glad to have you back so soon, Billie.'

Chapter 58

'May I speak to Helen Hawkins, please?'

'Can I ask what it's in connection with?'

'It's to do with the V2 rocket that hit Finsbury Park Cemetery.'

There was half a minute's pause as the switchboard operator cleared the call with Helen, then she announced, 'I'm putting you through now.'

'Helen Hawkins, how may I help you?'

'My name is Liz Morris, I was injured in the Finsbury Park bombing along with Billie Challinor. It's Billie I want to talk to you about. She's the niece of Cedric Elliker. Do you know him?'

Helen's pulse began to race. 'I know of him. Is this to do with, erm, Mr Elliker?'

'Oh, yes.'

'Then I'm interested. Where can we meet?'

'Do you know the Crazy Dazy Club on Denmark Street?'

'I do, yes, but isn't that a little noisy for an interview?'

'I live above the club, so does Billie. Ask for me at the bar, we can talk in our room.'

'When?'

'This evening at six thirty? It'll be well worth your while.'

'I'll be there.'

Cedric arrived home with the book, mightily relieved but angry at the way he'd been bested and humiliated by Liz, plus no longer having the Challinor fortune in his grasp. Lavinia greeted him at the door and was equally relieved to see the book. She looked at his arm which was in a sling.

'What happened?'

'The bitch shot me. I called in at the quack's on the way back.'

She took the book from him. 'There's a good fire going in the lounge. I think we should burn this.'

He shook his head. 'Not before I've made a coded version of it. We've lost the Challinor money. I need to stay in business.'

'You've got a business. You're a solicitor.'

'That pays peanuts compared to what we could be making.'

Helen Hawkins went straight into the club as directed by Liz. It had just opened up and there were very few customers in. Duke was behind the bar. Helen asked to see Liz and was shown upstairs by him.

Liz opened the door and introduced herself and Billie, who was sitting in the wheelchair. Helen showed appropriate concern for her welfare and that of Liz, but was really only interested in what they had to tell her about the Ellikers. Liz didn't disappoint her.

'Cedric Elliker keeps a written record of all his dealings: names, dates, amounts of money, people in their pay including police, judges, magistrates, council officials. Personally, I have little knowledge of his criminal activities but I'm told he's probably been involved in several murders. The book supports this. I believe there's enough evidence in it to send the whole Elliker family, plus a lot of their people, to the gallows.'

'Are you telling me you have this book?'

Liz looked at Billie. 'We did up to a few hours ago, but we had to give it back to Cedric when he abducted Billie on the street and threatened to kill her if I didn't give him the book back.'

'I stole the book and hid it when I lived with him,' explained Billie.

'I see, but you don't have it now?'

There was disappointment in Helen's voice. Liz spotted it and smiled. 'Not the actual book, but I did have time to have it all photographed by a professional photographer so we have all the information that's in it.'

The disappointment disappeared from Helen's face.

'Really?'

'Absolutely.'

Liz pointed to a dressing table on which stood a large box file. 'It's all in there. All three hundred and twenty pages of it. I'd give it to the police but there's evidence of widespread corruption in there and I couldn't be sure I was giving it to the right person.'

Helen went over and opened the box, which was full of expertly photographed pages, all written in Cedric's handwriting, as clear as the original, and numbered by him for his own convenience. Liz had pre-selected a few of them and placed them on the top of the pile.

'I picked out half a dozen, any of which should get the Ellikers locked up straight away. There're probably dozens more that'd do the same.'

Helen perused them and began to nod her head excitedly.

'You look a bit young, if you don't mind my saying so,' commented Liz. 'Are you sure this is something you can handle?'

Helen looked up at her and said, 'This is very big. A lot bigger than I was anticipating. I'm still a junior reporter and I doubt my editor will trust me to handle this story on my own. He won't take it off me, but I suspect I'll be working with a more senior person.'

'The reason I'm giving it to you is to make sure some bent copper can't bury it,' explained Liz.

'There are bad apples in every barrel but I don't think there are too many bent coppers in the Met,' said Helen.

'Then I'm hoping you can point me in the direction of one who definitely isn't,' said Liz. 'That's my price for giving you all the photos. I want you and the police to work on it together. There's also another story behind all this concerning Billie's paternal grandfather.'

'You mean Herbert Challinor?'

'You've done your homework then.'

'I did it some time ago,' said Helen, 'when the bomb dropped on you. I always thought there might be more to this but I wasn't given the time to investigate any further. So what's the story?'

'Well, as you know, Herbert Challinor died a few

months ago – two days before Billie's dad was killed in France, as it happens.'

Helen looked at the girl. 'I'm sorry to hear that, Billie. I understand he was a brave man.'

'Should have got the VC,' said Billie. 'He was recommended for one but for certain reasons it was downgraded.'

'Is there a story behind that too?'

'Yes,' said Liz, 'but not one that'd do Chas any credit. He was a lovely man but he was also a bit impulsive. The police wanted to speak to him over a very minor incident regarding a birthday present he gave his daughter, and the establishment need their VC heroes to be squeaky clean.'

'Can I have that story too after this is all over? If someone else gets wind of it they might paint Chas in a bad light.'

'I wouldn't want that,' said Billie quickly.

She looked to Liz for guidance. She shrugged and said, 'Okay, we'll let you have the true story, so long as you're kind to Chas.'

'I'll clear it with you first. Thank you.'

'Anyway,' Liz went on, 'it transpires that Billie is to inherit the bulk of the Challinor fortune. She was living with me in Leeds at the time and knew nothing of this when her grandfather died, but Cedric did. As the eldest of Billie's three uncles, he decided to become her guardian and get power of attorney over any assets she might acquire.'

Helen sat down and took out her notebook. 'I think you're right about giving it straight to the police. When this story breaks we need as many of the Elliker mob locked up as possible, for my safety as well as yours. Are there any negatives of these photographs?'

'Yes, we've got them.'

'Good. Then I suggest you have another set of copies made, just in case the police make you hand the negs over.'

'That's being done as we speak. What I need is the name of a cop we can trust.'

'I'd like to take you over to the office and have a word with my boss, Mr Cudlipp. He'll point you in the right direction. We'll get the copper to come to us, and you'll be doing me a favour if you tell my boss you'd prefer to deal with me when telling your part of the story. That'll be my exclusive.'

Chapter 59

Percy Cudlipp was looking through the photographed pages with mounting enthusiasm. Helen and Liz sat on chairs before his desk. He kept looking up at them, issuing mild expletives of amazement, then examining the photographs again.

'Helen, there's a file on the Ellikers in my filing cabinets. Could you get it for me, please? I'm sure there's something in Cedric's handwriting in there. I just want to compare it to this.'

Two minutes later he was making a comparison with a handwritten letter of complaint Cedric had sent to the paper about an article that had been written about him.

'This is from when he sued us for libel. He won as well. Got over two grand off us. Look at this – perfect match.'

Helen went around his desk to make the comparison. Liz didn't bother. She knew it was Cedric's writing. Cudlipp looked up at her. 'I'd like our legal people to take a look at all this and, if they agree, I want to print it before we take it to the police. It then becomes a fait accompli and the police are obliged either to arrest the lot of them or arrest us – and I don't think it's going to be us.'

Liz found herself nodding despite it not quite being her

plan. These people were professionals and they were on her side.

'Will I be writing the story?' asked Helen.

Cudlipp looked at her and smiled. 'I'd have been disappointed if you hadn't asked me, but I'm going to put you with Jack Lawson.'

'He'll just boss me about,' grumbled Helen.

'No, he won't. I'll tell him this is your story and it's his job to get the best out of you ... even if the best is mostly his own work. There's a long list of crimes to write about and you'll learn a lot from his experience: corrupt officials, coppers and judges. Enough to knock Hitler off the front page for at least a week, I shouldn't wonder.'

'There's another story that I'd like Helen to write,' said Liz. 'It's to do with Cedric Elliker trying to deprive Billie of her granddad's fortune.'

'First of all,' said Cudlipp, 'I'm going to clear tomorrow's front page for you and Jack to write me an article on the Bond Street robbery and the Ellikers' involvement. Take the relevant pages to him and concentrate on that. Quote verbatim from Elliker's book as much as you can. I want the article to be so watertight the police can't avoid arresting him. I want these whole entries reproduced on page two and three.' He handed her the relevant pages of the ledger, listing the timings and events of the jewel robbery, including what had been stolen, who had taken part, who had fenced the jewels and for how much, each gang member's share, and many other details that only the robbers could have known. A man had been shot dead. The gunman was named in Cedric's book as Edgar Elliker, the gun a Webley and Scott .38 revolver, three shots fired.

Much of this information was known only to the police and the perpetrators. Cedric was a meticulous record-keeper, it seemed. It was probably because of his legal training.

Two hours later DCI Dundas was at home when he received a call from the station for him to ring Percy Cudlipp. This raised a grumble from Dundas, but curiosity had him ringing the *Herald* editor.

'Mr Cudlipp, I trust this is important.'

'Sorry to disturb you at home, Detective Chief Inspector, but I'm aware you're not a fan of the Ellikers and we're running a most damning article on them in the morning. I've had it checked with our legal people and they assure me that our facts are unimpeachable. You may well wish to come in and take a look at what we've got as you might find it expedient to make arrests before the papers come out. You also need to alert your senior officers.'

'Most damning, you say?'

'That's correct.'

'I'm on my way,' said Dundas, who had no intention of alerting anyone.

Chapter 60

Neither of Cedric's brothers was too pleased at being summoned to his house later that night. Edgar and Albert were the worse for drink, and Lavinia was protesting that it was foolish even to contemplate taking revenge on Liz that night.

'If you must do it, leave it until tomorrow when you'll hopefully be sober and thinking clearer.'

'The bitches'll be away to bloody Yorkshire tomorrow!' snarled Cedric, who had his left arm in a sling after having four pellets removed by the Ellikers' doctor, who was used to tending such injuries within the family and was always well paid for it. 'I want this thing done tonight. The Elliker family has a certain reputation in London, and maintaining that reputation is vital to the smooth running of our business.'

'We can do this,' said Edgar. 'Just give us a couple of hours to sober up a bit first.'

Cedric looked at the clock. It was ten-past midnight. 'Okay, we do it at three o'clock in the morning. You lot get your heads down for a couple of hours. I assume you brought the necessary, Albert?'

'If you mean did I bring five gallons of petrol, yes, I did.'

'Good, three o'clock should see everyone fast asleep. Behind the club door is a wood-panelled corridor. Five gallons of petrol will get a hell of a blaze going in seconds. It should have taken hold by the time anyone wakes up – that's if anyone *does* wake up. I want them all dead: the woman, the girl, and that nigger piano player.'

'I don't like this one bit,' said Lavinia. 'You've got the ledger back. Can't you just be satisfied with that?'

'No!' snapped Cedric. 'We can't afford to be satisfied with that. We're the Ellikers. People cross us, they pay dearly.'

'Well, it won't take all three of you to pour petrol through a letterbox and set fire to it.'

'True,' said Edgar. 'I'll do it with Stuart. Albert can drive and keep lookout. A one-armed man will only hinder us.'

Cedric glared at him for a long moment then said, 'Just make sure it's done properly.'

Chapter 61

As the German war-making capability declined, the black-out restrictions were eased and a 'dim-out' had recently been introduced, allowing street lighting to the equivalent of moonlight. A full blackout would be re-imposed if an alert was sounded. This suited the Ellikers because any kind of lighting restrictions kept people off the streets. Their car headlights still beamed out through narrow protective slits, but were bright enough to pick out the Crazy Dazy. Stuart drove the Humber on to the pavement and shielded the club doorway from the eyes of any passers-by, although at three o'clock in the morning there were none. Edgar and Albert got out and carried the petrol drum over to the door. Edgar pushed a rubber tube through the letterbox and Albert poured the contents of the drum into a funnel attached to the other end of the tube. It took three minutes to empty all the petrol from the drum, after which Albert got back in the car while Edgar struck a fistful of matches and thrust them all through the letterbox. There was a satisfactory 'Whoosh!' as the petrol ignited. Within seconds the club hallway was an inferno. Upstairs, Liz and Billie, having been busy up to midnight at the

Herald offices, were sound asleep, unaware of the con-
flagration below.

Job done, Edgar got in the car and lit a cigar with
one of his remaining matches as Albert drove sedately
away.

'Drive around the block and park at the far end of the
street,' Edgar ordered. 'His Majesty'll want to know if we
did the job properly.'

'Okay,' said his brother.

He swung left down Charing Cross Road, left and left
again up St Giles High Street. The light from the blaze
down Denmark Street flickered across the road in front of
them. Two cars had stopped. A couple of people were
standing at the end of the street but no one was venturing
down. Edgar got out and joined them, acting the part of
a shocked observer.

'My God!' he said. 'Is anyone in there?'

'Dunno. It's to be hoped not.'

'No one's come out so far,' said the other watcher.

'No one could survive that. It can't have been a bomb,
can it?'

'Didn't hear anything.'

'Maybe a V2?' suggested Edgar.

'Oh, no, they make a hell of a racket when they land –
and it'd have blown up the whole street.'

'Yeah, probably,' Edgar agreed.

More bystanders were arriving. No sign of any fire
engines yet. The club's downstairs windows had already
exploded outwards, now the upstairs windows did the
same and very soon flames were licking through the roof.
Edgar was impressed by how quickly the blaze had taken

hold. He heard a police car approaching from a distance and strolled casually over to the Humber. He got inside and they cruised away down the road.

'Both the bitches are dead,' he said. 'Brother Cedric owes us.'

Chapter 62

Helen had stayed around, not wanting to miss any of what might well prove to be the most important hours of her career. Only Jack Lawson had left for home. Detective Chief Inspector Dundas was reading a fresh-off-the-press morning edition and wondering how best to approach the arrest of not only the Ellikers, but also certain members of the judiciary, parliament, the police and the London underworld. Cudlipp was reading his mind.

'What you're reading is just the tip of the iceberg.'

'I'm more than aware of that, Mr Cudlipp. I'm also aware that I'm just a DCI and I'm the only copper who knows about this. It's quite important I get things right.'

'I'm a good friend of Assistant Commissioner Goodhart. I could give him a ring right now, if you want.'

Goodhart, as head of the Metropolitan Police CID Division, was Dundas's ultimate boss. He wondered how Cudlipp came to know him so well. The Freemasons sprang to mind. Maybe, maybe not.

'He's as straight as they come,' Cudlipp assured the DCI.

'I'm sure he is.'

Cudlipp's phone rang. He answered it and looked at Helen with an expression of growing concern on his face. He put the phone down and shook his head.

'That was the police in Holborn. The Crazy Dazy Club has burned down.'

Helen was shocked. 'Liz and Billie are in there. Are they all right?'

Cudlipp shook his head. 'They don't know yet. Apparently the place has been completely gutted.'

'That has to be the Ellikers,' said Helen.

'Probably,' agreed Dundas. 'Fortunately we don't need to wait for proof of it to arrest them.' He turned to Cudlipp. 'I'd appreciate your ringing Goodhart. Meanwhile I'm going to the station to raise some troops and pick up as many bloody Ellikers as we can. I'll also need to take custody of those photographic sheets.'

Cudlipp looked at Helen, who said, 'Liz has negatives.'

'We'll need those as well,' said Dundas.

'Just remember who gave you this information,' said Cudlipp, sharply. 'I wouldn't appreciate it if our competitors got hold of those sheets.'

'I've no doubt you'll make copies before you hand them in.'

'That's fair,' said Cudlipp. 'I'll ring Goodhart and hope he doesn't mind getting up at this hour.'

'He'd mind very much if we didn't tell him. Perhaps if you ask him to come here, you can hand the sheets over. Tell him I'm off to arrest the Ellikers, that should get him down here. That damned family's tried to buy me in the past and this is where they realise that we're not all for sale!'

'Would you mind if I accompanied you?' Helen asked him.

'All this information originally came from her,' explained Cudlipp.

'Really? Oh ... okay then. Just stay well away from any trouble.'

'Can we call in at the Crazy Dazy on the way?' she asked. 'I need to see that Liz and Billie are okay.'

'Yes, yes, we need to do that,' said Dundas, 'but the odds are that they aren't.'

'I'm afraid he's right,' said Cudlipp. 'The police and firemen on the scene haven't found any survivors.'

Helen followed Dundas through the small crowd that had gathered at the end of Denmark Street. She was amazed that any sort of crowd would gather at that time of the morning. It was not yet four o'clock. All the time she looked around for any sign of Liz and Billie. An ambulance was parked nearby. Its driver was leaning against it, smoking a cigarette. She left Dundas and went over to the ambulance man, showing him her press card, which often elicited information from the most reluctant witness.

'Has anyone been injured?'

'They haven't found anyone yet.'

'That's a good thing, isn't it?'

'Not really. They daren't go in because the two adjacent buildings are on the verge of collapse.'

'Oh, so there might still be people in there?'

He flicked his cigarette end away into the darkness. 'I'm told there'll definitely be people in there, poor devils. Won't have stood a chance, I'm afraid.'

Helen took out her notebook and wrote this down, trying to remain professional despite the tears that threatened to spill down her face. She went over to where Dundas was talking to a fireman.

'I understand you can't go in to search because there's a danger of the adjacent buildings collapsing.'

'That's right, miss.'

Dundas introduced her. 'This is Helen Hawkins from the *Daily Herald*. She knows the people who should be in the club.'

'A woman, an eight-year-old girl and the club owner, a jazz musician. They all lived on the premises.

'Duke Wellington,' said the fireman. 'I already have his name.'

'The woman was Liz Morris and the girl was called Billie Challinor.'

'What I need to know is how the fire started,' said Dundas.

'We won't know until we get our investigation boys in, but in my opinion this fire was either a gas leak or arson.'

'We have reason to suspect arson,' Dundas told him.

'I'll tell them to bear that in mind.'

Dundas looked at Helen. 'There's nothing I can do here. I'm off to get on with the job in hand. Do you want to stay here or are you coming?'

'I'm coming.'

At five o'clock she was sitting in Dundas's car watching Cedric being taken out in handcuffs to a waiting Black Maria. Three miles away, Edgar and Albert had been picked up together at Edgar's house. All of them thought the arrest was to do with the fire, and all of them were shocked when they arrived at the station to find themselves charged with the Bond Street jewel robbery, murder, and other charges, to follow.

Dundas took great pleasure in showing them his copy of the *Daily Herald* with its unequivocal front-page head-lines.

Ellikers Charged with Bond Street Robbery

Edgar glared at Cedric and snarled, 'That bloody book's done for us!'

At eleven o'clock that same morning, after Goodhart and his team had taken a close look at the photographic copy of Cedric's ledger, many more arrests were made all over London. Helen Hawkins, who'd had two hours sleep, was given carte blanche to accompany whichever team of officers she chose. She stuck with DCI Dundas, who'd had no sleep at all, and was so pumped up with exhilaration he scarcely noticed how tired he was.

Chapter 63

Monty Finniston lived in Finchley, about five miles away from the Crazy Dazy. He was not as young as he used to be and relied quite heavily on gigs at the club to supplement his income. There had been nothing in the papers about it yet but he knew the place had been burned down. He knew because he'd been told as much by the people who were still safely asleep upstairs in his house. He'd gone out for a morning paper, and the headline in the *Daily Herald* had persuaded him to buy a copy. Monty was smiling broadly as he read the article. This would please the people upstairs, who had no time at all for the Ellikers.

He went into one of the bedrooms. 'Wakey, wakey! I bring news from the front.'

Duke peered over the bedclothes and blinked through smoke-reddened eyes. 'Man, I was fast asleep.'

Monty displayed the headline to him. Duke peered at it and sat up. 'Man, that was quick work. No wonder them Ellikers got mad and burned down the club.'

'I think they got mad before this wuz printed.'

Duke swung his legs out of bed and picked up his clothes, which reeked of smoke. 'Do you have any things I can borrow that don't smell so bad?'

Monty nodded in the direction of a wardrobe. 'There's a band suit in there that might just fit – never did fit me Might even have something for the lady that my darlin' wife left behind. Don't have nothing that'll fit the girl, though.'

'Maybe we should let them sleep a while longer,' said Duke. 'We had scary moments back there.'

'Scary moments you ain't prop'ly told me about. Is the club definitely gone?'

'It was definitely on its way when we left. No way back from a blaze like that, man.'

'So, how'd you get out? You wuz a bit vague about it last night when you arrived. Could hardly get a word o' sense out of none o' you. Maybe a cup of my coffee might jog yo' memory.'

'A cup of coffee would go down well,' said Duke, opening the wardrobe doors and examining the contents. 'Well, there's nothing in here that's gonna be too big for me, that's for sure.'

Duke was still collecting his thoughts as Monty brought him a cup of steaming coffee. They were sitting at the kitchen table when Duke began his story.

'Liz had a confrontation with Cedric yesterday over a book that Billie had stole from him.'

'What sort of book?'

'The one that I imagine caused them headlines. It had a record of all the Ellikers' dealings in it. In fact, Elliker kidnapped the girl to exchange her for the book, which was the confrontation I just mentioned. The exchange was done in the club. Liz was holding my shotgun as insurance, only she took a pot shot at Elliker and hit him in the arm.'

'Jesus, man! Don't she know who Cedric is?'

'She knows plenty, doesn't care. Anyways I was pretty sure they'd come back last night so I stayed downstairs. I actually fell asleep but woke up when the fire started in the hall. I ran upstairs and roused Liz and Billie, only we couldn't get back down with the flames spreading so fast. Jeez, it was wild, man! All of downstairs was ablaze. I got the women to a back window and did the old trick of tying sheets together. I lowered Liz down first and tied a sheet around Billie and lowered her down. By this time there were flames coming through the floor, man! I climbed halfway down on the drainpipe and jumped the rest. I had my van parked round the back, which was the only stroke of luck we had last night. Came straight here to be somewhere the Ellikers can't find us.'

'What're you gonna do now?'

'I'm gonna drink this coffee and mourn my piano, which went up with the club. Man, I loved that piano.'

'Yeah, you could make it talk all right. I mean, what're you gonna do about the club?'

'Well, I got insurance.'

'You got insurance? I am truly amazed, Duke. I never knew a piano player with such sense as to take out insurance.'

'But it don't solve our immediate problem. We need a new venue.'

A voice said, 'First we need new clothes.'

Duke and Monty spun round to see Liz standing in the doorway. She was wearing the nightclothes she'd arrived in.

'Luckily I managed to bring my handbag,' she said.

'Some sort of survival instinct, I suppose. When danger calls, grab your handbag, girl. It means I've got my purse, my bankbook, my identity card and my ration book, which means I have money to buy us both clothes, but I'm not going out dressed like this.'

'I happen to have some ladies' clothes on the premises,' said Monty, lowering his eyes modestly.

Duke held out the *Daily Herald* headline for her to read. It brought a smile to her face. 'I think I should ring Helen,' said Liz. 'Tell her what's happened to us – once I've had a cup of coffee.'

Helen was by now at home catching up on her sleep. Jack Lawson took the call and told Liz, 'The Ellikers are all in custody. If I send a car for you, would you like to come in and tell me your story?'

'I actually promised Helen that she could have our part of the story.'

'Fair enough. I'm going to give you her home number. You should call her right now. I must warn you, she thinks both you and Billie are dead and she's pretty upset about it.'

Chapter 64

February 1945

'I've been getting letters and stuff,' said Billie. 'Does that mean I'm famous?'

'What sort of letters?' asked Duke. He was sitting at his new piano, working out a jazz arrangement for 'Polka Dots and Moonbeams'. The club was being rebuilt around him but he'd insisted on the stage area being finished first so that he had somewhere to put his new piano. He'd negotiated with the insurers to replace his forty-year-old destroyed Shoninger upright with a like-for-like replacement, and had ended up with a much superior model – a 1907 Shoninger Louis XV Walnut Upright.

Billie had appeared beside him. He moved over, she climbed on to the stool. 'I got one from the people who I was sent to when Mum got killed and Dad was in hospital. They send it to the newspaper, and the newspaper sends all my letters on to me.'

'That'll be Helen Hawkins,' said Duke.

'Helen brings them round. And a man called Raymond Dunford sent me a lovely necklace with a real di'mond in it. He said he used to know my mum and that she left it with him, so it's really mine.'

Duke's face broke into a broad smile. 'Ah, your daddy told me about him ... and the necklace for that matter. Hey, I bet Helen would like that story.'

Billie shrugged. 'You can tell her, if you like.'

'Have you got the necklace with you?'

'No, Auntie Liz said I must keep it safe for special occasions.'

'Quite right. I imagine it's a very valuable necklace. I believe Mr Dunford was quite wealthy.'

'So, how did he know my mum?'

'He, er, he was her boyfriend before she met your dad.'

'But she preferred my dad, didn't she?'

'Billie, all the girls preferred your dad.'

'But I bet my dad preferred Mum to all the other girls.'

'Ah, yes. Once Chas Challinor met your mum there was no other girl for him.'

'Did you like my mum?'

'I did, yes.'

'Good.'

Billie began to tinkle on the keys, trying to pick out the tune of 'It's A Long Way To Tipperary'.

'They said I was welcome to visit them when I went up to Yorkshire.'

'Who did?'

'The people I stayed with ... I just told you.'

'Ah, sorry.'

'Auntie Liz said she'd take me the next time she went up there. Trouble is, they give you pom and sago. Have you ever had pom and sago?'

'I've tasted it, said Duke. 'Horrible. I hate pom, sago ... and swede.'

'I don't like swede either. Roy Morley says they make it from rotting spuds and donkey's tails.'

'Roy Morley knows his swede all right.'

Billie now concentrated on the piano. Within a minute she'd picked out the tune, laboriously at first, then she became more fluent. Duke tapped out the timing with his right forefinger, Billie immediately picked up on it as Duke accompanied her one-finger melody with left-hand chords. Billie was delighted with the result and played it over and over again until Duke brought things to a halt.

'Seems to me you've got your dad's musical talent, young lady. I highly recommend you find yourself a piano teacher immediately.'

'Do you think so? Honestly?'

'I honestly think so.'

'You could teach me.'

'I'm a piano player not a teacher. Teaching needs patience that I ain't got.'

She looked up at him. 'You've got a nice face, Duke. Why don't you marry Auntie Liz?'

'Where'd that come from? One minute we're talking about pom and saga and piano-playing, the next minute you're marrying me off to Auntie Liz.'

'She'd have married my daddy if he'd asked her, so you'd better ask her if you want to be her husband.'

'Is that so?'

'Yes. So why haven't you asked her? Don't you love her?'

'You're asking me some mighty personal stuff here, Billie.'

'I was just wondering, that's all. If you married her we could be a sort of family.'

364

'Well now, there's a bit of a problem insofar as my skin is a different colour from your auntie's.'

'Your skin is a very nice colour. It matches your piano.'

'Thank you, but it doesn't match your auntie's.'

'I didn't know your skin was supposed to match other people's skin. My daddy's didn't after the bomb and I bet Auntie Liz would've married him if he'd asked her.'

'Plenty of people think the colours should match.'

'That's silly.'

'I can't argue with that.'

'I thought it was only clothes an' stuff that had to match, and, if you don't mind me saying so, your tie doesn't match your shirt.'

Duke laughed out loud as Billie's butterfly mind fluttered on to another subject. 'Have we won the war?'

'Nearly.'

'I bet my daddy helped a lot.'

'He sure did, him and Mr Churchill ... and the Americans.'

'Adolf Hitler is a bad man.'

'He's as bad as he's stupid, which is a good job because him being stupid makes it easier for us to win the war. He thinks he can take on the whole world, but the world has other ideas. No one can take on the whole world, not even Jesus managed to do that. He just took on a bit of it and hoped the rest of the world would finish the job. The world is never gonna finish Hitler's work for him.'

'I bet my daddy would have tried to take on the world.'

Duke laughed again. 'Oh, I ain't gonna argue with that. Your daddy would have made a better job of it than Adolf Hitler. Your daddy won his hero's medal because he saw a problem and he saw the solution, and he had the brains and the skill and the courage to solve that problem. Mr Hitler had no brains, no skill and no courage. All he could do was talk loud and scare people.'

'Did you like my daddy?'

'I sure did, and what's more everyone who knew your daddy liked him. He was a real likeable dude was your daddy.'

'I loved him, you know.'

'I know . . . and shall I tell you something?'

'Yes, please.'

'Your Auntie Liz loves you.'

'Oh, I know that. It'd be good if you loved me as well then we could be a family who all loved each other.'

'You'd have to love me for that to work,' said Duke.

'Of course I love you – maybe not as much as I loved my daddy.'

'I don't expect you ever to love me as much as that. I could never be the great guy your daddy was, not in a million years.'

'I know, but you're okay though, and if we all got to be a family you'd have to have patience with me, which means you could teach me how to play the piano.'

Duke looked down in amazement at this child who was wrapping him around her little finger.

'Excuse me.'

They both turned round to see an elderly lady standing in the doorway.

Chapter 65

Duke got up from his stool.

'Can I help you, madam?'

The old lady looked nervous.

'I . . . erm . . . ' She seemed lost for words.

'Are you okay? Would you like to sit down?'

He picked up a chair from the stage and took it across to her. Billie followed him. The old lady looked familiar. She sat down on the chair. Liz, who had been in the kitchen, came through. She looked at Duke who shrugged as if to say, *I've got no idea who she is*.

'I've been away,' said the old lady. 'Away for so long.'

'Away from who . . . where?' said Liz.

The lady went quiet for several seconds as she gathered her thoughts. 'Oh, my family,' she said at last. 'They hated me, you know.'

'I'm sure they didn't,' said Duke, who wasn't sure of anything.

'The ones who are still alive hate me, but they'll soon be gone, which will be a blessing all round, I suppose.'

'Oh, dear,' said Liz. 'Look, would you like a cup of tea?'

'You're very kind, thank you, but I'm . . . I'm okay.'

There was an American drawl to her voice.

'Who are your family?' said Duke, who was wondering if he should know her. 'Why have you come here?'

The lady puffed out her cheeks and blew a long breath, then smiled a sad smile. 'Well, they're not gone yet, but it's just a matter of time – just a matter of time. They say time's a great healer, don't they? Such rubbish!'

She looked from one to the other of them until her eyes rested on Billie. There was affection in her eyes.

'What ... what is your name, young lady?' she asked, hesitantly.

'Billie ... Billie Challinor.'

The old woman gasped and clasped one hand to her mouth. Tears rolled down her face. Billie stepped forward and instinctively took the lady's hand. She held on to the child, shaking with emotion, eyes fixed on Billie's face. Liz leaned down beside Billie and placed an arm protectively around her shoulders.

'Who are you?' she asked their visitor.

The woman transferred her gaze to Liz. 'Promise you won't hate me?'

'Hate you? Why should we hate you?'

The lady frowned and began to take deep, firm breaths, as if to build up her strength.

'We promise not to hate you,' said Billie.

'My name ... well, my name used to be Anne Elliker.'

There was a stunned silence from all three of them. The lady's eyes were only on Billie, who said, 'That was my mum's name.'

'I know. I gave her that name.'

There was silence as Billie tried to unravel what she'd just heard.

'I'm your grandmother.'

Billie's mouth opened wide in amazement. The familiarity she'd seen in the woman's face was clear to her now. She had a faint look of Cedric.

'You're Annie Elliker's mother?' said Duke.

'Yes.'

'But she's dead.'

'Yes, I read in the paper that I was dead. Didn't believe it for one minute.'

'But Annie's mum died when she was a baby,' Duke said. 'That's what Annie told Chas.'

'Maybe I'm a ghost then.'

Duke touched her on her shoulder and withdrew his hand. 'You ain't no ghost, that's for sure.'

'I was sent away to America year after Annie was born and told never to come back or Montague Elliker, my husband, would have me killed. I assume he told his daughter I was dead.'

'I guess he did just that.'

'Still, better that than tell her I'd run off and left her to his mercy, which is what I did do.'

'What?' said Liz.

'I wasn't wanted any more. I asked if I could take Annie with me, but he kept her with him out of sheer cruelty to me. He was the most evil man. I lived out my life in America, not daring to come back because I knew he'd have me killed. I knew he'd had other people killed.'

She was still clutching Billie's hand. 'I'm so sorry. You shouldn't be hearing this, my dear.'

'She's heard a lot worse recently,' said Liz. 'This whole

Elliker family thing is beginning to make sense now. I assume Cedric and his brothers are your sons?'

'Yes,' she said. 'I believe all three of them are looking at death sentences.'

'Probably,' said Liz. 'I'm really sorry.'

'Oh, you mustn't be sorry. I no longer regard them as being any part of my life. I carried each of them for nine months but after that I was never allowed to love them or form any sort of relationship with them. I gave birth to three strangers who turned into cold-hearted monsters. It's better for the world that they all go back to where they came from – wherever that may be. I certainly have a good idea.'

'You know they burned this club down with all three of us in it, hoping to kill us?' Liz said.

'Oh, dear, I'm so sorry. I just don't know what to say.'

'You're really my grandma?' said Billie.

'Yes, my darling, I am. I only knew your mother for a year but she was my daughter and I loved her dearly. My sons were all strange boys, brainwashed by their father who would let me have nothing to do with them. He brought nannies in to feed and dress them, but he allowed me to look after Annie because she was a girl and he had no use for girls. The only reason he kept me was to satisfy his, er, other needs. My life with him was horrendous.'

'Then he sent you away?' said Duke.

'He did, yes. As soon as Annie was born he forced me into divorcing him and sent me packing. I was powerless. Divorcing him was the easy bit. Leaving Annie, that was hard to do.'

'You do know he's dead,' said Liz. 'He committed sui-cide, apparently.'

'I do, yes. But I only know what I've read in the news-papers. All this latest stuff was in the American papers, which gave me the courage to come over here.'

'The police found six ledgers in Cedric's house that belonged to his dad,' Liz told her. 'He really was a bad man. All sorts of people are being arrested for things that happened many years ago.'

'Back when I was around, I shouldn't wonder.'

'There was nothing in them about you. I asked espe-cially. He'd listed all sorts of people he'd had killed, but not you.'

'What? He'd written everything down? The arrogance of the man! What a shame he's dead. Oh, I'd have loved to have seen him get his comeuppance.'

'My mum's dead,' said Billie.

The old lady's tears streamed again. 'I know, my darling. I read about that in the States as well.' She squeezed Billie's hand. 'That's when I first learned about you. I learned I'd lost a daughter and gained a granddaughter. You're why I came here.'

'How did you get here?' asked Duke. 'There's still a war on.'

'I got a passage on a merchant ship – with the U-boat danger almost over it's a bit safer to travel, but passenger ships are few and far between.'

Duke and Liz stared at her. She looked such a frail old lady to have made such a dangerous journey. It was as if she could read their thoughts.

'I'm tougher than I look.' She smiled. 'If only I'd been braver before.'

'My daddy's dead as well,' said Billie.

'I know that, my darling, and I'm so sorry I didn't meet him. I should have come back years ago, but I was such an awful coward.'

'He was a war hero.'

'Yes, I know, and a brilliant musician.'

'I don't think you're a coward, Grandma.'

Anne's face crumpled with emotion at hearing herself being called Grandma by this delightful child. She let go of Billie's hand and opened her arms to give her a hug. Liz and Duke looked on with mixed emotions, neither of them knowing what to think about this new Elliker who had just come into their lives.

Anne looked over Billie's shoulder at them and smiled, once again reading their thoughts. 'Actually,' she said, 'I'm no longer an Elliker. My real name is Ellis. I got married in America to a lovely man who knew all about me. For obvious reasons he didn't want me to come back here to my old life before this. The darling man passed away four years ago.'

'I'm sorry,' said Liz, 'and for the record, I don't think you're a coward either. If you'd made a stand against the Ellikers you'd only have died.'

'I believe you took them on.'

'The three of us took them on,' said Liz, 'and we had a lot of luck.'

'Are you going to stay here?' Billie asked her grand-mother.

'Er, for a while, then I have to go back to America. I came here specifically to meet you and the people who are looking after you, and I must say I like what I see.'

'But why must you go back to America?'

'I have family there.'

'Really?' said Liz. 'What family?'

'I have a daughter and twin grandsons.'

She looked at Liz and explained. 'I had Cedric when I was nineteen. By the time I was twenty-one I had three sons. Annie arrived when I was thirty-five and Sarah was born in America when I was thirty-eight.'

Billie tried to work this out. Anne beat her to it. 'You have an Aunt Sarah and an Uncle Joe and two small cousins – Michael and James, or Mick and Jimmy as they seem to get called.'

'I have a family who aren't all horrible?' said Billie, beaming with delight. 'Can I go and see them?'

'I imagine so, when the war's over.'

'Do you need somewhere to stay?' said Liz.

Anne let go of Billie and dabbed her eyes with a hand-kerchief. 'Oh, you don't have to worry about my welfare. I have enough money to look after myself. My husband left me well placed financially.'

'Right. By the way, I'm Liz. I'm Billie's guardian.'

'I call her Auntie Liz,' said Billie.

'And my name's Duke. This is my club.'

'Yes, I've read all about you both. It seems my grand-daughter is in excellent hands. I would like to spend some time with you before I go back, if that's okay?'

'You talk American,' said Billie.

Anne laughed. 'That's not what they think when I'm over in the States. I'm known as Cockney Annie there.'

'The Americans are helping us to win the war,' said Billie. 'Them and my daddy and Mr Churchill.'

'I take it you won't stay for the trials?' said Liz.

'No, I won't. I have expunged those three foul men from my mind. I can't bear to think I ever carried them.'

'I find that so sad,' said Liz, remembering the child who had died in her own womb.

'Oh, it's much more than sad,' said Anne, 'but when the sentences are carried out I'll be back home with two of my three wonderful grandchildren.'

This drew a smile from Billie.

'Annie expunged her family from her life as well,' said Duke. 'She used to say it only began when she met Chas. Talking about the Ellikers was strictly forbidden.'

'Oh, did she really? That's such a relief. I wanted her to have some happiness.'

'Well, Chas gave her that all right. I never did see a lady so happy as Annie Challinor.'

Anne got to her feet then and gave Duke a hug. 'That's what I've come to hear.'

'Chas was quite a catch,' said Liz. 'Even after his injuries he was still a real charmer . . . and he loved the socks off Annie.'

Up until then Chas's deep love for Annie had always been a source of unreasonable hurt for Liz. This was no longer so, perhaps because of the lovely man smiling at her over Billie's head.

Epilogue

Wandsworth Gaol, London
4 May 1945

Liz sat in an empty visiting room, wondering why she was there, and why Cedric had agreed to see her. Well, she knew why she was there really; it was because she was Liz Morris and when she had to get something off her chest she couldn't rest until it was done, and some things had to be done face-to-face. This man and his brothers had come within a whisker of killing her and Billie. He'd snatched the child from her purely out of greed, and might well have had her killed once he'd done with her.

Edgar and Albert were due to be hanged in seven days. Two other gang members had been hanged the previous month. Cedric's death sentence had been commuted after he'd pleaded that he'd played no part personally in any of the eight murders the police had investigated. 'I was merely the accountant,' he'd said. The Home Secretary, Herbert Morrison, had commuted his sentence to life without parole.

All in all, two judges, four senior police officers, ten junior police officers, two members of parliament, five civil servants, seven local government officers, and fourteen members of the Ellikers' criminal organisation had been given sentences ranging from six months to hanging. Many of the gang's associates in the London underworld had gone to ground. Crime figures in the city were down by over twenty per cent. The cases had knocked the war in Europe off the front page of the *Daily Herald* for a total of six days. Helen Hawkins, under whose by-line the stories had been told, was now a fully-fledged crime reporter with the *Daily Mail*, who'd made her an offer the *Daily Herald* couldn't match – much to the relief of Jack Lawson who'd been working in the shadow of this young upstart all winter.

A prison officer appeared and asked Liz to follow him. She was led through two barred gates to the barred room where Cedric was already seated at a table, wearing handcuffs. Without saying a word to him she sat down opposite and asked the prison officer if it was okay to smoke. He said it was and she lit a cigarette without offering Cedric one.

'Why are you here?' he asked.

'I've come to gloat.'

'You're wasting your time. I won't be in here long.'

'True.'

He looked at her suspiciously, wondering why she was agreeing with him, this woman who had come to gloat.

'Your brothers are due for the drop, and your wife's gone off to America taking most of your loot with her. That's the problem with having secret accounts in the wife's name. Very helpful to the police was Lavinia. In return they turned a blind eye to her helping herself to your dosh. I gather even the house was in her name. I say *was* because she's just sold it, did you know that?'

Judging from the anger blazing in his eyes he obviously didn't. 'The bitch'll pay, don't you worry about that!'

'Well, *she's* not worrying because she knows you've got no influence inside or outside this prison. No one in London's scared of you anymore. You're a spent force, Cedric, a laughing stock. The kids have made up a skipping song about you. Have you heard it?'

She tapped her fingers on the table as she recited:

'Locked up for life, silly Cedric Elliker
His darling wife has left him and gone to America
Albert and Edgar are waiting for the rope
Brought down by a schoolgirl, what a bunch of dopes!'

'Pretty good, eh? It should be around for years, like the Lizzie Borden one.'

He said nothing to this taunt. Liz took a letter from her handbag and said, 'Anyway, this is what I've come about. It concerns you and I thought it better you heard it from me.'

'Why would I be interested in anything you have to tell me?' he grunted.

'Because it's to do with the Challinor millions. It's all been settled now. Everyone's been paid off including the taxman and all the creditors. With me being Billie's legal guardian I got this letter last week with a complete breakdown and a cheque in full and final settlement. If your scheme to get your hands on it through gaining power-of-attorney over Billie's money hadn't gone wrong, you'd have been banking this cheque. Let's face it, it was this scheme that led to the Ellikers' ruin. You might as well know what you've missed out on.'

'Okay, so the girl's now a millionaire. I'm delighted for her. She's my niece. Why shouldn't I be delighted?'

'Because you're a low-life, that's why. Don't you want to know how much she's getting? Which is what this was all about.'

'I imagine you're going to tell me.'

'One thousand two hundred and thirteen pounds, sixteen shillings and fourpence. Billie has already been paid a thousand, so the cheque was for two hundred and thirteen pounds, sixteen and four.'

She pushed the letter over to him.

'It seems,' she said, 'that Herbert Challinor conducted his business in an unorthodox fashion, which didn't include declaring overmuch to the taxman. It left him paying tax after his death, plus massive penalties. It also turns out he wasn't above a bit of bribery to obtain government contracts, plus the vultures started circling when they heard what was happening to his estate. Dozens of them sued and were all paid off in full to save expensive legal costs. This is the residue of the estate.'

Cedric shook his head. 'It can't be.'

'It is. It's amazing the rubbish that's sometimes left on a beach when the tide goes out.'

'That's ridiculous. His gross wealth was five point three million.'

'Read the letter. It's from his solicitors. I assume you know them – quite reputable apart from the one employee who was in your pay – the one who presumably told you what his gross wealth was before his affairs were settled.

She's been sacked, by the way. If it's any consolation, Billie's perfectly happy with the twelve hundred, which is now in a bank account earning interest.'

Cedric pushed the letter back to Liz. His prison pallor had turned a shade whiter. 'No ... no, I don't believe it.'

Liz picked it up and laughed. 'Oh, yes, you do. You're the idiot who destroyed his family and his criminal empire for a chance at getting a measly twelve hundred quid when you expected five million, so you can hardly blame me for wanting to see your face when you found out. All you had to do was carry on with your old criminal business and no one would ever have got to you – but you became too greedy and now you've been brought down by an eight-year-old girl. All the other cons will be laughing at you. I bet they've started already.'

She held his eyes with an intense gaze which he couldn't match. Cedric's shoulders slumped and he dropped his eyes, squeezing them shut and issuing a string of profanities to himself.

'I assume you knew that your mother wasn't dead.'

He shrugged as if to say, *So what?*

'But you let your little sister think she was, for the whole of her life.'

'What the hell do you know about the old hag?'

'I know she's alive. She came over from America to see her granddaughter. Very nice lady, actually. She got married again and she's quite well off now. Well rid of you lot.'

'So long as she doesn't want to come and see me.'

'No, she's gone back. She just wanted to make sure you were all hanged.'

379

'Well, that's not going to happen. Not to me.'

'Oh, but it is! Sorry.' Liz snapped her fingers. 'I knew there was something else I had to tell you. You'll be hanged for your father's murder.'

Cedric's prison pallor went even paler. He said nothing as Liz continued.

'Now this isn't supposed to come from me, it's just that I get on so well with a certain police officer who didn't know I was coming here. He made me swear not to tell anyone, the foolish man.'

'What the hell are you talking about?'

'It's about you murdering your father and arranging for it to look like suicide.'

'What?'

'It's a brand new murder charge, Cedric, and you've got the lovely Edgar and Albert to thank for it,' she said. 'With them having nothing to lose, they've both sworn independent affidavits about the day your father died. The police were always suspicious of the circumstances and your brothers' statements confirm those suspicions. You killed your father because he'd made a will for the first time in his life and you knew about it. He was leaving everything to his three sons – the lion's share to you. Nothing to his daughter or granddaughter, of course.'

The awful truth of her words hit Cedric like a sledge-hammer. His eyes widened in fear and he began to shake visibly.

'Do correct me if I'm wrong,' Liz continued. 'All three of you were in the house when he died, which was contrary to the statements you made at the time. Anyway, you alone went into his study and shot him through the head. The three of you then arranged the scene to look like suicide and afterwards you all went off to join the people you'd paid to give you an alibi. The cops have got their names by the way. Looks to me like your brothers didn't want to be the only ones to be hanged – close family you've got there. I'm guessing you'll be charged today.'

Abject defeat clouded Cedric's eyes. He gave a low moan of despair, got to his feet and shuffled from the room. Liz almost felt sorry for him.

Duke was waiting for her outside the prison. She linked his arm as they walked back towards his van.

'How did he take it?'

'He took it like a man who's suddenly found out he's going to be hanged. It was like I was the one sentencing him to death.'

'That good, huh?'

'Duke, it really wasn't my place to tell him. I did it to get him back for what he'd done to us. I thought I'd feel good about it, but I'm not sure I do.'

'The scales of good and evil need balancing in favour of the good. You needed to give him more than just a taste of his own medicine. It's messing with you and Billie that brought him down. You need him to wish he'd never met you.'

'I think I've achieved that.'

'Did you tell him about his mother coming over?'

'Yes. I told him she wanted to see him hanged, which was a lie I hope she never finds out about.'

'I'm not sure it's a lie. What about the painting, did you mention that to him?'

'What? No, that was never any of his business.'

After the affairs of Herbert Gordon Challinor had been wound up in court, Billie and Liz were invited round to his house to see if Billie wanted any of the effects left unsold. Most of the furniture worth anything had been disposed of at auction; there were various family photographs, some of them showing Chas as a boy that Billie wanted, plus photos of his mother, Billie's other grandmother, who looked a cheerful woman; a wall clock that had stopped after the winder was lost; various pieces of crockery and cutlery that Liz thought might come in handy for her café; a rocking chair that squeaked, dozens of books, and a large, dusty oil painting in a substantial frame of a group of fisherwomen.

'I bet that's the family heirloom your dad mentioned,' said Liz to Billie. 'Can't be much of an heirloom if it wasn't sold.'

'It was in the attic,' said the solicitor, 'in this condition. I imagine no one thought it worth the bother of putting it in the sale. It would have been surplus to requirements with all debts having been met in full.'

Liz looked at him. 'No doubt the debts would have been adjusted to include the value of the painting had it been worth anything.'

The solicitor didn't argue with this, other than to add, 'I doubt it's worth anything. It appears to be unsigned, and getting it cleaned would cost more than it's worth, although the frame's probably worth a pound or two.'

'I want to keep it,' said Billie. 'It's my daddy's family heirloom.' She licked her finger and rubbed away at the bottom right-hand corner. 'I think someone has written something here. Can't make out what it says, but it's writing not painting.'

'We'll take it with us,' decided Liz.

A week later a fine-art restorer and jazz fan, who had agreed to clean the painting at a reduced price simply because of its connection to Chas, rang the club. Liz answered.

'I've cleaned up the Homer.'

'What's a Homer?'

'Not a what, it's a who. The artist who painted the picture you gave me to clean. His name was Winslow Homer.'

'Who was he?'

'An American artist, very popular in the nineteenth century, and this was done pretty much at the height of his powers in 1886. It's cleaned up well. There was no overpainting or excessive varnish or damage to the canvas at all. It looks as good as new now.'

'Billie will be pleased.' Liz paused then asked, 'When you say popular painter, just how popular was he?'

'He's still very much sought after. His drawings and watercolours fetch a good price, so with this being a good-sized oil-on-canvas and a popular subject it should do well.'

'I'm not sure Billie wants to sell it. What do you mean when you say it should do well?'

'Well, the real market for this is in America, plus they've got a lot more money than we have. I'd guess that it'd go for around a hundred thousand dollars there.'

'What? How much is that in pounds?

'About twenty-five thousand.'

'That's more than a lifetime's wages!'

'Well, it's what it's worth.'

Duke gave Liz a hug as they walked away from the prison and changed the subject. 'No chance of Billie selling it, then?'

'Not at the moment. Apparently it was Chas who hid it in the attic. His father was about to ring the police until Chas told him where it was. He told his dad it wasn't worth anything and, amazingly, his father believed him so they left it there. Chas was full of stories like that and Billie hung on to his every word. That painting is part of one of his stories, part of his life. She really loves it. I quite like it myself. It's insured and it'll appreciate in value, so I'm told. If and when she sells it, she'll be set up for life. Chas would have liked that.'

'Did he know what it was worth?' Duke asked.

'Doubt it. I don't think he knew the value of anything other than his clarinet and Bluebelle. I think he told his dad the painting was worthless just to annoy him.'

'Yeah, sounds like Chas. The club's just about finished, by the way.'

'I know – the builders have done well.'

'They're used to putting buildings back together. They've had enough practice over the last five years. So, I've been thinking about a date.'

Her eyes lit up. 'What date?'

'A date to open my club.'

'Oh, that date.'

'I'm thinking next Tuesday.'

'Why next Tuesday?'

'Because I think the war's going to end officially on Tuesday.'

'How do you know that?'

'Educated guess. It's also Billie's birthday.'

'So it is,' said Liz. 'What if it ends on Monday?'

'I'll ring up Mr Churchill and tell him to leave it another day.'

'Good thinking. Will the club definitely be ready?'

'The fittings are all done, the decorators should be out today. I could stock up with drinks on Monday. All we need is some bunting and an advert in the papers. They're going to call it VE Day.'

'What's that stand for?'

'Victory in Europe. We can open the club with a VE Day party. The boys in the band are ready and waiting. It'll be a great night.'

'Right, I'll ring Helen,' said Liz. 'She'll be better than any advert.'

'Did I tell you I'm changing the name as well? You know, fresh start, everything changes. Tubby ain't coming back.'

'No word of him?'

'Other than missing in action, no. They saw his Mosquito going down and didn't see no parachutes, no word of him being captured. Same with Glenn Miller – he went missing back in December. His plane took off and was never seen again, no word of what happened to him. This war's taken too many good guys.'

Liz immediately thought of Chas, then asked, 'What are you changing the name to?'

'Billie insists on me calling it Bluebelle's Club after that beautiful doll of hers. I said I'd do it, but only if she lets me put Bluebelle on display inside. I reckon I'll get as many punters coming to see her as come to listen to the music. She'll be up in lights on Monday.'

'That'd bring a smile to Chas's face,' said Liz.

'I'd sure like to see that good old Chas Challinor smile one more time,' said Duke.

'You and me both.'

They arrived at Duke's van and got in. He didn't start it straight away, just sat there, thinking.

'Were . . . were you in love with Chas, by any chance?' he asked eventually.

'Why do you ask?'

'Oh, something Billie said.'

Liz gave his question some thought. 'Yes, I was.'

'Did you tell him?'

'I did, but he had no room in his heart for anyone but his Annie.'

They sat in silence, broken by Duke. 'We need to get the club rolling to keep Billie at St Ethelburga's.'

'Her fees have been paid up to the end of the summer term.'

'I was thinking more the long term. You and Billie can't keep living in that B&B, with you travelling up to Leeds every now and again to check on your house and café. There'll still be a room in the club, but it ain't much of a home for you.'

'I was thinking of selling up in Leeds and moving down here.'

'Why would you move down here?'

'Because Billie has grown to like her posh school, and because you're down here.'

It was the answer he'd hoped for, but hadn't expected. He wasn't sure what to say. He knew what he wanted to say, but for her to turn him down might end a beautiful friendship. Liz said it for him.

'I thought if you could pluck up the courage to ask me to marry you, we might pool our resources and buy a proper house.'

Still Duke said nothing.

'We do love each other, don't we?' Liz asked.

'I thought we did, but now you've told me about Chas ...'

'What? Yes, I loved Chas. He was an easy man to love, but he didn't love me back and he's dead and now I love you. So, what I want to know is, do you love me?'

'You know I do.'

'And we've told each other this?'

'Yes, we have, many times.'

'And we like each other? We get on okay?'

'We get on like a jazz club on fire.'

'So, why haven't you proposed to me?'

Duke started the engine and drove off. 'I haven't proposed to you because it might raise a few eyebrows among people who ... who frown on such marriages.'

'Ah, I assume you mean the ignominy of me marrying a piano player? Yeah, there is that. But you could always pretend you've got a much more respectable job. Tell you what, let's get married, buy a house and tell the neighbours you're something more respectable – like a cat burglar.'

Duke threw back his head and laughed. 'Lady – you've got yourself a deal!'

Acknowledgements

I need to acknowledge information given to me by my dad, Gunner 14354884 Wilf Myers of the Royal Artillery. His life in the army from call-up to being shelled by the Germans in Herouvillette on 8 June 1945 was exactly that of Chas Challinor. My dad's unit took 40 per cent casualties in that shelling, including the deaths of a young man who'd celebrated his twenty-first birthday the day before, the quartermaster and the cook, as in this story. But, thank heavens, my dad survived. He didn't play the clarinet and he didn't steal a doll but he regularly sneaked home from his training camp in Scarborough to Leeds without a train ticket. Unlike Chas my dad spent the war working his way through France, Belgium, Holland and Germany directing gunfire from observation posts, which wasn't the safest job they could have given him.

He came home in 1946 and, along with Mam, he gave me, my brother and my sister a good life, which was what he'd been fighting for.

Also by Ken McCoy

PERSEVERANCE STREET

When Lily Robinson sees the telegraph boy cycling down Perseverance Street, she knows that he's coming to deliver bad news. Clutching the telegram in her trembling hands, at eight months pregnant and mother to three-year-old Michael, Lily learns that she must now face life as a widow. Fortuitously, she is soon visited by acquaintances, Bernard and Edith Oldroyd, who, hearing of her plight, offer to take Michael home with them for the weekend and Lily gratefully accepts.

But to her horror, just days later, the Oldroyds disappear, along with her son. With the help of her redoubtable Auntie Dee and ex-Special Forces soldier, Charlie Cleghorn, Lily takes the investigation into their own hands, scouring the country and, ultimately, war-torn Europe in search of Michael, doing everything in her power to bring him home.

Available now from Piatkus . . .

Do you love historical fiction?

Want the chance to hear news about your favourite
authors (and the chance to win free books)?

Mary Balogh
Charlotte Betts
Jessica Blair
Frances Brody
Gaelen Foley
Elizabeth Hoyt
Eloisa James
Lisa Kleypas
Stephanie Laurens
Claire Lorrimer
Sarah MacLean
Amanda Quick
Julia Quinn

Then visit the Piatkus website and blog
www.piatkus.co.uk | www.piatkusbooks.net

And follow us on Facebook and Twitter
www.facebook.com/piatkusfiction | www.twitter.com/piatkusbooks